THE
HALF
KING

THE HALF KING

MELISSA LANDERS

Entangled Publishing, LLC
644 Shrewsbury Commons Ave., STE 181
Shrewsbury, PA 17361
rights@entangledpublishing.com

Red Tower Books is an imprint of Entangled Publishing, LLC.
Visit our website at www.entangledpublishing.com.

Edited by Molly Majumder
Cover design Bree Archer
Case design by Elizabeth Turner Stokes
Endpaper illustration by Zarin Baksh
Interior map art by Amy Acosta
Stock art by Alevtina Zainutdinova/GettyImages,
Ksyshakiss/DepositPhotos, in8finity/DepositPhotos,
carrollphoto/GettyImages, Cattallina/GettyImages,
and traffic_analyzer/GettyImages
Interior design and formatting by Britt Marczak

Hardcover ISBN 978-1-64937-713-5
Deluxe Edition ISBN 978-1-64937-410-3
Ebook ISBN 978-1-64937-491-2

Printed in Italy by Grafica Veneta SpA
First Edition November 2024

10 9 8 7 6 5 4 3 2 1

RED TOWER BOOKS™

MORE FROM MELISSA LANDERS

THE ALIENATED TRILOGY

Alienated
Invaded
United

THE STARFLIGHT DUOLOGY

Starflight
Starfall

To Nicole, for never giving up on this book,
and to Liz, for giving it a good home.
Thank you.

The Half King is an atmospheric romantasy set in a kingdom of curses, gods, and betrayal. As such, the story includes elements that might not be suitable for all readers, including violence, gore, injury, death, grief, classism, sexism, illness, loss of autonomy, religious trauma, burning, drowning, alcohol and drug use, and sexual activity on the page. Suicide, poisoning, and self-harm are discussed in backstory. Readers who may be sensitive to these elements, please take note, and prepare to enter the deadly court of the Half King...

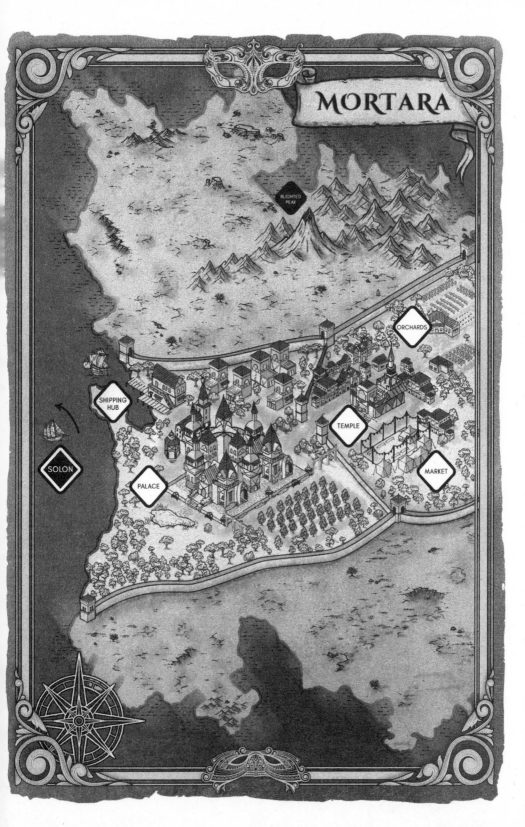

1

"Fetch me a youngling hare, Cerise. And be quick about it."

Cerise bowed to the Reverend Mother and spun on her heel toward the rabbit hutch situated at the opposite end of the courtyard. With haste, she wound her way through a maze of marble benches and shrines, moving her feet in an even glide—for ladies of the temple *never* ran—until she reached the hutch. She opened its roof, sending up the scents of wood dust and sweetgrass and revealing a new litter of kits resting inside. The babies blinked drowsily at her, twitching their downy ears and tiny pink noses. Cerise lifted the smallest kit from its nest and cradled it to her heart. As she glided back the way she had come, she stroked the rabbit's delicate pelt and smiled as it nuzzled her palm.

She lived for moments like these.

But when she approached the Reverend Mother's bench and noticed the thick serpent coiled in slumber beneath it, her footsteps faltered and her grin fell. She drew the kit closer to her chest. Now she knew why the Reverend Mother wanted it.

"Come and sit by me," the Reverend Mother ordered.

Cerise obeyed, though slower than she should have. As she lowered to the bench, she tried to exude the confidence of an oracle — to mask her fear like the other girls did — but her breath shook when she exhaled.

The Reverend Mother seemed to soften at the sound. She extended a withered hand, her long, mirrored fingernails glinting in the sunlight, and settled it atop Cerise's knee. "Tell me, girl. What do you feel for this animal?"

"Tenderness." Cerise cleared her throat and spoke more clearly. "Affection."

"Anything else?"

"Attachment."

"Do you feel a warmth inside your chest that drives you to protect it?"

"Yes, Your Grace. It's only a baby. It needs me."

"Good. I want you to focus on that instinct. The kit's life will depend on it." The Reverend Mother pressed a palm to her breastbone and delivered a pointed look from beneath her cap of short, gray hair. She was three, maybe four times Cerise's nineteen years. No one knew exactly or would even dare to ask. "Compassion is the source of our gift. Let it guide you, and you will See."

Cerise nodded as if processing the words, but she had heard them a thousand times before. Her earliest memories involved toddling through this very courtyard and admiring the teenage Seers as they honed their skills.

They had made it look so easy.

"Kneel on the ground there," the Reverend Mother said, pointing straight ahead of her at a stone paver located an arm's length from the bench…and the serpent resting beneath it. "Take the kit with you."

The edges of the stone pavers were sharp against Cerise's knees when she took her place, but she barely noticed the discomfort. She was too distracted by the serpent on the ground in front of her — now awake and flicking its forked tongue into the air. The kit seemed to sense danger. Cerise felt its tiny heart beating faster than angelfly wings.

"Now then…" The Reverend Mother reached behind her and produced a small wire cage, which she placed on the ground directly in front of Cerise. Approximately two hand-widths wide and deep, the cage was open at the top. Along the front wall were six evenly spaced holes, large enough to let the viper inside but too small to allow the rabbit to escape. The holes were facing the serpent, creating a short, straight path from its resting place to the six entrances. "Place the kit inside the cage."

Cerise did as she was told.

"The serpent will enter the cage," the Reverend Mother said, "through one of the six front holes. It will not enter from the top. I know this because it is a simple creature and I can See which path it will choose. Close your eyes, clear your mind, and you will See it, too. Once you know the correct entrance, point to it, and I will spare your kit." The Reverend Mother didn't speak the alternative, but it hung thicker than pollen in the air.

Before Cerise could prepare herself, the snake uncoiled into a slow, predatory crawl that revealed the pattern of red interlocking circles on its back. *A lowland flamewinder.* If there was a more excruciating way to die, she couldn't think of one. She clenched her eyes shut and focused on the warmth within her chest, holding tightly to the glow before it gave way to prickles of anxiety.

Which path will the serpent choose? she asked herself.

There was only darkness behind her eyelids.

She tried again to coax the answer from her mind's eye. *Which path?*

Nothing. Not even a flicker of divination passed through her. She had just exhaled to steady her nerves when something happened that curdled her blood.

The kit began to scream.

Cerise opened her eyes in horror. She had never heard a rabbit scream. She hadn't even known it was possible. It was an eerie sound, so charged with human emotion that she could easily mistake it for the cry of a child. The kit shrieked louder as it watched the snake approach; then, in hysterical panic, it hopped repeatedly against the wire walls, hurtling its tiny body into the barriers with an audible *thud thud thud*.

"Draw from your compassion," the Reverend Mother said.

Cerise refocused, drawing on not only her compassion but every single emotion within her until she feared she might burst from the strain. Sweat slicked her body, making her shiver. She cleared her mind and opened her heart. When that didn't work, she silently pleaded to the goddess for an answer.

Which path will it choose?

No matter how hard she tried, she couldn't See the snake in her mind's eye. The kit sent up a series of screams—death cries—as the serpent poked its head through the third lowest hole and drew back to strike.

Cerise plunged her hand into the cage at the exact moment the snake lunged forward. A pair of needle-sharp fangs sank into her forearm, and then came a pain so acute there wasn't a name for it. She screamed from the pits of her lungs without a care for her reputation as a lady of the temple. Let the goddess Shiera take her—death would be a mercy. Fire boiled the blood inside her veins. The scent of charred flesh filled her nostrils. She expected her sleeve to erupt into flames, but instead of bursting outward, the heat compounded from within, doubling in intensity until spots danced in her vision.

The next thing she knew, the Reverend Mother was at her side, using her power as a healer to draw out the venom. Blood flowed from the wounds in a thin stream that fell to the ground and congealed there in a burgundy pool. Beside the bloody pool lay the snake, either coiled in slumber or dead. She couldn't tell which. The venom left her veins, taking the fire with it, but even after the pain receded, she sobbed into her sleeve.

"Control yourself," chided the Reverend Mother. She sat back on her heels and shook her head. "Well, I certainly did not foresee *that*. Once again, you have confounded me. I don't know what to do with you."

"I tried, Your Grace. I promise—" Cerise cut off with a hitched breath, although there wasn't more to say. They both knew the truth and—more importantly—what it meant. Priests were the sole wielders of magic. Seers were oracles, foretelling paths to the future. A handful of exceptional Seers, like the Reverend Mother, also possessed the gift of healing. But Cerise's only gift was the ability to bewilder her mentors.

The Reverend Mother turned her attention to the stony ground and used her healing energy to separate the venom from the blood. The mass split into two liquid orbs, one yellow, the other red, until the venom formed a pearl of pure toxin. Blood was free, but poison was too precious to waste, especially when rumors buzzed of impending war. The toxin would be crafted into a weapon and stored for defense.

"Do not be discouraged," the Reverend Mother said in a voice devoid of hope. "We still have time."

Three moons. That was how much time Cerise had until she turned twenty and celebrated her Claiming Day, the final occasion upon which her gifts—assuming she had any—would manifest. If she didn't receive the Sight by then, she never would. It was the same for all second-born children given in service to the goddess. But in the nineteen years Cerise had lived at the temple, she had never met a Seer or a priest who had waited so long to receive a gift. In all likelihood, she didn't possess one, and then what was she meant to do? There weren't many options for ladies of noble birth, and as a second-born, she was forbidden to marry. The temple would keep her on, but only as a serving maid. She shuddered when she imagined what that would look like—cooking and cleaning for each new class of oracles, fading with age while they stayed perpetually young and full of promise.

Time would forget her. She might even forget herself.

The faint clicking of shoes sounded from the northern temple entrance, where a manservant strode toward them. As he crossed the courtyard, Cerise studied his clothes, which were simple and gray to match his station as a giftless second-born. Had the man dreamed of becoming a priest? Had he fantasized about changing the world with his magic? And had he been as heartbroken on his Claiming Day as she was bound to be on hers?

"Your Grace," he said, bowing to the Reverend Mother. "The Solon family is waiting for your student in the visitors' chamber."

Cerise blinked in surprise. What were her parents doing here? They had already visited her once during the last lunar cycle. She hadn't expected them to return until her Claiming Day.

"Show them into the garden room and offer them a tray of refreshments." The Reverend Mother lifted a hand to indicate Cerise's bloodstained dress. "Their daughter will join them once she has made herself presentable."

"Yes, Your Grace."

"And remove this"—pointing at the flamewinder venom—"to the arsenal, and this"—indicating the blood—"to the sacrificial altar."

"At once, Your Grace."

After the manservant filled two vials and carried them away, Cerise risked a glance at the Reverend Mother. "What will you tell them?"

"The truth, Cerise. Which I'm sure they would prefer hearing from you."

That wasn't the case. The last thing her parents wanted was the truth.

"Now go and change your dress," the Reverend Mother said as she placed something warm and soft into Cerise's hands. It was the rabbit kit, which had grown still—too still. "Calm yourself," the Reverend Mother added with a sharp glance. "The creature is alive. Its heart was strained during the ordeal. Return it to the hutch, where it can rest."

Cerise stroked the kit's long ears. "Will it survive, Your Grace?"

Instead of answering, the Reverend Mother regarded a droplet of blood on a stone paver near the cage. She scrubbed the spot clean with the toe of her shoe and repeated, "Go and change your dress."

2

Cerise descended the marble staircase from her quarters on the second floor, having donned a fresh gown and scrubbed her face and arms until they glowed. She brushed a hand over her pleated skirts, and as she did so, she admired the subtle shift in tone from stark white at the bodice to midnight black at the hem. The shades blended so seamlessly that she couldn't tell where one ended and the next began. Like all of her clothing, the gown reflected her status as a Seer in training—less elaborate than the Reverend Mother's gilded robes but finer than the gray linen of a servant. The satiny fabric was as smooth as glass and rustled when she moved, but mostly she loved what the shades represented: the balance between darkness and light, like the goddess Shiera herself.

Cerise dreaded the day when she would have to surrender it.

When she reached the atrium at the base of the steps, she glanced left toward the garden room and caught herself clenching her shoulders. She practiced her calming exercises, one slow breath after another, and while her muscles unwound, she turned her gaze to the domed ceiling, where murals painted in animated oils acted out the history of her people.

The first scene depicted Shiera crafting four land masses and setting the world in motion around the sun. Those four lands—Calatris, Mortara, Solon, and Petros—bore all known life, each ruled by a dynasty of corresponding name. As for Shiera, no one knew her true form. Her only visit to the world of men had been a thousand years ago during the Great Betrayal, and accounts from that time varied widely. Here, she was depicted as a fierce beauty, her limbs battle-strong and her face divided into equal halves: one beaming with mercy, the other contorted in wrath. That was how Cerise liked to picture the goddess, though the dark half would give her chills if she looked at it for too long.

A shiver passed through her, and she turned away.

She swept across the atrium toward the adjoining garden room. The sweet scent of moon blossoms greeted her before she reached the doorway. Once inside, she pushed through a wall of humidity to find her parents seated on a velvet divan, teacups in hand, their brunette heads—nearly identical in shade to her own—tipped close in conversation. They looked up, and she offered a tentative grin.

"Darling," called her mother, at once setting her teacup on the serving table and striding forward with her silk-draped arms open wide. Her amber eyes, which Cerise had inherited, were so bright with excitement that Cerise nearly forgot her worries. At least until after the embrace, when her mother pulled back with a silent question lifting her brows.

"Nothing has changed," Cerise admitted.

Her mother took an abrupt interest in the floor. Her father had dropped his gaze as well. Their disappointment was nearly as thick as the heated moisture in the air.

Still looking down, Father cleared his throat. "There's plenty of time, my dear."

"That's what the Reverend Mother says," Cerise told him.

"Well, she's right," came a new voice, and a lady's form stepped out from behind a vine-covered lattice near the rear wall. Tall and slim, the woman was dressed in silk finery and wore a dark veil that concealed every inch of her hair and face. "I've been telling you that for years."

Cerise gasped. "Nina!"

Temple rules forgotten, Cerise bolted to her sister and threw both arms around her neck in a running hug that knocked their bodies into the latticework. Nina didn't seem to mind. She drew Cerise more tightly against her and whispered, "I missed you."

"I missed you, too," Cerise muttered around a mouthful of veil. Now she understood why her parents had come: Nina was visiting. None of them had seen Nina since last spring, when she married a wealthy fourth-born Calatris gentleman and moved away to live on his estate.

"How long are you here?" Cerise asked.

"Long enough to visit you one more time before I leave." Nina stood back. "Now let me look at you."

"No, let me look at *you*." Cerise reached for her sister's veil. When Nina stiffened, Cerise glanced over her shoulder to ensure their family was alone. "No one will see."

"All right." Nina sighed. "But only for a moment."

Bouncing in anticipation, Cerise lifted the veil from her sister's head—and then promptly forgot how to breathe. Her blood refused to flow. Words lay dormant on her tongue. All she could do was gaze in wonder at the flawless contours of her sister's face because Nina was *that* stunning. She always had been. Nina had inherited their father's chestnut hair and emerald eyes, but she wore them in a way that made it impossible not to stare. No one could turn away from Nina, and no one could resist her.

That was her firstborn curse.

Not that destructive beauty seemed like much of an affliction. It was also rumored that firstborn Solons were unlucky in love, though couldn't the same be said of most people? Either way, Nina claimed that her appearance caused nothing but trouble, but the Solon allure was certainly preferable to the Petros bloodlust or the

Calatris delirium. Firstborns in those families would eagerly trade places with Nina. And then there was the Mortara curse. Theirs was truly chilling.

"That's enough." Nina let the veil fall back into place.

Cerise protested, causing their mother to intervene.

"Come and sit down, both of you. The Reverend Mother will be here soon."

As if on cue, the noise of swishing robes approached, and the Reverend Mother glided into the room wearing the polite smile she reserved for nobility. As High Seer, she outranked Cerise's father, but noble families had deep pockets, and the temple couldn't thrive on taxes alone.

"Welcome," the Reverend Mother said. "May Shiera's light shine upon you."

Everyone dipped their heads, chanting in response, "And may her wrathful eye look away."

Cerise sat in between her parents on the divan while Nina took the chair opposite the Reverend Mother. When everyone had settled, Cerise waited to hear the usual report regarding her progress or lack thereof. But as the Reverend Mother opened her mouth to speak, she gave a grunt of pain instead. Her posture slouched, both hands falling onto her lap as her head lolled forward.

Cerise extended her arms in front of her parents. "Don't touch her," she warned. "You'll break the trance."

"This is no ordinary trance," Nina whispered, watching the High Seer begin to tremble.

Nina was right. Any force powerful enough to drain the Reverend Mother had to be a revelation, an incredibly rare gift. Cerise had lived at the temple since birth, and she had only witnessed the phenomenon twice. The process was more delicate than a soap bubble — one errant move and the spiritual connection would pop.

The Reverend Mother drew a raspy breath and spoke in a guttural voice that raised the hairs on Cerise's arms. *"As above, so below. The flame you seek to dampen will consume you."*

As Cerise leaned forward, eager to hear more, her mother gripped her hand and squeezed it hard enough to grind her bones. Cerise wrenched her hand free. Glancing at her parents, she noticed they had paled. A revelation was a frightening thing to watch, especially for the first time.

"Don't be afraid," she whispered.

As abruptly as the trance had begun, it ended. The Reverend Mother snapped to attention in her chair, her chest heaving and her eyes wide with an emotion Cerise didn't know how to read. The Reverend Mother had always been so perfectly composed that any display of feeling on her face seemed foreign.

"Your Grace," Cerise said. "Are you all right? Do you want me to fetch a healer?"

The Reverend Mother peered back at her in an odd way, moving her gaze over Cerise's features deliberately, like an artist trying to memorize a vanishing subject.

"Your Grace?" Cerise repeated.

"Come," the Reverend Mother commanded, waving Cerise toward the exit. The Reverend Mother stood from her chair and told the others, "Please stay here and enjoy your refreshments. Cerise and I will return momentarily."

Her parents traded a look of confusion but said nothing.

After Cerise followed the Reverend Mother out of the garden room and into the adjoining atrium, she lowered her voice and asked again, "Your Grace? Are you well?"

"Oh, do be quiet," she dismissed. "I need to think."

Cerise pressed her lips together. She should have fetched a healer without asking for permission. If she summoned one now, she would be guilty of disobedience and thus barred from the supper hall.

"Listen to me," the Reverend Mother said. "I have an opportunity for you."

At that, Cerise inclined her head. She had only received orders until now, never opportunities.

"You may remain here with me at the temple," the Reverend Mother said. "But I do not believe this is your place. Today I learned that my oldest and most trusted servant has died. I believe your purpose is to replace her as the temple emissary to His Majesty Kian Hannibal Mortara."

"The Half King?" Cerise blurted. At once, her cheeks heated. She shouldn't have called him by such a vulgar nickname. "I mean, *the* king?"

"Is there another?" quipped the Reverend Mother.

No, there wasn't. That was why the Allied Realm sat on the brink of war. The king was the last surviving member of the royal line, and all priests were bound in service to him. But he was a firstborn noble and carried his bloodline's curse. Every night at sunset, he turned to shadow. Every dawn made him whole again. Eventually he would lose his daylight hours as well, until he vanished forever, like all of the Mortara firstborns who had come before him. When that happened, the Allied Realm would be without a ruler for the first time in recorded history.

"But why me?" Cerise asked. "I don't understand." She flinched as she said it, waiting for the inevitable rebuke.

But it didn't come. For the first time in nineteen years, the Reverend Mother looked torn, as though she were fighting an invisible battle inside her mind. Her indecisiveness scared Cerise more than the woman's temper ever had.

Finally, the Reverend Mother admitted in a quiet voice, "I have Seen more than the death of the king's emissary. I have foreseen a possible end to the curses."

Cerise gasped. "That's a miracle, Your Grace!"

"No, it is not," the Reverend Mother snapped. She glanced around as if to ensure no one was listening. "Not yet. That's why we must be discreet. The path for this outcome is narrow—more narrow than a strand of hair. To break the curses, the goddess must be appeased through tests and trials and sacrifices."

"*As above, so below*," Cerise repeated. "*The flame you seek to dampen will consume you.* Is that what you meant by the flame? Is it one of the trials?"

"I do not know." The Reverend Mother exhaled heavily through her nose. "I could not See any of it clearly. The details of this future are clouded because its path is entwined with yours."

Cerise felt her eyes go wide. "Mine?"

"Yes. And now more than ever, you confound me."

"But…" Cerise shook her head. None of this made sense. Had she somehow muddied the Reverend Mother's revelation? Even if she *was* a complete failure as an oracle, surely she didn't have the power to affect holy visions.

Did she?

"Have I done something wrong?" she asked.

The Reverend Mother arched an eyebrow. "You tell me, Cerise. Have you?"

"No, Your Grace," she promised, though that wasn't *entirely* true.

"Then you have nothing to worry about," the Reverend Mother said. "The goddess has allowed me to See precisely one clear vision of you."

Cerise perked up.

"In my vision," the Reverend Mother whispered, "you were seated at a desk in the palace, studying the notes and the journal entries left behind for you by the former emissary. You were learning her role—quite dutifully, I might add."

Cerise waited to hear more, but apparently, that was the end of it. She tried her best to hide her disappointment. She had hoped the vision would reveal something exciting, or at the very least help her understand why this "narrow path" intersected with hers.

"Is that all I'm meant to do, Your Grace?" she asked. "Is that my only role in breaking the curses? Being an emissary?"

"Is that *all*?" the Reverend Mother repeated, leveling her with a glare. "Have you taken leave of your senses?"

Oh, no. She'd said the wrong thing. Again.

"Have you forgotten your lessons?" the Reverend Mother went on. "Every element of a path—down to a singular insect—is critical to its outcome. We may not understand the insect's role until the future comes to pass. A hornet might sting a beast and spur the animal into a hunter's range, providing nourishment, sustaining the journey of dozens of men who might have otherwise starved. Your duties as emissary may lead you to uncover a critical detail, make a new ally, or inspire a discovery that results in breaking the curses. Whatever your role may be, it is no more—and no less—important than that of the hornet. So how dare you ask me *is that all*?"

The fire of ten suns blazed in Cerise's cheeks. "I'm sorry, Your Grace. I didn't mean it like—"

"Oh, save your excuses. You infuriate me."

The last thing Cerise wanted to do was ask another question. But there was no alternative. She raised her hand like a youngling seeking permission to visit the privy…and hated herself for it. If she only had the Sight, she would know the answers.

"Please, Your Grace," she said.

"What is it now?"

"May I ask what I would be expected to do as emissary?"

The Reverend Mother nodded. "Nothing beyond your scope. Your duties will include attending meetings with the king, advising him on matters of faith, and representing your goddess properly by conducting yourself as a lady of the temple."

That didn't help to clarify the role. Cerise couldn't visualize any of her proposed duties except for the last one. She knew how to behave like a lady, at least most of the time.

"So?" the Reverend Mother asked. "Do you accept?"

Cerise pushed down the fear that had risen in her chest. She couldn't possibly say *no*, not if there was a chance, however slim, that her role at court could end a thousand years of suffering. She had no idea how to be an emissary, but her predecessor had left behind notes and journal entries to guide her. That was a start.

"Yes, Your Grace," she said.

"Good. There is one other thing." The Reverend Mother leaned closer. "In my vision, I sensed enemies of the goddess—nameless, faceless men who serve false idols. It may not be easy to tell them apart, so be careful who you trust. And even within…" She cut off, seeming to consider her words.

"Even within…?" Cerise prompted.

"Even within our own Order," she whispered, her voice barely discernible, "there are overzealous servants of the goddess who believe that suffering is the only path to atonement. They may not want the suffering to end for the noble houses. The vision was fractured, incomplete. I could not discern what the goddess's will is in this, only that there is a chance. We must protect this fragile thing. Do you understand what I'm saying?"

Cerise didn't need the Sight to know exactly what kind of priest the Reverend Mother was describing. Most priests were calm and gentle. Then there were others—men with sharp, cold gazes who seemed to enjoy nothing more than catching a novice breaking a rule. She already did her best to avoid those men. And until the will of the goddess was clear, it was her sacred duty to protect the vision, much like a rabbit kit in her palm.

"Yes, Your Grace."

"Keep the revelation to yourself," the Reverend Mother said, "until you know who your allies are."

"Yes, Your Grace. When do I leave?"

"At once. I will order a carriage to take you to the harbor. The journey to Mortara will last several days, and there's not a moment to waste. Go and say goodbye to your family. I'll fetch a team of servants to help you pack."

At once? Cerise reeled. This was happening too quickly.

In a daze, she returned to the garden room to share the news with her family. She barely registered what she told them. When she had finished speaking, no one replied. Her parents sat frozen with their lips parted. Nina's expression was hidden by her veil, but she had gone unnaturally still, too. Cerise understood their shock—she felt it herself—but she had expected a hint of excitement from her family, or at least pride in her sudden rise in station.

"I know I don't deserve it," she said. "But to serve at court is a great honor."

Her mother blinked as if waking from a dream. "Oh, my dear, of course you deserve this honor and a thousand more. The king would be lucky to have you. We're just…"

"Concerned," Father finished.

"That's right," Mama said. "The temple is the safest place for you."

"For *anyone*," he interjected.

"Yes, for anyone," Mama agreed. "And it's close enough for us to visit you."

"The palace is too far for us to travel," Father said. "You should stay here."

Cerise shook her head. The time for making choices was over. "I'm supposed to say goodbye. The Reverend Mother told me I leave right away."

There was a collective silence, followed by an exchange of loaded glances. Then Mama forced a smile and patted the cushion beside her. Cerise sat down in between her parents, and Mama retrieved an object from her silk satchel.

"Take this." Mama pressed a smooth, flat disc into Cerise's palm. "Father has the other one. You can use it to talk to us while you're away."

Cerise glanced at the object and found it was a heartrending mirror, named for its use by parted lovers to communicate in secret. She had never owned one before, but she knew how it worked. Holding up the mirror, she saw the tan lining of Father's pocket. His fingers became visible, and then his face as he pulled out the mirror and delivered a grin that didn't reach his eyes.

"You were never allowed to have one of these before," he said into the glass. "But now that you won't live in the temple…"

Cerise didn't hear anything beyond the words *you won't live in the temple*. She couldn't conceive of such a thing. It would be easier to imagine wearing someone else's skin. She had never left the temple grounds, except for trips to the market. Now she would leave for an entirely new land. Part of her life was ending, and she hadn't even Seen it coming.

Moisture blurred her vision.

"None of that," commanded Nina, who had stayed silent for so long that Cerise had nearly forgotten she was there. "Mama? Father? May I say goodbye to Cerise in private?"

Their parents nodded and strode out to the atrium.

"Listen to me, because we don't have much time," Nina said as she sat beside Cerise on the divan. Reaching beneath the neckline of her dress, she retrieved a golden chain, which she pulled over her veil until it was free. The chain bore a misshapen, tarnished link that looked like it might once have been a ring. "I want you to wear this for protection."

Cerise took the chain and inspected its battered pendant. She had little experience with enchanted relics, but nothing about this one seemed particularly special. "What is it?"

"I can't tell you."

"Why not?"

"Because some magic is bound by secrets. Now put it on."

"But how does it work?"

"Never mind that." Impatiently, Nina looped the chain around Cerise's neck, then shoved a hand down the front of her temple dress and proceeded to stuff the ugly pendant between her breasts.

"Nina!" Cerise batted away her sister's hands.

"Bloody crows, Cerise. We have the same body parts."

"That doesn't mean I want you touching mine!"

"Fine." Nina held up her hands. "Just promise you'll never take it off."

"Not even to bathe?"

"Not even then. And don't let anyone see it—not the king, not his priests, not the Reverend Mother—no one."

"What about Mama and Father?"

Nina flipped back her veil and showed her face. That was how Cerise knew her sister was serious. "No one. Promise me."

Lost in the haze of Nina's beauty, Cerise heard herself say, "I promise."

Nina lowered her veil at the precise moment the Reverend Mother reentered the room. "Come, Cerise," she ordered. "Your carriage is here."

"Already?" Cerise glanced in the direction of her bedroom. Surely she owned more possessions than a servant could have packed by now.

"It's done. Now come, girl. Don't make me tell you again."

"Yes, Your Grace."

As Cerise made her way out of the garden room and noticed the luggage waiting for her on the other side, a thought occurred to her. She wondered what type of clothing the servants had packed for her. Would she continue to wear the gown of an oracle in training? Would she change into the robes of a novice Seer? Or would the king expect her to dress for court in the same silk finery that Mama and Nina wore? None of those roles fit. Cerise wasn't an oracle—at least she didn't think so—and her status as a second-born meant she belonged in service to the goddess, not to the world of men.

What was she now?

She wanted to ask, but she had already tested the Reverend Mother's patience too much to broach a topic as frivolous as clothing. So she remained silent and exchanged goodbye kisses with her family. After they left, the Reverend Mother settled a hand on Cerise's shoulder and said her own goodbye.

"This is where our paths diverge, my girl. I will miss you, even though you confounded me to the end of my wits."

"I'm sure I'll be back someday, Your Grace."

The Reverend Mother shook her head. "I do not know where your path ends, but you will never return to this temple."

Cerise chose not to point out all the times the Reverend Mother had been wrong about her path. The future could change. She had to believe it was possible to come home to her temple. Any other outcome was too frightening to consider.

"Remember, my girl, calm and compassion will guide you. Do not be afraid. Keep the vision alive, even if it means keeping it to yourself." The Reverend Mother turned her eyes to the animated murals on the ceiling. "The goddess has plans for you, Cerise."

When Cerise looked up, her gaze found the wrathful side of Shiera's face—one eye blazing, half an upper lip hitched above a lethal incisor. A chill skittered down her spine. She had no doubt the goddess had redirected her path.

But which side had plotted the course?

3

With no windows in her cabin, Cerise caught her first glimpse of Mortara when the ship docked and she made her way onto the deck. The first sensation to strike her was the heat. *Goddess.* Scorching and dry, it swept over her like the bellows of a flame, heady with the scents of lemongrass and musk. In the time it took for her to walk to the railing, she learned she would have to find a different wardrobe than the satiny dresses she had worn at the temple. Something loose and airy, like the clothes that the scurrying dockworkers and line-handlers wore, with long, linen sleeves to stave off the sun.

Voices tumbled over one another, creating a cacophony as workers used pulleys to unload boxes and trunks onto the dock. Cerise put on her best temple demeanor and nodded at some of the sailors as she passed, then looked away from the bustle of activity and surveyed the land that would be her new home.

To the west, greenish-brown clover rolled as far as she could see, leading to a mountain range on the horizon. The crags pushed to the sky—cruel, jagged peaks that sent a shiver down her spine.

That was the place.

The place where the Great Betrayal happened.

The very same mountain peak on which the four noble dynasties had gathered together and conspired to slay the goddess. Conspired and failed, resulting in a thousand years of curses for the noble firstborns and the lands of Mortara.

Very little of value was produced here, barring a few spices and rare gems from the mountains. Most of the vegetation was cultivated with the magic of the palace priests, or else imported from the other lands. She glanced down at the water sloshing against the dock, finding no trace of floating seagrass or saltweed.

Not even fish could thrive in such a cursed place.

To the east stood one of the city's outer walls, constructed from stone and tall enough that only the temple spire was visible above it. She didn't know what manner of protection the wall provided, but there were tales of strange beasts and anomalies created by the goddess's spilled blood. Cerise had assumed that some of the stories were fables.

Well, she was among fables now.

. . .

Dusk had fallen during the ride to the palace, which meant the king had vanished for the evening. Cerise couldn't deny the relief that swept over her as the sun dipped closer to the horizon. She didn't want to meet the king until she was fresh and rested. She didn't want to meet *anyone* until she'd had a proper bath. With any luck, she would arrive at suppertime and avoid introductions until morning.

Two guards met her carriage at the gatehouse, each man dressed in a lightweight tan uniform that bore the Mortara crest of a single mountain divided in half by a spear. The guards wore metal blades at their hips. Cerise studied the tapered edges and the needle-fine points of each sword. She had never seen a weapon up close before. There had been no need for them at the temple. Priests provided defense as well as instruction.

All thoughts of weapons disappeared as the gatehouse doors parted to reveal a crowd of palace workers waiting on the other side. She had just enough time to blink before the crowd erupted in a chorus of cheers.

Panic rose in her chest. What was happening?

Someone shouted, "She's here! The blessed oracle is here!"

The blessed oracle?

Did they have her confused with someone else? It was all she could do to remain in her seat and not run headlong back to the harbor. There were so many people surrounding the carriage — maids and cooks, grooms and groundskeepers — a hundred of them, at least, all rising onto their tiptoes and craning their necks to catch a glimpse of her through the window.

Just when she thought her heart might beat out of her chest, she heard a man call, "That is enough!" and in the span of a single breath, hundreds of voices went silent. The palace workers collectively backed away from the gatehouse, giving the carriage plenty of room to pull forward…and allowing Cerise to exhale.

The carriage came to a stop, the door opened, and a guard assisted her in stepping down onto the royal lawn. She peered through the crowd to identify the man who had tamed them, and she found him right away. There was no mistaking his gilded robes or the intricate, woven symbols that displayed his status. The high priest of Shiera, arguably the most powerful man alive, was gliding in her direction, leading two rows of priests behind him.

At once, Cerise stood with respect: backbone locked, chin high, fingers laced in front of her, blocking out every other person in her periphery. But as the distance between them closed, she had to fight to keep the shock from showing on her face.

The high priest was alarmingly young, with barely a hint of gray hair threaded among the blond at his temples and in the whiskers of his neatly trimmed beard. Even in the growing darkness, she could see his eyes were bluer than a peacock feather, set in a pleasant face that radiated confidence and calm. She wondered what powers the man possessed to entitle him to such a position at his age. His gift must be incredible.

He stopped in front of her, smiling with tenderness. "Welcome, child."

Cerise found her wits and lowered in a deep curtsy. "Your Grace."

"The Reverend Mother was right. I sense you have a generous spirit." He touched her cheek, indicating for her to stand. "You may call me Father Padron. I'm delighted to welcome you to the palace, Cerise." He offered his elbow to her. "May I escort you inside?"

"It would be my honor, Your Gr—" She cut off and corrected, "Father Padron."

She took his arm, but the oppressive heat made her wish that she hadn't. His added warmth sent a flush to her face, a reaction that didn't escape his notice.

"Ah, yes, you must be sweltering," he said. "I ordered a new set of gowns from the city temple and had them delivered to your chambers."

"That was thoughtful of you."

The crowd parted for them, and Cerise walked past the palace workers, smiling and nodding as she went along. She felt a pull at her skirts, and she glanced aside to find an elderly maid touching her gown with one hand while signing with the other. The old woman tapped her wrinkled forehead and then drew a triangle there. Cerise didn't understand what the sign meant, but Father Padron had seen it, too, and he stopped short, his arm tense beneath her hand.

Her stomach sank. Whatever the sign was, the priests didn't seem overly fond of it. Father Padron excused himself and circled behind her to speak in hushed tones with one of his men. Moments later, he rejoined her, and they continued on as if nothing had happened. When Cerise glanced behind them, the old woman and the priest were gone.

"The staring is harmless, but remember your place," Father Padron said. "You're an emissary and a lady of the temple. You're to be respected but not worshipped."

Worshipped? Was that what the old woman had done with her triangle sign? Engaged in idolatry—in plain sight of the priests? No, the sign must have meant something else. Nobody in their right mind would be so reckless.

"Yes, Your Grace," she told Father Padron. "I would never encourage idolatry."

"I know you wouldn't, Cerise," he said with a reassuring pat on her hand. "I also want you to remember that you are beholden to no layman. Everyone at court will address you as *my lady*, even the king. If you encounter any disrespect, I want to hear about it."

"Thank you, Your Grace," she told him.

Once they cleared the last vestiges of the crowd, she finally got her first unobstructed view of the palace…and gasped.

Dusk had cast shadows all around, and yet a glow emanated from the palace that was radiant enough to blind the heavens. She shielded her eyes and gazed ahead in wonder. The last flickers of sunlight glittered like countless stars across the castle's crystallized stone facade. The castle design was simple, a hexagon of walls with a tower at each point, but anything more ornate would have detracted from its beauty. Ahead of her, luscious trees laden with all manner of citrus fruit, all of them magically enhanced, lined the grass-carpeted pathway to the main doors.

Ten generations of priests had served this place well. They even seemed to have cooled the air in a protective bubble around the palace. The imprint of their magic was all around her. Though old and faded, she tasted the power on her tongue like the metallic tang before an electrical storm. She kept the observation to herself, though. She had never met an oracle in training who could taste magic, only priests, and she didn't want to give the Order any reason to investigate her for unnatural tendencies.

"Ah, yes," chuckled Father Padron. "The palace is a spectacular sight, especially for a newcomer."

The sky dimmed to a purple haze, and strands of overhead globes illuminated to take its place.

"Indeed," she agreed. "Thank you for your kindness in welcoming me here."

"It's nothing. I remember my first excursion outside the temple." His lips twitched in a wistful grin. "It was a rather… *trying*…adjustment. Now I do my best to make the transition more comfortable for others."

"In which temple were you raised?" she asked.

"Calatris," he said. "Northwestern Calatris to be exact, where summertime means a thin sheet of snow beneath your boots instead of a drift knee high."

She pictured him at her age, innocent and wide-eyed, his face smooth-shaven and perspiring in the Mortara heat. The mental image made her smile. She still couldn't believe how young he was— or that he had honored her with a personal escort to the palace. It was a rare treat to speak with him at all. Most ladies of the temple— gentlemen, too—went their entire lives without meeting the Order's high priest.

"It's important for your mental wellness that you maintain a worship schedule," he advised as they continued up the path, passing neatly planted rows of blossoming pear trees. "You may join the Order in using the palace sanctuary. It's in a detached building near the east gardens. Laymen aren't permitted inside."

Ah. Cerise understood his message. The sanctuary was an escape from court. She was glad to hear it, especially with the press of people behind her. She could almost feel their gazes on her back. She couldn't imagine what she had done to merit such a reception.

"And His Majesty asked me to convey his regrets at not being able to greet you in person." Father Padron used a hand to indicate the shadows tumbling down the stone steps of the entrance in front of them. "He is indisposed until morning."

"I look forward to meeting him," she said. "May I inquire about

His Majesty?"

"You may ask me anything, Cerise."

"When he vanishes at night…where does he go? Is he in *all* of the shadows?"

She glanced at the dark silhouette of her own form, and her imagination conjured a pair of invisible eyes looking back at her. She had heard stories that the king's nights in the shadows had acquainted him with demons and that he'd made deals to prevent his parents from conceiving another heir. She didn't believe that—not *really*—but there had also been chatter in the market last year, whispers of unnatural deaths at the palace. The former king and queen had been found dead in their chambers, their rigid bodies an identical shade of bluish gray. And according to palace servants, Kian hadn't seemed surprised by the news.

Rumors and nonsense. Probably.

There was a smile in Father Padron's voice when he answered. "His Majesty once told me that he has no memory of his nighttime hours and that he awakes at sunrise as if he'd merely blinked. I have no reason to doubt him."

She preferred that answer to the thought of the king spying on her through the shadows. She wanted to ask another, more delicate question. The Mortara curse differed from that of the other noble dynasties. For Solon, Calatris, and Petros firstborns, their curse manifested fully on their twentieth birthday, their Claiming Day. After that, the nobles lived on for any number of years, or at least survived, if *living* was too generous a word. But Mortara firstborns began disappearing at sunset on their Claiming Day, and in the year that followed, the curse consumed their daytime hours as well, until the firstborn faded out of existence. Few Mortara firstborns survived beyond twenty-one. The king likely had six more moons before he vanished forever and left behind a war for his empty throne. The exact timing would depend on how far the curse had advanced, how quickly it was consuming him during the day.

"After sunrise," Cerise began, "is His Majesty fully present until the sun sets?"

"Fully present?" Father Padron asked. "No, unfortunately he is not. The curse has infringed on His Majesty's daylight hours, though I'm unable to say to what extent. His Majesty keeps to himself during the day, as is his privilege."

"I see."

"You may consider asking his courtesan," Father Padron suggested. "She would know better than I how the king passes his time."

Cerise doubted that would provide an answer. If the king's courtesan had any regard for him, she would never betray his secrets.

"Here we are," Father Padron said as they climbed the steps and entered the castle foyer. "Ah, there's Daerick." He nodded at a tall, dark-haired boy loitering at the base of the staircase. The boy was dressed in a blue silk shirt tucked into slim-fitting trousers, and there seemed to be something akin to bean sprouts dangling from his chin. On closer inspection, she found it was a beard...more or less. He was watching her, too, but with an expression of interest instead of morbid fascination. "I'll let him show you to your quarters. I have a matter to attend to."

Cerise wondered if the "matter" was about the elderly woman who had been ushered away. Father Padron seemed gentle, but some of his priests might not be, and Cerise didn't want the woman punished too harshly for the sign she had made. But despite Father Padron's invitation to ask him anything, the topic seemed too charged for their first meeting. She would ask him about it tomorrow.

"Cerise," Father Padron said, "this is Daerick Calatris, the king's private historian. No one knows more about the sacred scrolls than he does. In fact, I believe he can recite them from memory—"

"In ten languages," Daerick interjected. "Not that I'm counting."

"So if anyone can assist you in your new role, it's him."

"I'm grateful for the help," she said. "My appointment as His Majesty's emissary was abrupt. I have much to learn. I look forward to working with you, Lord Calatris."

Daerick bowed. "Not nearly as much as I do, my lady." He spoke without a hint of sarcasm, smiling in a way that crinkled the skin around his eyes. Cerise noticed that his irises were deep brown, brimming with a sharpness that reflected his intelligence.

He must be a firstborn.

Sympathy tugged at her ribs. The Calatris curse was one of the cruelest. Scrolls about the Great Betrayal said that a Calatris scholar with a brilliant intellect had devised the method to slay the goddess. As punishment, his firstborn descendants were cursed with more knowledge than the mortal mind could bear. Cerise didn't want to imagine what Daerick's smiling eyes would look like when his Claiming Day arrived and filled his mind to the breaking point with all the secrets of the universe.

He extended an elbow. "Shall we?"

As she settled a hand on his forearm, her insides stirred with guilt. She had always felt a deep connection to the goddess, even the vengeful side of Shiera, because darkness was just as important as the light. But after all this time, surely the goddess would let them break the curses. Surely the debt had been paid.

"The king dismissed his court a while ago," Daerick said, leading her up the stairs, "so there are plenty of empty suites. I chose your quarters myself. They're situated in the best spot. Yours has the most shade during the day, and the windows face east so the sunrise will wake you for morning prayers." He added, "I know your schedule because my brother lives in a temple on Calatris."

"Is he a priest in training?"

"Yes, his gift manifested on our nineteenth birthday."

"*Our* birthday?"

"We're twins. I'm the oldest by three minutes." Daerick gave a dry laugh. "Lucky me. I inherited the threat of impending delirium, and he inherited the magic. Can you believe in common families it's the oldest child that has the advantage?"

Yes, she could believe it. Only noble families bore a curse.

"I envy the commoners. They have more freedom than they

realize." Daerick covered her hand with his own. "I hope to share that freedom. You can't imagine how excited I was when I heard the rumors about you."

"What rumors?" she asked.

"That you're destined to break the noble curses."

She stopped and gaped at him, nearly tripping on her own shoes. *"What?"*

"You're destined to break the noble curses," he repeated. "Aren't you?"

Oh, goddess. That explained the crowd at the gates. "Who told you that?"

Daerick turned his gaze to the ceiling as if to recall a memory. "I heard it from the groundskeeper, who heard it from his wife, who heard it from a stable hand. I think he heard it from someone in the kitchens, and I believe they heard it from a man making a cider delivery to the temple, and after that, I don't know where the story goes."

Cerise suppressed yet another surge of panic. She knew that gossip ran rampant at court, but she never imagined she could be the subject of it before her own arrival. How had anyone gotten such a twisted version of the truth—or *any* version of the truth? The revelation was supposed to be a secret. And besides, she was completely ordinary. The goddess hadn't even gifted her with the Sight. This rumor was a problem, a big one, because it spread false hope. How many firstborn nobles would be crushed to learn that she hadn't come there to perform a miracle? And what about the king? Did he believe it, too?

Oh, stars, she hoped not. His expectations of her would be impossible.

"Is that why people think I'm here?" she asked.

Daerick lowered one brow. "Isn't it? Everyone knows you're gifted. Why else would the Reverend Mother send a nineteen-year-old girl to replace the old emissary?"

Gifted. The word hit like a punch to the chest.

Daerick was right: an emissary was supposed to be gifted, a person who'd earned the role through decades of experience, not a novice with no talents apart from rescuing rabbit kits and confounding Seers. So when the people of Mortara had learned that the new emissary was nineteen, of course they'd assumed she was remarkable. She should have expected as much, but ironically, she wasn't even gifted enough to See the most predictable path in front of her.

She would need to let Daerick down easily.

"Lord Calatris," she began.

"Please call me Daerick."

"Daerick," she said. "I don't understand my purpose here, because the Reverend Mother couldn't fully See it. But I do know the rumor you heard about me is wrong." Her stomach sank along with Daerick's expression, but she refused to lie to him. Nothing was crueler than a false promise. "I believe in Shiera's mercy, and I believe the goddess is ready to forgive the world of men. But I don't know what that looks like. I don't even have the Sight."

"You're not twenty yet," he said. "When is your Claiming Day?"

"In three moons."

"Then there's still time."

She heaved a sigh. She was tired of hearing that. "When is yours?"

"Five and a half moons, shortly before the king's birthday." He paused thoughtfully for a moment. "Did the Reverend Mother specifically say that you *couldn't* break the curses?"

"Well...no," she admitted. She had somehow clouded the revelation and stopped the Reverend Mother from Seeing whose role that was. "Not in so many words, but I'm sure that's not why I'm here."

"Did she tell you how the old emissary died?" he asked.

Cerise shook her head. "I assumed it was from old age."

"Oh, she was ancient, no doubt about it. But time didn't kill her."

"Then what did?"

"*She* did."

Cerise felt her eyebrows jump. "Do you mean the emissary ended her own life?"

"With poison," he said. "No one knows why. She left behind a note, but it made very little sense. I think the nature of her message might have contributed to the mysticism surrounding your arrival. It sounded prophetic."

"What did the note say?"

"Just a single line," Daerick said. *"As above, so below. The flame you seek to dampen will consume you."*

Chills broke out along Cerise's arms.

"At first, I thought it was a reference to something in the sacred scrolls," Daerick continued. "But I've been searching my texts for any mention of dampened flames, and I haven't found anything."

"When exactly did the emissary die?" Cerise asked.

Daerick considered. "Four days ago, midafternoon."

That was when the Reverend Mother had received her revelation. The timing couldn't be a coincidence. The Reverend Mother had referred to the old emissary as her most trusted servant. More than likely, the two of them had shared a spiritual connection. But what did that have to do with Cerise? Maybe the woman's journal would provide a clue—a discovery that might lead to breaking the curses, like the Reverend Mother had said.

"You know something," Daerick said. "I can tell."

She hesitated to say more. She didn't mind Daerick knowing that she was ordinary. Her lack of Sight was no secret. But any mention of the Reverend Mother's vision could plant a new crop of harmful rumors, and she wouldn't let that happen.

"You don't trust me," he said in a matter-of-fact way.

"It's not that."

"Don't worry, my lady." He patted her hand as he led her toward the eastern corridor, through halls carpeted in silk and lined with bejeweled mirrors. "Trust is earned. But for the record, I'm doing my part to help you. I've already gathered a few of the old emissary's notes, and I'm hunting down the rest. Organization wasn't her strong suit, I'm afraid."

"What about her journal?"

"That's on the list. It hasn't turned up yet, but I'll find it for you. Until then, all I can do is promise that your secrets are safe with me, just as I hope mine are safe with you. The only way to help each other is to speak freely." He lowered his voice to a teasing whisper. "Besides, I like you."

Cerise couldn't help smiling. She liked him, too. Even though she didn't fully trust him, she felt safe enough to ask him a question that had seemed too charged for Father Padron.

"What does this mean?" she said, imitating the triangular sign she had seen the elderly maid perform.

"Flaming hell!" Daerick snatched her hand before she could complete the sign. "Don't do that." He glanced all around. Only when he confirmed they were alone did he exhale and release her fingers. "Never let anyone see you do that."

"Why?"

"Because it's apostasy, that's why."

Cerise gasped, glancing over her own shoulder. The Order had discretion in handing down their penalties, but the traditional punishment for apostasy was death by a thousand stones. She shuddered to think about that happening to the elderly maid. What had possessed the old woman to make that sign in front of the priests?

Daerick guided her fingers back to the crook of his elbow. "I don't suppose you learned about the Triad."

She shook her head. She had never heard of it.

"You know the story about Shiera's lover?" he asked. "From the Great Betrayal?"

"Of course." As a Solon, she knew better than anyone. A member of her own dynasty had seduced the goddess from the heavens and convinced her to take mortal form so the other nobles could slay her. That was the reason for the Solon curse of destructive allure.

"Well, there's an old rumor," Daerick went on, "that the Solon seducer was a woman and that Shiera impregnated her and sired a race of demigods. The Triad believes that Shiera's descendants should be in control, not the priests or even the king. They have followers in all four lands, but the sect is especially popular here."

Cerise wiped her hand on her gown, mortified that she had made such an abominable sign. She knew there were nonbelievers scattered throughout the realm—people who worshipped coin or flesh—but this was just *wrong*. There were no other gods than Shiera. That anyone would organize a sect and recruit others to glorify false deities offended her on the deepest level. The Reverend Mother had been right to warn her about enemies in this land.

"Heretics," she spat.

Daerick glanced at her as if amused.

"What?" she asked.

"You and Father Padron are going to get along beautifully."

Whatever he meant by that, it didn't sound like a compliment.

"Here we are." Daerick flourished a hand at the last door along the eastern corridor. He opened it and gestured for her to precede him inside.

"Oh, stars," she murmured as she entered her suite. She hadn't expected anything this sprawling. Her quarters' entryway opened to a sitting area furnished with a plush divan and two armchairs, beyond which stood a four-poster bed draped in white netting. A cool breeze wafted inside from the open doors to her private balcony. The air smelled of sugar vines, which she noticed grew wild along the balcony railings.

"It's cruel, really," Daerick mused with a grin. "Now you're spoiled for any other kind of life."

She laughed because he was right. Her former quarters had consisted of a single bed, a wardrobe, and a corner shrine for prayers. She didn't know how long she would serve as an emissary or where life would take her afterward, but she doubted her rooms would ever be this luxurious again.

She crossed the suite until she reached the open balcony. Outside, the moon bathed the land in its glow, allowing her to see into the walled city beyond. At the heart of it lay the temple. From there, narrow streets wound outward among boxy structures of varying heights. She was too far away to see any activity, but the nearby rustle of fabric drew her attention to a garden below, where a young woman strolled among rows of exotic greenery. With her long, glossy hair and regal features, she was almost beautiful enough to pass for a Solon firstborn. But what really struck Cerise was the haste in the young woman's steps. She seemed restless, pacing the garden instead of enjoying it.

Cerise waved Daerick over to the balcony and whispered, "Who's that?"

As he peered down, he grinned. "Lady Delora Champlain. The king's courtesan."

"Oh, I heard about her, or at least I think I did," Cerise said. "Does His Majesty have any other courtesans?"

Daerick muffled a laugh. "Believe me, one is enough. Even though Delora's low-born, the king gave her a title and promised to marry her if she can conceive an heir. Let's just say she's highly motivated to be the next queen."

Cerise turned away from the balcony. That was more information than she wanted to know. She would have to face the king in the morning, and the rumors about him had made her nervous enough as it was.

"Thank you for your hospitality," she told Daerick. "I think I'll rest now."

"Of course." He bowed after she walked him to the door. "Make sure you lock this after I leave. And close the balcony doors."

"Why?" she asked. "With all the magic here, what could happen?"

"You would be surprised. Good night, my lady."

4

Cerise slept fitfully, dreaming of heretics and demigods and living shadows. Twice she awoke to urgent whispers in her ear, only to find herself alone and panting for air. The voice had seemed so clear when it had called her name, but she convinced herself it was a trick of the mind and closed her eyes until she fell asleep again.

She finally rose for good with the sun and dressed in one of the gowns from the local temple. The frock was identical in style to her old gown but constructed from a light, gauzy material that made her feel exposed, even though she wasn't. On her way to the first floor, she found the palace abuzz with nervous chatter. The staff was so consumed by gossip that the servants barely took notice of her. She caught snippets of conversation as she glided along the corridor, murmurs of *a horrible beast* and *in her bed*. It wasn't until she strode into the foyer and glanced through the open doors onto the lawn that she realized what had caused the stir.

An animal lay on its side in the grass. It looked like a desert panther with its limbs outstretched, rigid in death. She felt an odd mingling of regret and fascination as she eyed the panther's hairless body and its long, hollow claws, known for drawing moisture from the ground. She had never seen anything so magnificent except in books at the temple library.

She descended the steps for a closer look and found Father Padron outside with several of his priests. He gave her a grim smile when their eyes met, as if apologizing for whatever had taken place during the night.

"What happened, Your Grace?" she asked him.

"Lady Champlain retired to her chambers at midnight and found this"—indicating the panther—"waiting for her. She owes her life to Father Bishop's weakness for sweet cakes. He was halfway to the kitchen when he heard her screams and ran to help. After he killed the beast, it took three royal guards to drag the carcass outside."

Cerise noticed there were no wounds on the animal's leathery hide. The priest must have slain it with his magic. She had seen it done once before, when a badger had burrowed under the courtyard wall to attack the temple hens. With a wave of his hand, Father Diaz had stopped the creature's heart, but then Father Diaz had collapsed and lost consciousness. It had taken a full day for him to awake. Nothing required more magical energy than dispatching death.

"Lady Champlain should send sweet cakes for his recovery," Cerise said. She recalled what Daerick had told her about the woman. "Isn't she the king's—"

"Courtesan, yes," Father Padron finished. "His Majesty is understandably upset. He insisted on accompanying the guards into the city for an investigation." Using his shoe, he nudged the cat's hindquarters, where a circular brand was singed into the flesh. "This is the mark of a local trader."

Cerise doubted any trader would be careless enough to unleash a panther into the palace with his brand on display, but she supposed the investigation had to begin somewhere.

"Do you think His Majesty will return before sunset?" she asked.

She had just worked up the nerve to meet the king, and delaying it for another day would have her stomach dancing again.

Father Padron shook his head. "Probably not. And he's wasting his time. The trader didn't do this, and I doubt the courtesan was the real target."

"Do you mean His Majesty was the target?" Cerise asked. "How could anyone kill him after sunset? He disappears into the shadows."

"And awakes at sunrise wherever his spirit is drawn, which at the moment is to Lady Champlain's bedside."

"Oh, I didn't know that." Cerise had always assumed that the king's mortal body appeared in a place of significance, not in the presence of a particular person. For his body to follow the pull of his spirit was an oddly romantic element of his curse that she hadn't anticipated. "Is it the same when he loses daytime hours? Does he reappear beside Lady Champlain then, too?"

"For the time being, yes," Father Padron said. "Like all young people, his feelings have been known to change."

A king with a wandering eye? That was no surprise. "But who would want him to die any sooner than he has to? An empty throne would mean war. That's everyone's greatest fear."

Father Padron shifted his focus to the foyer, where the noise of approaching boots grew louder. His gaze tightened. "Not everyone's greatest fear."

The moment Cerise turned to regard the owner of those boots, she took an instinctive step backward. Storming toward them was the largest man she had ever seen, at least two heads taller than Father Padron and twice as broad. Tattooed flames covered the skin on the man's shaven scalp, and his chest stretched the limits of his guard uniform. But it was his expression that turned Cerise cold. His lips were hard as slate, his eyes wild with fury.

If violence had a face, his would be it.

Father Padron rested a hand on her forearm. No words passed between them, but his touch held a promise of protection. "General Petros," he greeted coolly.

Now Cerise understood Father Padron's comment about war. It was a Petros who had forged the weapon to slay the goddess during the Great Betrayal. As punishment, Petros firstborns carried the curse of bloodlust. A man like General Petros would love nothing more than a battle for the throne. Scarier still, his dynasty would probably win.

"Your Grace," the general rumbled through clenched teeth. "I just received word of another incident, this time in southern Calatris." He looked from one priest to another, glaring at them hard enough to engorge the veins at his temples. "I swear by the blood of Shiera that if you don't get your—"

His voice went mute, and his body froze. Cerise tasted the coppery tang of energy and glanced at Father Padron, who hadn't moved a muscle. He stood calm and relaxed, as though paralyzing a mountain of a man caused him no strain at all.

"You will not threaten me," Father Padron said smoothly. "Or anyone in my care. As much as His Majesty values your tactical advice, he values the Order more. You will remember your place, or I will continue to remind you of it."

He released the enchantment and freed the general, whose body trembled with rage. For a moment, the general curled his hands into fists and held still. Then he gave a throaty roar and punched the ground hard enough for Cerise to feel a tremor beneath her shoes. His bones cracked. When he stood up, his hand swung limp and mangled by his side. He didn't seem to notice. He simply turned toward the gatehouse and stalked away.

"Don't worry about his hand," Father Padron said as he watched the general enter the gatehouse. "He's on his way to the temple to visit his mistress. She will heal it." He added darkly, "He thinks I don't know. It's a disgrace."

"You know of the affair?" Cerise whispered. "And you..." *haven't stopped it?* She caught herself before she rudely questioned his judgment, choosing instead to file away the information for later. At this rate, she wouldn't have any space left inside her head.

"Some battles are best saved for the future," he said.

She held her tongue because there was nothing more she could add. Temple Seers, even those with the added gift of healing, weren't magically bound to celibacy like members of the Order were. Priests couldn't engage in physical intimacy. They didn't even desire it. That was the price they paid for their gift. But while the act of love wasn't expressly denied to Seers in the sacred scrolls, it dimmed the Sight. Most Seers refused romantic company for that very reason. Those who took a lover were encouraged to repent or else sent away to parts unknown until they atoned. Cerise had never seen it happen. She had only heard stories.

"I'm sure I don't have to worry about your virtue," Father Padron added, but in a questioning tone that negated his words.

"You don't," Cerise told him. Her inner eye was sightless enough without inviting a lover to muddy her vision.

He lifted an apologetic hand. "I don't mean to offend you. It's just that I've lived at court long enough to know how laymen think. They'll consider you a prize. You're special, so they think that winning you will make them special, too. But they care nothing about your future or what a dalliance will cost you. Do you understand?"

Cerise nodded, trying to look somber while her lips begged to smile. The high priest of Shiera thought she was special. She couldn't imagine a greater compliment than that.

"The goddess will test you," he said. "I only want you to be prepared." He offered his elbow. "Let's put it behind us. Will you join me for morning prayer?"

By way of answer, she took his arm and let him lead her to the sanctuary. The small, domed building stood slightly apart from the palace, connected by a long, covered, open-air corridor that bordered one of the palace gardens. The sanctuary earned its name the moment she stepped across the threshold. There were no silken carpets or magical embellishments in the prayer room, only the familiar black and white floor tiles to symbolize balance between darkness and light. As she lowered onto a floor cushion and closed her eyes, she felt something no enchantment could provide.

Peace.

She spent most of the day there, praying for guidance, and at his invitation, she enjoyed lunch with Father Padron in his sitting room. He listened without judgment as she told him the truth about her lack of Sight. He didn't even flinch when she asked about the elderly woman who had touched her skirts the day before.

"I thought you would be angry," she confessed, "that I brought it up."

"Angry?" His face softened into a smile. "The fact that you want to save the fallen is a testament to your purity of heart. How could I feel anything but admiration for you, Cerise?"

A blush crept into her cheeks. "Then the woman hasn't been… dispatched?"

"Dispatched?" He drew back. "My goodness, is that what you think happens under my watch? Abuse? Murder?"

"No, Your Grace," she said, but in truth, the Order wasn't known for its tolerance. "Of course not. I shouldn't have assumed the worst."

"I assure you the maid was given a warning and released," he told her. "Her punishment was the loss of her position here at the palace, but I believe she has already found another posting in the city. I'm nothing if not merciful. How can we expect the goddess to forgive our sins if we're unable to forgive others?"

Relief washed over her, and not simply for the elderly woman's sake. Father Padron was the head of Shiera's Order, and she was glad to find he wasn't cruel, that he was a good man. She was still obligated to protect the revelation, but today, in her heart, Father Padron had taken a step toward being an ally.

His kindness mattered more to her than he probably knew.

"May I ask one more question?" she said.

"As I've told you, Cerise, you may ask me anything."

"Nothing was explained to me when I was sent here," she began. "I've heard that the people in the city expect me to do miracles. I'm already going to disappoint them by being ordinary. I don't want to be incompetent as well. How can I impress the king when I meet him tomorrow? What will my first day as emissary look like?"

"Let me put your mind at ease," Father Padron said. "The king will expect very little, if anything, from you in the way of political guidance. And as for spiritual guidance, you needn't waste your efforts."

"What do you mean?"

"Do you remember how His Majesty spends his days?"

"In his chamber with his courtesan."

"The king is seldom seen and rarely heard," Father Padron explained. "He dismissed the majority of his court several moons ago. Since then, he has withdrawn from the daily business of rule. The people you saw yesterday were mainly palace servants, along with a few courtiers who chose to remain. There are no meetings for you to attend, no public audiences or hearings, because he cancelled them all."

"Are you saying I have nothing to do here?"

"That is exactly what I'm saying," he told her. "Try not to worry."

Oddly, it didn't make her feel better to learn that she had no role in the palace. There must be *something* for her to do; otherwise, the Reverend Mother wouldn't have Seen the image of her studying "quite dutifully" at the emissary's desk. But she kept that thought to herself, and she left Father Padron to his duties.

She didn't realize how long she had spent inside the sanctuary until she noticed the low sunlight slanting across the foyer. Judging by the scent of roasting meat, dinner would be served soon. There seemed no point in returning to her room only to leave it again, so she drifted outside in search of the garden she had seen last night from her balcony.

The air began to surrender its moisture as the sun slid closer to the horizon. She decided this was her favorite time of day in Mortara, and when she reached the garden, she noticed with pleasure that she had it all to herself. The flowers in Mortara were different than the ones in Solon, blooming in vibrant blues, pinks, and purples, but not as delicate. They were thicker to the touch and less satiny, with tough stems. The harsh climate had made them strong. She wanted to be strong, too.

A sweet chirping from nearby drew her gaze to a wooden trellis, on which perched the tiniest frog she had ever seen. She had never come across anything like it in her books. Vivid blue and about the size of her thumbnail, its form was delicate, unlike the tough plants all around it. Its eyes were large for its face, giving it an undoubtedly cute appearance. She crept slowly toward the trellis, trying not to startle the frog. Once she had moved close enough to touch it, she stretched out a hand to welcome the tiny creature into her palm.

A sudden rush of movement whizzed past her ear, followed by a *thud*. The next thing she knew, the frog was dead, pinned to the wooden trellis by a dagger. Gasping, she whirled around to see who had thrown the weapon.

That was when she met His Majesty Kian Hannibal Mortara.

A thrill passed through her at the sight of him. She had seen his official portrait many times—shoulder-length ebony hair parted down the middle, framing a copper-hued face and a pair of gray eyes she considered more dangerous than attractive. But in person he commanded a bold presence that oils couldn't capture. Instead of his royal military jacket, he wore canvas pants and a black silk shirt rolled at the sleeves, revealing strong, tanned forearms made taut by clenching fists. He hadn't smiled for his portrait, and he wasn't smiling now. He was glaring at her as though she were something vulgar he had discovered underneath a rock.

"Didn't they teach you anything at the temple?" he demanded. For a sliver of a second, she thought she saw more than anger in his eyes. He seemed...disappointed.

Catching herself, she dipped in a low curtsy.

"Not that, you insipid girl!" He flung a hand toward the frog. *"That."*

Insipid girl? Her lips parted in offense. She was of noble birth, and king or not, he had no right to treat her like a serving wench.

"I am…" Her voice trembled, and she lifted her chin to try again. "I am a lady of the temple, and you will address me as such."

The king broke into laughter—a slow, menacing chuckle that did nothing to warm his gaze. "I see you've met my high priest."

She didn't like the way he said *my* high priest, as if the sacred Order was a commodity to be traded among laymen. "I've met Father Padron, yes."

"A pity he spent more time overinflating your ego than teaching you which creatures to avoid." He jutted his chin at the frog while striding toward it. "Like that one. It emits toxins through its skin. One touch, and not even Padron could have saved you in time." He pulled his dagger free and pointed the blade at her. "You're welcome, by the way."

Cerise realized she was backing up, and she stopped. She wouldn't let him bully her. "If that's true, then I owe you my gratitude, Your Highness."

"If that's true," he repeated while raking a disdainful gaze over her. "You're the emissary they sent here to deliver me from evil? Forgive me if I lack faith, *my lady*, but you don't look like much. You don't even have the Sight, do you?"

She clenched her jaw, refusing to answer him. Clearly, he had heard the same rumor that Daerick had told her about. And she had been right in predicting that the king would hate her when he learned the truth.

The king's gaze dipped to the throbbing pulse point at the base of her throat. One corner of his lips curved up. He thrust his dagger into the trellis and then began inching toward her. "Do you want to know how I can tell you have no Sight?" he asked. "True Seers possess a calm that comes from the ability to See the paths around them. But you're more frightened than a rabbit staring down a viper, aren't you?"

Her confident mask slipped. He couldn't possibly know about the rabbit kit and the lowland flamewinder, could he?

"Let me predict something for you, my lady of the temple." His voice, already deep, turned sinister. "You *will* find evil here, in the most unexpected places. By the time the shadows consume me and I dissolve into nothing, you'll wish you could forget all the things the temple has hidden from you."

Cerise swallowed hard and held her ground at first. But as he quickened his steps, advancing toward her with no hint of stopping, she scurried backward, nearly tripping over the hem of her gown. His tall, broad frame began to fade at the edges, curling into smoke. Still he advanced, until she was certain their bodies would collide. She balled her fists and closed her eyes, tensing for the blow, but instead of impact, a cool breeze rushed over her, brushing back her hair.

She opened her eyes and blinked.

All that remained of the king was a pile of clothing at her feet.

5

The next morning, Cerise made it her mission to seek out Daerick Calatris. Her face hadn't stopped flushing with embarrassment since her disastrous first meeting with the king, and after another long night of restless sleep, she no longer cared whether His Majesty had dismissed his court, or if his meetings had been cancelled, or if he had withdrawn from his responsibilities and absolved Cerise of hers.

She was tired of feeling like a failure.

The title of emissary belonged to her now—for better or for worse—and she would perform her duties with honor. Sightless as she was, she had other skills. She was better read than anyone else at the temple, having spent night after night with her nose buried in books, trying to find a way to bring about her gift. With any luck, Daerick would teach her what her duties entailed.

And she didn't have to leave her room to find him. He appeared at her suite before she had even finished her breakfast. He knocked twice and announced himself from the corridor.

When she opened the door to let him inside, it took her a

moment to recognize him, dressed as he was in the gauzy linen of a laborer instead of silk finery. "Lord Calatris," she greeted in a tone that was more of a question.

"Good morning, my lady." Daerick indicated his plain clothes and extended a matching bundle of folded garments to her. "I know what you're thinking: *How is Daerick so devilishly handsome, even in the garb of a peasant?*"

"Yes, you read my thoughts," she said, playing along with his game. She took the folded clothes and smelled them. She found them clean, which was a relief, as it seemed she was meant to put them on. "Please don't keep me in suspense, my lord."

"I have a surprise for you." He pointed at the clothes he had given her. "But first, you have to change into that cap and dress."

She arched an eyebrow. Impersonating a stranger didn't seem like a good sort of surprise.

"The king has invited us to accompany him into the city," Daerick told her. "I accepted on behalf of both of us, because there's someplace I want to take you. And in that particular part of the city, it's best if we don't draw too much attention to ourselves."

"So you want us to dress as commoners," Cerise said. "But won't we draw attention to ourselves anyway by traveling with the king?"

"Yes and no. He won't be with us for long."

"Where is it you want to take me?"

"So many questions!" he complained.

"And so few answers…"

"All right," he said, "I'd rather tell you when we get there. Strictly speaking, our destination isn't considered fitting for a lady of the temple. I don't want to put you in a position of having to lie to anyone like Father Padron, who might intercept you and ask where we're going today."

"I don't like the sound of that." And though Daerick didn't know it, he'd already put her in a position of having to lie by telling her she was going somewhere that was not appropriate for a lady of her station. "I was hoping you would show me the former emissary's office and help me learn her duties. Did you find her journal?"

"Not yet, but I will. I promise." Daerick leaned down and peered intently at her. "The emissary's office isn't going anywhere. But for the errand I have in mind, we have only today. Do this one favor for me, and then I'll teach you anything you want."

"Do you promise it's safe?"

"I give you my word."

"All right, then. We have a deal."

She ushered Daerick out of her suite so she could change from her temple gown into the plainsmen clothes he had brought her. The outfit was a simple one that included a beige linen dress with long, loose sleeves to protect her arms from the sun and a long hemline to cover her legs to the ankles. She tucked her hair into a matching beige cap, slipped her feet into the plain leather sandals she had worn during summers at the temple, and then met Daerick in the corridor.

To her relief, she didn't have to lie to Father Padron because she passed neither him nor anyone else she knew on the way out of the palace. Daerick guided her outside, beyond the spot where she had seen the desert panther the day before, and then the two of them continued along the grass-carpeted path leading to the front gate. A small group of people had formed in the shade of the fruit trees lining the path. As Cerise approached the group, she identified several royal guards, and with them, the king and his courtesan, Lady Delora Champlain.

The king sat on a stone bench beneath a citrus tree, one arm curled around Lady Champlain's waist and the other tipping a leather flask to his mouth. He seemed to be wearing the same clothes that he had abandoned the previous night in the garden: badly wrinkled canvas pants and a black silk shirt rolled at the sleeves.

For a brief moment, Cerise wondered if his body had reappeared in the garden at sunrise, but then she remembered that he materialized where his spirit was drawn, which was to Lady

Champlain's bedchamber. Perhaps Delora had collected the king's clothes and brought them to her rooms. Regardless, His Majesty hadn't bothered to dress properly for the day. And judging by the looseness of his limbs and the sloppy grin he delivered when their eyes met, he was drunk.

At breakfast time.

Half a king, indeed.

"My lady of the temple," he slurred while feigning a seated bow. Liquid dribbled from his flagon down the front of his shirt. "You're looking quite…" He squinted at her clothing. "*Peasantly* this morning."

"'Peasantly'?" Daerick repeated with a snigger. He brushed a bit of lint from the sleeve of his own tunic. "Did the Royal Academy of Linguists add that delightful nugget to the lexicon when I wasn't looking?"

"Oh, shut up," the king spat. "I can invent whatever words I want."

Cerise dipped her head in a show of respect that she didn't feel. "And you're looking rather…*relaxed*, Your Majesty."

Kian chortled from low in his belly, but it was a disingenuous sound, no more pleasing to her ears than the cold laughter he had used as a weapon against her the day before. As she approached him, she smelled the tang of hard cider, and she turned her eyes to Daerick in a silent question. Was the king always like this? Intoxicated and childish? As rude and spoiled as an entitled schoolboy?

"His Majesty has honored us with an invitation to the city," Daerick said with a hint of sarcasm in his voice. "He even cancelled all of his royal engagements to do so. Isn't that generous of him?"

"Long live the king," Kian muttered. He fished a pillbox from his trouser pocket and tossed a handful of stomach soothers into his mouth, then threw back his head, draining the last few drops from his flask. He frowned at the empty container. "I want something stronger than cider, and I know just the place to find it." The king stood and stumbled before offering his arm to Delora. "My lady. Shall we earn our wicked reputations?"

"It would be my pleasure," Delora said. She smoothed a hand over her silk-draped curves, drawing attention to the swells of her breasts. "They say the lower a lady's neckline, the worse she can behave."

Kian chuckled. "Then you'll get away with murder, my dear."

While Cerise resisted the urge to roll her eyes to the heavens, she caught something in Lady Champlain's smile—a hint of wariness that made her look twice. No one else in the group had seemed to notice; certainly not the king. If he had paid attention to more than Delora's breasts, he might have noted that her grin didn't extend beyond her mouth. He might have detected the stiffness in her shoulders and the way she held too tightly to his arm.

The king's courtesan seemed afraid. But of what? Or of whom?

Perhaps she'd read too much into Delora's mannerisms. She fell into step behind the pair, watching their body language as the group strolled beyond the armored gatehouse doors and toward the city entrance, which was equally guarded by dozens of uniformed soldiers.

Cerise waved Daerick over and asked him in a low voice, "Are you ready to tell me where we're going?"

"Not yet," he whispered. "There are too many ears around us. But we'll be alone soon. There's a gambling hall no more than three paces inside the city gate. The king won't be able to pass it up."

She cast him a doubtful glance.

"Believe me," Daerick said. "Kian and I have been friends for a long time. If there's one thing I know, it's his vices."

"Friends?" she asked. "He doesn't treat you like one."

"He's not himself today."

"Was he himself yesterday?" she challenged. "Because I met him in the garden, and he introduced himself with a blade." At Daerick's wide-eyed response, she told him about the tiny frog and how the king had taunted her after killing it. "He hates me. He couldn't have made it any plainer."

She expected Daerick to deny her claim or at least to make an excuse for the king's behavior, but he didn't. She almost wished that he had.

"My lady of the temple," the king called over one shoulder while stumbling ahead on the grassy path. "You're a second-born Solon. Who bears your family curse?"

"My sister, Nina," she told him. "She's married and has an estate in Calatris."

"Are you close in age?" Delora asked.

"Oh, no, she's much older than me," Cerise said. "I think she was meant to be an only child, and I was a surprise."

"Is your sister beautiful?" the king asked.

Cerise touched the pendant beneath her dress and caught herself smiling. "No, Your Highness. She is not."

The king stopped short and swung his dark gaze to her, setting his ebony waves in motion. Delora peered around his shoulder, equally intrigued.

"A sunrise is beautiful," Cerise explained. "A flower is beautiful. A sky full of stars is beautiful. My sister is something else entirely. She casts a shadow over beauty. I forget my own name when I see her face. All I want to do is keep looking at her. I would stare at her all day if she would let me."

For some reason, the king didn't seem to like her answer. He stood there furrowing his brow until Delora grinned and said, "We have a firstborn Solon at the palace. His name is Cole. Half of the old court was in love with him."

The king snorted a dry laugh and continued walking a crooked path. "Maybe my father was one of them. That would explain why he never killed the slippery bastard." He glanced at Cerise. "My mother and Cole Solon were lovers."

Cerise felt her eyes go wide.

"It was no secret," Kian said, facing away from her again. "Well, no secret to anyone but *you*...the blessed oracle."

Cerise probably should've stayed quiet, but instead, she blurted, "Blessed as I am, even I have my limitations, Your Majesty."

"True," he agreed. "So tell me, my lady of the temple—if you hold a hand in front of your face, will you be able to See it? Or is that another one of your limitations?"

She glared at the back of his head. She had a hand gesture in mind, but she chose to behave like a lady instead of showing it to him.

They continued in silence until they reached the armored gate that separated the palace grounds from the city marketplace.

"Here we are." The king spread his arms wide. "My glorious city, filled with subjects who adore me as much as you do, Lord Calatris."

Daerick laughed. "Then it's a good thing your men are armed."

"And that my subjects aren't," the king added.

Cerise glanced at the guard in front of her and the broadsword holstered to his hip. The law forbade common folk from owning any weapon deadlier than a dagger, but even the smallest of blades could make a man bleed. Surely the king wouldn't visit the city if it was unsafe for him.

Or would he? Was he that reckless?

That would explain his courtesan's fear. Though looking at Delora now—concealing a yawn behind her delicate hand—she seemed more bored than afraid.

The heavy gate began to lift. Each slow inch admitted a new chorus of sounds: first the steady hammering of mallets, and then raised voices followed by hooves clopping against stone. When the gate reached Cerise's knees, she detected the scents of grilled meat, rotting garbage, and unwashed bodies. Despite the unpleasantness of it all, a grin found its way to her lips. The odor was a familiar one that had reached her Solon temple grounds when the wind had blown from the west. Her visits to the city market had been a rare treat. She was eager to see what this one had to offer.

A tingle of excitement stirred inside her. Before the gate had fully risen, she crouched slightly to peer beneath it. The city was an exotic delight, like something out of a storybook. A wide, stone-paved street stretched out before her, lined with clay stucco buildings of varying height and width. Each structure was connected to the next by a second-story wooden walkway that allowed foot traffic from above as well as below. Plain folk bustled to and fro, outfitted in thin linen and simple sandals, or else in bare feet and exposed chests. Men and women alike wore their hair tucked into a cap or cropped close with just enough growth to protect their scalps from the sun. She noticed only two women with braids coiling in spirals around their heads. Both of them wore an extra layer of linen in a colorful sash over their dresses. Clearly, that was the mark of wealth here, proof that one could remain indoors and cool for the bulk of the day.

From the porch rafters of a meat shop hung several beheaded chickens with bat-like hides instead of feathers. Other creatures had similar traits to thrive in the Mortara heat, like the furless dogs sniffing for scraps along the gutters, and above them, the naked squirrels dancing along a roof's ledge. The animals looked odd compared to those Cerise had known, but they were cute in their own way.

A bead of sweat trickled down the back of her neck. She wiped away the perspiration and stood to find Daerick and Kian watching her, one with amusement and the other with disdain. She glanced away from the king. She didn't know what she had done to earn his low opinion of her. It was true that she had no Sight, but she wasn't the one drunk before midday.

As Daerick predicted, the king soon led Delora into the nearest gambling hall. Half of his soldiers followed him inside while the other half stood sentry by the doorway.

"Is he safe here?" she asked Daerick. "You made it sound like he's not well loved by the people."

"He has his critics, like all kings do," Daerick said. "But they're outnumbered by his supporters, at least for now. He'll be all right."

"Now can you tell me where we're going?"

Nodding, Daerick led her forward until they reached the first intersection, where they scaled a set of stairs and resumed their walk on the second-story pathway. There was less bustle above the street—and more privacy. "There's an old man staying in the city," Daerick murmured as they strode briskly across the wooden planks. "He's a traveler. He only passes through here once or twice a year. That's why we couldn't wait."

"What's so special about this man?"

"Are you sure you want to know? You might not like the answer."

"Tell me."

"He's a soothsayer."

She cut her eyes at him. "There's no such thing as soothsayers. Oracles have the Sight, and priests have magic. Anyone else is fooling you with tricks or illusions. You of all people should know that."

"All right," Daerick said. "Then let's call him an acutely perceptive individual with a talent for discerning truth from fiction."

"Perceptive how?" she asked. "What truth do you expect him to tell you?"

Before Daerick could answer her, a Seer rounded the corner ahead of them, followed by a pair of oracles in training, all three of them gliding toward Cerise with an elegance she had never quite mastered. One of the novices carried a tray laden with coins and trinkets—offerings that had been made in exchange for healing or divination. The other had a small animal on her shoulder, a scaly primate with a long tail that curled at the tip. As the Seer glided closer to Cerise and Daerick, the woman slowed her steps, eventually stopping to regard Cerise in confusion.

The Seer moved her sharpened gaze over Cerise's face until the woman frowned and tilted her head to the side. "Your future path..."

"Yes, my lady?" Cerise asked.

"Why can I not See it?" the woman demanded. She flicked a hand at Daerick. "His fate is clear enough. Tragic but clear." She peered harder. "But yours? Nothing."

Cerise traded a glance with Daerick, who had paled a shade. She took his hand and squeezed it. "The goddess works in mysterious ways. Our paths can change according to her will. Don't you agree?"

Nobody answered.

The scaled monkey gave a light *squeak* and climbed down the length of his owner's arm. He blinked owlishly at Cerise, and then, with no warning whatsoever, he leaped into her arms. Though startled, she caught him. He gripped the front of her dress and wasted no time in rubbing his cheek against hers. The dry tickle of his skin made her smile.

"He must be friendly," she said while stroking his warm back.

The novice stared open-mouthed at her. "I didn't See this," the girl said, whirling to face her superior. "My mind's eye showed me our walk to the temple. Imp hissed at everyone we passed."

"You see?" Cerise said. She gently gathered Imp and handed him back to his owner, who had to tempt him with a fig to make him stay in her arms. "Paths can change."

"You have a way with animals," Daerick told her a while later, when they had descended the stairs to the street level and then turned left at an intersection where the buildings were thin and grouped closer together.

Cerise caught herself rubbing the fang-shaped scars on her forearm. "Mammals seem to like me. Reptiles, not so much."

"What's your secret?" he asked.

"I adore animals," she said simply. "I always have." For all its glory, the temple could be a lonely place for a child. "If I wanted affection, I knew better than to go to a Seer. I visited the rabbit hutch or the kennels. The kits and pups were always happy to see me. They gave me love. I needed that, and I think they could sense it."

"Animal instincts don't lie," Daerick said. "It's one of the advantages they have over mankind."

"*One* of the advantages?" she asked as she peeked farther down the street. The upper level was mostly residential. Everything of interest took place below. She saw a vendor selling palm-sized winged creatures that she desperately wanted to hold. "What are the others?"

"Freedom from the micromanaging of polite society." He hesitated before adding, "And from the Order."

Cerise stopped in her tracks, taken aback by his words. "The Sacred Order is a gift from the goddess. She gives us priests for enrichment and protection, and oracles to heal us and guide our paths. The Order doesn't take. It gives."

"Says the girl taken at birth from her family."

"It was my honor to serve in the temple."

"But you didn't volunteer for that service." Daerick glanced left and right, then lowered his voice. "It was forced on you—on all second-borns. No one should have the right to take away your freedom."

"But Shiera decreed it as part of the atonement for the Great Betrayal."

"Did she?" Daerick asked. "How do we know? We didn't hear her decrees. We have only the words of priests to tell us what Shiera wants."

"And scrolls," she said. She had read every word and every line.

"And scrolls," he conceded. "But that leads me to a deeper question: Why are the priests in control of an Order dedicated to worshipping a goddess? Shiera is a woman, so why aren't the Seers in higher positions of power?"

"For equity," Cerise said easily. She had gone looking for the same answer when she was a child. "Shiera is darkness and light, wrath and mercy. She creates balance in all things, so for her to give more power to her own sex would create instability."

"But I don't see balance," Daerick argued. "It's the priests who decide what constitutes a sin. It's the priests who determine the punishment for that sin, and it's the priests who carry out the sentence. Seers have no real say within the Order. Even your Reverend Mother would have to bend the knee to Father Padron if he required it."

Cerise tried to come up with a counterargument, but she

couldn't. Memorizing the scrolls hadn't prepared her to debate a firstborn Calatris. Discussing theology with Daerick was akin to arguing with a library that had come to life.

Daerick pointed above the rooftops to the nearby temple. Alongside the temple spire stood a statue of Shiera, her marble arms and shoulders thick with muscle, a spear in her mighty hand. "Look at her," Daerick said. "What makes you think that a goddess as fierce and as powerful as Shiera—a woman strong enough to craft this world and perhaps others, to give life and to take it away— would allow her sex to be dominated by men?"

Cerise could only repeat what the Order had told her since birth. "It is not our place to question the will of Shiera."

"Says who?"

"The...priests."

"Well, how convenient for the priests," Daerick said. "To do whatever they please in the name of the goddess and then forbid anyone from questioning them. That kind of unrestricted control would almost make them gods themselves, wouldn't you say?"

A flicker of anger rose in her chest. "That's sacrilege."

"Says who?"

"The scrolls."

"They were written by mortals."

"Mortals inspired by the goddess."

"Says who?" Daerick repeated. "What proof did the Order give you?"

"I don't need proof," she told him. "I have faith."

Daerick smiled sadly at her. "And that's why the Order will win."

"Win?" she asked. "Win against what? You make it sound like we're at war."

"Let me show you something," he said, and they began walking again.

They strode across two more streets, passed the city temple, and continued to an open-air vegetable market where the homes and shops were smaller and beginning to crumble at the edges. The farther they ventured from the palace, the fewer merchants peddled exotic wares. Soon the vendors disappeared altogether. There were no braids or colorful sashes in this part of town. Most of the children were barely wearing clothes.

They stopped at the fringes of a packed-dirt courtyard, where two priests were administering to a group of plain folk. Magical advancements were reserved for royalty and the Order, but priests helped the plain folk in other ways, using their gifts to mend plows, enrich the soil, and cast enchantments of honesty to settle disputes.

Daerick took her by the hand and guided her to a shaded alleyway situated behind the priests. He stopped and indicated for her to listen.

At first, she heard nothing beyond the ordinary. One man wanted his mule made fertile. Another man begged to have his broken loom restored. Both requests were granted. Then a trio of men approached the priests and bowed their heads.

"May Shiera's light shine upon you," one priest said.

"And may her wrathful eye look away," came the joint reply. The group spokesman stood tall and stated his request. "Please, fathers, we beg you. Use your magic to bring back the rains. Our honey fruit orchard is dying. You gave us rain for many years, and now—"

"You know I cannot," the priest interrupted. "The king has forbidden it."

Angry murmurs broke out among the crowd.

"But why?" demanded the man. "All of the magic in the realm is at his disposal."

"It is not our place to question His Majesty," the priest said. "Only to carry out his will."

This response drew an even more turbulent reaction from the plain folk, who shouted *It's not right!* and *Down with the Half King!* Just when Cerise began to worry that the crowd might lash out at the priests, she tasted the coppery tang of magic and felt a sense of calm wash over her. The first priest shouted, "Return to your homes," and then he staggered weakly against his partner, exhausted from using his energy to calm the crowd.

Within moments, all of the plain folk dispersed.

The enchantment drained away as soon as the priests left. Cerise looked to Daerick for an explanation. "Why would the king inflict a drought upon his own people?" she asked. "There are already so many blighted crops here."

Daerick responded with a question of his own. "Have you ever tried one of Mortara's native fruits, like sand melon?"

She shook her head.

"Sand melon tastes exactly like it sounds. Everyone raises honey fruit instead, which doesn't grow here naturally. The royal family imported the saplings hundreds of years ago when they started using priests to multiply the rainfall."

"So?" she asked.

"So now farmers are dependent on weather patterns that shouldn't exist. No one wants to raise native crops anymore. They want to grow imports that need steady rain to thrive."

Cerise turned up both palms.

"Who do the priests serve?" Daerick asked.

"House Mortara."

"And when the Mortara line ceases to exist?"

"I…I don't know."

"No one knows," Daerick said. "Not even me, and that's saying a lot. We don't even know why the priests are bound in servitude to the Mortara dynasty in the first place. But I can tell you one thing: the priests aren't going to stay in this dusty hellhole if they're free to go wherever they want. If Kian vanishes without an heir, it's possible that no one will be able to command the priests. And if that's the case, it's only a matter of time until they leave Mortara."

Now Cerise began to understand about the rain.

Daerick touched her wrist. "A good king protects his people. And if he knows his time is coming to an end, he makes sure they can survive without him. The priests know that, but they didn't explain it to the farmers. Doesn't that make you wonder who they *really* serve? They rely on faith, but it's not faith to ignore common sense. It's foolishness."

Cerise considered Daerick's words. She didn't want to believe that the priests had intentionally misled anyone, though it did seem odd that they hadn't explained their reasoning to the crowd. But more than that, she couldn't reconcile Kian, the stumbling drunkard, with the selfless ruler Daerick had described. "Does a good king skip his council meetings to drink ale and gamble on fighting birds?"

"He might, if he was a firstborn with only six moons to live."

She drew a breath to argue, but Daerick beat her to it.

"You're not a firstborn," he said. "You don't know what it's like to count down the days until you disappear, either inside the void of your own mind or into the shadows."

Cerise glanced at her toes. He was right. She didn't know that pain.

"Try to picture it," he said. "Imagine how you would prepare for your curse, how you would harden yourself to face your inevitable suffering. Now imagine that after years of detaching yourself from everyone and everything that brings you joy, you finally grow a thick enough callus over your heart that you no longer fear the end. You're prepared for it. You've made peace with your fate…until one day, news arrives that a mighty oracle is coming to save you."

Her guilt multiplied.

"Your first reaction wouldn't be excitement," Daerick said. "It would be fear. Because the callus on your heart took years to build, and you're terrified of reopening that wound. But you can't help it. Despite your better judgment, you allow yourself to hope."

"And then the mighty oracle turns out to be ordinary," Cerise said. She remembered the way Kian had looked at her in the garden, as if she had failed him. He wasn't punishing her for her lack of Sight. He was punishing the both of them because he had allowed himself to hope, and in return, he had doubled his pain. "He's given up on life."

"Don't take it personally," Daerick told her. "I imagine it's hard to have faith when nobles are already killing each other to eliminate competition for the throne."

"That's happening?"

"Two dead in Calatris already. There will be more. That's just the way the wind blows." Daerick lifted a shoulder. "So you can probably understand why hope is a cruel mistress for the king. Almost as brutal as the shadows."

Two dead in Calatris. That must have been the incident General Petros had referred to the day before, when he had confronted Father Padron on the palace lawn. But before Cerise could give it any more thought, her attention was drawn by something else Daerick had said.

"Brutal as the shadows?" she repeated. "Father Padron told me the king has no memory of his nighttime hours."

"That's what Kian told me, too," Daerick said. "But I wonder… what healthy twenty-year-old carries a tin of stomach soothers in his pocket?" He arched a brow. "All firstborn nobles feel anxiety. They all have ways to dull it, but few have to medicate themselves."

"What do you think happens to the king at night?"

"I have no idea. But I recognize torment when I see it."

Cerise didn't want to hear any of this. She didn't want to believe that Kian was suffering when the shadows claimed him after sunset, because that would mean an eternity of torment for him when he vanished completely. According to lore, Mortara firstborns didn't truly die. They remained in darkness forever.

"Why did you bring me here?" she asked. "What was the point of telling me all of this? What is it you expect me to do, apart from feel horrible?"

"Remember the perceptive old man I mentioned?" Daerick said. "The man who's definitely not a soothsayer because you don't believe that soothsayers exist?"

"Yes. And I asked you what truth he perceives."

"He perceives the dark and forbidden. Specifically blood curses — and how to break them. Now can you see why I would like to meet him?"

Cerise grimaced. She had heard stories of dark priests, fallen members of the Order who had deserted their temples and now slunk throughout the lands, hiding in caves and casting enchantments for coin. Was this the sort of man Daerick wanted her to meet? If so, he didn't understand what he was asking of her. To encounter a rogue priest—and then fail to report him—would make her complicit in his crime of sorcery. Even if she kept the truth to herself, someone in the Order might eventually suspect her, and then Father Padron could compel a confession out of her as easily as blinking.

But when she opened her mouth, the eager look on Daerick's face stole her words. He had hope. He had put his faith in her, even though she didn't deserve it. She couldn't stand by and wait for his Claiming Day to ruin him. Nor could she watch the king disappear into the shadows without lifting a finger to try to help him. If there was the slightest chance that Daerick's "perceptive" acquaintance could lead them to breaking the noble curses, she had to take it.

6

Cerise didn't know where she had expected Daerick to take her, but an underground hovel on the fringe of the city's pleasure district was the last place she'd had in mind. She frowned at a set of uneven clay steps descending steeply into the ground. Beyond the packed dirt at the bottom, she could see nothing but shadow. Her only clue as to what she might find down there was the occasional sound of violent retching.

"Delightful," she whispered, gathering the fabric of her neckline around her face. "I won't ask how you know about this place."

"Best that you don't," Daerick agreed. "I've never met this particular soothsayer before, but I've had many dealings here, and I doubt you would approve of any of them."

"I thought you were a gentleman."

"Well, sometimes the pursuit of knowledge comes before propriety."

She wrinkled her nose at him. "Do I have to come in? I would rather wait here while you..." She trailed off when a man from the other side of the street whistled to her and offered her a copper bit for five minutes of her company.

"You were saying?" Daerick asked.

"Never mind. Lead the way."

She kept her nose covered and her eyes fixed on the back of Daerick's head as she followed him into the bowels of the den. They crossed through a dim, open room littered with bodies, some of them unconscious, others engaged in activities that she blocked from her peripheral vision by adjusting her cap.

Soon they reached a door, and Daerick knocked on it in a code of three slow raps followed by two quick ones. Someone from the other side spoke in a language she didn't understand. Daerick answered in the same language, and the door opened.

Musky incense enveloped her. She entered a tiny room, clean and brightly lit by an assortment of candles resting on the polished floor. It seemed like the perfect meeting place, cleverly concealed as it was in a hovel where no one would think to look. Plush seating cushions were scattered about. Two of the cushions were occupied, one by a young man the approximate size of an ox, and the other by a withered elder who was clearly the "perceptive" man that Daerick had brought her to see. As she approached the pair, she noticed with a start that the elderly man had no eyes. His sockets were covered by skin and sunken with age, as though he had been born that way.

The younger man stiffened protectively and glared at Cerise. "Who is this? She's new."

"She's my cousin," Daerick said. He indicated the difference between his pale skin and her olive tone and clarified, "Twice removed."

The old man wheezed a laugh. "No, she's not. I can smell the difference in your blood."

Cerise glanced at Daerick, who nudged her a step closer toward the man.

"Come," the elder said and patted the spot in front of him.

With some reluctance, she sat beside Daerick on a floor cushion, leaving an arm's length of distance between herself and the two men facing her. As soon as she and Daerick were situated, the elderly man leaned forward and inhaled deeply through his nose.

"You're a Calatris," he said to Daerick. "A firstborn. I can smell the curse on you."

That didn't necessarily impress Cerise. Daerick was a member of court, a public figure of sorts. Maybe the elderly man had recognized his voice or his cologne.

"But the girl," the man said and then inhaled again. "She is something else."

She waited for him to go on.

The elder drew another deep breath through his nose. "I detect a hint of Solon in your veins."

"My father is a Solon," she said.

"Do you mean your mother?" he asked.

"No, my father," she told him.

The man made a noise of contemplation. "There's something stronger in your blood than your Solon roots. But I don't recognize it. The scent is…confusing."

"*That* could be my mother," Cerise said. She and Mama bore such a strong resemblance to each other that they could easily pass for twins born in different generations. "My mother is common-born. She was adopted by a merchant when she was a baby, so we know nothing about her lineage."

The old man waved her off. He didn't seem to care about her story.

His enormous young companion, however, *did* seem to care. His eyebrows flattened into a slash, and he told Daerick, "You shouldn't have brought her here."

"Does it matter?" Daerick asked. He pulled a coin pouch from his pocket and jangled it in his palm. "I can vouch for her."

"It matters," the young man growled.

Suddenly, the elder man lunged toward Cerise and snatched her hand with a quickness and strength that surprised her. Before she could object, he reached beneath his cushion and retrieved a short, double-edged blade. She tried to pull away, but he held firm and pricked the pad of her index finger.

"Ow," she cried. "Let go of me!"

Ignoring her, the man squeezed a fat bead of blood to the surface of her skin and sniffed at it. When that didn't satisfy him, he took her finger inside his mouth and sucked it clean.

Disgusting! This was *not* her idea of keeping an open mind!

He released her, and she yanked back her hand. She was so busy trying to wipe off the wetness from the old man's mouth that she missed his initial reaction. When she glanced up at him, she found his gray eyebrows poised high above his sunken, skin-covered sockets.

"Umbra sangi," he whispered to the younger man, who jerked his gaze to Cerise and stared at her as though she had sprouted horns and a tail.

"What does that mean?" she asked.

The old man spat her blood onto the floor and scrubbed a hand over his mouth. She looked to Daerick, who stared blankly ahead, his forehead wrinkled in confusion. It was the first time she had seen him perplexed.

Daerick asked the men, *"Hara 'umbra sangi'?"* but they ignored him and began whispering urgently to each other.

Cerise felt a sense of foreboding, a sickening twist low in her stomach. She didn't understand what was happening, but her instincts warned her to leave. Despite that, she remained pinned to the ground by her own curiosity.

"What does that mean?" she repeated. "What's wrong with my blood? What do you know that you're not telling me?"

"Nothing," the old man blurted. "That's the problem. Your blood has revealed nothing to me."

"Why would that be a problem?"

"Because of his gift," Daerick murmured to her. "He can sense the living history in blood the same way an oracle can See paths to the future."

"And no blood has ever refused me." The elder man wiped his lips again. "Not once in all of my many years. All veins have revealed their secrets to me, except for yours. I don't know what exists beyond your Solon roots. You have confounded me."

The flesh on Cerise's arms prickled into bumps. *You have confounded me.* How many times had the Reverend Mother spoken those same words? How many Seers had complained that they couldn't See the path in front of her? She had confounded them all, and now this man, too. What if she was so far removed from possessing the Sight that she blinded the inner eye of others? What if there was something truly wrong with her?

The large young man pointed at the door. "Leave," he ordered, but in a softer voice than he had used before. "You're not welcome here."

The young giant knew something. She could tell from the change in his demeanor. He was still unfriendly toward her but no longer hostile. It seemed he either feared or respected her now, and she wanted to know why.

She locked eyes with the young man. "Tell me what you're hiding."

"Leave," he repeated.

Daerick held up an index finger. "Please. Just answer one question for me, and then we'll go." He jangled his satchel of coin. "I promise to compensate you for your time."

The elder man turned his face to Daerick. "I know your question, young Calatris. I've heard it on the lips of half of the nobles in the market. You want to know if the rumors about the king's emissary are true."

"Yes," Daerick said. "Can the noble curses be undone?"

"Any curse can be undone," the old man told him. "In one of two ways. The first is to end the life of the individual who cast it. I don't recommend that for you. The goddess has proven herself difficult to kill."

The younger man raised an eyebrow in agreement.

"Your other option," the elder continued, "is to reverse the offense committed against the spell caster."

"But he committed no wrong," Cerise argued.

"The offenses of his ancestors, then," the man said. "The solution for generational curses is the same as any other. You must appease the spell caster by reversing the injury that was done to them."

Cerise tried to imagine reversing the Great Betrayal. She couldn't picture such a thing. "Are you suggesting that we find the Petros Blade, lure the goddess down from the heavens, seduce her into taking mortal form, and then...*un*stab her?"

"Of course not," the old man said. "The penance is different for each wrongdoing. You'll have to discover this one for yourself. But I can tell you the reversal of blood spilled is almost always blood sacrificed."

"Blood for blood," Daerick mused. "But how? What would that look like?"

"I wish I knew," the old man said.

The elder's young companion extended a hand for payment. "Your question has been answered. Now honor your deal and go."

Daerick didn't argue. He tossed his pouch of coin to the large man and then escorted Cerise out of the room. The two of them left the den the same way they had entered it, saying nothing until they had climbed the steep clay steps that led out of the hovel and into the street.

Cerise squinted against the sunlight while her nose acclimated to the strong scents of the city. "I don't feel like we learned much," she told Daerick. "I hope that satchel was full of copper and not silver."

"Oh, I paid him a fortune," Daerick said, scratching the bean sprout beard on his chin. "And he earned every coin."

"Do you really think so?"

Daerick began walking in a different direction than the route they had taken to get there. Cerise followed him, though not before casting a wistful glance over her shoulder. She had hoped to take the same route back to the palace so she could inspect the tiny winged creatures she had seen earlier in the market.

"I do," Daerick answered. "He gave us three valuable bits of information for me to research. First, he told us how curses can be broken, and second, he told us that you're an anomaly."

Cerise didn't appreciate being called an anomaly, but she couldn't think of a more fitting label to replace it. "What's the third?"

"The term *umbra sangi*," he said. "I don't know what it means, but I intend to find out. I think it will explain the soothsayer's reaction to you."

"The younger man's, too," Cerise added. "Did you see the way he looked at me?"

"Like a demon had sprung from your chest?" Daerick asked with a twitch of a grin. "Yes, I noticed. He didn't hide his shock very well."

Daerick quickened his pace and lengthened his stride, forcing Cerise to hasten her steps in an unladylike manner. She thought of asking him to slow down when they reached an open-air farmer's market, but he seemed fueled by excitement and nervous energy. The prospect of breaking the curse had clearly given him a renewed sense of purpose, so she couldn't bring herself to complain.

They made their way out of the city and returned to the royal grounds. When they reached the entrance to the palace, Daerick paused at the bottom step and faced Cerise like a proper gentleman.

"My lady." He took her hand and bowed low, placing a kiss on her knuckles. "Thank you for the pleasure of your company. I hate to leave you without an escort to dinner, but I want to do some research before we begin our emissary lessons tomorrow."

"Of course," she told him, grateful to hear that he had remembered his promise to teach her about her duties. She glanced at her freshly kissed knuckles and smiled. No one had ever kissed her hand before. She rather enjoyed it. The act made her feel older somehow. "I'll see you in the morning, Lord Calatris."

"Daerick," he corrected.

"Only if you call me Cerise."

"Happily, *Cerise*." He climbed the stairs and paused before entering the foyer. "It's still early in the day. I suggest you ask Father Padron for a tour of the archives."

"What archives?"

"In the catacombs beneath the sanctuary. There's a collection of relics and texts down there. I wouldn't know exactly what the archives contain because laymen aren't allowed inside the sanctuary." He lifted a shoulder. "Couldn't hurt to have a look around and see if you can find any useful lore to help us."

She smiled. "I'll look for the volume titled *Reversing the Great Betrayal: A Guidebook for Novices*."

Though she teased, inwardly she felt dark and heavy, a sensation that could only be described as the pain of broken trust. Father Padron could have mentioned the archives to her at any time during the hours she had spent with him in the sanctuary. She hated to think that he'd deliberately concealed the archives from her, but the interaction with the priests in the city weighed heavily on her mind. Perhaps the Mortaran priests had a taste for deception. Even though they toiled in the service of the goddess, they were still human.

She followed Daerick inside the palace and continued up the sweeping staircase to her suite, where she changed out of her peasant garb and into a fresh temple gown. She washed her face and hands and then tidied her hair. When she had made herself presentable, she returned to the first floor, crossed the open-air corridor, and pushed open the sanctuary doors.

The prayer room was empty, the priests having been dispatched to the dining hall for lunch or into the city to perform their duties. When she peered down the adjoining hallway to Father Padron's private chamber, she noticed his door was slightly ajar, indicating he was inside. She could ask him for a tour of the archives, but what if the catacombs were forbidden to novices? If so, then she would have no choice but to accept his rule. But if she discovered the catacombs on her own—before learning they were forbidden—she could claim ignorance if anyone caught her.

Yes, she decided. Better to ask forgiveness than permission.

As she crossed the prayer room, her shoes clicked against the floor tiles with an echo that loosed a chill down her spine. A sudden urge compelled her to stop and look over her shoulder. She turned slowly and checked behind her.

No one was there.

Releasing a breath, she continued to the altar and walked in a circle around it. As she studied its marble construction, she ran her fingers along the sides to check for any hidden hinges or cracks. When that yielded no results, she hitched up her dress and knelt on the floor, using both hands to probe the tile for irregularities.

"What are you doing?"

She gasped so hard she nearly collapsed her lungs. Craning her neck, she discovered a priest standing a few paces away from her—a middle-age redheaded man who seemed to have appeared out of nowhere. Though he stood poised and tranquil with both hands folded in front of him, his eyes betrayed a cold edge that prompted her to crawl backward an inch. This was exactly the kind of man she had avoided at the temple.

"You startled me, Father." She brought a palm to her sternum and attempted a smile. "You must have silent feet. I envy you. It's a skill I never mastered."

"I said," he gritted out, "what are you doing?"

She licked her lips. She couldn't lie and risk him using magic to extract the truth from her, so she chose her next words carefully. "I was looking for something, but it's not here." Before he could press the issue, she stood up from the floor and curtsied. "We haven't met. I'm Cerise Solon, emissary to the king."

The man picked a bit of lint from his robe. "Yes, I know. I'm Father Bishop."

"Oh, yes. I've heard of you," she said. "You're the priest who rescued Lady Champlain from the desert panther in her chambers. I'm glad to see you recovered from the ordeal. Did the sweet cakes help?"

He lowered one brow. "How did you know…"

"Father Padron told me you have a weakness for them."

"I do," he said. But the way he raked his gaze over her face made it clear that he considered her unworthy of the information.

"Yes, well"—she inched toward Father Padron's office—"I should go and find His Grace. It was an honor to meet you, Father Bishop. Shiera's light upon you."

"And may her wrathful eye look away," he replied, but probably only because decorum compelled him to.

As she strode briskly out of the room, she blotted her dewy palms on her skirts. She hadn't decided whether or not to mention the encounter to Father Padron when she knocked twice on his door, and the motion pushed it farther open. But as soon as she saw him standing behind his desk with his back to her, her mind emptied of everything other than the patches of blood seeping through his gilded robes. He turned and met her gaze with a grin that instantly fell when she rushed forward, calling, "Father, you're hurt!"

His sea blue eyes blinked.

"Your back is bleeding," she said.

"Oh, is that all?" He smiled again and settled in his chair. "It's nothing but a little atonement. We are all sinners in our own way."

A *little* atonement? Cerise shook her head. He clearly didn't know how badly he was wounded. "Let me call for a healer. The temple isn't far. It won't take long to—"

"If I require a healer," he interrupted, "I'm fully capable of summoning one. Or healing myself. I possess many gifts."

"But—"

"Cerise." In the single utterance of her name, he warned her to remember her place.

She held her tongue, feeling like a scolded child and hating it.

"Now tell me." He folded both hands atop his desk as if their quibble had never happened. "What brings you here?"

Seeing no other option, she decided to be direct with him. "Lord Calatris told me there are catacombs and archives below the sanctuary. If that's true, I would love to see them."

If her words surprised the high priest, he didn't let it show. "That's true. But I'm afraid the catacombs aren't as intriguing as they sound. There's not much down there except urns and dust and a few scrolls of parchment too ancient to read."

"That sounds intriguing to *me*..."

"Would you like me to give you a tour?"

"I would, Father. If you please."

"Well, then," he said and strode around his desk to present a gentlemanly arm to her. "We will go and see them at once."

He escorted her into the sanctuary, which was beginning to stir with activity as the priests returned from lunch for their afternoon prayers. The men gathered kneeling cushions and dropped them onto the floor. Very few of the priests took note of Cerise, not even Father Bishop, whose eyes were closed in worship. But when she and Father Padron passed the altar and continued to the great stone wall on the other side of it, she felt the sensation of being watched and turned to find every gaze in the room fixed on her.

Not on her. On Father Padron.

"They're staring at you," she whispered to him.

He stopped in front of the wall and lifted a haughty chin. His pride took her by surprise because she had considered him above it. He was the high priest of Shiera, the most powerful man alive. Why would he crave validation from ordinary priests?

"They love to watch me open the catacombs," he murmured. "I'm the only one who can do it alone. The others have to pool their energy."

A charge thickened the air and raised the tiny hairs along the back of her neck. She had never felt magic so strong. It covered her in chills and sent a pleasurable shiver down her spine. The wide section of stone in front of her made a grinding noise as it separated from the wall. It inched forward and then slid aside to reveal a dark entrance that smelled of damp air.

So this was the entrance to the archives. She never would have found it on her own.

She peered into the shadows and saw that the slate floor sloped on a gradual decline, leading deep belowground. With one last flicker of energy from him, dozens of wall sconces caught flame and illuminated the passage. She drifted forward, her hand still resting on Father Padron's forearm, which hadn't so much as tensed during the ordeal of moving the wall.

"May I ask you something, Father?"

He patted her hand. "I have told you, Cerise — you may ask me anything."

"It's about your gift," she said over the crunch of dust and light debris beneath her shoes. "Was it always this powerful, or did it grow with training?"

"In a way, it was both," he said. "When a priest receives his gift, it manifests at full strength from the onset. Each of us is born with a finite amount of transformable energy. My supply happens to be larger than most. Training helped me use my gift to my fullest ability, but it only increased my skill and my efficiency, not my power."

She nodded. It was the same for Seers. An oracle's gift of foresight, however weak or strong it was, remained consistent for life. "Did your gift manifest early?"

"Actually, no, it arrived the morning of my Claiming Day. I suppose you could say I was late to bloom." He slid her an amused glance. "Much like someone else I know."

An unexpected jolt of hope lightened her step. *Maybe she was a late bloomer instead of a weed?*

The corridor led to a stone archway constructed from alternating black and white blocks of polished marble. They passed beneath it and emerged into what appeared to be a mausoleum. Hundreds of silver plaques were affixed to the marble walls in many rows from floor to ceiling. Each plaque bore an engraved name.

"This is the Arch Sanctum," Father Padron said, his voice echoing in the chamber. "Every high priest who has served the Mortara dynasty rests in this room. One day, my ashes will join my brethren who came before me. To be interred here is the greatest honor the Order can bestow upon a man." He teasingly added, "Though I'm in no hurry to accept it."

Cerise glanced around by the light of a flickering torch, searching for relics or scrolls but seeing only cobwebs and dust. For the Order's highest honor, the priests didn't keep the mausoleum very clean. Perhaps they thought the dead didn't care about cobwebs. "You mentioned ancient scrolls?"

"Yes, over here."

He released her hand and strode to the rear left corner of the crypt, where he used his energy to create a slim doorway to another room. She joined him in the antechamber, which bore a slight resemblance to the tomb, only in miniature. Its marble walls, also dulled by neglect, had been hollowed out to create shelves, some of which were lined with leather-bound books. Others were heaped high with scrolls of parchment lying haphazardly on top of one another. She didn't know what the scrolls contained, but the Order must not have considered them important. She could tell by the thick, undisturbed carpet of dirt on the floor that no one visited the room. Still, she took the time to peruse the volumes and found that most of them were a compilation of names and dates.

"These aren't the original sacred scrolls, are they?" she asked.

"Oh, no," Father Padron said, laughing. "Those are kept in Calatris, under so many protective enchantments that not even I could read them." He jutted his bearded chin at the shelves. "These are mundane records that have long since been transcribed—births and deaths and such. We only keep them because it seems a shame to destroy anything so ancient."

Another failure. Another dead end. If the answers weren't down there, she couldn't imagine where else they would be.

"Is there anything else?" she asked.

"I'm afraid this is all we have." Father Padron backed up, grinning apologetically before he turned and strode out of the antechamber. "I did warn you it wasn't intriguing."

With sagging shoulders, she followed him. "I'm still grateful for…"

She trailed off as a flame leaped in her peripheral vision. One of the wall sconces was burning more brightly than the others. She didn't think much of it until she glanced down and noticed an imprint of a shoe in the dirt. But only half of a shoe print: the small, square-heeled portion of a boot or a dress loafer. The rest of the imprint disappeared beneath the marble—as though someone had parted the wall and stepped through it.

There was another antechamber. One Father Padron had hidden from her.

She felt a pinch in her chest. She tried telling herself that perhaps he was unaware of the room's existence, but that was a lie, and she knew it in her bones. Her instincts had been right. He had deliberately chosen not to tell her about the archives because there was something in the hidden room that he didn't want her to find.

Maybe some ends weren't so dead after all.

. . .

Hours later, she paced the garden, seeing nothing, feeling nothing. She wished Daerick were there. With him holed up in the palace doing research, she had no one to talk to about the archives. She wanted so desperately to give Father Padron the benefit of the doubt, but the truth was that he had deceived her, and it stung. And then there was his embrace of suffering as atonement. Exactly what the Reverend Mother had warned her about. What else had been a lie? Had she been mistaken about his kindness? Did he secretly view her with the same contempt that Father Bishop displayed so openly?

She didn't know, and that was maddening.

Distracted, she reached out to skim a rosebush and pricked her little finger. She hissed and brought the finger to her mouth. The pain turned her focus outward, making her aware of her surroundings once more. She heard a noise coming from a maze of hedges at the back of the garden: a muffled grunting, the sound of someone in pain.

She followed the noise to the center of the maze and discovered she was right. There on the grass knelt the king, pale in the face, more drunk than ever, clutching his stomach and trying not to lose its contents. Oddly enough, she empathized with his pain, having once enjoyed too much sacramental cider at the temple. She lifted her skirts and sat far enough away from him to avoid any unpleasantness.

"Your Majesty," she greeted. "I would say you're going to feel worse in the morning, but I don't know if you will." Perhaps the alcohol in his blood would disappear at sunset, along with the rest of him. "Your body is different than mine."

The king sniffed a laugh and darted a glance at her chest. "Maybe you're not as ignorant as I thought."

"I know why you're doing that," she told him.

"Doing what? Defiling the garden with half-digested ale?"

"Belittling me," she said. "The rumors you heard about me raised your hopes, and it hurt to learn that I'm ordinary. Your insults are a way of retaliating against me and also against yourself for believing the rumors in the first place." When he opened his mouth to deny it, she added, "Daerick told me so."

"Daerick," the king grumbled. "One of these days he's going to talk himself into a broken nose."

"He told me more than just that," she said. "He told me you remember your nights in the shadows. Is that true?"

For a sliver of a second, fear widened Kian's gaze. If she had blinked, she would have missed it. But she didn't miss it, and in that moment, she saw the king for who he truly was—a wounded young man who dreaded the night. Sympathy prickled behind her ribs, but she hid the emotion, afraid that he would mistake it for weakness and lose whatever respect he had for her.

"Daerick is mistaken," Kian said.

"I don't believe you."

"So you're an oracle now?"

"I only need eyes to see that you're afraid."

Kian spat into the grass and then shamelessly changed the subject. "You were wrong when you said I would feel worse in the morning. No matter what I do to myself—even if I lose a finger, which has actually happened—I wake up whole." He tapped the visible patch of skin on his upper chest. "You can pierce my heart if you want to. As long as it's beating when the sun goes down, I'll have a new one at sunrise."

"I'll keep that in mind," she told him. "If you can be polite and stop insulting me, I'll wait until twilight to stab you."

He released a soft, breathy chuckle that made his eyes crinkle at the edges. This time his laughter was genuine, and she found herself searching for another funny remark so she could hear it again.

"No one prepared me for my curse," Kian said. "After my Claiming Day, it took me a fortnight to learn that my body restores itself at dawn. I found out the hard way when I fractured my elbow." Absently, he rubbed the crook of his left arm. "That was the day I lost a finger, too."

"Sounds like an eventful day," she said. "What happened?"

"Daerick and I might have liberated a bottle of my father's finest and then consumed it in the stables." Kian grinned. "Did you know that horses dislike being dressed in men's breeches?"

She laughed. "I can't say I've ever given it a thought."

"Well, now you know," he said. "And the only thing worse than a mare's bite is having to face your father's physician while drunk, bloodied, and naked."

Still smiling, the king stared off into the hedges as if replaying the memory. Cerise enjoyed this version of him, of Kian the mischievous young man with an easy grin and a story to tell.

But as the wind shifted, the king turned his gaze skyward, where streaks of orange and purple tinted the last rays of sunlight. The corners of his lips turned down. All of the cheer left his face, peeling away until only dread remained.

"Your Majesty, please listen to me." Cerise moved closer to him and reached for his hand. At first, he hesitated, but he allowed her to hold one of his hands in between both of hers. She took a moment to savor the pleasant heat of it, the feel of it, rough and callused and large. "I don't have the Sight, and I don't know if I ever will. But today Daerick and I learned something about the noble curses, and he came back from the city so full of hope that he was practically glowing. You know Daerick, his standards and his brilliance. He wouldn't be excited about an idea unless it had merit."

"What did you learn?" Kian asked.

"That the curse can be broken through atonement."

"And how would we do that?" He looked into her face, hope and despair warring in those smoky gray eyes.

Cerise bit her bottom lip. "I don't know yet."

The king dropped his gaze, though not before a wall went up behind it. She couldn't blame him for wanting to protect himself. She hadn't earned his trust yet.

"I do know this," she told him. "The goddess sent me here for a reason. I'm certain of it. She has a plan that's bigger than all of us."

Kian peeked up through a fringe of dark lashes, his gray eyes latching onto hers. Again she noticed a subtle hint of emotion, a need for hope and an even greater fear of it.

She squeezed his hand. "Shiera doesn't make mistakes."

"No," he agreed. "The suffering she inflicts on me is deliberate."

"The goddess can be vengeful; that's true. But I've seen her merciful side."

Kian scoffed.

"I have," she promised. "There was a girl who came to the temple with hells bane—horrible red scales all over her face and a fever out of control. None of the healers could help her. But then the girl put her favorite doll on the burning altar, and just like that"—she snapped her fingers—"she was cured."

"A miracle," Kian droned with an eye roll.

"It *was* a miracle," Cerise insisted. "They don't happen often, but by definition, miracles are supposed to be rare. Shiera answers prayers. Even when the answer is no, I've felt her presence inside me like a second heart."

"When has she ever answered *my* prayers?" An undercurrent of bitterness flowed heavily in those words.

"Maybe when she sent me here to serve you. Or again today, when she guided my path into the city so Daerick and I could learn how to break her curse. I think she's decided that the noble houses have suffered long enough."

"Or maybe she's twisting the knife."

Cerise huffed a dry laugh. "Do you think she sent me here to give you hope and then take it away? That's arrogant, even for a king. Of all the men who ever lived, what makes *you* so special that our creator would go through the trouble of toying with you?"

He didn't have an answer for that.

"This is bigger than both of us," she said. "It has to be. But I need you to have a little faith, or at least pretend to. Breaking the curse will be hard enough without you fighting me and making me feel small."

The king opened his mouth to speak but faltered.

"Promise you won't quit," she added. "Promise that when you wake up at dawn, you'll rule like you mean it, like a king with a hundred years to live. Your people need you more than you know. Think of how your subjects will suffer if you continue to neglect them."

His throat shifted as he swallowed.

"I need to hear you say it."

With a slow nod, Kian murmured, "I'll try."

She wanted to press for more than a halfhearted try, but his hand dissolved into shadow, and he slipped like an onyx breeze through her fingers. The last parts of him to vanish were his eyes, round and unblinking and filled with a hundred silent pleas that rang louder than a thunderclap inside her head.

Don't leave me stranded and alone. Don't give up on me. Don't fail.

Those eyes imprinted on hers and lingered long after they were gone.

7

Cerise.

The whisper tickled her inner ear, rousing her from dreams.

Wake up, Cerise.

She batted at the sound.

Wake up!

She came to with a gasp, whipping her gaze around her bedchamber for the owner of the voice. Much like her previous nights in the palace, only darkness surrounded her, the deep black that came before dawn. But as the haze of slumber faded, she detected a slight difference in the air. A scent that didn't belong. Sniffing again, she realized—it was smoke.

She scrambled out of bed, ran through her suite, and continued all the way into the lamp-lit corridor, not bothering to change out of her nightshirt. She knew there were no hearths in Mortara outside of the kitchens, so if there was a fire in the palace, it wasn't the good kind.

She called out, "Fire!"

When no one responded, she remembered that the other suites

along her corridor were empty. A tint clung to the air, growing thicker at the opposite end of the hallway. The source of the fire was close. Even though the king had dismissed his court, maybe a visitor had arrived during the night and was trapped inside a burning room.

Cerise followed the trail of smoke until she reached a suite with blackened fumes pouring from underneath the door. Again, she shouted, "Fire!"

This time, someone heard her call. A royal guard rounded the corner at the other end of the hallway. He saw the smoke and ran toward her, but as he approached, his footsteps slowed and grew clumsy. He made it within ten paces of her before he dropped to his knees and collapsed onto the floor. A moment later, two more guards rounded the corner, but both of them tripped over their boots and crumpled, unconscious, beside the first man.

Cerise shook the guards' shoulders, but she couldn't rouse them. Since it was clear that no one else was coming to help her, she used the back of her hand to test the doorknob's temperature. The metal was only warm to the touch, so she opened the door and immediately cringed as heat tightened her skin.

She dropped to her knees, scanning below the smoke. She identified two more unconscious guards on the suite floor. In the adjoining bedchamber, a woman was slumped halfway over the mattress as though she had lost consciousness while trying to escape. The source of the fire was contained near the balcony, where flames engulfed the curtains. The fire hadn't spread to the furniture or the carpets yet, but it would if she didn't extinguish it soon.

She crouched low and darted into the room. Smoke stung her eyes and blurred her vision. Blinking furiously, she snatched the blanket off of the bed and used it to bat at the curtains. The gauzy fabric disintegrated into spirals of ash, which she then smothered with the blanket before she pushed open both balcony doors to clear the smoke.

With the flames extinguished, she pulled in a cool lungful of air, then another. Had a breeze ever tasted this good? A gentle wind swirled inside the suite, pushing the smoke out of the opposite doorway and into the hall. Cerise blotted her eyes with her nightshirt and turned in a clumsy circle to survey the damage.

Numbly, she took in the room, feeling like a spectator in someone else's dream: debris scattered everywhere, chairs overturned, the blood-orange glow of sunrise on the horizon, the murky cloud that tumbled through the balcony doors. But when the cloud blew back her loose hair, smelling of clean, male skin, she realized what she was witnessing.

The king had arrived.

She watched a ball of shadow gather at the foot of the bed and materialize into flesh. The king's feet appeared first, long and bronze, followed so quickly by a pair of lean calves and muscular thighs that before her heart could finish its beat, Kian was fully formed.

And completely naked.

Her breath caught. She knew that she should look away, but her eyes only widened to take in more of him. She had never seen a man's body—not like this—and she found herself captivated by the dusting of hair that covered his skin. Dark and glossy, the king's curls were sparse in some places, like along the contours of his chest, but they converged at his abdomen and led south, where they encircled his navel and formed a thick trail that drew her focus between his hips.

Oh, stars.

Cheeks heating, she jerked her gaze to his face.

Thankfully, the king hadn't noticed her watching him. He glanced around the room and muttered, "What in damnation?" until he caught sight of Cerise's bare legs and arched a brow. "My lady of the temple, you are not dressed."

She studied the carpet at his feet. "Neither are you, Your Highness."

There was a rustle of fabric as he ripped the top sheet from the bed and wrapped it around his waist. "My apologies. I don't suppose priests flaunt their nudity at the temple."

"Only the toddlers," she said to the floor. "They remove their clods every chance they get."

"A natural male trait, the disdain for pants," he told her.

She peeked up with a grin that she found reflected in his eyes. They looked at each other for a moment until he seemed to remember his surroundings, and then he peppered her with questions. "What happened? Was there a fire? What are you doing here? What am *I* doing here? I usually wake up with—"

"Lady Champlain," Cerise interrupted. She rushed to the side of the bed, where the young woman was still unconscious. "This must be her." She rolled the woman face up and discovered she was right. "I was so focused on putting out the fire that I forgot to check on her."

Kian gently pried open Delora's eyelids, revealing pupils so wide they nearly eclipsed her irises. He glanced over his shoulder at the guards while he sniffed the air. "Do you smell that?"

"Smoke?"

"Not just smoke. Something else, almost…sweet."

Cerise inhaled again and noticed it, too—a nearly imperceptible layer of scent below the acridity of scorched linens. "Yes, it reminds me of burning leaves in the fall."

The king strode to the balcony and picked up what appeared to be a bundle of charred twigs. He sniffed at the bundle and then recoiled. "Dream weed," he said. He pointed at Delora. "She would have burned in her sleep. They all would have."

"Dream weed?" Cerise asked. "Is that a drug?"

"A strong one. The stalk makes an anesthetic when it's dried and burned. But it's not easy to find." Kian crushed the charred bundle in his fist. "There are at least a dozen stalks here. Someone went to a lot of trouble to collect these."

"So the fire was set on purpose," she realized.

"With the intention of killing everyone in this room."

"Was it the same person who loosed the panther, do you think?"

The king didn't seem to be listening. His eyes were still fixed on Delora. "She was supposed to sleep in my chambers last night. She must have thought I was the target of the panther attack, so she moved to a different suite to protect herself. She even stationed guards at the door, for what little good it did."

"You *are* the target," Cerise told him. "It's no secret that you appear next to Lady Champlain each day at sunrise. And it can't be a coincidence that both attacks happened moments before dawn. Someone is trying to kill you. If Father Bishop hadn't slain the panther, it would have sliced you to ribbons, and you would've bled to death before the sun could have set and made you whole again. And if I hadn't smelled the smoke from my chambers, you would have materialized in a burning room, too drugged to—"

"Save myself, I know," Kian interrupted. "It's lucky for all of us that you…" He trailed off and narrowed his eyes, first at the guards and then at her. "My lady of the temple, why didn't the dream weed affect you? You should be asleep like the others."

Cerise realized he was right. Every guard who had responded to her call had collapsed in the hallway, and she had inhaled more smoke than all of them. She suddenly became aware of her sister's pendant resting slightly heavier than before between her breasts. She touched the warm metal ring through her nightshirt and wondered if Nina had been right about the necklace's protection.

"The goddess works in mysterious ways," was all she said.

The king cocked his head to the side and studied her with an intensity that raised the tiny hairs at the back of her neck. His gaze bored uncomfortably into hers, almost as if he were trying to see beneath her skin. She could swear that it worked. Those slate-gray eyes made her feel exposed, and for the first time, she remembered she was undressed.

She crossed both arms over her chest. "I should put on some clothes."

"Should you?"

There was a flirtatious tone in his question that brought a blush to her cheeks. She hoped he didn't notice, but he probably did.

"Yes, and so should you, Your Majesty," she said. "I'm meeting with Daerick so he can teach me about my role as emissary. I want to be prepared to assist you when you resume your duties today. And you will resume them, won't you? You remember our talk in the garden?"

Instead of answering her, the king stared silently at Delora's sleeping form. Cerise couldn't tell if he was worried for his courtesan or simply deep in thought. Just when he opened his mouth to speak, Delora began to stir, moaning and clutching her head in both hands, and Kian moved to her side to comfort her.

"Lie still," he murmured to Delora, brushing back her long, brown waves with so much tenderness that Cerise had to avert her gaze. She didn't know why, but watching him attend to Delora made her chest ache. When he started making gentle shushing noises, she decided it was time to return to her suite.

"I'll take my leave now, Your Highness," she said. "Will you please remember that you made me a promise?"

"I haven't forgotten," Kian answered. After a long pause, he added, "Enjoy your lessons, my lady of the temple."

With a dip of her chin, Cerise made her exit.

. . .

Gossip about the fire spread through the palace faster than the actual flames. By the time Cerise had bathed away the stench of smoke and dressed herself in a fresh temple gown, a trio of young maidservants had arrived in her suite and arranged a breakfast fit for a queen.

A small, round table had been delivered to her sitting room. Draped in a starched white cloth that bore a gold-embroidered Mortara crest, the table offered the finest place setting Cerise had ever seen, each plate rimmed with precious metals and gilded art. A sparkling crystal decanter of juice stood alongside a silver teapot, and etched silver trays offered an assortment of berries and melons, eggs and salted meats, and crème-filled pastries so delicate and enticing they made her mouth water. One of the maidservants placed a single pink rose on the edge of the table, along with a note that read:

With gratitude from His Majesty's Royal Guard.

Cerise placed a hand over her heart. She thought back to her years at the temple, to the shame and the envy she had felt watching the other Seers succeed where she had only failed. All she had ever been was a disappointment. Now, to look upon the lavish display of appreciation from the palace guards made her eyes water. She blinked furiously to stop herself from crying in front of the maidservants.

She cleared the thickness from her throat and said, "Shiera's light upon you."

"And may her wrathful eye look away," came the joint reply.

Though the maids had finished their work, they made no move to leave her suite. All three of them were young—barely fourteen, by Cerise's estimate—with round, freckled faces and even rounder eyes that regarded her in the same way a child might gaze at a stack of presents left behind by the Harvest Fairy. In unison, the girls dipped into low curtsies, their gray linen skirts brushing the floor.

"If you please, my lady," the first girl said in a voice that trembled. "May I have the honor of braiding your hair? I know the best plaits. All of the ladies at court used to request me to style them for parties."

Before Cerise could respond, the second girl lifted a gilded plate from the table and asked, "May I serve you, my lady?"

The third girl quickly added, "And may I prepare your tea?"

Pressure built behind Cerise's eyes. As she struggled to maintain her composure, she visualized the Reverend Mother standing in front of her, tall and regal, narrowing her gaze, shaking her head in disapproval, and chiding, *Calm yourself, girl!*

The mental image dried her tears at once.

"Thank you for your kind offers," Cerise said. "I would love nothing more than to accept."

All three of the maids beamed and then flew into action. Within moments, Cerise was seated on a plush, cushioned dining chair in front of the breakfast table while one maid tenderly brushed her hair and the others prepared to serve her. She briefly wondered what Father Padron would say if he could see her now, being showered with appreciation for her bravery. Would he join in and praise her? Or would he criticize her for enjoying the attention? She didn't want to care about his opinion of her, but she couldn't help it. She did.

Fortunately, the girls made it easy to forget him. She learned that they were triplets, and their mother had named them after her favorite birds: Wren, Lark, and Dove. As the girls attended to her, they took turns explaining their troubles—everything from unpleasant dreams and painful courses to diseased relatives and unwelcome proposals of marriage—and asking her for guidance. Cerise didn't pretend that she could See their paths, but she promised to mention Wren, Lark, and Dove in her prayers, and that seemed to be a comfort to them. Then they told her some of the stories they had heard about the fire. Cerise had to bite her lip to contain a laugh when she heard a description of how she had extinguished the flames with the power of her prayers.

When Cerise had finished her breakfast of fruit pastries, honeyed oats, and spiced tea, a knock sounded at the door to her suite. She was still seated for her braid and unable to move, so she asked Wren to answer the door.

"It's probably Lord Calatris," Cerise said. "I'm expecting him."

But it wasn't the royal historian on the other side of the door.

The king's courtesan had come to pay a visit.

Delora Champlain strode into the sitting room and smoothly

lowered in a curtsy. Her glossy hair was loosely pinned in chestnut waves that spilled down the back of her silken gown, which was royal blue to match her eyes. She seemed as lovely and regal as ever. If not for the slight redness in her gaze, no one would guess that anything was amiss.

"My lady of the temple," Delora greeted in a voice raw from smoke.

"Good morning, Lady Champlain," Cerise said.

Delora looked from one serving maid to the next. "Leave us, please."

"But my lady," objected Lark, the maid braiding Cerise's hair. "The plait is only half—"

"I will finish it," Delora interrupted. She glided behind the chair where Cerise sat and then took over her loose sections of hair so gently that Cerise didn't notice the transfer until Lark bowed and joined her sisters in leaving the suite. Delora resumed the braid in silence for a few moments, her fingers light and deft as they slipped through Cerise's hair. Finally, she softly coughed and said, "I must apologize, my lady."

"Apologize for what?" Cerise asked.

"The king explained what happened while I was incapacitated," she said. "And when I listened to his story, I realized that he failed to thank you."

"Did he?" Cerise asked. "I assure you I didn't notice."

"Nevertheless, the king owes you his gratitude, and I owe you mine."

Delora completed the last section of braid and used a hairpin to secure the plait. With her long fingernails, she combed the stray hairs into place along the nape of Cerise's neck, the gentle scraping raising chills on her skin. The sensation felt exquisite, and before Cerise could stop herself, she pictured Delora using that same sensual touch on the king. Her stomach sank an inch. She didn't want to imagine them together. She shouldn't be thinking of the king in that way.

Delora glided around the chair and faced Cerise, peering at the intricate braids as if to inspect her work. She nodded in approval. "Perfect."

Cerise delicately touched her hair. "Thank you."

"No, thank *you*. I could have died today." Delora released another quiet cough and then shook her head. "And to think that I became the king's courtesan because I believed it would save me."

"Save you?" Cerise blinked. "Save you from what?"

"That's a story for another day. I'm quite tired, my lady. I hope you don't mind if I excuse myself."

Cerise stood from her chair and gave a farewell nod. A small part of her wondered if Delora was exhausted from the dream weed...or if she had finally conceived the king's heir.

Instead of asking, Cerise said, "Rest well, Lady Champlain."

8

Daerick arrived at Cerise's suite shortly after the departure of Lady Champlain.

"Your hair looks like a work of art," Daerick exclaimed with a smile as Cerise opened the door and welcomed him into the sitting room. But when his gaze found the breakfast table, his eyes widened, his mouth formed a perfect oval, and he murmured, "But this...this is a masterpiece."

Cerise laughed. "Help yourself. If I eat another bite, I might burst."

"Well then, I must remove the temptation of these delicacies from your sight and spare you from bursting."

"You're such a gentleman."

"I am, aren't I?" he said while filling a plate with salted meats and eggs. "I'm saving your life with this selfless act." He grinned and teasingly fanned his eyes. "I'm getting misty. Is this how it feels to be a hero, Cerise?"

She laughed again and poured him a cup of tea. "I'm no hero."

"That's not what everyone in the palace is saying." Fluttering his lashes, Daerick mimicked a maiden's high voice. *"Did you hear about the king's emissary? She walked through fire to save a dozen men, and then she put out the flames with the power of her mind!"*

"I thought it was the power of my prayers."

"Yes, I heard that version, too," Daerick said, adding several pastries to the rim of his plate. "There's another one claiming that you blew out the flames with your sacred lungs. That one is my favorite."

"My sacred lungs?" she repeated. "It seems I'm more talented than I thought. When I'm finished becoming a legendary emissary and helping you break the noble curses, I think I'll use my spare time to conquer death."

"You should invent a male enhancement while you're at it." With a grin, Daerick added, "Not that I need one. I'm only thinking of my less fortunate brethren."

"How saintly of you."

"It's true. Not even Father Padron can match my piety."

Father Padron.

She'd been so distracted by the morning's events that she had forgotten to tell Daerick about her visit to the catacombs. While Daerick sat at the table and devoured his breakfast, she paced the sitting room and relayed the story to him, starting with Father Bishop's open hostility toward her in the prayer room and ending with a description of the antechamber she had visited and the half footprint near the wall.

Daerick frowned and blotted his mouth with a silk napkin. "Are you sure the imprint wasn't made by something else? Furniture or a walking stick?"

She slid him a dirty look. "I may not have sacred lungs, but I can recognize a boot print when I see one."

"Did you confront Father Padron about it?"

"Of course not." Now he was just insulting her intelligence. She was a novice at court, but not when it came to matters of the Order. She knew better than to accuse the high priest of lying to her.

"Good," he said, seemingly oblivious to his own patronization. "Are you certain that Father Padron doesn't know that *you* know about the hidden chamber?"

"I'm certain."

"Then don't do anything to change that. We need him to believe he fooled you. He hid the antechamber for a reason. Whatever he's keeping in there, he's willing to lie to protect it. And if he's willing to lie, we have to assume he's willing to do more than that to stop you from finding it."

"Are you implying he would hurt me?"

"People have done worse things to bury their secrets."

"He's no ordinary person," she pointed out.

"No," Daerick agreed. "And that's what makes him dangerous."

She wanted to argue that Father Padron would never harm her. But what reason did she have to believe that? He had broken her trust. Logic would say that she didn't truly know him at all. The Reverend Mother had warned her of overzealous priests—maybe he was one of them. He had certainly atoned like one of them. So then why did she still want to defend him? Why did she crave his approval and his company even though he had deceived her? Why was she still drawn to him?

"You're only human," Daerick said. "It's natural for you to see the best in Father Padron. There's a reason for that." He sipped his tea and went thoughtful for a moment. "I don't suppose the Silent Soul ever visited you at the temple."

Cerise shook her head. She had never heard of the Silent Soul.

"She's a legendary figure," Daerick explained. "Like the Harvest Fairy or the Winter Mouse, but she brings sweets instead of presents or coins. Parents use the Silent Soul to manipulate their children into obedience. If you do what you're told and you don't complain, she will leave a bundle of goodies on your doorstep when her soul's day arrives. But you have to *believe*. Otherwise, she won't come."

"Did you believe in her?" Cerise asked, her lips twitching in a grin. "I can't imagine that you did."

Daerick frowned as he set down his teacup. "I wasn't always a genius, Cerise. My parents fooled me a time or two."

She patted him on the shoulder. "At least you're human like me."

"Yes, well," he went on. "My mother was strict with sweets, and the Silent Soul always brought my favorite toffee. So I followed my parents' orders without questioning them—which, believe me, was a struggle. Then one year I overheard a serving boy telling his friends that the Silent Soul wasn't real, that it was parents who left sweets at the door. What he said made sense to me. My intellect told me he was right." Daerick lifted an index finger. "But I was afraid to admit to myself that the Silent Soul was a myth. Because what if I was wrong?"

"Then you would get no toffee."

"Exactly. I wasn't prepared to take that gamble, so against my better judgment, I forced myself to believe in the Silent Soul until enough time passed that I couldn't deny the truth anymore. And by then I had lost my taste for toffee. I used to feel foolish for how easily I let myself be manipulated by sweets and lies, but the experience taught me about the power of persuasion, and that was a lesson worth learning."

Even though she saw his point, it felt like he was patronizing her again. "You equate my respect for Father Padron to your belief in the Silent Soul."

"And who could blame you?" Daerick asked. "You lived at the temple since birth. Nineteen years is a long time for the Order to teach you their version of the truth. Their doctrine is a part of you. It's in your bones, and it's going to take longer than a few days to admit to yourself that some of what they told you is a lie." He stood from his chair and took Cerise by the hand. "Don't be ashamed for feeling confused about Father Padron. He's powerful and charming, and he represents everything that's sacred to you. But don't let your confusion make you reckless. Not all priests are safe. There's a lot you don't know about them."

"Fine," she said. *Enough with the lectures.* "Then teach me."

Daerick gave her a resolute nod. "With pleasure."

While Daerick escorted Cerise to the east wing on the first floor of the palace, where the former emissary's office was located, he quietly discussed what he had learned from his research. He still hadn't translated the term *umbra sangi*, but he had sent an encrypted letter to a colleague in Calatris who specialized in linguistics. Daerick had spent most of his time poring over ancient writings related to the Great Betrayal.

"I realized something that should've occurred to me before," he whispered as they descended the main staircase. "I haven't spent as much time immersed in religion as you have. I think that's why it took me so long to notice there are no records of the Mortara dynasty's role in the Great Betrayal."

Cerise had always known that the Mortara dynasty's role was absent from the scrolls; she had read them so many times she could recite whole passages from memory. She did so now. "'To house Calatris, which devised the method to slay the goddess, she unleashed more knowledge than the mortal mind could bear. To house Petros, which forged the weapon against her, she gave the curse of bloodlust. To house Solon, which seduced her from the heavens, she bestowed self-destructive beauty. And to house Mortara, she gave the curse of darkness, to disappear into the shadows for eternity.'"

"But why?" Daerick asked.

"It's not recorded in the scrolls, but I assumed the Mortara dynasty was the house that brought together the other nobles— that the betrayal was their idea," Cerise said. "And that's why the Mortara curse is the worst of them all."

"It's not just absent from the scrolls; it's absent from *all records.*

That's what I spent this morning confirming," Daerick replied. "But if that's the reason for their curse, why would the goddess reward house Mortara with dominion over the priests?" Daerick quieted his voice as he led her down the first-floor eastern corridor, where silken carpets gave way to tile that caused their sounds to echo. "No priest, not even Father Padron, can refuse a direct order from a firstborn Mortara. Most people would kill for power like that."

"Do you think the reason matters?" she asked. "Can the curse be broken without us understanding why the priests are bound to Kian?"

"Perhaps," Daerick said in a tone that hinted otherwise.

They reached an office suite situated about halfway down the corridor. The office must have been built along an exterior palace wall, because beams of sunlight streamed through the open door and into the hallway, bathing the floor tiles in brilliance. Cerise entered the suite and found a small sitting room furnished with a tastefully simple red velvet sofa and two end tables. Spanning the rear wall was a window that offered a view of the east lawn and the rows of citrus trees in the distance. While Daerick closed the door behind them, Cerise inspected the sitting room. The greeting area was pristine, without a trace of dust on the furniture or on the glossy floor. She continued beyond the sitting room to a side-facing doorway that led to an office carpeted with colorful, plush rugs and featuring an etched mahogany desk with a matching chair settled behind it. In the corner stood a cushioned divan and a side table bearing a silver tea set.

She wondered if this was the office the Reverend Mother had Seen in her vision. Cerise could picture herself behind the desk, reading and learning and sipping tea like a proper lady. The mental image made her smile. She felt older and wiser simply by standing here.

"Here it is," Daerick said with a flourish. "The old woman's office, and now yours, unless you'd prefer a different one. The king created a lot of vacancies when he dismissed his court, so you can have your pick of any of the office suites along this corridor."

"No, I like this one." She slipped behind the desk and found that she could still see the window through the doorway. "The view is perfect, and besides, the late emissary's notes are in here."

Daerick winced. "Only a few pages. She wasn't much of a recordkeeper. Everything I could find is in the top drawer of her desk."

"And the elusive journal?" Cerise asked. It had to be somewhere around here if the Reverend Mother had Seen her reading it. "What does it look like?"

"It's quite distinctive," Daerick said. "The cover is made from black and white leather squares stitched together to look like temple floor tiles. Kian's father gave it to her as a welcome gift. It's impossible to miss."

"Did you look for it in her bedchamber?" Cerise asked. "If the journal was important to her, it was probably with her when she died."

Again, Daerick winced. "This is where she died."

Cerise felt her eyes widen. Her gaze drifted to the chair behind the desk, to the plush divan, to the carpeted floor, while her mind conjured images of an elderly woman slumped across the various objects in death.

Daerick gently elbowed her. "Change your mind about one of those vacancies?"

While Cerise was still trying to adjust to the knowledge that her predecessor had poisoned herself in this very room, someone from the outer corridor opened the door to the sitting room and then walked into the office. Cerise stepped around her desk and was met with a startled reaction from Father Bishop, who had clearly assumed the suite was empty.

Father Bishop glanced back and forth between Cerise and Daerick. His mouth moved, but no words passed his lips.

"May I assist you, Father Bishop?" Cerise asked in her most ladylike tone. Not that he deserved it. He looked more guilty than a child with his hand in the sweets jar.

He composed himself and fixed his icy glare upon her. "Excuse the interruption. I only came to return this." Then, from the billowy left sleeve of his robe, he retrieved a small book bound in alternating leather squares of black and white.

Cerise gasped. "The emissary's journal!"

"That's the one," Daerick said. He folded both arms and lifted his chin, looking down his nose at the priest. "That explains why it was missing. What were you doing with it?"

"The emissary had a name," Father Bishop snapped. "She was Mother Strout. And yes, I borrowed her journal. What of it? I came to put it back. I did nothing wrong."

Cerise had been so fixated on the journal that she hadn't noticed the changes in Father Bishop. Now that she studied his face, she detected a hint of redness in his eyes and rimming the bottom of his nose. His eyelids were swollen, and his voice seemed a note rougher, more raw than it had been yesterday when he'd chastised her in the sanctuary. It almost looked like he had been crying.

Crying for the old emissary?

"Lord Calatris didn't accuse you of wrongdoing," she told Father Bishop. "He asked you a question, which you still haven't answered."

"You want an answer?" he asked in a tone that sounded like a threat. "All right. I'll tell you why I took it." He shook the journal in the air. "Because her death made no sense—that's why. I knew Mother Strout. I knew her longer than anyone else at the palace. Before she was the old king's emissary, she was a Seer in the temple where I was raised. Mother Strout was the most devoted oracle that ever existed. She lived to serve the goddess, so why would she dispatch herself without saying a word to anyone?"

"Did you find your answer?" Cerise asked, nodding at the journal.

By way of reply, Father Bishop slammed the book on the desk and then turned on his heel and stalked out of the room. A moment later, the suite door clattered shut.

She would take that as a *no*.

She picked up the journal and traced a square with her fingertip. At least now she understood why Father Bishop hated her. The late emissary had been like a mother to him. He had respected and cared for Mother Strout, and when she had died, the Order had sent a novice in training to replace her. That must have felt like an insult to her memory.

"The crotchety priest did make an interesting point," Daerick said.

Yes, he did. Based on everything Cerise had heard about Mother Strout, it did seem strange that the woman had poisoned herself. "Was there an investigation when she died?"

"There was an inquiry," Daerick said, "but it turned up nothing. She had no enemies and no heirs, so there was no one to benefit from her death. And the note she left behind was in her own handwriting."

As above, so below. The flame you seek to dampen will consume you. Cerise wished she understood what it meant.

"If there was foul play involved in her death, it was meticulously planned and flawlessly executed." Daerick shrugged. "I can't tell you why old Mother Strout is dead, but now that we have her journal, I can help you resume her work. There are only six moons remaining with Kian on the throne. In that time, you might as well be the best emissary you can be. That will have to do."

A heavy silence fell between them.

"You're right," Cerise agreed softly. "Let's get started."

She still didn't know her purpose along the narrow path to breaking the curses, but the journal felt like a stepping stone—with any luck, the first of many.

Finally, it was time to set destiny in motion.

9

After the lesson ended, Daerick returned to his chambers to continue his research on the origins of the noble curses and how to undo them while Cerise sat alone at her desk, eating a luncheon of cold meats and cheeses and thumbing through the late emissary's journal.

She worked her way backward through a year's worth of entries, not only to learn what an emissary's daily life should look like but in hopes of discovering what might have driven Mother Strout to cut short her own. So far, the journal contained nothing more than a collection of painfully mundane details from palace meetings. Strout must have been bored out of her wits, because she'd sketched odd designs in the margins of each page. The images weren't recognizable, just the casual scribbles of one with a restless mind. Unless boredom had stripped Mother Strout of her will to live, the answer to her death wouldn't be found in her entries, and there was no mention of curses. Not a single clue to be found.

So much for destiny.

Cerise closed the journal and rubbed her weary eyes. Each day at the palace seemed to pass like a year at the temple. She gazed through her open doorway to the window, where the afternoon sun struck the edges of the glass panes and sprayed colorful prisms on the floor. As she peered beyond the lawn to the trees stirring in the breeze, she felt something wistful building inside her, a longing of sorts. She recognized the feeling from her years at the temple.

She needed to find the palace kennels.

She took the journal with her as she walked out of her office suite, and she noticed Lark, the young maid who had braided her hair, carrying a tray of scones toward the open-air corridor that led to the sanctuary, possibly for Father Padron's afternoon tea.

"Excuse me," Cerise called to Lark. "Can you direct me to the kennels?"

Lark colored visibly, grinning. She attempted a curtsy that was more of a wobbling of knees. "Yes, my lady. I'll take you there myself."

"There's no need—"

But Lark was already placing her tray on the floor, insisting that a priest would have to come and fetch the scones anyhow, as maids weren't allowed inside the sanctuary. She waved Cerise toward the kitchens, and as they walked, Lark continued to blush and avert her gaze.

The two of them exited the back of the castle and continued through the rear gardens, near which stood the stables, the barracks, and beyond that, presumably, the kennels. But what drew Cerise's attention was the sight of the king administering his duties. Two companies of guards were running drills, presided over by Kian, who looked very royal indeed as he nodded in approval and clapped General Petros on the shoulder.

"Now that's something I haven't seen in a while," murmured Lark.

Cerise turned to her. "What do you mean?"

"Oh, my lady, I'm sorry. I only meant that the king stopped his drill exercises with the soldiers, and I know the men have missed his presence. It's nice to see him do it again."

Cerise couldn't help but smile as she shielded her eyes from the sun. "It certainly is," she said quietly.

Kian was keeping his promise to her.

She and Lark stood in silence for a moment as the soldiers finished drilling. Some of them formed pairs and began to spar. Another group converged around General Petros while the rest headed back to the barracks.

"I can find my way all right from here, thank you," Cerise said. She added, "Shiera's light to you," and flourished a hand as if dispensing blessings.

"And may her wrathful eye look away," came the reply.

Lark smiled and hurried back to the castle, and Cerise veered toward the practice field. As she neared it, the knot of soldiers around the general seemed to grow more boisterous, and those who remained on the field quickly came over to join the crowd. Curious, she picked up her pace as much as propriety would allow. Soon she drew close enough to hear cheers and groans, punctuated by the smacking of fists against flesh. It seemed a fight was underway — and a sensational one, judging by the thick audience. It didn't take long for her to identify General Petros as one of the opponents, light armor now shed, his tattooed head easily visible above the spectators. All she could see of the other man was an occasional blur of skin as his knuckles connected with the general's face.

No one noticed her as she joined the crowd and made her way closer to the front. When she could go no farther, she stood on tiptoe to peer over the shoulders in front of her. At first the general stood with his back to her, his fists raised, his massive frame concealing his opponent. But then the pair circled around, and she recognized a familiar male torso, dewy and bronze with a trail of ebony hair that ringed his navel and disappeared below the waistband of his pants.

She tugged a nearby sleeve. "Why is the king fighting?"

The steward beside her kept his gaze fixed on the match, cringing when the general landed a fist in Kian's stomach. "Sparring practice.

These two are the best in the city. I used to watch 'em all the time, but the king quit his lessons moons ago. Now that he came back to drill the men, they talked him into it. The general's taking it easy on him, if you ask—" The man cut off when he glanced at her for the first time. "Oh, apologies, my lady. I didn't know who I was talking to."

His comment prompted the guard in front of them to turn around. Cerise didn't recognize him, but the gratitude in his eyes hinted that he was one of the men she had saved from the fire that morning. "Make room," he ordered, shoving onlookers aside to create an opening at the front of the circle. "Make room for the blessed oracle!"

The gap in the crowd gave her a perfect view of Kian, who paused and locked eyes with her. He lowered both fists, his dark gaze holding her spellbound, and in that moment, General Petros landed a shattering blow to his ribs.

The crowd gave a collective, "Ooooh!"

Kian doubled over and dropped to his knees. He sucked a breath through his teeth, eyes clenched, hair glued to his face by sweat. Cerise cringed in sympathy. She couldn't help feeling partly to blame for distracting him.

"I'm sorry, Your Highness," the general said in a tone that implied the opposite. "I didn't realize we had taken a break. Speaking of *breaks*, I believe I felt some of your ribs crack. Shall I send word to the temple? I know a healer there."

"*Intimately*, I've heard," Cerise blurted. The crowd broke into laughter. She hadn't meant to speak the words aloud, but when the king glanced up and rewarded her with one of his rare smiles, she was glad that she'd said it.

"No need," Kian told the general as he stood and gingerly brushed himself off. He squinted at the sky. "The sun will go down in a few hours. Your healer can save her energy for…other pursuits."

There was another round of laughter, at which point the general's face turned the shade of ripe summer berries. He glared at Cerise with mild annoyance, but then his gaze moved to the journal tucked in the crook of her elbow, and in the time it took for her to blink, he erupted into a rage so explosive that the entire crowd took a step backward. Cerise clutched the nearest arm, watching as bloodlust consumed the general's eyes. He snarled—actually *snarled*—while scanning the crowd as if daring someone to fight him. All of the men wisely scattered back to their posts, including the owner of the arm Cerise had been holding.

"General," Kian warned.

In that single utterance, Cerise caught her first glimpse of a true king.

The general closed his eyes in an obvious struggle for control. He snorted like a bull, clenching and unclenching his fists until he turned on his heel and stalked away toward the garden.

Kian blew out a breath as he watched the general's retreating form. "Don't worry. The fountain is his happy place. He'll stay there until he calms down."

Cerise took the journal in her hand and turned it to and fro. "This seemed to trigger him. Did he care for Mother Strout?"

Kian laughed, quickly wincing and cradling his ribs. "Only in the way that a tree cares for an axe."

"Do you mean they were enemies?" Cerise asked. "Daerick told me she had none."

"Not enemies but definitely rivals. Old Mother Strout didn't think the general was worthy of his woman at the temple, and she made no secret about it." He smiled as if recalling a memory. "If looks could kill, Strout would have sent Petros to his grave a hundred times over."

Cerise peered at the journal, thinking it odd that Mother Strout hadn't mentioned the general in any of her entries.

"You surprise me, my lady of the temple," Kian said, grinning at her.

"How so?"

"You told a joke about the general's mistress. Not that I'm

complaining," he added with a lifted hand. "But it was almost distasteful. I didn't think you had it in you."

"You make it sound like I'm perfect."

"Hardly," he disagreed. "But your imperfections are annoyances—flea bites, really. Let's cover some sins with real teeth. Have you ever killed a man?"

"No, but the day is young, and you *did* offer to let me stab you."

A grin tilted the corner of his mouth. "Have you ever gotten drunk on ale?"

"Sacramental cider, and only once. The sickness cured me of ever wanting to try it a second time."

"Any adultery? Conceived a love child?"

"I'll leave that to the courtesans," Cerise said, smiling sweetly. "And the kings they serve."

Kian clapped a hand over his heart, feigning injury. "Deny it all you want, my lady of the temple, but I'll wager you've never even been kissed."

Her smile fell—a detail that didn't escape his notice.

"Did I pluck a nerve?" he teased.

Yes, he had. But he was wrong. She'd been kissed—quite thoroughly, too—one time, in a dark, hidden corner of the temple grounds. It had begun innocently enough. He had been a dark-haired delivery boy with a dimpled smile. She had been a lonely sixteen-year-old with a head full of curiosity. On delivery days, they had met behind hedges or inside sheds to trade stories about their lives. Then one day the talking had turned into something more, and they'd explored each other's mouths until their lips had grown chapped. Cerise had looked forward to the boy's next visit, but he'd stopped making deliveries to the temple, and it had taken three new litters of rabbit kits to make her smile again.

What she hadn't realized at the time—what she wished she had known—was that she wouldn't receive the Sight. The Order had warned her about sins of the flesh and how acts of love could ruin a woman's gift. At the time, she hadn't believed them. Now she wondered how things might have been different if she had never kissed the boy.

But then she thought of Daerick's story about the Silent Soul. Maybe kissing had changed nothing about her life. The general's mistress had taken a lover without the loss of her gift. Far from it. She possessed both the Sight and the ability to heal. Could that be a coincidence?

She didn't know what to think anymore, what to believe. Everything felt upside-down now. She couldn't even trust Father Padron to tell her the truth.

"I'm sorry," Kian said, bringing her back to the present with a featherlight touch to her wrist. "I was only teasing. I didn't mean to upset you."

She shook her head to clear it. "You didn't."

"Want to tell me what's bothering you?"

Her first inclination was to say no. In all honesty, she wanted nothing more than to put it all behind her and lose her worries in the kennels. But then she reminded herself that Kian was trying to keep his promise to her. She still didn't want to give him false hope, but he deserved to know what she and Daerick had learned. So she told him what they had been up to, even details about her visit to the soothsayer and the hidden antechamber in the catacombs. She didn't mean to share quite so much, but Kian listened with such intensity, hanging on her every word, and when he watched her with those storm-cloud eyes, she couldn't hold anything back.

"I came outside to visit the kennels," she said when she had finished. "Animals make me feel at ease, and I need that today."

The king was thoughtful for a moment, pushing back his dampened hair and staring into the grass. "So your path is a blank to Seers?"

"Well...yes. Or it diverges from what they've already Seen. That used to happen with the Reverend Mother." Cerise hadn't expected him to fixate on that part of the story, and she hoped he wouldn't linger on it. She didn't like keeping things from him, but she wasn't ready to tell him about the revelation. Anyway, what was there to tell? Her involvement in the vision had clouded all of the details that could have helped them.

"Interesting," was all he said. He retrieved a white linen shirt from the grass and put it on, the thin fabric clinging to the contours of his chest. He extended an elbow to her. "My lady, may I escort you to the kennels?"

She felt a blush rise to her cheeks as she slid her arm through his. They began an easy stroll toward the gated fence that separated the paddock from the kennel. With each motion of their footsteps, the king's muscled arm pressed against her and stirred a fluttering behind her navel. His nearness and his warmth unsettled her. The scent of him dizzied her senses. To distract herself, she cleared her throat and broached a new subject.

"Your Majesty, may I ask you an uncomfortable question?"

"That's the best kind," he told her.

"How many daylight hours do you lose?" She fixed her gaze straight ahead, afraid that direct eye contact would make him uneasy. "When Father Padron told me you keep to yourself during the day, I assumed you were trying to hide how far your curse has advanced."

"You have good instincts," Kian said. "Each day is different. Today I lost parts of only two hours. I meant to accompany Lady Champlain to your suite to convey my thanks, but...now you understand why I didn't."

"She didn't tell me a thing about it. She kept your secret."

"Lady Champlain is loyal to me."

Now Cerise looked to him. She wanted to read his expression. "Is that why you're protecting her?"

The king blinked. "I beg your pardon?"

"Lady Champlain mentioned to me that she became your courtesan to save herself. She wouldn't tell me why, but don't you think she's in more danger now because of her closeness to you and the attempts on your life?"

The king didn't seem to like hearing that. His lips flattened into a line.

"Oh, was that too uncomfortable a question?" she asked while playfully bumping his shoulder with hers. "I thought that was your favorite kind."

Kian slid her an amused glance. "You're right. I've been negligent in seeing to Lady Champlain's safety, and I intend to correct that oversight now."

"How so?"

"With the assistance of my high priest."

They reached the gated fence, and while Kian unfastened the latch, Cerise peered behind them to look for a servant who could convey a message to Father Padron.

He noticed her search. "There's no need to send a message to him," Kian said as he opened the gate and swept a hand for her to enter the enclosure. "I can call for him myself. Watch this." Turning his face toward the castle, Kian murmured, "Come to me, high priest," and then he offered his elbow to Cerise again, and they resumed striding onward.

"You can summon him like that?" she asked.

The king's devilish smile was answer enough. "He despises it."

"Because priests exist to serve the goddess, not the whims of kings."

"Obviously you're wrong, or else your goddess wouldn't allow it."

"She's your goddess, too," Cerise told him. But though she didn't say so, she couldn't deny the truth in Kian's argument. For whatever reason, the goddess had given him power over her priests to use in whatever way he chose. The bond of service made no sense. She wished she understood it.

Kian pushed open the kennel door and spurred a chorus of barking. "Let's talk about something more pleasant, like our new litter of pups."

"Pups?" she squeaked. Oh, stars, that was the magic word to make her forget everything else in existence. All that mattered now

was holding one in her arms. After tucking the journal into her pocket, she tugged on the king's elbow to rush him forward—most unladylike, but who cared?

There were pups in the kennel!

"All right, all right," Kian said, hurrying his pace. "Just this way."

He led her past dozens of wooden pens, each housing a Mortara brush hound so flawlessly bred that they shamed their encyclopedia illustrations. The hounds ran to greet her as she passed, wagging their stump-like tails, beaming at her with wide, expressive eyes, their tongues lolling to the side as they panted in excitement.

Goddess, they were beautiful! And well adapted to the heat, too, with short, fuzzy coats that were resistant to sunlight. But best of all was the intelligence brimming in those dark eyes. They studied her every move, taking her in, missing nothing. She'd heard that Mortara brush hounds were so smart they could detect illnesses in their owners and even hunt down medicinal herbs. Seeing them now, she didn't doubt it. These hounds would make a razor look dull.

"Here we are." Kian stopped in front of a waist-high door and ruffled the head of the fuzzy hound who had come to greet him. "This naughty girl is Stella. She ran away during a hunt and came back pregnant by…well, none of us are sure. If I believed in goblins, that would be my guess." He peeked beyond the door and shuddered. "The pups are so hideous they're almost cute."

When Cerise leaned over the gate and caught sight of the pups, her heart nearly burst. Oddly, Kian wasn't wrong. Sometimes a creature went so far beyond ugly that it came back around and reached adorable. Stella's pups had done just that.

There were five of them, all engaged in an energetic game of bounce and tumble. They had inherited their mother's hindquarters and stumpy tail but little else. Their chests were much too broad to belong to a hound, as were their jaws, and instead of floppy ears, theirs stood on end, tall and pointed. Their coats were bald and stacked with dozens of folds, as though their pelts were ten sizes too big. Judging by their clownishly large paws, they would soon grow into their wrinkles.

"May I go inside?" she asked, already hitching up her skirts to climb over the gate.

Kian chuckled. "Be my guest."

Her shoes had barely reached the pen floor when the pups bounded over to her and began tugging on her dress hem. She sat down, giggling as half the litter climbed on her lap and the other half chewed on her skirts. Stella padded over and lay down on her side, exposing her milk-engorged belly. Cerise nudged one of the pups in an encouragement to nurse, but it only yipped and rejoined the game.

"They self-weaned," Kian said. "Much to Stella's dismay."

"They don't look old enough for solid food."

"They're not. The kennel master's been feeding them congealed chicken blood." Kian reached down to pet the largest puppy and received an earnest nip on the finger. "Ouch. Little monster."

"A taste for human flesh," she teased. "Maybe they *are* half goblin."

One of the pups scampered around in front of her and bounced in place as if asking to play fetch. Doing the best she could with what she had, she tossed him a piece of straw, which he retrieved with zeal. But while carrying back his prize, he drew the attention of his siblings. Two pups ran to him and tried to steal the straw, and then two more. He made a valiant effort to defend his trophy, but it wasn't long before the litter had him on his back, and then playtime shifted into something primal. The pup cried as his siblings attacked his throat and belly. He squirmed, pawing at the air, but he couldn't right himself. Stella didn't lift her head. To her, the attack was a lesson in establishing pack dominance, but Cerise couldn't stand to watch it.

She crawled to the fray and nudged aside the litter until the injured pup was able to wriggle to his feet. He stood in place, legs shaking, head bent low in fear. Even now, the poor thing was so terrified that he wet the floor. Cerise lifted him up without a care.

She could wash her hands later.

Cradling his trembling body to her chest, she swayed gently from side to side and stroked the pup until his heartbeat steadied and he stopped shaking. The litter had resumed tugging on her dress, the piece of straw forgotten. She considered setting down the pup, but he was so warm and snuggly that she pressed her cheek to the top of his head and let him lick her chin.

"You have too much love in you," Kian said. He was watching her in amusement, both arms resting on the wooden gate. "If you don't find an outlet for it, you might explode. And we can't have that. Think of the mess!" He nodded at the pup. "You should keep him."

"For my own?" Even as she asked, her arms tightened around the puppy. "But he's worth his weight in coin, half-breed or not."

"I can afford it," Kian whispered behind his hand. "I'm the king."

An emotion swelled inside her—a happiness so complete that all she could do was hug the puppy and try not to split her face in half from smiling.

"Unless you'd prefer a purebred." He thumbed toward the adjoining pen. "The kennel master will breed a litter as soon as—"

"No," she interrupted. "I want this one."

"Then the lucky beast is yours. No one will cherish him more." He reached down and patted Stella's resting head. "Not even his own mother. Take him with you; the staff will give you whatever he needs."

"Isn't he too young to leave his mother?"

"He self-weaned," Kian reminded her. "He's more of a nuisance to Stella than anything. Trust me, you'd be doing them both a favor."

"Thank you," she said. "I've never had a pup to call mine. Or anything, really."

In response, Kian abruptly changed the subject and asked her, "Why did you braid your hair today?"

Cerise touched a section of the intricate plaits. "You're just now noticing?"

"No, I noticed the instant I saw you."

But he hadn't complimented her hair like Daerick had. "You don't like it?"

"It's not that I don't like it. You're as lovely as any of the women I ever hosted at court." His gray eyes softened as they moved over her face. "But you're not a woman of court. You're my lady of the temple, aren't you?"

A bubbling sensation arose inside her chest. She had to battle the urge to unpin her plaits right there and unbraid every last one of them. She decided that tomorrow she would wear her hair loose.

From down the hall, the kennel door squeaked open. Cerise craned her neck to look over the pen, expecting to find Father Padron. But instead of the high priest, a middle-aged man strode into view. He was tall and slender with thick, brown hair and a face so handsome he could charge people to look at it.

"You must be Cole Solon," she said. "I've been waiting to meet you."

Cole bowed to the king and then to her. "And I you, my lady."

"The two of you haven't met at dinner?" Kian asked.

Cerise shook her head, offering no explanation. She didn't want to admit that she had taken her evening meals in her suite.

"I just passed General Petros in the garden," Cole said. "He told me the king's emissary was near, so I came straight away."

Cerise turned up a dirty palm. "I would greet you properly, but you wouldn't want to touch this hand."

Cole responded with a chuckle that sounded rehearsed. Something about his eyes reminded her of the painted goose eggs the Reverend Mother collected in her office: intricately decorated on the outside and hollow within. His Solon allure wasn't as strong as Nina's. He was undeniably handsome, but Cerise had no problem looking away from him.

Cole started to speak, but then he tipped his head to the side and studied her. "There's something familiar about you… The eyes, I think. I can't place it. Who are your parents?"

"Elaina Igalsi and Edwin Solon," she told him.

"Were they ever at court?" Cole asked.

"I don't think they were," she said. "But I never thought to ask."

"Maybe what you see is a Solon family resemblance," Kian offered.

"Maybe," Cole repeated in a tone that said *no*. "Regardless, I'm glad to have met our resident hero."

Just then, the kennel door squeaked open again, and Father Padron joined them. He stood as serenely as ever in front of the king, but he spoke with exaggerated precision, as though each word caused him physical pain. "How may I serve His Majesty?"

"I require your expertise, high priest," Kian answered in a playful tone, almost taunting. Cerise didn't like it. Despite her mistrust of Father Padron, the high priest of Shiera deserved respect. She couldn't look at Kian as he continued. "You will investigate the attacks against me. Direct your priests to question every resident and worker in the palace. Use honesty enchantments if you have to. I want to know who released the panther and who set the fire."

"As His Majesty commands," Father Padron answered.

"And tonight, while I am indisposed," the king added in a sharper tone, "you will cast an enchantment of protection over Lady Champlain. If she is injured in any way, I will tear down one temple for every hair on her head that is harmed."

Cerise drew a loud gasp. "Kian!"

All three men swiveled their gazes to her, two of them shocked that she had dared to call the king by his name and the third clearly amused at having scandalized her.

"I mean, *Your Highness*," she corrected. "You mustn't threaten the goddess. It's blasphemy. She is your creator."

"Even so, my order stands." The king glanced out the nearest window as if gauging the position of the sun. "Now if you'll excuse me, I have only two hours until sunset, and there are love children to be made."

Something cold and sick churned in Cerise's stomach as Kian strode away. She told herself it was the meats and cheeses she had eaten for lunch that bothered her, not the king's parting words. Then she pushed aside the thought altogether and nuzzled her puppy, who licked her cheeks in response. She stood up to take him to his new home.

"He's mine," she announced with a smile, hoping to dissipate the tension from the king's abrasive command. "Isn't he the most precious creature you've ever seen?"

Father Padron chuckled while assisting her over the gate. "*Precious* isn't the word I would use to describe the creature, but happiness suits you. Don't you agree, Lord Solon?"

"Mmm," Cole replied absently. His eyes weren't on the puppy. "Between your parents, my lady, who would you say you favor more?"

"My mother," Cerise told him. There was very little of Father in her face. Nina had inherited all of his traits. "Why? Do you think you might have met her?"

"Perhaps," Cole said, but it was in the same doubtful tone. "I'll look into it."

His talk of family reminded Cerise that there was a heartrending mirror tucked beneath her mattress. She couldn't wait to tell Mama and Father about her time in the palace and show them her new puppy. The pup needed a name, too—and food, and toys, and a bed. There was so much to do to prepare. She dipped in a curtsy to excuse herself. "I should go and clean up."

"If you'll permit me," Cole said, "I would be honored to escort you to dinner." He winked. "You can't hide in your suite forever."

Cerise hesitated. She didn't want to eat dinner with Cole Solon, but to refuse him would be an insult. Besides, he was right. One of her duties as emissary was to conduct herself properly as a lady of the temple, and that included dining in polite company. She doubted that Mother Strout had taken dinners in her suite.

"Yes, of course," she said, forcing a grin. "It would be my pleasure."

10

"My sister, the miracle worker." Nina's face was predictably hidden by a sheet of black muslin, but her voice smiled. "I like the sound of that."

"I'm sorry," Cerise said, lying sideways on her bed with her puppy curled against her chest. She cuddled him with one hand while using the other to hold up the heartrending mirror. "You claim you're my sister, but you could be anyone behind that veil. I'm going to need proof of your identity before this discussion goes any further."

"Oh?" Nina said. "Your *sacred ears* can't discern a lie?"

"Are you mocking the blessed oracle?"

"Never."

"Good, because we take that sort of thing seriously here."

"All right," Nina said. "Here's your evidence. You have a birthmark on your bottom. Left cheek. It's pink and small and shaped like a squashed bug."

Cerise drew a breath. "How do you know about that?"

"From visiting days at the temple. I used to change your clod when you were a baby."

"So did a lot of people," Cerise pointed out. "That proves nothing."

"Hmm. I guess I'd better show myself, then."

"Yes, you'd better."

"Very well."

Nina flipped back her veil, and at once, Cerise's lips drifted apart in a sigh. By the goddess, Nina was so beautiful that it was impossible to know where to focus. Cerise drank in the curve of her sister's face, her flawless lips, her smooth skin. But most breathtaking of all were Nina's eyes, fringed by thick lashes, greener than springtime, and made infinitely more stunning by the warmth and affection brimming behind them. It was then that Cerise understood why she couldn't look away from her sister.

Love.

"Your curse," Cerise murmured, still entranced. "Does the Solon allure grow stronger when someone loves you?"

Nina's eyes went wide. She seemed bothered by the question. "Why do you ask?"

"Because I met another firstborn Solon today," Cerise said. "He's handsome, but I don't want to stare at him forever and ever." She lost track of her thoughts, caught up in a haze as she traced the high angle of her sister's cheekbones. But then Cerise noticed a slight change in the sharpness of Nina's cheeks. She had lost weight.

The veil fell back into place. "That's enough."

"Wait, your face looks thin. Are you sick?"

"I am," Nina said with a smile in her voice. "Every morning. I'm going to have a baby."

Cerise gasped in excitement. She would be an aunt! But her happiness quickly sank when she remembered that Nina's baby would carry a firstborn curse, and it might not be the Solon allure.

"You married a Calatris," Cerise said.

"Yes. What of it?"

"His family curse…"

"There won't be one," Nina said. "Not for this baby. His late wife already gave him a firstborn—and a second-born. This will be his third child."

Cerise shook her head. That wasn't how it worked. It didn't matter how many children Nina's husband had sired with another woman. Nina had never been pregnant before. This baby would be *her* firstborn, which meant the child would bear a curse.

No. Enough was enough.

The curses needed to end—now. Cerise no longer cared what her role was supposed to be in the Reverend Mother's "narrow path" to the future. She was done searching for clues that might inspire someone else to break the curses. Since no one seemed to have any idea how to earn the goddess's forgiveness, she would do it herself.

"I'll break the curses," she promised. "Or I'll die trying. I swear it."

"Don't say that," Nina snapped. "I don't want to hear any talk of dying. Do you hear me?" Her veiled head turned as if she was seeking support, and then Mama took the mirror.

"Darling," Mama said as her face appeared in the glass. "I think what your sister is trying to say is that you're every bit as important to us as the child she's carrying. We don't want you to risk your safety. The baby will be fine. We'll make sure of it."

"You can't make sure of anything," Cerise said. "Do you really think you can change the baby's fate? Do you think any noble firstborn was ever saved by their family's love? The curse is beyond your control, but it might be within mine. I already have to help break the noble curses to save the king, so why wouldn't I double my efforts if it means saving Nina's baby, too?"

"The only thing you *have* to do for the king is serve as his emissary," Mama corrected. "That was the task the Reverend Mother assigned to you."

"You have no idea what the Reverend Mother assigned to me, because I didn't tell you." But maybe it was time they knew the truth. "It might be time for the curses to be broken. The Reverend Mother couldn't See how, but she said there's a path to make it happen. And I'm going to find it."

"Cerise," Father called from outside the frame. "Do you want to upset your sister in her delicate condition? Because that's what you're doing. Your sister is in tears now."

She let go of a long breath. Instead of making Nina feel better, she'd made her cry. Why couldn't she say the right thing, just this once? The puppy seemed to sense her agitation and licked the edge of her jaw. "No. That's not what I want."

"Then we won't speak of it again." Mama nodded, closing the topic. "Now tell me more about the Solon gentleman you met at the palace. Is there any relation?"

Cerise hated the subject change. For her, the discussion was far from over. But she rubbed her pup's ear and said, "Not a close relation. He kept asking about you, though."

Mama touched her chest. "Me?"

"Yes, he thinks I look like someone he used to know. Were you ever at court?"

Mama shared a glance with someone outside the frame—Father, no doubt. Her eyes widened a fraction before they returned to the mirror. "How strange," she said. "He must have me confused with someone else."

Something about her tone seemed odd. Cerise studied her mother. She didn't believe her parents had ever lied to her, but she couldn't help feeling like there was a story in play and her family had just tried to close the book. "I'll ask him tonight at dinner," Cerise said, watching her mother's expression closely. "He's my escort."

If there was any doubt that her parents were hiding something, their reactions put it to rest. Mama's lips parted, and Father snatched away the mirror. The image movement caught the puppy's eye, who yipped and snapped at the glass. Cerise held the mirror beyond his reach.

"That's not necessary, my dear," Father said. "Simply tell the man that we've never met him and change the subject if he asks again."

"How do you know you've never met him?" Cerise asked, raising an eyebrow. "I haven't told you his name."

Father stammered.

"What are you hiding?" Cerise demanded. "Because I know there's something wrong, and you're not helping me by lying about it. I'm sick to death of being lied to!"

Father opened his mouth and paused to breathe. The frustration etched onto his face reminded her of the way General Petros struggled to tame his temper. "You've lived a sheltered life, Cerise. You don't know how dangerous court politics can be. Nothing at court is as it seems. Behind every honest word, you should expect a hidden meaning. No one will be transparent with you. They've learned it's not safe to be."

"The king dismissed his court," Cerise said. A silent voice inside her head added, *It's the priests I have to watch out for, and the ones who serve false idols.*

"Even so, information is power," Father told her. "Don't give anything away unless you have to." His eyes, nearly identical to Nina's, were serious in a way that turned Cerise cold. Whatever he was hiding, it frightened him, and that shook her because she had never seen him afraid. "The temple taught you to be obedient and kind—admirable traits for a Seer but not for a lady in service to the king. Trust no one and say as little as possible." He pointed a stern finger at her. "Do you understand?"

"Yes," she told him, but she understood less than ever.

That night at dinner, Cerise kept her eyes fixed on her plate, nodding as she pretended to listen to Cole Solon's prattle but secretly wondering why her parents hadn't trusted her with the truth about him. The simplest explanation was that Cole and Mama had been lovers many years ago, before Mama married Father. But an affair wasn't frightening or scandalous enough to lie about...unless it had happened *after* Mama married Father.

Could that be the case? Had Cole Solon seduced Mama into betraying her husband? Kian's mother had fallen deeply enough for Cole's charms to betray her king. But despite that, Cerise couldn't imagine that her mother had done the same. It just didn't feel right.

During the first course, Cerise snuck glances at Cole. She didn't know what the late queen had seen in him. The longer she studied Cole's chiseled features, the less human he seemed. By the second course, she agreed with Kian's prior assessment of Cole as a *slippery bastard*. Flattery slid like oil off of Cole's tongue. He complimented Daerick's beard (something no one would do), remarked on Lady Champlain's "healthy glow" (clearly a means of fishing for pregnancy news), and praised the way General Petros filled out his dinner jacket. It wasn't until the general growled in annoyance that Cole finally returned his attention to Cerise.

"My lady," Cole said to her as he buttered his dinner roll, "I admire how well you seem to have adjusted to palace life. It must have been a shock, leaving your temple."

She nodded in agreement. "It was."

"Well, clearly you were destined for court." He delivered a grin that didn't reach his eyes. "You're a natural, my dear."

She barely managed to stifle a laugh. If lies were gold, Cole Solon could build a palace out of coin.

"How are you settling in to your duties as emissary?" He lifted an apologetic hand and added, "Please forgive me for broaching such a vulgar topic as politics at the dining table. It's just that our beloved Mother Strout left us far too soon. As much as we miss her, it's a comfort to know that you're here to carry on her legacy."

"I can't say that I'm carrying on her legacy just yet," Cerise said. "I'm still learning what my responsibilities are. It certainly helps to have her journal as a guide, though."

Cole paused, his dinner roll halfway to his mouth. He recovered quickly, but the slip hinted that she had revealed too much. For some strange reason, both Cole and General Petros had reacted to Mother Strout's journal. Cerise couldn't imagine why. She had read the whole thing from cover to cover and found not a word of interest. But regardless, Father had told her to say as little as possible, and she had failed him before the dessert course.

She would have to do better.

She wished Kian could be there to distract the group in that bold, scandalous way of his. Though she wouldn't enjoy watching him escort Delora to dinner, not to mention flatter her with endless compliments, he would make up for it by telling a funny story. She smiled just thinking about it. She had come to crave his company more than she'd realized.

For the rest of the meal, she answered each of Cole's questions in no more than a word or two. She could hear how rude she sounded, and she sensed Father Padron's chiding gaze on her. She avoided that, too, by refusing to look up from her plate. Finally, Daerick asked if she was all right, and she used a heat migraine as an excuse to leave the table.

Away from the group, she felt free for the first time all evening, as though a boulder had been lifted from her chest. On her way back to her suite, she stopped at the kitchens for a bowl of water and a plate of congealed chicken blood. Then she asked the groundskeeper to lay a length of sod on her balcony for housetraining. After that, she returned to her chamber to spend the evening with the only creature that had never lied to her, criticized her, or vexed her in any way. Her puppy.

Truly, the world of men didn't deserve dogs.

Remarkably, her pup was advanced well beyond his age. She was even able to teach him a few basic commands. As she did so, she tried to think of a fitting name for him. The answer came during a game of fetch, when she noticed a streak of color peeking out from between the folds on his back. She parted the loose skin to reveal a blotchy indigo birthmark.

"I have a birthmark, too," she told him. "But mine's pink, not blue."

The pup rolled onto his back and hugged her wrist between his front paws—a move the brilliant rascal had learned would result in a belly rub.

"Blue," she repeated, testing the name as she used her fingertips to tickle his skin. "What do you think? Do you like it?"

Eyes closed, he made a contented sound that she took as a *yes*.

"Then *Blue* it is." She leaned down, rubbing noses with him. "We're a family now, Lord Blue Solon. And that's forever."

When he opened his dark eyes and looked at her, she could swear that he had understood every word. Something seemed to pass between them: an unspoken promise that neither of them would ever feel alone again. For the first time in her life, she could say that her heart was truly full.

At bedtime, they snuggled on their sides between the linen sheets, Blue's head tucked beneath her chin. He licked her neck once as if to say good night, and then they drifted into dreams.

The next morning, when the sun was no more than a purple stain on the curtains, Cerise awoke to a growl and a shrill bark. She opened her eyes and found Blue standing alert in front of her pillow, his dark eyes focused on something she couldn't see. She didn't think much of it at first. She assumed Blue had caught sight of an insect or a lizard. But then she heard the *click* of her suite door closing, and she sat bolt upright, peering all around.

Someone had just been in her room.

The intruder had left, but that didn't stop her heart from racing. She must have forgotten to lock the door last night when she returned from dinner. It was a mistake she wouldn't make twice. She hated to imagine what could have happened if Blue hadn't barked at the intruder and scared them away.

"Good boy," she praised Blue while rubbing his head. "You're my tiny hero." Only he wasn't as tiny as she remembered. Picking him up, she noticed that his rump no longer fit within the palm of her hand. "Let's go find this growing boy some breakfast."

Her miniature protector scampered alongside her in the corridor, his stumpy tail wagging and his head held high...until he approached the top of the staircase, where he halted as though he had reached the edge of the world. Cerise picked him up and carried him the rest of the way. They ate a breakfast of scones and sausages in the garden, then played hide-and-seek in the hedge maze until it was time to meet Daerick in her office.

Leaving Blue behind simply wasn't an option, so she fashioned a sling out of an old scarf and tucked Blue inside it to rest with his head near her heart. By the time she reached her office suite, the motion of her footsteps had rocked him to sleep.

The door to her suite was already open. Beyond the sitting area, a male figure stood as still as stone in front of the window, peering out at the palace lawn as if deep in thought. He must have recently come in from outdoors, because he wore a cloak of gauzy linen to protect his head and his shoulders from the sun.

Cerise recognized him easily. "Good morning, Your Majesty," she whispered so as not to wake Blue.

Kian pulled back his hood and turned to face her. "How did you know it was me?"

"You're the only person who looks at the lawns as if you own them," she said.

But that was only partly true. She had noticed other details about him—the casual tilt of his head, the confidence in his stance, the way he rubbed his thumb against his index finger when he checked the position of the sun. She kept those observations to herself. She didn't want to admit to him how quickly she had learned his habits...and she didn't want to admit it to herself, either.

"Impressive," he said with a crooked grin that made her stomach dance. "You're rather brilliant, except when it comes to toxic frogs."

She pressed a hand over her abdomen to still it. The sensation was familiar. She recognized it from a dozen delivery days at the temple, when she had been naive enough to think the thrill was worth the cost.

She peered absently around the sitting room to avoid the slate-gray eyes that made her talk too much and feel unwelcome things. "Where's Daerick?"

"He should be on his way." Kian strode toward her and stopped near enough to fill her space with the scents of fresh hay and male skin. He removed his cloak and tossed it onto the velvet sofa. "I visited the stables and the kennel master this morning."

"Did you?" Cerise asked while her pulse thumped from the closeness of him. She didn't realize how quickly her heart was racing until Blue awoke and licked her chin as if to calm her. "I named the pup," she blurted. "Lord Blue Solon. Blue for short."

"Hello, Blue." Kian rubbed the puppy's head and pulled a treat from his pocket—a small, sand-colored nugget, which he sniffed at before recoiling. "The kennel master's secret recipe. I don't want to know what's in this."

Blue gobbled the treat in a single bite. When it became clear that there wouldn't be any more, he smacked his chops and then rested his head squarely between Cerise's breasts, causing her to blush and Kian to laugh.

"He's the one living like a king," Kian said. "I should be taking lessons."

Thankfully, the moment ended when Daerick walked into the sitting room, noticed Blue, and wrinkled his nose as if he had encountered a mountain of horse dung.

"My lady," Daerick said with feigned alarm. "There seems to be a goblin fastened to your chest. Is this some new form of punishment the priests have invented?"

Cerise shushed him while covering Blue's ears. "He's not a goblin, and you know it."

"Half of him might be," Kian muttered.

Cerise glared at the king and reminded herself that her purpose was to serve him, not to kick him in the shin. "His name is Lord

Blue Solon."

"Blue for short," Kian added.

"Well, he's hideous, but I suppose that isn't his fault." Daerick smoothed a wrinkle from his satin tunic. "We can't all be handsome."

"I think he's perfect." Cerise dropped a kiss on the top of Blue's head. "And he's smart, too. Brilliant, in fact. He already learned all of the commands I taught him, and this morning he saved me from an intruder in my bedchamber."

Daerick and Kian widened their eyes at her.

"I was never in any real danger," she added. "Blue scared away the person before I even knew they were there."

Kian scrubbed a hand over his face. "Make no mistake, my lady of the temple—the danger in this palace is real."

"I told you to lock your door," Daerick said. "The night you arrived, remember?"

"I thought I did," she said. "I'll be more careful."

Daerick glanced at Kian. "I saw the priests going from room to room last night. They questioned me before dinner. What did the investigation turn up?"

"It turned up nothing." Kian folded his arms. "I summoned Padron at sunrise. He told me that his men finished their inquiry and that no one in the palace knows who's responsible for the fire or the desert panther."

"But they couldn't have finished their inquiry," Cerise said. She lifted Blue out of his sling and placed him on the floor so he could explore the office. "They didn't question me."

"Well, it's obvious you had no part in the attacks," Kian told her. "My parents were the first victims, and they died while you were still living at the temple."

Cerise had heard stories that the late king and queen had died from unnatural causes, but she had dismissed the talk as gossip. "I thought that was a rumor."

"Not all rumors are lies. This one had merit."

"All right," she said, "but if the priests thought it was unnecessary to question me, doesn't it make you wonder who else they failed to investigate?"

Daerick smiled at her like a proud parent. "Now you're thinking like a Calatris who no longer believes in the Silent Soul."

"You taught me well," she told him.

Kian sat on the arm of the sofa and exhaled a bitter laugh. "Padron lied to me. I don't know why I'm surprised."

"But how can any priest lie to you?" Cerise asked. "They're compelled to obey you."

"To obey my direct commands," Kian said. "I can't control the way their minds work. I can't compel them to respect me or to support my rule. Even if I order them to speak only the truth, they can choose words that are misleading. Trust me, my lady of the temple. The priests are dutiful to me in body but not in spirit. All it takes for them to disobey me is creativity, and they have it."

Cerise instinctively checked over both shoulders before she asked her next question. "*Could* a priest have set the fire?" she whispered. "Or turned the panther loose?"

Kian shook his head. "The first order I give every priest is to take no action that could result in my harm. The actual command is longer than that. I worded it in a way to eliminate loopholes. They can't hurt me directly. I made sure of it."

So if the priests weren't trying to kill Kian, then who was? Cerise couldn't think of any group that stood to gain more from Kian's death than the priests who resented their bond of service to him. "Who else benefits?"

"Anyone who wants my throne," Kian said. "Take your pick."

But an empty throne would lead to war, and Cerise refused to believe that any of the noble houses wanted that, not even the Petros dynasty. A firstborn Petros would certainly enjoy the bloody battles, but their victory wouldn't win them control of the priests. At least she didn't think so. The Mortara dynasty had used their dominion over the priests to unify the four lands and create the Allied Realm. Without magic, the Petros dynasty would have to use their own troops to hold the realm together and to enforce peace. The cost, both in coin and in lives, would be more than the throne was worth.

"What's the point of killing you and stealing your throne if the new monarch won't have command over the priests?" she asked.

"Who says they won't?" Kian countered. "We don't know what would happen, because we have no idea why they're bound to me in the first place."

Daerick made a noise of disagreement. "I think the priests have an idea. They must believe that your death will set them free. Otherwise, they wouldn't be making a play for the throne."

"What?" Cerise asked. "What play?"

"Kian knows," Daerick said, peering somberly at the king.

"He's referring to the recent deaths in Calatris," Kian told her. "General Petros thinks the murders were facilitated by the Order to eliminate competition for my throne."

"What evidence does he have of that?" Cerise asked.

"It's circumstantial," Daerick said. "The heads of the two most powerful families in Calatris were summoned by the Order to attend a meeting, supposedly to discuss temple taxes or some such. But when the men arrived for the meeting, they found no one there…except for an assassin who just so happened to be waiting for them. The priests arrived too late to stop the killings. They claimed a wheel had broken on their carriage."

"A wheel that any priest could mend with magic," Cerise murmured. If the story was true, then General Petros was right. The priests had been complicit. "I was there when General Petros confronted Father Padron about the deaths."

"Oh?" Daerick asked with a lifted brow. "And did Father Padron apologize on behalf of his men? Did he happily agree to control the priests who follow his every whim and worship him like he's a god?"

"No," she said. Father Padron had paralyzed the general in a show of dominance.

Cerise chewed on the inside of her cheek. She absently stroked

Blue's head and remembered what Kian had told her when they first met. *You will find evil here, in the most unexpected places. By the time the shadows consume me and I dissolve into nothing, you'll wish you could forget all the things the temple has hidden from you.*

His prediction had already come true. She wished she couldn't believe that the Order coveted the throne, because it upended everything she had known about the world. But she couldn't ignore what she had seen of the Order since she'd come here. Was that what the Reverend Mother had been trying to tell her? She knew there had to be *some* priests who were loyal to the goddess. But what were their numbers? Were they willing to stand against their brothers? No second-born given in service to the temple had been raised to question the Order's teachings, only to follow them.

One thing was certain: any person, priest or otherwise, with unchecked power on the throne would be a nightmare.

"Your Majesty," Cerise said. "I need to ask you another uncomfortable question."

Kian swept a permissive hand. "If you must."

"Is Lady Champlain carrying your heir?"

Kian parted his lips, momentarily at a loss for words. "No. And that information is not to leave this room. Do you understand?"

Cerise nodded. She could see why he would want the Order to fear the possibility of having a new commander. "It seems to me the only way to stop a priest from taking the throne is to keep you on it—and to make sure your bloodline continues. And to do that, we have to put all of our focus on breaking the curse before it takes you. We have to make it our only goal. Because if we fail and the Order has no master..."

Daerick shuddered. "Say no more. Let's start with what we know about undoing curses: the soothsayer told us that blood spilled requires blood given."

"All right, so who stabbed the goddess?" Kian asked, looking to Cerise as if she would know the answer. "Which dynasty spilled her blood?"

Cerise tipped up her palms. It was common knowledge that the Petros dynasty had forged the weapon used in the attack. The weapon was known as the Petros Blade, but none of the scrolls mentioned who had actually wielded it or what had happened to the blade following the Great Betrayal.

"Maybe it doesn't matter," she said. "All four houses are equally guilty of trying to kill Shiera. If a firstborn from each noble dynasty makes a blood offering to the goddess, maybe that will repay the debt."

"But how much blood is enough?" Kian asked. "A thimbleful? A whole body full? And in what manner should it be spilled in order to appease your goddess?"

"She's your goddess, too," Cerise reminded him. Other than that, she didn't know the answers to his questions.

Kian groaned and rolled his eyes to the heavens. "Perhaps you can pray to the goddess you adore so much and ask her for a hint—just a shade of transparency to clarify the water she deliberately muddied for us."

A shade of transparency. The words stood out in Cerise's mind. She recalled what her father had told her about the dangers of court politics: *Nothing at court is as it seems. Behind every honest word, you should expect a hidden meaning. No one will be transparent with you. They've learned it's not safe to be.*

All of a sudden, she thought of Mother Strout's journal and how little information it contained. There was nothing of use on its pages, only scribbles and secretarial details, so why had the old emissary bothered to keep a journal at all? Unless there was more to it…a hidden meaning behind the words, like Father had said.

Cerise slipped to her desk and opened the middle drawer to retrieve the journal. She lifted the black-and-white book and flipped through its pages, studying them with fresh eyes. Now that she paid special attention, she could see how the outer edge of each nonsensical drawing along the margin aligned with the inner edge of the drawing on the next page. Mother Strout hadn't scribbled in her journal out of boredom. She had left a message for her replacement, and Cerise had nearly missed it.

"Help me with this," she said, then told Kian and Daerick what she had learned.

Together, they worked for the next hour to carefully cut each drawing from its margin and lay it atop Cerise's mahogany desk. There were hundreds of pieces in all—a handmade puzzle to solve without a single guiding clue. Next came the task of arranging the pieces into something recognizable. The process was laboriously slow, but eventually the matches began to reveal a rough sketch of a lady's gown. After that, the puzzle came together more easily. Daerick found the final match, and then they stood back to study the picture.

The sketch showed a group of people, five of them in all, gathered at the base of a mountain. One of the figures appeared to be a priest or at least a man dressed in robes. Two figures were depicted as women, and another two were depicted as men. The priest stood at the center of the group, holding a sword in his outstretched hands while the four other figures touched the blade with their index fingers. The image was titled CONTRITION in tiny block letters and dated a hundred years in the past, as if Mother Strout had discovered the artwork and sketched from memory.

"Is this…" Cerise began, nearly afraid to hope. "Could this be…"

"A visual set of instructions for breaking the curse?" Daerick offered. "It certainly looks that way."

Cerise had never seen anything like it. "I wonder where the original is."

Kian exhaled bitterly. "If Strout hadn't poisoned herself, we could ask her."

But *had* she poisoned herself? Especially after making such an important discovery?

"I can't believe she kept it a secret," Cerise said. The world of men had been looking for a way to break the noble curses for a thousand years. Uncovering this knowledge would have made Mother Strout a hero to every noble family in the world.

"I know; it doesn't make sense," Daerick agreed. "If I found a way to end generations of torment, I would tell anyone with ears."

So would Cerise. But then she remembered her father's warning about transparency being a danger at court. Maybe Mother Strout had hidden her discovery because she'd felt unsafe. And considering her recent death, her fears had probably been justified.

Kian pointed at the sword. "Well, this answers my question. A drop or two of blood from all four dynasties, given to—"

"The Petros Blade," Cerise breathed, touching the sword in the drawing. Her heart was beating too fast, and there was a strange buzzing in her ears. The revelation was real. Her *purpose* was real. She might actually have a chance of doing this. "But where do we get it?"

"I heard it's frozen in the northern ice caps," Kian said.

"No," Daerick told him. "You're thinking of the Chalice of Champions, and that's not a real thing."

"Of course it's not real. I wasn't thinking of the Chalice. Everyone knows it's made up."

"Not everyone."

"Everyone with a brain."

"Well, I'm just saying…"

While the two of them bickered, Cerise squinted at a miniature detail she'd just noticed in the background. There was more to the picture. A series of numbers had been cleverly drawn into the curves of the mountainside. "What's this?"

Daerick leaned over the puzzle and inspected it for a silent beat before his face transformed into a smile. "It's a cipher."

"To a code?" Kian asked.

"To a code," Daerick echoed. He picked up the journal and strode closer to the window, where he thumbed through its marginless pages in the morning light. Thank Shiera they hadn't just ripped the pages out.

"And to think," he muttered to himself, "I accused the old woman of flimsy recordkeeping. She was more brilliant than any of us gave her credit for."

"I knew her journal entries didn't make sense," Cerise said. "I should have put it together sooner."

"Don't be too hard on yourself," Kian told her. "I doubt the temple prepared you for a life of code-breaking and intrigue."

"Well, either way, we're lucky that Father Bishop brought the journal back." She peeked at Daerick, who was furiously scanning a new page. "Do you think he noticed anything suspicious about the entries?"

"I doubt it," Daerick murmured absently. "Otherwise, he would have kept it and tried to decode it himself."

She supposed he was right. Still, she worried that Father Bishop might have discovered more than he'd let on. If Mother Strout had helped raise him from infancy, he would have known her better than anyone else at the palace.

Kian tapped his booted foot as he watched Daerick scan the journal. "Do you need parchment?" Kian asked him. "A quill?"

"Only silence, thank you," Daerick said, his eyes wide and fixed on the page.

The waiting was torture. Even Blue, who had curled up to nap in a patch of sunlight, seemed to sense the tension in the air. He lifted his head from the carpet, peered sleepily at Cerise, and then gave a tremendous yawn before setting his head down again.

"I've got it!" Daerick closed the journal between his hands with a loud *snap* that caused Blue to flinch. "I know the message she was hiding."

"Which was…" Kian prompted.

"The location of the Petros Blade." Daerick wobbled a palm in a *so-so* motion and added, "Sort of."

Kian growled, pinching the bridge of his nose in annoyance. "Lord Calatris, I am not in the mood for riddles."

"All right, all right," Daerick said. "Cutting right to the chase."

"Please do," Cerise told him. She wasn't in the mood for games, either.

Daerick held up the journal for show. "Here's the short of it: I don't know where Strout found her information or even if it's correct, but according to her, the Petros Blade was hidden on the blighted mountain by Shiera's followers. It's under an enchantment that moves it to a new location at every full moon. The only way to find it is with sunset runes."

Kian wrinkled his brow. "Sunset runes are real? I thought they were a myth, like the Chalice."

"So did I," Daerick said. "But Mother Strout believed otherwise."

Cerise had never heard of sunset runes. "What are they?"

"Imagine a set of dice," Daerick said. "But with distances carved on one and directions carved on the other. You cast the dice before sunset, and they show you which way to travel the next day and for how far. Supposedly, they can lead you to any object in the world, and then they vanish when you find it."

"But what leads us to the runes?" Cerise asked, trying not to think too hard about why the temple hadn't taught her any of this. She could worry about that later. "How do we find *them*?"

Kian chuckled under his breath. "There lies the irony."

"Ah, but Mother Strout had an answer for that as well," Daerick said, holding up an index finger. "She claimed the runes will present themselves to a worshipper of pure faith who makes an offering of darkness and light at the Blighted Shrine."

Of course. The Blighted Shrine! Cerise knew of that. It had been built as a tribute to Shiera's resilience, named for its location on the mountain peak where the Great Betrayal had taken place. As for the nature of the offering, Cerise had an abundance of light to give. But she didn't know what manner of darkness the goddess would require.

"A worshipper of pure faith." Daerick teasingly tapped his chin while grinning at Kian. "Does that describe anyone you know?"

"Hmm," Kian said, pretending to think about it. "That's a tough one. We might have to turn the kingdom upside down to find a person like that."

Both of their smiling gazes turned to Cerise. She knew they were making fun of her, but she couldn't help but smile in return. Now that she had hope—real hope—of breaking the curse, she was finally in the mood for games.

"I might know someone," she told them, playing along. "And she might be willing to help you, but she insists on traveling with her pup."

"Is her pup at least handsome?" Daerick asked, biting back a grin.

Cerise glanced at Blue, who had rolled onto his back and now lay asleep on the carpet with his limbs splayed out, his wide jaw open at an awkward angle, and his tongue lolling to the side. "He's the most breathtaking hound to have ever been sired."

"...by a goblin," Kian added with a snigger. He held up an apologetic hand to fend off a glare. "All teasing aside, we need to make a plan."

Yes, they certainly did. Mother Strout had given them a lead—maybe at the expense of her own life—and now they owed it to her to follow it. And with just under six moons until the king's last sunset, there was no time to waste.

"The blighted mountain is a death trap," Daerick said. "We'll need a guide—someone discreet who can tell us which routes are safe to travel and where to find water along the way. It will cost us a lot of coin, but I think I know where to find one."

"Take as much from the treasury as you need," Kian told him.

"I can start gathering supplies," Cerise volunteered. "How many people will be traveling with us? And how long do you think we'll be gone? Do we need to arrange a caravan?"

Kian jutted his chin toward the journal. "Old Strout kept this a secret for a reason. Until we find out why, I want to keep our group as small as possible. Let's plan a day trip for the three of us, just an exploratory visit to see what we're up against. Then I can decide who else to include. I know I can trust General Petros. But Father Padron... I only want to bring him with us if our lives depend on it. A priest's protection isn't always worth the cost of his presence."

Cerise couldn't argue with that.

"Then it's decided," Kian announced. "We'll take the rest of the day to prepare, and we'll leave tomorrow morning. Meet me at the stables an hour past dawn."

11

With their tasks divided, the three of them set to their work. Kian left for the stables to select the hardiest horses for the mountain journey. Daerick went into the city in pursuit of a guide. And Cerise and Blue visited the kitchens to secure provisions for the following day. In hopes of minimizing gossip among the staff, she enlisted the help of Wren, one of the young serving maids who had come to visit her after the fire. Wren promised to quietly set aside an assortment of dried meats and fruits, flatbreads, and several flagons of water. Cerise thanked her, and then she found a snack for Blue and carried him outside to the palace gardens to exercise his rapidly growing legs.

Though it didn't seem possible, Blue had gained nearly half a stone in the hours since dawn. The adorable stumpy-tailed rump that had once fit in the palm of her hand now stood almost halfway to her calf. If Blue kept growing at this rate, she would only be able to carry him in her sling for another day, two at the most.

"Slow down, my sweet boy," she told Blue as she knelt in the grass to scratch his neck. "Can't you stay a baby for a while longer?"

As if in response, he yipped and rolled over for a belly rub. But then his head jerked up and he froze, tense and alert with a predatory instinct. He must have caught a scent on the breeze, because in an instant, he was on his paws and loping toward the hedge maze faster than Cerise could catch him.

"Blue, stop!" she called, but she hadn't taught him that command yet, and so he darted onward and disappeared into the maze.

Cerise scrambled to her feet while glancing behind her to ensure she was alone, and then she hitched up her dress and sprinted in a most unladylike manner into the maze. She caught sight of Blue and ran after him as fast as her legs would carry her. It was all she could do to keep him in her line of vision. Blue led her around so many twists and turns that she feared she might not find her way out again. He reached the center of the maze and continued around two more corners until he finally stopped at a small, grassy nook hidden by an extra layer of hedges. The space was so well concealed that Cerise never would have found it on her own. But as she caught up with Blue, she discovered that the alcove was occupied by two young ladies seated on a marble bench, their silk-draped bodies pressed together in a passionate kiss.

Cerise gasped in embarrassment and startled the ladies, who pulled apart and released gasps of their own. One woman splayed a hand over the swell of her left breast as if to still her heart. She stared at Cerise with round, unblinking eyes, and with equal shock, Cerise recognized Delora Champlain. The other woman was unfamiliar. Slightly older than Delora, she had the face of nobility—a long, straight nose, smooth skin, high cheekbones, and a strong chin—and her auburn hair was worn in a twist secured by golden combs.

Blue broke the silence with a shrill bark directed at a basket of food resting on the grass near the bench. Both ladies started at the noise, but their gazes remained fixed on Cerise.

They weren't afraid of Blue. They were afraid of *her.*

"I'm sorry for the intrusion," Cerise told them. "I'll go."

"No, wait!" Delora exclaimed. Her mouth was still swollen from the kiss, but the blush on her cheeks had turned to wax. "Please let me explain."

"You don't need to," Cerise said. Delora had done nothing wrong. She had taken a lover in addition to the king, and that lover happened to be a woman. Both of those things were within her rights as a courtesan, though she was wise to be discreet about it. If Kian's spirit was drawn to Delora, he probably wouldn't enjoy the idea of sharing her.

But then something occurred to Cerise. She noticed the tender way Delora stroked the woman's back. Delora had never shown that kind of affection for Kian—no warm gazes, no kisses, no embraces, no touches of any kind other than to accept his arm in escort. It almost seemed like Delora didn't share a connection with the king.

For some odd reason, Cerise's heart lifted.

"My lady," Delora began, pausing to lick her lips. She wrung her hands, the patch of skin at the base of her throat visibly pulsing. "You won't tell, will you?"

"It's not my place to tell," Cerise said. "But to be fair, don't you think the king has a right to know…" She swept a hand toward the women. "…about this?"

"I'm not worried about the king." Delora lowered her voice. "He already knows."

Cerise blinked. But that made no sense. Kian could have any woman in the kingdom as his courtesan. Why would he choose someone who clearly didn't want him? There was no shortage of young, desirable ladies who would leap at the chance to conceive his heir and become the next queen.

"But…" Cerise began. "I thought he offered to marry you if…"

"If I conceive his child," Delora finished. "Yes, that's the story."

The story? Was it a lie, then?

"Will you allow me to explain?" Delora asked again.

Cerise moved closer to the bench so they could talk quietly. She lowered onto the grass in front of the bench, and Blue padded along beside her. Blue sniffed at the lunch basket and whined. The woman with the auburn hair lifted the basket onto her lap and began feeding Blue nibbles of cold chicken while Delora spoke.

"This is Philippa," Delora said, indicating the other woman. "She was my harp tutor when I lived at home. I loved her from the moment we met, but I couldn't tell my father. He was raised in the old ways, to believe that women belong only with men. So when he hired a matchmaker to find me a husband, I didn't object. I thought my suitors would be old and ugly and that I could turn them down and never get married." Delora released a dry laugh. "But the matchmaker was good at her job. Too good. She kept bringing me handsome, wealthy men no reasonable girl would refuse. I started to run out of excuses to say no, and I knew it was only a matter of time until my father made the decision for me."

"So you asked the king to intervene?" Cerise guessed.

"He's a good friend," Delora said. "Good enough to lie and give me the perfect excuse to end the matchmaking once and for all. His idea was brilliant. He said that no man would risk offending the king by proposing marriage to his courtesan. So that was the role he gave me. My father was furious at first, but then Kian added the bit about making me his queen if I conceived an heir. He even gave me the title of *lady*. After that, there were no complaints. Every father dreams of his daughter being a queen."

"That's what you meant by becoming a courtesan to save yourself." Cerise could see the irony now. "The king's friendship made you free, but that same friendship draws his spirit to you and puts you at risk."

"I don't have as much freedom as you think." Delora reached for Philippa's hand and gripped it. "The priests here are a lot like my father—believers in the old ways. They don't care about the law of the land. They wouldn't dare to act against me while the king is alive, but if they knew about Philippa, they could find a reason to send her away. Or worse."

Anger rose in Cerise's chest. She didn't say so, but the priests had no grounds to object. The goddess had never been controlled by a man. Shiera loved all of her creations equally, men and women alike. Some of the priests in Mortara needed to learn their place.

"The priests won't find out from me," Cerise promised. "But are you saying the king has never tried to produce an heir?"

Delora tilted her head to the side, her eyes softening. "You've seen the way he suffers, my lady. Do you believe he would pass that agony on to a child?"

The answer formed in Cerise's heart. No, of course he wouldn't want his firstborn child, or any child, to bear his curse. But still, wasn't it reckless of him to let the Mortara bloodline die out before the curses were broken? They had only just discovered how to find the Petros Blade, and that was assuming Mother Strout's information was correct. What if they failed? Then the Order would try to take the throne, and that was an outcome more chilling than the shadows.

. . .

Much like the day before, Cerise awoke to a loud bark from her pup. Her eyes flew open, and she sat bolt upright in bed, peering around her room by the faint, orange glow of dawn. She found no one in her chamber except for Blue, who seemed perfectly content standing beside her, now as tall as a fawn, wagging his stumpy tail and licking his chops as if he had just finished eating.

"Did you swallow a bug?" she asked. "They always make you throw up. When will you learn?"

Blue licked her chin, and at once, Cerise recoiled from the scent of his breath. The odor was unmistakable. He had eaten a treat from the kennel master. But Cerise couldn't imagine where Blue had found it. She didn't remember bringing any treats back to her room. Surely she would have smelled them if she had.

Something wasn't right.

She pulled back the sheet and tiptoed across the bedchamber until she reached the doorway to the sitting room. When she peeked into the sitting room and found it empty, she continued all the way to the suite door and turned the knob.

The door was unlocked.

"No, that's impossible," she murmured to herself. She had locked the door last night. She was certain of it. She had even tested the door afterward by trying to open it, and it hadn't budged.

Someone must have stolen a key to her suite. But if the intruder had a key, why hadn't they locked the door behind them? Did they *want* her to know that they had been in her bedchamber? That they had watched her sleep and could have violated her at their leisure? Was someone in the palace purposefully trying to scare her?

"Well, it's not working," she announced, though her trembling voice made her a liar. She returned to her bedchamber and ruffled Blue's head. "Never mind what I said yesterday about staying a baby. I want you to grow big enough to eat the person who's sneaking into my room. Do we have a deal?"

Blue yipped and turned in a circle—his way of communicating that he needed to go outside to relieve himself.

Cerise dressed quickly in riding clothes—a gauzy linen tunic over pants—and covered her hair in a light scarf to protect her from the sun. She had already packed two changes of clothes and her heartrending mirror in a small bag, which she strapped over one shoulder. She fastened her homemade sling around the other shoulder, and after squeezing Blue inside it, she was ready to start the day's journey.

She stopped at the kitchens to procure a bowl of honeyed oats for herself and a whole raw chicken for Blue, and also to verify that the provisions she'd ordered the day before had been delivered to the stables. With that handled, she swept outside to the gardens, where she and Blue ate their breakfast and exercised their legs while they still could.

After Blue had run through the hedge maze and expended his energy, Cerise tucked him inside the sling and then walked across the paddock to meet Daerick and Kian. When she arrived, she noticed three horses tethered outside the stables, each bearing water and supplies and saddled for the day's ride. Kian lingered in the shade, dressed in the light tan linen of a farmhand, surveying the castle grounds with a cool gaze and a lifted chin.

"Good morning, Your Majesty," she called to him, searching his face for any hint that Delora had told him about their encounter yesterday. The subject seemed delicate, or at least private, and Cerise didn't know if she should bring it up. When Kian only greeted her with a nod, she added, "Where's Daerick?"

"At the cleric's office for *yet* another bag of coin." Kian waved her over to the shade to wait with him. After she joined him, he eliminated the polite distance between their bodies and stood close enough to make her pulse hitch. "This guide of his had better be worth it," he said while scratching Blue's ears.

Cerise wished he wouldn't stand so near. A new kind of heat radiated from her chest. She fanned her cheeks, but that didn't stop them from flushing. "What about General Petros?" she asked. "I think we should invite him, too."

"I already did," Kian said. "He's away on an errand for me, but he's an excellent tracker and an even better rider, so I have no doubt that he'll catch up to us on the trail."

Cerise didn't like the idea of leaving without the general. She recalled the angry voices she had heard in the city, chants of *Down with the Half King!* "What do we know about our guide? Can we trust him? I would feel better if we brought some of the royal guard along, at least until General Petros can join us. A king should be protected."

"A king should be," Kian agreed. "To show my face outside these palace walls without protection would be lunacy. That's why I intend to wear someone else's face."

Cerise raised an eyebrow.

"This morning, I summoned Father Padron," Kian explained. "I ordered him to transform my appearance into something more... pedestrian...for the day."

"That explains the clothes," she said with a glance at his outfit.

"Nothing escapes your notice, my lady of the temple." Kian winked at her. "Padron should begin the transformation any moment now."

As if on cue, Cerise tasted the metal tang of magic, and Kian's hair began to shorten and change color to a ruddy brown. His eyes remained unchanged, but his nose formed a slight hook, his forehead lengthened, and his lips thinned.

In a blink, the king looked like a stranger.

She glanced around for Father Padron but didn't see him. "Did he transform you from inside the palace?"

"He did indeed," Kian said, frowning while he probed the slope of his new nose and the wide expanse of his brow. "Isn't it disturbing how easily he can do that?"

She understood what Kian meant, but even though her trust in the Order had been shaken, she was still amazed by the scope of Father Padron's power. "I'm grateful he's in your service."

Kian laughed. "Spoken like a politician. You're becoming a real emissary, my lady of the temple."

"I only mean to say the Order has its use," she told him. "And not all of the priests are after your throne. Some of them are loyal to the goddess."

Kian grinned at her like one of the temple workers had done years ago, when she had asked if hot cocoa came from brown goats. "There's the Cerise I met in the garden. The starry-eyed girl who sees no evil. I knew she was still in there."

"I'm not wrong, though," she insisted. "There are some good priests in the Order."

"You overestimate them. You can't help it. It's how you were raised."

"Perhaps I'm biased," she said. "I can admit it if you will, too."

"Me?" he asked, touching his chest. "How am I biased?"

"It's simple," she told him. "Shiera's curse sends you to the shadows every night, and she's the one the Order serves. You resent the goddess for punishing you, and by extension, you resent her priests and those who worship her."

"That would make sense if…"

"If?"

"If I resented you, too." Kian rubbed Blue's ear, and while doing so, he reached up with his thumb to touch her chin. "But I don't. And you're more blindly devoted to that goddess of yours than any priest under my command."

It took a moment before Cerise found her voice. All she could say was, "She's your goddess, too."

"Is that so?" he murmured, drawing closer while his gaze lowered to her mouth.

The next thing she knew, she was angling her face toward his. Her mind warned her to stop, but her heart refused to obey. It didn't matter that Kian looked like a stranger. Her spirit knew him, craved him, and as she held her breath in anticipation of feeling his kiss, her body stirred with equal parts fear and hunger.

From far behind them, Daerick shouted a greeting, and she drew back from Kian. The king seemed to recover from the moment quickly. He returned his attention to scratching Blue behind the ears, casually grinning as if nothing had happened.

"I've got it!" Daerick jogged into the paddock while brandishing a sack of coin. "Now who's ready to ride a sweaty beast across the desert?"

"Sweaty beast?" Kian made a show of looking around, trying and failing to hide a smile. "I don't see your mother here."

"She's at home," Daerick said flatly. "Recovering from the ten seconds you gave her last night."

Kian clapped a hand to his heart. "You wound me, Lord Calatris."

"Yes, well, I'd shoot you an ugly look to go with it, but you already have one." Daerick squinted at Kian's new features. "What did Padron do to your face?"

"You don't like it? I think it's rather—"

"Uncanny?" Daerick offered.

"I was going to say roguish. Uncanny works."

Cerise caught herself smiling. She ducked her head and whispered to Blue, "These boys are a silly breed, aren't they?"

"I heard that." Daerick stroked his wiry beard. "Could a mere boy produce anything as fine as this?"

Kian snorted. "Unlike your other parts, at least the beard can keep growing."

"Would the two of you like to trade insults all day?" Cerise asked. "Or should we go and meet our guide?"

Daerick glanced at Kian. "No reason why we can't do both."

"Indeed. Mount your sweaty beast, Lord Calatris." Kian chuckled under his breath. "I think I'll name mine after your sister."

Daerick tapped his ear. "Sorry, I can't understand you. *Buffoon* isn't one of the many languages I speak."

Cerise bit back a laugh as she approached the horses, all of which greeted her with bowed heads. While she took turns rubbing their forelocks and listening to the jokes unfold in the background, a horrible feeling bloomed in her chest.

How fleeting this moment was. How soon it could all end if they failed to find the Petros Blade. And even if they did find the blade, they still had to learn the exact method of undoing the curse. Only five moons remained until Daerick's Claiming Day. And not much longer after that, Kian would run out of time. To lose either of them was unthinkable.

The thought made her breath hitch.

"We'll ask Cerise," Daerick said, returning her to the present. "What do ladies want more: brains or brawn?"

As Daerick tapped his head and Kian playfully nudged him aside to flex his biceps, she focused on both of them, painting a mental picture to preserve the memory. She took in Daerick's scraggly beard and his easy smile, the wit that glowed within him like a second sun. Then she moved her gaze to Kian, to the storm-cloud eyes that could see parts of herself she hadn't known were there. At some point during her short time at the palace, both of them had become her family. It had happened by accident, but she knew without a doubt that the bond was real.

She wanted to remember them exactly like this.

"Neither," she teased, smiling and blinking her eyes dry. "The goddess achieved perfection when she created women. We want for nothing."

12

Several hours later, Cerise was in want of a great many things, chief among them a bath and a generous dusting of medicated powder. She never wanted to travel on horseback again. She felt sorry for the animals, adapted as they were to the Mortara heat, but she felt even sorrier for her backside and her sweat-dampened thighs, which chafed with each bounce in the saddle. She gave her horse—a gray-spotted gelding she'd nicknamed Ash—a scratch on the neck to thank him. He probably wasn't enjoying himself, either.

She hadn't fully appreciated how strong an enchantment the priests had woven over the royal lands. Magic shielded the palace in a protective bubble that dulled the sun's fury by a few precious degrees. She missed that bubble. The scarf covering her head provided protection from the sun but gave her little relief from the heat. The scorching wind blowing over the fabric made her feel like an acorn roasting on a harvest bonfire.

Daerick and Kian were more accustomed to the elements, though they had no more insults to share. All teasing died as soon as they left the palace grounds. The only member of their party seemingly unaffected by the sun was Blue, who rode in his sling, barking at desert lizards, sniffing the wind, and consuming so little water that Cerise suspected he had been sired by a camel instead of a goblin.

"I'm not saying it's hot out here," Daerick announced from his horse in front of her. "But rumor has it the goats give evaporated milk."

Cerise laughed. "And the beets come from the ground fully cooked?"

"No beets," Kian said from behind. "But you might find a sand melon if you know where to look." He pointed to a brown tangle of thorns growing in the shade of a long-dead tree. The brambles were so well camouflaged that she had to squint to see them. "The fruit grows at the bottom, all the way under the thorns. You'll tear up your arms trying to get one, but it's worth it if you're desperate enough."

Cerise tucked away that knowledge and hoped she would never need it. "What about our guide?" she called ahead to Daerick. "You haven't told us who you hired."

"That was deliberate," Daerick said. "To give you plausible deniability, in case Father Padron asked you any questions about our plans today."

"He hasn't said a word to me since I saw him in the kennels," Cerise told Daerick. "I think he's lost interest in me."

"Even so, the less we all know about our guide, the better," Daerick said. "Not even I know his name—or what he looks like. He doesn't interact with the public. I hired him through one of my contacts in the city."

"Why the need for secrecy?" she asked. "Is it because of the sunset runes? Do you think someone would try to steal them from us?"

Daerick wobbled a hand as if to say *partly*. "It has more to do with the talents our guide will use to lead us on the right path and to help us find water."

"Talents?" she asked. "What does that mean?"

"You won't like the answer," Daerick warned her.

"Oh, just tell her," Kian said. "She has to grow up sometime."

Cerise turned and glared at Kian, who grinned and winked in response.

"If you must know," Daerick called over his shoulder, "he'll use magic."

"Is he a rogue priest, then?" she asked. "Like the soothsayer?"

"Neither one of them are priests."

"Well, not anymore," she clarified. "They ran away from their temples."

"I mean they never were priests," Daerick told her. "They're not second-born, and they never lived at a temple."

Cerise shook her head. *Impossible.* That contradicted everything she'd been taught. "But priests are the only wielders of Shiera's magic. Any other abilities are unnatural."

Daerick turned and gave her a look of disappointment. "I thought I taught you better than that. There's no such thing as an unnatural tendency. If something occurs within nature, it is by default natural. What's *un*natural is to vilify it and criminalize it and force people into hiding for being born the way they are."

"But…" Cerise stammered, trying to make sense of it. "Are you saying there's no such thing as sorcery or dark arts, that there's only *magic*, and all of it is the same?"

"Maybe not the same," Kian interjected. "I've never seen magic in the wild that can match the power of my priests. But all gifts, whatever they may be, originate from the same source, wouldn't you say?"

"From the goddess," Cerise said. She began to see the logic. "If Shiera created all things and all life, then everything in creation has to be in accordance with her will."

"I agree," Daerick told her. "But the priests don't see it that way."

"Which is why our guide operates in secret," Cerise said. "All right. So where are we supposed to meet him?"

"Just there, up ahead." Daerick nodded toward a boulder, or rather two halves of what used to be a boulder, flanking the entrance to a small cave at the base of the northernmost mountain. He slowed his horse and shielded his eyes. "I don't see him yet."

"If he's smart, he's inside that cave," Kian said.

"That's where I would be," Daerick agreed.

They rode ahead until they reached the split boulder, where they tethered the horses within the shaded mouth of the cave. Cerise unfastened her sling and let Blue walk beside her, though she kept a close eye on him. She had taught him to stay on command, but even though his abilities were uncanny, he was still just a pup.

The air was marginally cooler in the cave, growing more crisp with each forward stride and smelling faintly of animal dung. From the darkness ahead of them, a young man stepped into view, dressed in linen and standing so tall that Cerise had to tip back her head to look him in the eyes. She recognized him at once, even without his elderly soothsayer companion.

"You," she said. "The one from the city."

"Me," he answered flatly in a deep voice. "Your guide."

The young man didn't seem the least bit surprised to see her. Clearly, he had known that she would be there, which made her wonder what had changed since their meeting in the secret den in the pleasure district, when he had bristled at her and ordered her to leave.

He hitched his upper lip and pointed at Blue, who stood faithfully beside her, tipping his wrinkled puppy head to and fro and studying the guide. "What's *that*?"

"*He* is my hound," she answered. "His name is Blue."

"That's no hound," he said.

"Half of him is, I assure you," she told him. "What I want to know is why you agreed to come here if you knew Lord Calatris and I were the ones who hired you. The last time I saw you, you couldn't wait to be rid of us."

"You were a stranger to me then," he said. "I don't make a habit of trusting strangers. It's a sure way to die."

Cerise didn't believe him. The real answer probably had more to do with what the soothsayer had said about her blood: *umbra sangi.*

"So does that mean you trust me now?" she asked him.

He responded with a grunt.

"What about me?" Kian asked, lifting his chin in a regal way that clashed with his farmhand facade. "I'm a stranger to you. Is that going to be a problem?"

The young man laughed without humor. "You're no threat to me, Half King. I'm glad for your company. The two of us will have much to discuss."

Cerise drew a breath and looked to Daerick and Kian, neither of whom seemed shocked to learn that the young man had seen through Kian's transformation. It took her a moment to remember that the guide possessed magical talents, perhaps even the same ability as the soothsayer to detect bloodlines through scent.

"Well, now that we've established who we can trust," Kian said to the guide, "by what name shall we call you?"

"You can call me Nero," he said, and then he extended a massive palm toward Daerick. "Do you have my fee?"

Daerick snickered as he handed over the satchel of coin. "Straight to business. I can respect that. Now we can be on our way."

Nero glanced above their heads at the horses tethered in the shade. "Is that all you brought with you? Provisions for one day's ride?"

"Two days," Daerick corrected. "But yes. Without meeting you, we had no way of knowing how long the journey to the Blighted Shrine would last or how many resources we might need."

"More than that," Nero said.

Daerick paused as if waiting for more information. When it didn't come, he asked, "Can you be more precise?"

Nero shrugged. "The Blighted Shrine is at the top of the mountain. How long it takes to get there depends on many things, but I can promise you no one has ever done it in a matter of days.

And then if you earn the runes, you'll have no way of knowing where they will take you or how long you'll travel until you reach the object you seek. Plan for weeks or even moons. And don't forget to bring feed for the horses. There's not much for them to eat on the mountain. That's why I travel on foot."

Kian swore under his breath. "We'll need wagons for all of that."

"Which will slow us down and make the trip last even longer," Daerick said. "But there's no way around it. We won't survive long without supplies."

A distant roar sounded from outside the cave, and Nero added, "Protection wouldn't be a bad idea, either. Creatures mostly hunt at night, but some will come out during the day if they're hungry enough."

"Creatures?" Cerise asked. "Do you mean predators like the desert panther?"

Nero shook his head. "Predators that *hunt* the desert panther."

Blue whined, seeming to share her fear.

"Well, that decides it." Kian put his hands on his hips and peered outside at the position of the sun. "I'll ride back to the palace and assemble a caravan. The three of you get started and make it as far as you can before dark. I'll send General Petros to lead the caravan immediately so you'll have protection overnight."

Suddenly, it occurred to Cerise that they hadn't discussed Kian's disappearance at sunset, or more importantly, his *re*appearance at the bedside of Delora Champlain each dawn. And then there were the spontaneous daylight hours that the king lost to the curse. Kian could vanish at any moment and then awaken at the palace with Delora.

"Your Majesty," Cerise said, "may I have a word with you in private?"

Kian walked with her to the horses at the mouth of the cave. He positioned them behind his horse and turned away, blocking Nero's view, and lowered his voice to a murmur. "What is it?"

"Lady Champlain," Cerise whispered. "If you want to travel with us, then she'll have to join the caravan. And that would risk her safety more than if she stayed at the palace. Do you think we should find the runes and the blade without you?"

Kian froze for the span of a heartbeat, seemingly at a loss for words. Then he abruptly cleared his throat and told her, "Let me worry about Lady Champlain's safety. I'll see you at sunrise, my lady of the temple."

"But...there's another problem," Cerise said. She paused to consider how to voice her fears and her mixed feelings. She wanted protection from the creatures Nero had mentioned, but not enough to risk the safety of the caravan by asking them to travel in the dark while those same creatures came out to hunt. "General Petros is only one man. Will his protection be enough for the group?"

"No, it won't," Kian said. "That's why I'm sending Padron with him. There's not a beast in these mountains that can survive my high priest. The general can drive the wagon and Padron can ride on horseback. The two of them are all the protection we need."

"But we don't trust Father Padron."

"We certainly don't," Kian agreed.

"So why not send the royal guard instead?"

Kian heaved a sigh. "Do you know how many men it would take to equal the power of one priest?" Before she could answer, he did: "Dozens—or more. And each guard requires provisions and rides a horse that requires provisions, and before you know it, we're traveling with twelve wagons instead of one, and our journey will last until the end of time."

Cerise hadn't considered any of that.

"I don't like it, either," Kian told her. "But Padron is the strongest weapon in my arsenal. I would be a fool not to use him to my advantage."

"But what about Nero?" Cerise whispered in her softest voice. "Whatever magic he has, he would never use it around Father Padron. The Order would stone him for sorcery."

"Nero can use his magic when Padron isn't looking. No one has to know."

"What if he refuses to help us?"

"Then we won't give him a choice," Kian hissed. "We need the runes so we can find the Petros Blade."

"What are we going to do, chain Nero to us?" she asked. "He knows these mountains. We don't. He can slip away whenever he wants and leave us stranded."

"You really do underestimate my high priest," Kian said darkly.

His words plucked a note of dread inside her. She wondered if he was right.

Kian must have decided the discussion was over, because he mounted his horse and, without another word to anyone, rode off into the desert the same way they had come.

Daerick and Nero joined Cerise at the mouth of the cave. Nero crossed both arms over his massive chest, and for a long moment of silence, the three of them watched the king ride away. Then Nero swiveled his gaze to Cerise and told her, "We need to talk before we leave."

She waited for him to go on.

"Alone," Nero clarified, giving Daerick a pointed look.

"I have no secrets from Lord Calatris," Cerise said. "Whatever you have to say to me, you can say to the both of us."

Nero heaved a sigh and rolled his eyes to the cave ceiling. He then used a thumbnail to open a thin cut on his palm, and after that, several things happened at once. Nero pressed his bloodied palm to the cave wall while his other hand shot out and gripped Cerise's wrist. She opened her mouth to object, but no sound left her lips. She seemed suspended in time, as though the world had stopped turning. Abruptly, she felt the sick sensation of falling. Then she closed her eyes, and when she reopened them, she was standing in the middle of a dim cavern with Nero still gripping her wrist and Daerick nowhere to be found.

"What..." She jerked free of Nero's grasp. "What did you do? Where is Lord Calatris? Bring him back at once!"

"Your friend hasn't moved," Nero told her, holding both palms forward in a gesture of surrender. "We have. I only want to talk to you in private. After we talk, I'll return you to your friend. I give you my word."

Cerise released a breath and peered all around her at the black slab walls, which were glossy from moisture leaching through the stone. Strangely, it was the moisture that provided the only light, the drops emitting a faint glow reminiscent of moon-flies. The air was cool and smelled metallic, like the charge before a storm, but it was a welcome relief from the desert heat. Distantly, she could hear Daerick shouting her name, but she couldn't tell where his voice was coming from.

"Where are we?" she asked, her fear fading and giving way to wonder. "Lord Calatris is worried for me. I can hear him."

"He won't worry for long," Nero told her. "Time passes slowly here. A moment for your friend out there is like an hour for us in the Below."

"The Below," she absently repeated as she took in her surroundings.

The cavern floor was carpeted in thick, lush mosses and silken grass, and if she looked closely at the ground, she could make out an occasional lavender blossom peeking out from between the grassy tufts. She bent down and plucked one of the flowers, admiring the way its petals seemed to glow from within. Now that her panic had receded, she could appreciate the cavern's unusual beauty. She even detected the babble of gently falling water echoing from somewhere out of sight.

"What is this place?" she asked. "It looks like an underground oasis."

"In a way, it is," Nero said. "The blood of Shiera was spilled on this mountain. The ground absorbed her darkness and her light. Her wrathful side created the blight you see from above. And here below"—indicating the luminescent walls of the cavern—"is what grew from her merciful side."

"Darkness and light," Cerise murmured, gazing at the lavender blossom. She tucked the delicate flower in her pocket. It would make a perfect addition to her offering at the Blighted Shrine. "How does your magic allow you to come here?"

He chuckled without humor. "How are the stars born?"

"Fair point," she admitted. Her question had been a stupid one. Nobody understood how magic worked. "Are there places like this everywhere on the mountain? Or only here?"

"The *Below* exists only here," Nero said. "But my blood can carry me here from any place on the mountain."

"So you have an escape," she said. "No wonder you can survive out here for so long."

Nero shrugged a massive shoulder. "The better question is why you want the sunset runes. What do you hope they will help you find?"

"Why do you care?"

"Because if I lead you to the runes, I'm complicit in what you do with them."

"My intentions are good. I can promise you that."

He chuckled again. "Intentions are more meaningless than grains of sand. It's your actions that matter."

Cerise chewed the inside of her cheek and considered whether she should tell Nero the truth. She didn't know Nero well enough to trust him. But to be fair, he didn't know her, either, and he had trusted her enough to display his magical talents, which—knowing as he did of her proximity to the Order—was akin to putting his life in her hands. Besides, if Nero was as skilled a mountain guide as he had claimed, the caravan would need his help after she secured the sunset runes. Sooner or later, he would learn what object she sought.

"Very well. I'll tell you," she decided. "I want the Petros Blade."

That didn't seem to surprise him. "For what purpose?"

"To break the noble curses."

"Shiera's curses?"

"Yes."

"Why would you do that?"

His question confused her. "Why *wouldn't* I do that?"

"Because I know who you are," he said. "A failed oracle sent here to play politics with the king. It's the goddess you really serve, not the royal line."

Cerise gaped at Nero. He could have learned her identity from any number of sources, but only three people on Mortara knew that she had no Sight. Her reputation as a "blessed oracle" had only gained momentum since the fire at the palace, so how could he know that she was a failure?

"It's true," she admitted. "I serve the goddess."

"Then why break her curses?"

"Because I don't want to see anyone suffer," she said. "Why is that so difficult to understand?"

Nero must not have expected that response, because he watched her for a long, silent moment before he finally said, "Then I need your vow."

"What vow?"

"The Petros Blade is no ordinary weapon," he told her. "If wielded by the correct hand, it can kill any living creature, even a goddess."

"Do you think I don't know that? I'm well aware of the blade's history. That's the whole reason we want it—to atone for the Great Betrayal."

"Do *you* think you're the first one to try?" Nero retorted.

"Well..." Cerise stammered. "Yes, actually, I did."

"You're not," Nero told her. "Generations of nobles have hired guides like me to lead them to the sunset runes, hoping to find the Petros Blade so they could break Shiera's curse and save themselves."

"And none of them found it?"

"None of them were *worthy*," Nero said.

Cerise shook her head in confusion. "But I thought only a worshipper of pure faith can earn the sunset runes. How can a person be unworthy if Shiera entrusted them with a map to the

Petros Blade?"

"Because faith is not the only thing that determines a person's worth," Nero said in the same lecturing tone that Daerick often used. "The Petros Blade never should have been forged. The only reason it still exists is because it can't be destroyed. A weapon like that could do terrible damage, even in the hands of the faithful, so it's been safeguarded by more than just a vanishing hiding place. That's why it hasn't seen the sun in a thousand years."

"Safeguarded by what? Beasts? Magic?"

"I wouldn't know," Nero told her. "I've never looked for it before. Others have tried to hire me to take them to the Blighted Shrine, but I knew better than to waste my time on them. And now I want to know that I'm not wasting my time on you."

"So you want my vow that I'm worthy?"

"You won't know you're worthy until you're tested," he said. "What I want is your vow that *if* we find the blade and *if* you're able to retrieve it, then the blade will never leave your side. You will sheathe it to your body, day and night. You will allow no other to lay hands on it, and you will kill anyone who tries." Nero towered over her, his lethal gaze boring into hers until Blue growled at him. "Do you promise?"

"I promise," she said. Even if Nero hadn't insisted, she would have been vigilant in protecting the blade. "I swear it."

Nero nodded, seemingly satisfied by her oath. "Then we will return to your friend."

He extended a hand to her, she took it, and with a violent lurch and a dip of her stomach, she was back at the mouth of the cave, squinting against the sunlight.

"Charred bones!" Daerick cried, grabbing Cerise in a hug before she had fully opened her eyes. He muttered a strand of curses and pulled away but kept a grip on her upper arms. "Are you all right?" He fired a glare at Nero. "Did he hurt you?"

"No, he didn't hurt me," Cerise assured him. "He only wanted a word in private."

Daerick cast her a skeptical look. "Well, it must have been an incredibly loaded word, because you weren't gone long enough to exchange a full sentence."

Cerise glanced at Nero, recalling what he had said about the passage of time in the cavern. The minutes they had spent "Below" had passed like mere seconds for Daerick. Nero grinned at her as if to say *I told you so*.

"Now we can begin," Nero told them. "I know a safe place to make camp in the next ridge. Your horses will slow us down, but we should be able to reach it before nightfall."

13

And so began their quest for the Petros Blade.

Cerise learned that in its entirety, the mountain range extended so far that it continued beyond the horizon. But their journey would take them to the nearby blighted peak, the site of the Great Betrayal. That was where the Blighted Shrine had been built and where Cerise would make her offering of darkness and light to the goddess in exchange for the sunset runes. What she intended to offer to satisfy the goddess's vengeful side remained to be seen.

She kept glancing at the dark peak, expecting it to grow closer as the hours passed, but it remained as distant as ever. Even with her gelding, Ash, doing all of the work, she found the trip up the narrow, winding path comparable to running headlong into a flaming hearth. She didn't know how Nero could bear it on foot, setting the pace ahead of the horses without breaking a sweat.

"The horses could use some water," she called to Nero. "Don't you think?"

"They can always use water, but they don't need it," he replied over his shoulder. "They're not like your beasts in Solon."

Daerick spoke from behind her. "Most of the species indigenous to Mortara are accustomed to the heat. They can regulate their temperature, and they have special kidneys that recycle water through the bloodstream several times before it's excreted. That's why your horse's urine smells so pungent."

Cerise sniffed the air. Their trail would certainly be easy to follow.

"Most mountain creatures stay in their dens during the day," Nero added. "And only come out at night. That's why I want to reach camp before we stop."

"What's so special about your camp?" Daerick asked.

"You'll see."

And they did, hours later when the sun hung dangerously low on the horizon. Cerise could barely feel her lower half by that point. Nero led them off the trail to a small plateau, walled in on three sides by great slabs of sienna-colored stone. The area had been cleared of brambles, weeds, and desert saplings. There were scorch marks on the ground where someone, probably Nero, had cooked meals and a packed dirt area backing up to the far wall where he had presumably slept. The space was wide enough to contain all of them, including the horses, but aside from the flat terrain, she didn't see what made the spot particularly special.

Until Nero strode to the front left wall and reached high above his head, resting his hand on the stone. The air thickened with the tang of metal. A crack appeared in the slab, and a trickle of pure, clean water flowed out.

Cerise had tasted magic. *His* magic.

There was no denying it anymore.

Thunderstruck, she dismounted Ash, barely noticing the ache in her legs. She was too busy processing what she had witnessed. Ash ambled to the stone and lapped up the water. Blue pawed at the sling, and she set him down to quench his thirst.

"You *do* have the magic of priests," she said to Nero. "I tasted it."

One corner of his mouth curved up. "Like dirt on your tongue?"

"No, like copper."

"It tastes different for everyone. I know a man who says the flavor reminds him of honey." Nero muttered under his breath, "The lucky toad."

Daerick dismounted and lightly slapped his horse's rump to send it to the spring. He massaged his lower back while pinching his eyebrows together. "Who trained you?"

"My father taught me how to control my energy," Nero said. "His father taught him, and his grandfather before him, and so on."

Cerise realized she'd been shaking her head the entire time. She couldn't fathom the idea of magic being passed down from parent to child. Her entire life, she'd believed that only second-born servants of the goddess could possess a gift. That was what *everyone* believed. It was common knowledge, written in scrolls: magic and foresight were rewards for a lifetime of devotion at the temple.

How many others like Nero were there?

How had they hidden their existence?

Nero clapped his hands as if to refocus and then pointed at the sky, which had colored with the first blush of dusk. "There's much to do before dark and not enough time to do it." He jutted his chin at Daerick. "Tether the horses at the back wall, in the corner if you can. Make sure they're facing the stone. We don't want them to see what's outside the camp."

That tore Cerise out of her thoughts. "What can I do to help?"

"Climb up there." Nero indicated a pair of hooks hammered midway up both of the front walls. He dug through his pack and handed her a roll of thin, gauzy fabric. "And hang this."

"Like a curtain?"

"Exactly like a curtain."

She turned the fabric over in her hands. As transparent as it was, she didn't understand how it would hide them from anything. Then there was the matter of their scent. Any predator in creation would be able to smell them through the fabric.

"I don't have time to explain," Nero said. "Just do it. I'm going to check my traps. With any luck, we'll eat more than jerky tonight."

Nero jogged away, his leather satchel bouncing against his hip. Cerise set to her task of unrolling the gauze to find which way was up. She had no trouble scaling the rubble that led to the first hook, but she needed Daerick's help with the opposite side, which was steep and difficult to climb. She sat on his shoulders, and they used their combined height to thread the second hook.

"I thought Nero was like the soothsayer or like Seers," she told Daerick. "That he has a talent supplied by magic, not magic itself."

"I was surprised, too," Daerick admitted. "But I also didn't expect him to disappear with you inside the cave. I didn't know *anyone* could do that."

"We didn't really disappear. I think we moved to another part of the cave."

"Well, it was still an impressive trick," Daerick said. "Can you tell a difference between Nero's magic and the Order's? Anything at all? Even the slightest distinction?"

"No, it all tastes the same to me."

"The Mortara dynasty has always commanded the priests. I wonder what would happen if Kian gave Nero a direct order…" Daerick trailed off at the sound of approaching footsteps.

Nero came running back into camp, clutching two dead jackrabbits by their long, mulish ears. He closed the spring and motioned for them to hide behind the curtain. "Hurry," he said. "We'll skin the rabbits inside."

While he cleaned his kills, Cerise and Daerick built a fire from dung pellets Nero had packed in his bag. Under the light of the moon, they roasted both jackrabbits on charred, wooden spits. Nero tossed the entrails and pelts into the fire, remarking that he hated to waste a good pair of hides but he didn't have time to tan them.

"Can't you use magic to do it?" Daerick asked with one cheek stuffed full.

Nero paused to pick his front teeth. "I could. But I would rather save my energy for more important things." He pointed at the curtain. "Like this."

Cerise felt a charge thicken the air and tasted the familiar tang of metal, but she didn't notice that anything had changed. She peered around while she fed Blue a bite from her meal. "What did you do?"

"I cast a charm on the fabric." Nero sat a little taller, clearly pleased with himself. "No creature on the outside can see or smell us. The curtain will look like a wall of stone to them."

"What about from above?" Daerick glanced at the night sky, where the eyes of a million stars winked down at them. "The harpy vulture hunts at night, too."

"True," Nero agreed. He nodded at Blue. "Better keep him close. Even ugly pups make tasty snacks."

Cerise shot him a dirty look.

She gathered Blue onto her lap while they finished eating. She found that the jackrabbit didn't agree with her. Each bite felt like lead in her stomach, so she fed the rest to Blue, who happily gobbled it up and licked her hands clean.

After the fire died out and the night air puckered their skin with chills, the group curled up on the ground, which was still warm from the heat of day, and tried to sleep.

Tried.

A saddlebag was no substitute for a pillow, and the hard, dry soil didn't feel good to a body that had spent twelve hours in the saddle. Then there were the noises from outside the curtain—scratches and clicks, guttural growls, shrieks of pain cut short. Cerise kept glancing at the sky, expecting to find a deer-sized vulture circling the camp. She gathered Blue closer, and for good measure, she pulled the sling over his entire body and face so that only his tiny nose peeked out.

Only then was she able to relax.

Her dreams took her back to the Solon temple, where the Reverend Mother was standing alone in the courtyard, her gilded robes ruffling in the breeze as she warmed her hands in front of a blazing fire. When Cerise peered deep into the flames, she could see flickers of the goddess looking back at her, smiling with the merciful side of her face. Cerise clutched her heart in amazement, but before she could bow to the goddess, a robed priest appeared in the courtyard. The priest's face was vague, easily forgotten. No matter how hard Cerise stared at the man, she couldn't hold his image in her mind.

The priest held both palms toward the fire, but it was clear that he didn't intend to warm himself. He meant to extinguish it. The Reverend Mother asked him to stop. She told him that her sisters needed the fire's warmth, but he refused to listen to her. He summoned a rush of water and doused the flames, leaving the Reverend Mother shivering and hugging herself to stave off the cold.

The Reverend Mother glanced at Cerise as if noticing her for the first time. "Do you See what he has done, Cerise?"

"Yes, Your Grace," she answered.

"He will be sorry." The Reverend Mother spoke in a voice as hard as steel. "The flame he seeks to dampen will consume him, Cerise."

"Yes, Your Grace," she repeated.

"Cerise."

Her shoulders shook.

"Cerise!"

Gasping, she awoke to find Daerick jostling her shoulder while Nero chased Blue, who had wriggled out from beneath her arm and was running in circles with his head raised to the moon, howling *awooooo* in his high-pitched puppy voice. Nero was hissing furious curses, but Cerise didn't understand what was wrong.

Then something howled back at Blue.

An icy finger traced her spine. The animal howled again, closer now. It was a haunting noise—not the smooth, graceful baying of a hound or a wolf but an off-key distortion that reminded her of a warped bell.

Blue ran under the horses, where Nero couldn't reach him. "Shut him up," Nero growled. "Or I will."

"Blue," she called frantically, slapping the spot next to her on the ground. When he only peered back at her, she felt her heart seize, and she commanded, "You come here right now, Blue Solon!"

He whined and padded over to her, hanging his head like a scolded child.

She snatched him up and muzzled his snout, but the eerie howling continued. Each cry caused Blue to squirm and whine in her arms. Soon other howls joined the first, louder and growing closer. At times, Blue burrowed his face into the crook of her arm, but then he would go back to wriggling and trying to escape. What was he *thinking*?

Nero glared at Blue. "If you don't keep that mongrel quiet, I'll—"

A loud snuffling interrupted him, like the snorting of a bull, coming directly from the other side of the curtain. There was another exhale, and the fabric billowed.

"Um." Daerick swallowed. "You said the sheet looks like stone from the outside. Does it *feel* like stone, too?"

The answer came when a creature pawed at the fabric and four long, yellow, saber-like claws poked through it. Fear rose in Cerise's chest. Whatever was on the other side of that curtain knew the fabric wasn't made of stone. The horses whinnied, stamping at the ground. They couldn't see the threat, but they sensed it.

She clutched Blue to her chest while her breathing shuddered. She glanced at Nero. "You can kill that thing, right?"

His frozen expression didn't fill her with confidence. Nothing required more energy than dispatching death—and that was for an ordinary creature, not a beast with claws longer than her whole hand.

Nero drew his blade and indicated for her to do the same. "I can shield us..." He didn't say *temporarily*, but she heard it in his tone. "Be ready to fight. All creatures bleed, even monsters."

"Monsters," she repeated. *Plural.* "How many do you think—"

"I heard four," Daerick said. "Four distinct howls."

"Stand back-to-back," Nero told them, then formed part of a

circle. "I can shield us longer if we stay close."

Cerise moved into position, numbly tucking Blue inside the sling. Her hands were sweaty and trembling. It took two tries to unsheathe her knife. "Mother Shiera, mistress of worlds," she murmured under her breath. "Guide my hand and...and..." She wanted to finish the prayer for courage in the face of battle, but she couldn't remember the words.

Then the curtain was torn completely away, and the camp spiraled into chaos.

Her mouth filled with the tang of magic as a static wall went up around them. Sweaty backs pressed against hers. Horses neighed in panic. Blue barked. And on the other side of the rippling shield stood a beast she couldn't have conceived in her darkest nightmares.

Tall as a mule and covered in patches of mottled brown fur, the creature looked like it might have been a hyena once, before the mountain's blight had taken root and curved its spine into a gnarled hunch. Its ears were pointed, its chest absurdly broad. Drool hung from the edges of its jaws, and as it bared its teeth, Cerise could see chunks of animal flesh in between them. But scariest of all were its eyes. Black and calculating, they spoke of an intelligence that set her hair on end. When those eyes narrowed on Blue, she understood why it had come.

"I think I know what sired Stella's litter," she said.

"Titan hyenas," Daerick muttered behind her.

She glanced around and noticed three smaller beasts, one other male and two females. Blue shook his mouth free and barked at the pack, sending them into a frenzy. They scratched and snapped at the shield, howling in turn at Blue, who howled back and pawed at the sling.

"No, Blue," she commanded, putting as much authority in her shaky voice as she could. "Stay."

"Let him go," Nero said. "It's him they want, not us."

Daerick huffed a nervous laugh. "That's not celery between their teeth. I'm pretty sure they want us, too."

"Not as badly as the pup. If he's part of the pack, they won't leave him." Nero panted with the strain of maintaining the shield. "Let him go!" he shouted over the riot of growls and barking. "I can't hold on forever. If you give them what they want, they might lose interest in us and run away!"

Cerise shook her head wildly. She had read about titan hyenas. "The alpha female will kill him as soon as she delivers the next litter. He's not her pup."

"I don't care!" bellowed Nero. "His life isn't more important than ours or the horses'. They are going to die if I can't hold this—" He cut off in exhaustion, and for a sliver of a second, the static barrier faltered. In that instant, the smell of hot, rancid breath filled the circle. "Do it now!"

She clutched onto Blue in his sling, despite his wriggling, despite the advancing beasts, because she had made a promise to him. *We're a family now, Lord Blue Solon. And that's forever.* She'd just opened her mouth to tell Nero there had to be another way when the shield dropped again. She felt a tug at her neck, followed by a sudden lightness, as if a weight had been lifted.

Too late, she realized that Nero had cut the sling.

By the time she saw Blue on the ground, he had already bounded away to sniff the pack leader, who bent low and sniffed Blue in return. Then the great beast lifted Blue by the wrinkly scruff of his neck and turned to run.

Cerise didn't remember leaving the circle, and she didn't remember charging toward the hyena or dropping her knife along the way. But the next thing she knew, she was on top of his hunched back with both arms wrapped around his neck. As the beast roared and tried to buck her off, Blue dropped out of his mouth to the ground.

"Blue, *run!*" she yelled.

In the next moment, the hyena shook her off. She felt herself fly and then hit the ground with a sickening thump. When she opened her eyes, she was flat on her back, staring up at a set of open jaws.

The animal didn't hesitate. He went for the kill.

The hyena tore at her throat. She screamed as something hot and wet dribbled down the sides of her neck. Uselessly, she shoved against the beast. Then she heard a yapping sound, and the hyena pulled back slightly—just enough for Cerise to turn her head and see Blue frantically attacking his sire's leg.

"Blue, no!" she shrieked.

The beast shook him off and in the process gave her a glimpse of Daerick and Nero standing back-to-back, swinging their blades to fend off the rest of the pack. The alpha lunged at her again. Teeth clicked and slid against her flesh. It was then that she realized she felt no pain. The beast should have shredded her windpipe by now, but it kept gnawing at her as though she were covered in alloy.

The pendant between her breasts grew warm.

It was protecting her, just like Nina said it would.

Hope swelled within her. She glanced around for her knife and spotted it just beyond reach. She stretched her arm as far as she could and yelled, "Blue! Fetch!" He understood and finally listened this time, using his nose to push the handle within her grasp. As soon as her fingers curled around the grip, she drove the blade upward with all her strength.

The hyena yelped in pain. It was a horrible sensation, feeling the creature's muscles and tendons grip the knife, but she jerked the blade free and drove it in again. Enraged, the hyena attacked her with twice the ferocity, biting her face, her scalp, her arms—anywhere he could reach. Her fingers were slick with blood, causing the knife to slip. When she picked it up again, she barely had enough strength and grip to pierce the animal's hide. Her pendant was burning hot now. Its protection couldn't possibly last much longer. Blue snapped his tiny jaws at the hyena, which, wild with fury, turned on his pup, growling and tensing his haunches.

Then the air turned thick with an energy so powerful that Cerise lost touch with her senses. The world fell away. She was on fire with the rush of magic, the raw force filling her veins. Her neck arched, and as she fought to regain focus, she noticed the hyena's eyes roll back in his massive head. The beast crumpled halfway on top of her, dead. Three more heavy thuds told her the entire pack had fallen.

The wet lapping of Blue's tongue on her cheek finally nudged her out of the haze. She dragged herself out from beneath the heavy corpse and pushed to her elbows to find the source of the magic that had saved them all. As if there was any doubt. Only one man could wield such power—the same man she hadn't wanted to come to the mountain, though now she was infinitely grateful that he had.

Father Padron must have heard the howling and ridden ahead of the wagon, because he was alone. Sitting astride his horse, he was the picture of a storybook hero: fierce and triumphant with the moonlight shining in his hair. But when she peered more closely at him, she saw his skin was pale and his eyes glassy.

"Cerise," he whispered. "Are you…"

"I'm all right," she told him. "Thank you."

He gave her a weak smile, and then his chin dipped, his shoulders rounded, and he slid sideways out of his saddle and onto the ground.

14

Cerise awoke the next morning when Blue squirmed out of the sling she had repaired. She reached for him, but her hand landed instead on a warm knee, and she opened her eyes to find Kian sitting cross-legged beside her, scratching Blue's ears and wearing nothing except for a shawl draped over his lap. He must have just materialized, because the sun was barely aglow behind the mountains.

The king smiled. He glanced at the fingers curled atop his knee and whispered, "Good morning to you, too, my lady of the temple."

It was lucky she hadn't lost any blood last night, because all of it seemed to be rushing to her face. She snatched away her hand, which awoke the rest of her muscles. She groaned in pain and rolled onto her back. Her arms and shoulders were tender from the fight, her back and thighs sore from a day in the saddle. And if that wasn't enough, her stomach felt like a wet fist clenched around a ball of ice.

She was never eating jackrabbit again.

"Seems I missed quite the party," Kian added, hooking a thumb toward the remains of the titan hyena pack that they had burned last night, along with her bloody clothes. Cerise had saved a single incisor from the alpha male she had battled. She could think of no greater offering of darkness to the Blighted Shrine than a piece of the monster that had tried to kill her.

"You shouldn't have all the fun in the shadows," she whispered back. "The rest of us are entitled to a little suffering, too."

A smile played at his lips as he glanced around the cluttered camp. She followed the direction of his gaze, first to the covered supply wagon, below which slept General Petros. She'd learned that the general had a phobia of birds and refused to sleep in the open because he was afraid they would peck at his face. He had packed tents, but in the aftermath of the attack, the group had been too tired to pitch them. To the left of the wagon slept Daerick and Nero, still positioned back-to-back, daggers in hand. At the rear of the camp stood the horses—six of them now—and in the opposite corner lay Father Padron, unconscious on the blanket pallet Cerise had made for him.

The one person Cerise didn't see was Delora Champlain. In the chaotic haze of the previous night, she hadn't given a thought to Delora. But now that she looked around the camp, she realized the king's courtesan wasn't there, not even in the covered back of the wagon.

Cerise pushed onto her elbows. "Where is Lady Champlain? How are you able to sit here if—" She cut off as a realization struck her like a blow to the skull. Kian hadn't appeared at Delora's bedside because his spirit was drawn to someone else now—to *her*—and it had been for days. "It was you in my room," she whispered, turning her wide eyes to him. "I locked my door each night, and you unlocked it when you left."

Kian offered her an apologetic grin. "I didn't mean to frighten you."

"And yesterday," she realized. "You gave Blue a treat from the kennel master. I wondered how he got it."

"I hid a few of them on the balcony," Kian said. "I couldn't have him barking at me every morning and startling you awake."

"Why didn't you tell me?" she asked, a little hurt because she had known there was a fondness between them. The king had made that much clear with his flirtatious words and touches. So why had he concealed the extent of his fondness from her? Was he ashamed of her? Did he wish that he was drawn to someone else?

Kian released a quiet breath and dropped his gaze for a long moment before looking up at her again. There was a new softness in his eyes, a tenderness that warmed the deep, hidden parts of her that she hadn't known were cold.

"I should have told you," he said. "Kings are stubborn creatures. But now that my secret is out, you might as well know that I like you, my lady of the temple. I like you very much."

Cerise felt her cheeks go up in flames. Not only her cheeks—her whole body.

He tried and failed to hide a smile. "I've made you uncomfortable."

"No," she denied but then quickly admitted, "well, yes…" She didn't know how to tell him that she liked him, too. That she liked the way she felt around him, and the low timbre of his voice, and his storm-cloud eyes, and even the way her chest erupted into flutters whenever he stood too near.

"Yes, and…?" he prompted.

Her racing mind made it impossible to say the right thing. Her emotions were all in a jumble. He was the *king*, and she was a lady of the temple. What did it matter how much she cared for him? Her life belonged to the goddess. She could not marry. And until her Claiming Day, she couldn't even take a lover without risking her chance of gaining the Sight. Her duty had to come first—not just to the goddess but to the king himself, as well as to every cursed firstborn. Only a worshipper of pure faith could earn the sunset runes. She had to stay faithful. She had to stay focused.

She had to stay away from him.

"I'm glad your spirit is drawn to me," she finally said. "You don't have to sneak off anymore. We're friends now, aren't we?"

Friends. Her fluttering heart called her a liar.

"Certainly," Kian agreed, though he couldn't hide the disappointment in his eyes. He peered around the camp as if searching for a new topic of discussion. He found it when his gaze landed on the nearly lifeless face of Father Padron. "Gods alive," he breathed. "What did you do to my high priest?"

Cerise didn't say so, but it was more a matter of what Father Padron had done to himself. Last night after his fall, she'd noticed blood soaking through the back of his robe, much like several days ago, when he had shown her the catacombs. So she had removed his robe to see what was the matter. She hadn't been prepared for the mutilation she'd found. From the look of the gashes on his back, he had used a cattail lash, and not for the first time. His back was woven in scars, some of them fresh and pink, others old and white, and far below them, the silvery ghosts of another decade. There were so many layers of injury stacked on top of one another that no healthy skin remained. What he had done wasn't overzealous atonement. It was self-loathing. He had been punishing himself savagely for at least half his life.

Cerise would give nearly anything to know why.

"He dispatched a pack of titan hyenas," she said, keeping Father Padron's secret to herself, at least for now. She owed him her life, and she felt obliged to protect him in return. "That's more than twenty priests could do."

Kian grunted in disagreement. "It's nothing for him. You don't know the man like I do. When I was still in clods, my father sent Padron to put down an uprising in Solon. They say he stopped the hearts of fifty men before he broke a sweat. And he was practically a boy then. He's grown more skilled with time. Killing a pack of hyenas shouldn't have fazed him."

"War stories," she dismissed. "I don't care what anyone says. A priest has to rest after dispatching death."

"I wonder if he's ill." Kian pushed back his hair, which was long again, as the transformation had worn off and restored his true appearance. "Come to think of it, he looked a bit rough when I saw him yesterday. It was only for a moment, right before sunset, but his face seemed waxy, like he'd eaten a tray of spoiled oysters for lunch."

Or like he had brutally whipped himself? Cerise thought.

On the other side of the camp, Nero stirred and pushed onto one elbow, looking rather pale and weak as well. Cerise still hadn't forgiven Nero for cutting Blue's sling, so she scowled at him and glanced away.

"If you'll excuse me, Your Highness," she said and gathered Blue in her arms. Her pup was heavier by at least two stones, which made sense, considering he was half titan. Luckily, Blue had inherited Stella's good nature and not that of his sire. But the titan half of Blue would require more food to eat. "We're going in search of a suitable bathroom. And if we're lucky, breakfast."

"And I should find my clothes."

"Everything is in the wagon," she said, pointing. "Though I must say that shawl looks lovely with your complexion."

"Mmm," he agreed, extending an ankle. "Makes my legs look fetching, too."

"Better put on some pants before the horses swoon."

She left Kian with a smile, which was her favorite way to go, and then she walked along the trail until she found a secluded spot to freshen up. She set down Blue, keeping watch over him as she used the water from her flagon to wash her chest and arms. While her blouse was unbuttoned, she caught sight of her pendant and stopped to take a closer look at it. The metal had changed. It was twisted and mangled, as if a team of oxen had trampled it. Maybe each act of protection weakened the metal. That would explain why it was dented when she had received it. She wondered how many uses it had left.

Footsteps sounded from nearby, and she quickly buttoned her shirt as Daerick and Nero strode into view. Daerick still hadn't let go of his knife, and Nero was so exhausted from the walk that by the time he reached her, he had to stop and brace both hands on his knees. Casting the shield must have drained him more than she'd realized.

But Nero had enough strength to complain. He jerked a thumb toward camp and hissed, "I didn't agree to this. To *him*. Gods be damned, you brought the high priest of Shiera to my door!"

"You didn't seem to mind when he saved us," Cerise pointed out.

"I could have handled it."

She rolled her eyes. "Of course. Because we were doing so well on our own."

"None of this would have happened if you had just let the mongrel go!"

At that, Blue growled.

"Shhh. Guard your words," Daerick reminded them. "Let's focus on what's important." He nodded at Nero. "By the time Father Padron rode to the rescue, you had already dropped the shield. He has no reason to believe you're anything except an ordinary mountain guide."

"What about the curtain?" Nero asked. "He'll sense the energy when he wakes up. He might have sensed it last night."

"We'll tell him it was a gift, blessed by priests to protect you," Daerick said. "They do that sort of thing all the time." He shifted his gaze to Cerise, splaying both hands in confusion. "And *you*. I saw that monster use your throat like a chew toy, and there's not a scratch on you. Want to share your secret with the rest of us?"

Cerise touched the pendant below her blouse. She wished Nina hadn't sworn her to secrecy. "The goddess works in mysterious ways," she said again, and then she closed the subject by turning her attention to Nero. "Are you strong enough to reopen the spring? We have three times as many horses now."

"Yes." Nero frowned. "Maybe."

"Maybe?" she repeated. "That would have been nice to know *before* I used my water to wash."

"Either way, I won't use my energy around the high priest." Nero shifted nervously and glanced higher up the mountain. "There's another spring close by. I'll ride ahead and open it and pretend I found it that way." His stomach grumbled loudly. "And check my traps, too."

"Anything but jackrabbit, please."

"Sand melon tastes no better."

"I don't care about the taste—"

"Jackrabbit," Daerick interrupted, tilting his head as if solving an equation. "The second largest Mortara hare. Its flesh is rich in protein, but it hosts a wide variety of parasites such as hook mites and sand lice. You were wise to burn the pelts, Nero."

The statement had come out of nowhere.

Cerise shared a worried look with Nero, who had already known that Daerick was a Calatris but had clearly just realized that Daerick was a *firstborn* Calatris. But Daerick's Claiming Day was still moons away. Why would his curse begin affecting him now?

Daerick blinked and returned to himself, blushing and refusing to look at them. He had always joked about his curse, but now it seemed the joke wasn't funny anymore.

Cerise drew him into a sideways hug and rested her chin on his shoulder. She thought of Nina's baby and the countless other Calatris children whose only crime was being born in the wrong order. Despite what she had told her sister, she *would* break the curse or die trying.

Daerick peeked up at her. "I don't suppose you woke up with the Sight today."

She wished she could tell him yes, but with just over two moons until her Claiming Day, her hope was dwindling. Still, there were special cases—late bloomers like Father Padron. She tried to put on a brave face. "I don't need the Sight. Who says I have to be an oracle to change the world?"

"You're not an oracle," Nero said. "And you never will be. You're *umbra sangi*."

Cerise whipped her gaze to him. "What does that mean—what does any of that mean?"

"I want to know, too," Daerick agreed. "I think the direct translation is *hot blooded*, but that's all I could find out."

"Fire blood," Nero corrected. He jutted his chin at her. "You're a descendent of the goddess. Her life force runs in your veins."

Cerise sucked in a breath. It sounded like Nero believed in the heretical Triad nonsense that Daerick had told her about — that the Reverend Mother had warned her about. "You can't be serious."

"I was surprised, too," Nero said. "But it was my grandfather who tasted your blood, and he's never been wrong."

"Well, he lied, either to you or to me," Cerise pointed out. "Your grandfather told me my blood wouldn't speak to him, remember? He said my origins were blank to him, just like my path is blank to Seers."

"That was the truth."

"How can it be true?"

Nero pointed back and forth between them. "Because I'm *umbra sangi*, too, and my grandfather can trace our fire blood back through the ages. But not yours. In your blood, he could taste nothing beyond the flame. That was why he spat it out. Your blood was too rich for him. It could have consumed him if he'd swallowed it."

A chill puckered Cerise's flesh, despite the growing heat of the day. She heard the Reverend Mother's voice echoing from her dreams: *He will be sorry. The flame he seeks to dampen will consume him.*

"My grandfather is afraid of you," Nero went on. "He thinks the flame in your blood is too strong for you to control. But I think anyone with your fire would make a good ally. That's why I agreed to be your guide." He considered for a moment and then pointed at her. "Have you ever burned your blood before? Set fire to it?"

Cerise wrinkled her forehead at the odd questions. "No."

"It would burn black if you did," he said. "What about the clothes you wore last night? You burned them with the others. Did they burn darker than the rest?"

"Not that I noticed," she said. But none of the blood on her clothes had belonged to her. It had all come from the titan hyena. And besides, she had heard rumors of black flame omens. There were many reasons for an object to burn darker than usual.

"Pay attention next time," Nero told her. "You'll see."

Cerise looked to Daerick with a question in her eyes. None of what Nero had said could possibly be true, could it? But *stars*, everything about him contradicted what she'd learned at the temple, every single text that she'd read. The Order had lied to her before. Could this be another one of their lies? Or was Nero the liar in this case? She didn't trust him, either. After all, he'd tried to sacrifice Blue.

She had to get her Sight. She had to.

Daerick shrugged. "The Triad has never been proven, but it's never been disproven, either. If you believe that Shiera created all life, it's not a stretch to believe that she could impregnate a woman."

"But fire blood is inherited, right?" Cerise asked Nero.

He nodded.

"Then I can't possibly have it," she said. "There's no magic in my family. My father can trace his Solon roots back for ten generations, and even though my mother doesn't know who her parents are, I can promise you she has no gifts. None of us have one. Not even me. So if I'm a descendent of Shiera with fire in my veins, explain why I'm ordinary."

"I wish I could," Nero said.

"Me, too," Daerick added. "But there's an unfortunate lack of reference materials on the subject of demigoddesses."

"Don't call me that," she told him. There were limits to how far she was willing to stray from her teachings. To consider herself a demigoddess was heresy, and besides, she hadn't seen enough evidence to convince her that Nero was right. Sure, he had magic, but maybe there was a segment of the Order that had defected at some point. There were too many things they didn't know, like why the priests were bound to the Mortara kings.

And none of this mattered right now.

"Whatever's in my blood, it won't save you or the king or my sister's baby from the curse. For that, we need the Petros Blade. So let's focus on what we can control."

Nero and Daerick were wise enough not to argue with her. The two of them returned to camp while Cerise finished washing. She brushed the tangles from her hair and then twisted it off her neck and secured it with a pin. When she was done, she pulled her scarf over her head and shoulders and followed the trail back the way she had come.

At the outer fringe of the encampment, Nero stood holding his horse's reins. He had saddled the animal, but he hadn't mounted it. Instead, Nero seemed distracted by something that was happening behind the supply wagon.

Cerise drew closer to camp, cocking an ear as she picked up bits of conversation.

"...never seen him this weak," the general rumbled. "...might not get another chance."

Kian's voice followed. "...can't...uprising...my armies couldn't..."

"...madness," Daerick answered hotly. "And I know a thing or two on the subject."

Cerise had walked close enough to the group to see what they were discussing—or, rather, whom—because at the center of their huddle lay Father Padron, still unconscious. It seemed the group had carried him as far as the wagon, and now there was some debate over what to do next.

"I don't suppose we can just leave him here." General Petros raised a hopeful eyebrow at the king. "Can we?"

Cerise made a noise of disgust, causing all three men to whirl around. "I can't believe this is a question after what he did for us last night. No matter how you feel about the Order, you should want him by our side. There are creatures on this mountain far more dangerous than titan hyenas." She glanced at Nero. "Tell them I'm right."

Nero scratched his neck and pretended not to hear her.

"Make no mistake, my girl," General Petros muttered through his teeth. "The most dangerous creature on this mountain is the one lying on your blanket."

"General," the king warned in that way of his. "Load the priest and be done with it. We do need him, and we have ground to cover."

The general obeyed, but when he set Father Padron in the wagon atop the folded canvas tents and sacks of feed, it was with more force than necessary.

Nero mounted his horse and pointed at the trail winding up the mountain. "You should all follow this path and stay together. I'll come back for you as soon as—"

"Come back for us?" Kian interrupted. "You're not leaving my sight. Dismount your horse until the rest of us are ready."

A muscle ticked visibly in Nero's jaw. He remained in the saddle. "We won't last long without water. I have to ride ahead to find a spring." He begrudgingly added, "Your Majesty."

Cerise felt the sensation of being watched, and she turned to find Daerick arching a brow at her. She nodded in return. Now they knew the answer to whether or not Nero was subject to the king's command. He wasn't. Nero's magic truly must be different than that of the priests. If Nero was right about inheriting the blood of the goddess—and that was still an *if*—then it would seem Shiera had allowed her descendants to use their magic freely while she required her priests to repay their gift of magic through servitude to the king. But for what reason remained a mystery.

"Very well." Kian clapped General Petros on the shoulder. "My general will go with you to make sure you don't lose your way. He's an excellent navigator. Aren't you, Petros?"

"The best, Your Highness," the general said while staring at Nero. "But I'm an even better killer."

Kian grinned. "Have a pleasant ride."

The general stalked toward his horse—a mammoth stallion at least twenty hands high—and hoisted himself into the saddle. With one last regretful look at Father Padron, he spurred his horse onto the trail ahead of Nero, who heaved a sigh and followed.

Cerise shielded her eyes as she watched them leave. At least when Nero used magic to open the spring, it would be in the company of someone who despised the Order as much as he did.

D aerick drove the wagon, which was pulled by his horse and trailed by Father Padron's mare. Cerise rode in front of Daerick while Kian led the group. When the trail was wide enough, Cerise fell back and rode side by side with Daerick, sharing the shade from the wagon top and listening to his stories about the old court.

Cerise enjoyed listening to Daerick's tales, which were mostly collections of gossip—the schemes and scandals that had filled the castle before Kian had grown weary of his guests and sent them away.

"In my defense," Kian called over his shoulder, "I thought I would die soon. I didn't want to spend the time I had left in the company of depraved bastards."

Daerick snickered as he loosened the reins. "To give proper credit, depraved bastards make the best entertainment."

He launched into another story, this time about a lord and his three adult sons, all of whom were unknowingly trying to bed the same woman—a redhead who was secretly having an affair with the lord's wife. In an added twist, both women were conspiring to kill the lord for control of his fortune.

"The family that betrays together stays together," Daerick added with a snort.

Next came a tale about a common girl who passed herself off as a lady at court for half a year and during that time received eleven proposals of marriage before she disappeared into the night with a wealth of engagement jewels. Then there was the viscount who'd had an unnatural affection for goats; the royal tailor with a fetish for dirty socks; a colonel running a brothel out of the military stockade; and a young stable boy, no older than thirteen, who had made a sizeable income from keeping all of their secrets.

"No wonder you sent them home," Cerise called ahead to Kian. "I would take a thousand lifetimes in the temple over one year at court."

Daerick leaned aside in his wooden seat. "It wasn't that bad," he admitted. "I might have embellished the story about the goats."

As Cerise rode on, she thought about what her father had said: court politics were dangerous, and she should remain silent. But she couldn't resist the chance to find out what her parents were hiding. "What about Cole Solon?"

"You'll have to be more specific," Kian told her. "We could spend a fortnight telling you stories about him."

"He thought I looked familiar when we met in the kennels," Cerise said. "He kept asking about my family. I told him I resemble my mother, but he claimed he didn't know her. When I talked to my parents about it, they reacted...very strongly."

Daerick arched a brow. "Interesting."

"Were there any rumors about Cole and a common girl named Elaina Igalsi?" she asked.

"Not that I can recall," Daerick said. "But Delora is the real keeper of scandals at the palace. She would know better than any of us if Cole bedded your mother."

"I doubt that he did," Kian said. "Cole isn't one for commoners. He tends to invest his affection where it will reap the most rewards."

Right then, the trail narrowed again and required them to ride single file, so Cerise turned her attention to Blue, whose growth spurt had strained the limits of his sling. She had just shared the last sip from her flagon with him when Nero and General Petros appeared ahead of them on the trail. She suspected from their relaxed body language that they had bonded over their mutual loathing of Father Padron.

"There's a spring just ahead," Nero said, pointing. "We'll stop long enough to water the animals and refill our skins, then move on." He squinted at the wagon. "Without the protection of your priest, it's more important than ever that we reach the next camp before nightfall."

The king nodded his consent, and the caravan continued to a wide section of the trail that had probably once been a watering hole. Though a spring bubbled freely from the ground, it was obvious from the lack of mud and animal tracks that the hole had only recently been filled.

Cerise set Blue down and led her horse to drink, and then she dipped her flagon until it was full. After quenching her thirst, she filled a bucket with water and added some healing herbs to make a poultice for Father Padron's back.

To her surprise, she found Father Padron awake in the wagon, lying with one arm curled beneath his head and blinking sleepily at the canopy.

"You look better," she told him.

He gave her a tired smile. "Then I can only imagine how ghastly I looked before."

She lifted the bucket for show and set it on the wagon's edge. "If you'll give me your shirt, I'll soak it in this. It will help you heal faster."

Father Padron's smile died. He probed the fabric at his chest, seeming to realize for the first time that she had removed his robe and exposed the mutilation on his back.

"It's all right," she told him. "No one else knows."

He avoided her eyes. "Thank you, Cerise, but all I need is a drink."

She climbed into the wagon and helped him into a sitting position before offering her flagon. "I understand why you don't want to heal," she whispered as he drank. "You mean to suffer, and it's not my place to question you. But this is cursed land, and you're our only defense. We need you strong and whole." She gently blotted the water droplets from his beard and implored, "Please let me help you."

He rewarded her with one of his rare soft gazes—the kind that made her want to forget everything she had learned about him: his lies about the hidden antechamber, his possible ambition for the throne, his willingness to let other priests facilitate murder on his behalf. She hated to believe that any of it was true, but she refused to live in denial. She would respect his power and station while keeping her head clear and her heart guarded.

"When you put it that way, how can I refuse?" he asked.

After peeling off his shirt, she let it soak while she tended to his wounds. When she wrung out the garment and helped him put it back on, his resounding sigh told her the medicinal water brought relief. Once he was settled comfortably, she crawled out of the wagon.

Father Padron caught her by the wrist. His grip was surprisingly strong. "One thing before you go." He peered around the wagon. "I sense magic here, and it's not mine."

Cerise made a special effort to hold his gaze, to give him no reason to doubt the lie that was about to follow. "Our guide has some blessed objects—gifts from priests," she said. "And it's a good thing, too, because their blessings kept us safe until you arrived. The goddess was watching us with her merciful eye. Don't you agree?"

Father Padron said nothing at first, only looked at her in silence until her pulse ticked and she had to remind herself to breathe. She sensed that her deception hadn't fooled him, though she hoped she was wrong, because she didn't have a better story to tell.

"Yes, Cerise." The grip around her wrist loosened. "The goddess rewards the faithful. But her betrayers *will* suffer until the end of days. You would do well to remember that."

15

They made camp with hours to spare before sunset, but the distant screeching of harpy vultures reminded them that daylight was no guarantee of safety on the blighted mountain. No sooner had they tethered their horses and pitched the first tent than a shadow passed over the sun. They glanced up at a pair of dark, leathery wings spanning at least ten men in width, each tipped by a razor-sharp talon. It was lucky that Father Padron had recovered enough strength to cast a protective enchantment over the camp.

After that, tensions unwound and postures relaxed. Even General Petros seemed lighter, letting loose an occasional smile as he helped Nero clean the ram they had killed earlier in the day. When the mutton was done roasting, the general carved the beast and offered the first serving to Father Padron.

"With your permission, Your Majesty," General Petros added.

"By all means," Kian said, sweeping a hand. "Our high priest has earned it."

Father Padron accepted the honor, but he elected to eat inside his tent, where he could spend the rest of the afternoon in meditation. As soon as he excused himself, Nero released a breath and unclenched his shoulders. Clearly, not everyone felt safer under the Order's protection.

The group gathered around the roasting pit and swapped stories while they ate. General Petros had the most to say, recounting his favorite hunting tales as he paced a circuit to burn off his perpetual anger. Cerise sat in between Daerick and Nero. On the other side of the fire, Kian reclined against a tree stump with his long legs crossed at the ankles.

Every time Cerise glanced at Kian, she found him watching her. It wasn't an absent stare or the blank look of someone deep in thought. He wasn't peering through her or even at her. More like *inside* her. And he didn't bother trying to avert his gaze when she caught him. If anything, his focus deepened. He held her with his eyes and made every soft part of her dance. The contact was so intense that she only lasted a moment before she had to glance down and feed Blue another slice of meat from her plate.

"You don't like my mutton?" Nero pointed at her untouched food. "Is there no pleasing you?"

"I'm not hungry," she told him, which was true. Maybe the heat was to blame, or the stress from the journey. Less than a day ago, she had bloodied her blade for the first time. That would crimp anyone's appetite.

"Eat," General Petros muttered while chewing. His gaze darted to her full plate, and for a moment, his eyes went wild. But he clenched them shut and breathed deeply through his nose. His eyes were still closed when he growled, "You do us no favors by starving yourself in penance for whatever sins you think you've committed."

"Penance?" Cerise repeated. "Is that what you think I'm doing?"

The general fixed his gaze on the fire. "Lanna, my woman at the temple, does it, too. She punishes herself for loving me. It began with fasting, and when that wasn't enough, she moved on to cutting her flesh. There's a new scar every time I see her. She used to hide them from me, but now she's run out of places—" He cut off, clenching his teeth and his fists in a struggle for control. "I hate what they taught her, what they taught all of you. For twisting her mind and making her feel ashamed—" He shut down again. The skin on his head was so flushed it nearly blended with his tattooed flames.

Cerise didn't know what to say to him. He loved an oracle who was slowly killing herself with the guilt of loving him back. There were no words to fix that. She wondered for the hundredth time if the Order had lied to her about sins of the flesh dimming the Sight. The general's mistress had incredible power; meanwhile, a chaste second-born like Cerise had no gift. Could it be that the act of love made the Sight stronger, not weaker? But if that was the case, then why would the Order try to weaken a woman's ability to serve the goddess? That would benefit no one. Perhaps the Order was right and the general's mistress would've been even more powerful if she had refused physical love.

Cerise hated that she had no way of knowing. And she would have to swallow her feelings for Kian until she did.

"I promise I'm not starving myself," was all she could think to say.

The general drove one fist into his opposite hand. He muttered an apology to the king and then charged out of sight.

"Should we go after him?" Cerise asked. "He's outside the line of protection."

Kian shook his head. "Any beast that crosses his path will find itself relieved of its limbs. Let him be." He nodded at her plate. "And please do eat."

She tore off a bite and chewed mechanically. The mutton felt as greasy and dense as the jackrabbit had the night before. When she swallowed it, her stomach churned. She forced down one more bite and had to spit the next mouthful into the fire.

"I can't," she said over the saliva flooding her mouth. She pushed her plate to Blue and let him have the rest. "I think the jackrabbit made me sick. I haven't felt right since."

Nero cast her a disbelieving glance. "You didn't eat enough jackrabbit to make a bird sick."

"Maybe these will help." Kian drew his tin of stomach soothers from his pocket. He started to toss it to her, but he changed his mind and walked around the fire. He crouched down by her side and placed the tin in her palm, curling both hands around hers. It was such a tender gesture that for one moment, she forgot that she even *had* a stomach. "The sun will set soon," he murmured to her. "Will you allow me to escort you to your tent?"

A smile lit her heart. "I would love that."

He extended a palm to help her stand, and then he kept her hand and settled it on his rounded bicep. He guided her the short distance to the outskirts of camp while Blue trotted along behind them. When they reached her tent, Kian held open one of the canvas flaps for her and ushered her inside. Cerise ducked low and inched her way to the blanket pallet she had made on the floor. She didn't expect Kian to follow her, but she was glad when he did.

"Lie down," he whispered, closing the tent flaps behind him.

She couldn't help but grin. "Are you going to tuck me in?"

"Would you like that?" he countered in a low, wicked voice that caused her pulse to hitch. "Would you like me to put you to bed, my lady of the temple? Or would you prefer that I take you to bed?"

Her pulse quickened. The king had never spoken so brazenly to her before. The mere suggestion of Kian in her bed stirred her blood and sent it rushing to the juncture of her thighs. She didn't know how to answer him. She was no good at this game of teasing and wordplay.

"Lie down," he repeated with that smile of his.

So she did as he asked, settling face up on top of her blankets, as the lingering heat was still too thick to allow for a cover. She felt Blue curl up against her, but she hadn't taken her eyes off of Kian, who now knelt down on the canvas floor and leaned over her, propping himself on one hand while using his other hand to brush the hair back from her face. The lapels of his shirt hung open just wide enough to give her a glimpse of the glossy, black curls that led from his chest to his abdomen. She recalled from memory the way those curls encircled his navel and created a trail to the thicket between his thighs. She could still picture him naked, and the mental image forced her to release a trembling sigh.

Kian clearly noticed her reaction because he had been watching her mouth. His eyes remained fixed there as he slowly trailed an index finger down the slope of her nose and continued all the way to her bottom lip, where he skimmed her flesh with his fingertip and peered down at her with more longing than a blossom for the sun.

Her breath caught. No one had ever given her that look before. She wanted to feel him, to taste his mouth, to gently sink her teeth into the side of his neck. But when she reached up to lace her fingers through his hair and pull him closer to her, he began to dissolve at the edges, and one blink later, the only trace that remained of him was a pile of clothing.

S leep didn't come easily that night. Cerise was plagued by unmet desire and bad dreams, along with a persistent ache in her stomach. When she awoke the next morning, her tent was empty except for Blue. She had hoped to see Kian at sunrise, but she had been so exhausted from a night of tossing and turning that she had slept through breakfast.

Not that she could have eaten. The sight of sand melon, oatcakes, and mutton jerky made her insides harden like a stone. She could barely tolerate feeding Blue. After giving him a few slices of jerky, she had to ask Daerick to finish the job. As for Kian, he was nowhere to be found. She learned that he had gone hunting with General Petros and Nero.

She barely saw Kian during the day's ride. Instead of leading the caravan, he elected to ride behind the wagon, saying so little to the group that no one noticed when the curse had taken him until his horse wandered off the trail. It was hours later when he reappeared. He said nothing to her then, either, and she didn't know why. That night, she couldn't manage a single bite of dinner. Kian continued watching her from the other side of the fire, though with more concern now than longing. There was a distance between them that she didn't know how to close.

He didn't offer to escort her to her tent after dinner. By the following day, she began to worry there was something wrong with her. She had never felt like this before, like her stomach belonged in a different body. At times it seemed there was a fish thrashing inside her trying to get out.

"Maybe you have a parasite," Daerick mused that morning, after she had discreetly called him into her tent to ask for advice. She had considered asking Father Padron for help, but her inner voice warned that if she truly did have fire in her blood, he might be able to detect it. "You're new to Mortara," Daerick went on. "So you wouldn't have developed the same resistance that the rest of us have." He frowned. "But you're missing the main symptoms."

"How do we know for sure?" she asked.

Nero poked his head through the tent flaps. Obviously, he'd been eavesdropping. He handed her a tin cup and said, "Make water in here. I'll be able to tell."

She raised a brow. "You want me to urinate...in your drinking cup?"

"I'll wash it," he said, shrugging.

Eventually, she gave him a sample, and he took it off to a secret place to do some manner of testing on it. He returned with an empty cup and a wrinkled forehead. He said he couldn't find anything wrong with her.

She could barely stay in the saddle as they traveled through the day, and when they stopped to make camp, she wanted to do nothing but curl up with Blue inside her tent. The thought of food repulsed her. Even water tasted sour. She refused to drink anything until Father Padron threatened to compel her to do it. Then she held her flagon to her lips and tried to force herself to swallow. The liquid sputtered out of her mouth. She couldn't get it down.

"I'm sorry, Cerise," Father Padron said. "I hate to do this."

But he did it anyway.

His energy filled the air, and then, like a puppet with its strings pulled, her body moved according to his will. She swallowed one rancid mouthful after another, unable to breathe except when he allowed it. She had never been compelled before, and she couldn't think of a worse violation of her body. When it was over, she made drinking her only goal so he didn't feel the need to do it again.

By the third day, she gave up any pretense of wellness and asked to travel in the wagon. She had just settled in among the folded tents and the sacks of oats when Kian strode toward her, flanked by Daerick and General Petros. The king moved with the sort of purpose that told her he had made a decision—one she wouldn't like.

"We're turning back," he said. "I'm taking you home to see my physician." When she opened her mouth to argue, he cut her off with a lifted palm. "The Petros Blade has waited for a thousand years. It's not going anywhere. There are other faithful servants of the goddess who can get the sunset runes for us. We just need to find one."

"We'll try again," the general added. "While you heal."

Cerise shook her head. Kian had mere moons to live unless she broke the curse. There was no time to hunt for another person who may or may not have the purity of faith to earn the sunset runes, and in her heart, she doubted that Father Padron could do it. To turn back now would mean failure. They had to keep going. Cerise scrambled for a lie to explain her symptoms, an excuse that no man would question.

The answer presented itself.

"I was hoping to keep this private," she said. She avoided their eyes, doing her best to look embarrassed as she pressed a hand to her lower abdomen. "This is what happens during my courses. Some women have a hard time of it, you know."

She glanced up to find their expressions blank.

"I promise I'll be fine in a few days." She made a pained face. "The cramps are the worst part. They start in my back and move around to the front. Sometimes the pain is so severe that I get sick to my stomach."

That was all it took to set the caravan in motion again.

And so passed another day.

Cerise was almost certain that she didn't have a parasite, because her symptoms had changed. Instead of the sensation of a thrashing fish in her stomach, she felt pressure rising behind her ribs. She kept patting her chest to release a bubble that didn't exist.

To add to her troubles, Blue had grown so large that his sling wouldn't hold him. His head came up past her knees. Now that he was the size of a hound, he could jump in and out of the wagon. Cerise couldn't stop him from running away from the caravan, which he did several times a day. Often, he stayed gone for hours before returning with a dirty root or a sprig of leaves. She finally realized what he was doing when he nudged her hand toward the plants. It was the Mortara brush hound in him. He had sensed that she was sick, and he had brought remedies to make her feel better.

"My brilliant boy." She hugged him close while turning the roots over in her hand to study them. "I don't suppose you can tell me what to do with these."

"We'll give them to Nero," Kian said from the other side of the canopy, where he had been riding so quietly she hadn't known he was there. "If anyone knows how to use them, it will be him."

When the caravan stopped for water, Nero ground up the roots and steeped them with the leaves to make the foulest tea Cerise had ever tasted. The drink didn't spark her appetite or shrink the bubble in her chest, but it sent her into a deep, tranquil sleep for the rest of the day, which was the next best thing.

For the first time since the trip had begun, she felt no pain or fear. Instead, she dreamed that someone had carried her out of the wagon and into her tent and placed her atop a bundle of blankets. She crouched at the foot of her own body and studied herself. Her cheekbones were too sharp, and her eyelids were slightly sunken. Blue was asleep with his head resting on her thigh. He heard the sound of footsteps and jerked awake, but he noticed it was only Kian, and he yawned before laying his head down again.

The king patted Blue and stood next to Cerise, unaware of her dreaming body standing right beside him. His gaze was fixed on her sleeping form. She could tell from the way he kept rubbing his face and forgetting to breathe that he was worried about her. She tried to comfort him with a touch, but her hand wasn't solid, and it passed through him.

He knelt down and placed a kiss on her sleeping forehead. The kiss was no more than a brush of contact, but Cerise touched her own skin and wished that she could feel it, wished that he could kiss her when she was awake.

The king glanced outside the tent at the last glimmer of sunset, and his body began to curl into shadow. She had seen him vanish before, but this time was different. Now a portal appeared in the air behind him, round and wide and swirling with gray mist. As Kian disappeared and his clothes fell to the floor, the doorway flashed, and all of a sudden, he was on the other side of it, naked and fully formed and walking away.

Slowly, the portal began to close. Cerise crept closer to the mist, wondering if she should try to enter it. This might be her only chance to find out where the king went at night. She glanced at her sleeping body and knew Blue would keep her safe. So she gulped a breath, stepped through the shrinking doorway, and followed Kian into the darkness.

On the other side of the portal, she became instantly solid—she could tell from the press of stone beneath her shoes and the air caressing her skin. Unlike Kian, she had kept her clothes, though she didn't know why. She stood still and let her eyes adjust to the cool, colorless world.

A feeble glow emanated from above, like the moon filtered through a veil of clouds. It was enough to show her that nothing grew there, not a single weed or shrub. There was no dirt for anything to grow *in*. All that existed was rock—tall, gray slabs forming passageways that sprawled in all directions. She couldn't tell what the place was supposed to be. From her vantage point, it seemed like an enormous labyrinth. She looked down and noticed a glossy path on the ground, buffed smooth by countless feet. She hugged herself against a chill and stepped forward to see where it led.

The first passageway was deserted, so she continued around two more corners, where she reached an open courtyard strewn with crumbling marble benches arranged around a long-dry fountain. At the opposite end of the courtyard, four arched doorways led in different directions. She approached each one, finding them vacant. At the fourth doorway, she noticed a distant sound—a low drone like the buzzing of insects. Curious, she followed the noise for quite some time, turning corner after corner until her feet ached from rubbing against her sandals.

The louder the noise grew, the slower her steps became—not from the pain of walking but because she began to realize that insects weren't making the sound.

It was human voices, hundreds of them, all groaning in a harmony of anguish.

At one point, she stopped.

Every instinct urged her to turn back. But she forced herself onward, thinking of Kian. If he could endure this every night, then she could experience it one time.

Before long, she happened upon two young men...if she could call them that, for each of them seemed to have lost whatever had made him a person. Their skin was waxy, their cheeks sunken. They looked at her as she passed, but there was no thought behind their eyes. The men swayed from side to side, wailing deliriously.

Around the next corner was a young woman on her hands

and knees, sweeping aside imaginary objects as if searching for something. The woman froze, seeming to forget what she was looking for, and then she lowered her head and released a racking sob that was so heartrending—so completely devoid of hope—that Cerise had to blot the tears from her eyes.

None of the men or women looked older than twenty, and all of them had the dark skin and hair of the Mortara line. Legends had long claimed that firstborn Mortaras didn't die, that they remained in the shadows forever. Now that Cerise had seen for herself that the rumors were true, she wished she could erase the knowledge from her mind. She didn't want to know of such suffering. She didn't want to see the evidence of how wrathful the goddess could be. It simply wasn't fair.

Cerise backed away from the woman and retraced her steps to the vacant courtyard to try a different passage. She didn't know how long she wandered. Hours must have gone by, because her eyelids were heavy, and twice she tripped over her own feet. She had nearly given up when she passed the entrance to a stone room, and there was Kian: his head down, sitting naked in the corner with both knees drawn to his chest.

He had never looked so small.

A piece of her heart fell away when she imagined all the nights he had spent like this. She crouched down in front of him and sighed. "No wonder you need stomach soothers."

His head snapped up.

"Oh," she said, waving a hand. "Can you see me?"

He stood up slowly and clung to the wall, inching away from her while shaking his head in horror. "No," he breathed. "No, no, no."

"Kian, it's me." She touched her chest. "It's Cerise."

He clapped a hand over his mouth. His gaze shimmered as if he might cry.

"It's just me," she added softly.

"I knew it," he choked out. "I knew I shouldn't have listened to you. Daerick told me you were lying about your courses. He has teenage sisters; he knows about these things."

"Kian, it's—"

"I waited too long." Still pressed to the wall, he raked a trembling hand through his hair. He seemed to be talking to himself now. "I should've taken you home when I had the chance. I knew it in my gut, but I didn't listen because I wanted the Petros Blade."

She moved toward him cautiously. "It's all right. I followed you here from my tent. I was dreaming. You couldn't see me, but I could see you. I watched you kiss my forehead. Do you remember doing that?"

Something within him seemed to break. He closed the distance between them and took her face roughly in his hands, tilting their foreheads together until the only thing that separated their mouths was a mingled breath.

Her insides sprouted wings and took flight. Her head was dizzy with the scent of him. She lifted a hand to touch him, hesitating once, twice, before she rested her fingertips on his chest and skimmed the soft, dark curls there. Her breathing shuddered. So did his. Swallowing hard, she smoothed her hands over his shoulders and clasped them behind his neck. With one small step, she leaned into him until every part of her body was flush with his.

The closeness was too much and not nearly enough.

She raised her face and parted her lips without meaning to. She wanted him to kiss her more than she wanted her heart to beat, but then she remembered why she couldn't.

A worshipper of pure faith.

To earn the sunset runes, she had to prove herself worthy. She couldn't take the chance of damning Kian to this hell forever. She turned her face aside, peering at the stone walls because she couldn't look him in the eyes. The moment sobered her enough to remind her of another reason not to kiss him: he'd been avoiding her.

"I don't understand you," she murmured. "Your spirit is still drawn to me, but you've been colder than ever. You haven't said a kind word to me in days. It's not fair to treat me like that—like you don't even care for me anymore."

He moved one hand to the curve of her neck while gripping her lower back and crushing their bodies together. "I do care," he whispered in a pained voice. "I want you, Cerise, more than I've let myself want anything in a long time. Then I imagined spending eternity here, missing you, tortured by the memory of you. I thought it would be worse to have you and lose you than to never have you at all. But now look. I've lost you, and it hurts so badly I can't stand it."

She gazed up at him and found his eyelids pinched shut. "You haven't lost me."

He whispered, "I'm sorry."

"Kian, look at me." She cupped his cheek and told him, "I'm not sorry."

He exhaled into a sad smile. His hands tightened around her as if he meant to pull her inside him. "My sweet, brave lady of the temple. That's because you only just arrived." He stroked her skin with his thumbs and added in a choked whisper, "You don't know where you are." A tear slid down his cheek, hot and wet against her fingertips. "You don't know that you're dead."

16

Falling.
Falling endlessly.
Falling through time and space.

Cerise jerked awake so violently that Blue yelped and rolled off the blankets onto the canvas floor. She clapped a hand over her heart, its wild beat confirming that she was, indeed, still alive. Silently, she sent up a prayer of thanks to the goddess while Blue righted himself and licked her chin.

"I'm sorry, boy," she whispered to him, holding him tight.

She pulled in a deep breath and let it out slowly, repeating the process until her heart stopped pounding. As the remnants of the images faded away, she rubbed her eyes and tried to gauge whether it was morning or night. The surrounding darkness had a faint glow to it that could indicate either dawn or dusk. Still lying on her back, she glanced first at the canvas ceiling, then to her left and right, and realized she was in her tent. She wondered how long she had been there. Peering through a thin gap in the canvas flaps, she noticed the sky growing half a shade brighter.

Morning, she decided. That meant the king would arrive soon, assuming his spirit was still drawn to her. After the way he had behaved recently, she had her doubts.

She licked her lips and felt around for her flagon. She must have slept for a moon's age, because she was thirsty enough to drain a pond. When she found the flagon, she rolled onto her side and took a deep pull. The water tasted incredible, so clean and pure that she didn't stop gulping until she finished the last drop. Panting, she wiped her mouth while her stomach rumbled. Oatcakes and sand melon sounded incredible at the moment. Mutton jerky and jackrabbit, too. She would eat the tent floor if she could. She gave her chest a few testing pats. The bubble behind her ribs had popped. As for her stomach, the only sensation she felt was the ravenous need to put food inside it.

"I'm starving," she told Blue, ruffling his head. "I don't suppose you can hunt me down some food?"

Blue bounced in place and yipped as if agreeing to the challenge. Then he turned around and darted outside.

Cerise was still lying on her pallet and debating whether or not to get up and follow him when a cloud of smoke blew open the tent flaps and washed over her, cool and intoxicating and smelling of clean, male skin. The ball of shadow gathered at her bedside and materialized into flesh. The king appeared, fully naked, seated on her blanket with his head tucked low and his knees drawn to his chest, exactly the same way she had found him in her dream. He didn't look up at first, until she quietly cleared her throat to get his attention.

At the sound, he snapped his gaze to hers. His eyes were wide, his face slack. He peered at her as though she were a ghost. He even seemed to have stopped breathing.

"Your Highness, are you all right?" she whispered.

He inched his hand forward to touch her arm and gave it a testing squeeze. "You're alive," he breathed. "You're actually alive."

As she nodded slowly at him, realization struck. Had she

experienced a *vision*? Had she finally received the Sight?

What about her strange "dream" involving the Reverend Mother? Had that been a vision, too?

Where were all the oracles when she needed one?

"How?" the king asked in a barely audible whisper. "How is it possible? No one has ever followed me into the darkness. You were solid—flesh and bone. I felt you."

If she'd been solid, then it couldn't have been a vision. Her searing hope turned to confusion. "I was actually with you in that place? It happened in real time?"

Was there a Sight like that?

"How?" he repeated, but then he immediately shook his head as if he didn't care anymore. His storm-cloud eyes locked on to her, and he delivered a look so raw and primal, so full of hunger that it stilled her lungs.

She froze like prey in the thrall of a predator. He crawled over her and took her face roughly in one hand, much like he had done in the stone room. She lay flat between her blankets as she peered up at him and splayed both hands by her side. A rush of anticipation flooded her senses, but she couldn't forget her purpose. She pressed a palm against his chest to stop him.

It was the hardest thing she'd ever done.

"We can't," she told him.

He removed his hand from her face, but he drew nearer to her, lowering himself onto one elbow until she could feel the heat of his naked flesh radiating through the blanket that covered her legs.

"I'm sorry I was cold to you," he whispered. "What I said in that place…I meant it. My spirit doesn't belong to me anymore. It belongs to the girl with too much love inside her, the girl whose light scatters the darkness. My spirit wants the patron saint of ugly pups, toxic frogs, and foolish half kings." His gaze moved over her face, burning her everywhere it landed. "I want you, Cerise. I'm sorry I gave you any reason to doubt that."

He reached for her again, but now with deliberate slowness, as if seeking her permission. This time, she didn't have the strength to turn him away. She took his hand and placed it on her cheek, holding it there.

"Kian," she began, but before she could finish her thought, he lowered his mouth to hers and wiped her mind clean.

This was no dream, no strange vision. The king was kissing her… if she could call it that, because the way he used his mouth redefined the act of kissing as she had known it.

This was more than two pairs of lips pressed together. His every move was lethal, each tender sweep and teasing nibble touching her in the places his hands didn't wander. She opened to him, tasting his mouth, stroking his tongue with hers, probing deeper and deeper and never getting her fill of him. With her pulse thrumming in her ears, she tugged him closer, pulling his chest on top of hers, needing to feel more of his weight for fear that her body might float away if he didn't anchor her to the ground.

He moved his lips to her ear, where he whispered her name in an urgent breath that raised chills on her skin. She bared her neck to him and squirmed as he kissed a trail from her ear to her collar. Tugging aside her shirt, he bit the top of her shoulder and sent her eyes rolling back in her head. Then he used a knee to part her linen-clad thighs. She didn't know what to expect next, and she wasn't ready for the rush of sensation that followed when he rocked against her. Pleasure bloomed between her thighs, so hot and so intense that she couldn't stop a groan from rising in her throat.

At that moment, Blue burst through the tent flaps. He must have thought her moans were of pain, because he delivered an earnest nip to the king's backside.

Kian flinched away, hissing a curse. As he rolled aside to inspect his bottom, he gave her a view of Blue, who had dropped a lifeless jackrabbit on the tent floor.

Cerise clenched her jaw and exhaled a long, calming breath through her nose. All the blood in her body seemed to have pooled between her legs, creating a new, throbbing pulse point that ached for more of Kian's touch. She tried to will away the sensation. She had to get control of herself; she'd already let things go too far.

Kian rubbed his backside and cast a glare at Blue. "I think someone's jealous."

Blue lay down and rested his head next to her pillow, seemingly confident that the threat to her safety was over. Cerise blew out another breath. Her body still fought her, but at least she was coming to her senses. She snuck a peek at the king's rear end, finding his skin unbroken. Thank the goddess Blue had interrupted them.

Kian leaned down. "Now where were we?"

She placed a palm against his chest. "We can't."

"What's wrong?" He pulled back to look at her, his eyes heavily lidded with desire. "Are you afraid that someone will hear?"

"No," she said. "Well, yes, but that's not why we have to stop."

When he raised an eyebrow in question, she told him her worries surrounding the act of love—how the Order had claimed it would dim the Sight or prevent her from receiving it in the first place.

"And that's not all," she whispered. "Mother Strout's journal said the sunset runes would only give themselves to a worshipper of pure faith."

"You have the purest faith of anyone I've ever met."

She shook her head. Faith of the heart wasn't enough. "The Order says I have to give myself completely to the goddess, in body and in soul."

"And do you believe them?"

She bit her lip. She didn't know what to believe anymore.

"Would it help to tell you they're wrong?" he asked, but then he immediately shook his head. "Of course it won't. They sowed their seeds in you when you were just a child. Now those roots run deep."

She took his face in her hands. She needed to break the curses; she needed to be worthy of the sunset runes and then to receive the Sight so she could use her gift to restore him. Her ability to follow him into the darkness last night, whatever it meant, didn't seem to serve much of a purpose. If there was a chance that she could receive a *real* gift, a useful one, she had to protect it.

"It's not long until my Claiming Day," she said. "I don't see the harm in waiting."

"And what if you *do* receive the Sight?" he asked. "What then? Will you be so afraid to dim your gift that you end up dimming your own light in the process?"

She peeked up at him. She didn't know what to say.

"Cerise, I respect your decision," he whispered. "But as a king, I know a thing or two about control. The kings who came before me ruled by fear. My father was one of them. And strictly speaking, fear works. It's a powerful motivator. But anyone who has to terrorize their people into submission is a poor and unimaginative leader. A strong ruler inspires others to follow them. The same is true of faith. Any order worth your prayers will lead by inspiration, but a false order will create illusions of fear to control you. They'll make you confused, just like you're confused now. They'll tell you not to question them. They'll invent rules and consequences that don't exist to make you afraid of disobeying them—just like you're afraid of disobeying them now. So ask yourself: Why can't the priests inspire you by grace? Could it be because they have none?"

"But why would they lie about this?" she asked. "What would they stand to gain from keeping me a maiden?"

"Maybe nothing. Maybe they're manipulating you just because they can."

She didn't believe that. No one lied without a reason; it required too much effort. "I don't know what's true," she admitted. "I only know what feels right."

"Does that mean my touch feels wrong to you?"

"No," she told him at once. She refused to let him believe for even one moment that his touch was anything less than her greatest joy. "Maybe I am afraid of something that's not real. But I don't want to take the risk. There's too much at stake—not just for you and me, but for Daerick and my sister's baby and all of the firstborns who will suffer if I fail. Please tell me you understand."

A flicker of disappointment crossed the king's face, but he cupped her cheeks in both hands and placed a chaste kiss on her forehead. "If it's important to you that we wait, then it's important to me." He winked. "Though I may have already ruined your reputation, my lady. These canvas walls are thinner than you think."

She froze, her eyes wide. "Do you think anyone heard?"

"I suppose we'll find out," he told her.

And they did, a while later, after they had dressed for the day and walked out of her tent to a host of downturned gazes. The group had definitely heard her moans. She flushed hot with embarrassment. She could only imagine what everyone was thinking.

Nero slid her an amused glance, chuckling to himself as he stuffed his folded tent into a bag. She wordlessly handed him the jackrabbit Blue had retrieved and then strode to the fire to prepare a bowl of oats. Daerick and General Petros were also preparing their breakfasts. They scratched the backs of their necks and studied their shoes when she joined them. They put her in mind of two overprotective brothers working up the courage to give her an uncomfortable talk about men. And if she was the sister in this imaginary family, then Father Padron was the patriarch. He pierced her with a reproachful look that made her want to thrust out her tongue and remind him that he wasn't her real father.

"I might expect this from the king, but not from you," Father Padron hissed as soon as he got her alone. He had finished saddling his horse and insisted on helping with hers—an offer she had known better than to refuse. "The goddess gave you a body of flesh so you could serve her will, not so you could make yourself a vessel for male lust."

Cerise whirled to face him, leaving the saddle unfastened. She had never heard a more twisted view of love or of women. It wasn't simply the crude words that offended her, but the implication that the only thing Kian wanted from her was pleasure. As if that was all she had to offer. As if no man, least of all a king, could have any other interest in her than that.

"I'm sorry you think so little of me," she said and then immediately corrected herself. "No, I'm not sorry, because I haven't done anything wrong. The king barely laid a hand on me."

"It didn't sound that way."

Another wave of heat flushed her cheeks. None of this was his business. She had chosen to stop Kian out of an abundance of caution, not because the act of love was shameful. "Nothing happened. But even if it had, it's not forbidden by scrolls for an oracle to love."

"It dims the Sight."

"But how do we know that?" she asked. "I've heard of powerful Seers who engage in love. Where is it written that it dims the Sight? If the goddess didn't intend for oracles to love, then why wouldn't she relieve them of the desire for it, like she did for the priests?"

He must not have had a logical response for that, because instead of answering her question, he chose to prey on her heart's worst fear. "It won't last," he said. "Even if you break the king's curse, he will eventually discard you."

She shook her head. She refused to believe that.

"Kings marry for power and for peace," he went on. "Not for love. Even the late queen was no ordinary commoner. She had influence over the people. Respect. The old king believed a union with her would make the people respect him, too. He never loved her, and he made no secret about it."

Father Padron leaned down so she could see him better. It wasn't so much a gesture of tenderness as a means of inflicting more damage. "You could be his *concubine*." The word made her flinch, exactly as he had intended. "Is that what you want? A life spent waiting in your chambers for the king to come to you when he's finished bedding his wife? Feeding on the scraps of another woman? Watching him make a legitimate family with the queen while your belly swells with his bastard?"

Cerise couldn't bear to think of it, let alone answer.

"Then by all means, give yourself to him. Forsake your calling to a higher purpose. But I don't think that's the life you want, Cerise. So tread carefully around those who matter most; otherwise, your path will be a lonely one that leads to ruin." He mounted his horse and left her with one parting thought. "*That* is what you stand to lose."

17

There was no muting the echo of Father Padron's voice during the day's ride. It chanted in time with Ash's hooves: *won't-last won't-last, concu-bine concu-bine*. A new fear tightened her chest and reminded her of what Kian had said in the dark, stone room—that he had dreaded the pain of losing her more than the disappointment of never having her at all. At the time, she had thought it silly of him to let his fear of tomorrow steal his joy from today. But now she understood him all too well.

Mere hours had passed since the king had promised his soul to her, and already the fear of losing him had begun. A ball of ice formed in her stomach when she imagined giving her love to him, freeing him from his curse, and then watching him marry another woman. But that was the inevitable outcome. A king needed legitimate heirs, and ladies of the temple weren't permitted to marry.

Father Padron was right. Her time with Kian couldn't last.

She tried to tell herself it didn't matter, that there was a purpose for every season, and now was the summer of her life. She could enjoy summer's warmth or not, but dreading winter's arrival wouldn't stop the cold from coming. She had to be brave in order to love... Such a deceptively simple idea, but in truth, it was the hardest challenge she had ever faced.

She distracted herself from her troubled thoughts by riding alongside Daerick at the back of the caravan, where she shared with him in whispers the details of her visit to the Mortara underworld the night before. Daerick had already been watching her intently since her sudden recovery from her ailments that morning. As Kian had told her, her excuse about her courses hadn't fooled him. She also suspected that her recovery was linked to her visit to the shadows. The timing of the two events couldn't be a coincidence.

"At first I thought it was a vision," she added in her softest voice, so Father Padron wouldn't overhear. "And that I was finally receiving the Sight. But my spirit left my body and came back to it. That's unlike any trance or vision I've ever heard of."

Daerick held up a hand. "Wait a minute. So you're telling me the underworld is a place—a place that actually exists—but it's a purgatory for firstborn Mortaras?"

"It seems that way." For a moment, she forgot her worries. She couldn't imagine anything worse than returning to that place every night, except staying there for eternity. Now more than ever, she felt the weight of Kian's curse on her shoulders.

"It almost sounds like you experienced astral projection," Daerick murmured. "But you say your body was solid when you followed Kian through the portal?"

"Yes," she said. "I'm certain of it."

"Then I don't know how to label this new gift of yours."

"Gift?" she asked. It had only happened once. "How do we know it's a gift?"

"I suppose we don't," Daerick admitted. "Not until you can repeat it. But you said Kian told you you're the only one who's ever followed him into the shadows. You've done something no one else can do. If that's not the definition of a gift, then I don't know what is."

"All right, let's say it *is* a gift," she said. "Do you think it's the only one I'm meant to receive? My Claiming Day is soon. Am I fooling myself by hoping for the Sight?"

Daerick laughed without humor. "In these unusual times? Who could say? My Claiming Day is still moons away, and you saw my lapse in sanity. The rules of nature don't seem to matter anymore."

At that moment, she glanced at the front of the caravan and found Kian's horse in want of a rider. Kian must have only just vanished, because his clothes were still balanced on his saddle. As the linen pile slid onto the packed dirt trail, General Petros smoothly dismounted his beast and rescued the king's clothing before resuming his ride as though nothing had happened. No one seemed surprised by Kian's disappearances anymore. The loss of his daylight hours had become commonplace, and that worried her.

"Why, though?" she asked Daerick. "Why do you think the curse is breaking through the veil of time?"

Daerick cast a heavy look at the landscape on either side of the trail—the cracked and barren ground, the dried tumbleweeds, the vastness of death all around them. "I think it's this place. The blight here runs deep. Nothing good has ever happened on this mountain."

Cerise touched his hand and gave it a reassuring squeeze. "Let's see if we can change that."

• • •

The group approached the mountain summit at midday. The Blighted Shrine hadn't come into view yet, but as Cerise peered ahead of Nero, she noticed there wasn't much higher to climb... unless he meant to lead them off a cliff.

She used one hand to fan the back of her neck. The temperature at this altitude was unbearable, and the air was too thin and stank of decay. No matter how many breaths she took, she couldn't satisfy her lungs. Blue was struggling, too. He panted as he jogged alongside her horse, and poor Ash had slowed his pace as well, his ribs expanding between her knees.

"Not much farther." She rubbed Ash's neck and asked Nero, "Right?"

Nero nodded, seemingly too exhausted for words. The group continued in silence for a short while, until the path inclined so sharply that the horses couldn't hold their footing and the wagon threatened to capsize. The caravan stopped there, and they tethered the horses in a thicket of dried brush before following Nero up the path to the mountain summit.

What they found next explained the foul smell.

The Blighted Shrine stood above them at the highest peak of the summit. The shrine was simple in its design, constructed from three narrow onyx slabs that formed a waist-high table. At the base of the shrine lay the putrid remains of what appeared to be a stag or perhaps an elk, a once majestic beast that now writhed with maggots. The goddess had rejected the offering. If Shiera had accepted it, the carcass would have been consumed by her sacred flame.

"Shameful," Father Padron muttered.

Cerise shared a heavy look with Father Padron while pulling her headscarf over her nose. It was sacrilege to defile a holy place with the odor of death. If the shrine had been located in a more hospitable place, priests would protect it and ensure that failed offerings were removed and burned. Whoever had left the carcass behind to rot in the sun had truly been unworthy of Shiera's favor. The goddess had been wise to reject their plea.

Blue whined and buried his snout beneath his paws. The odor had to be especially unbearable for a nose as sensitive as his. While Cerise bent down to stroke the back of Blue's neck, she tasted the electric tang of magic and found Father Padron extending a palm toward the shrine. The carcass began to sizzle and smoke until all that remained of the enormous beast was a pile of ash, which Father Padron then swept off the summit with a wave of his hand. He cleared the air and then indicated that it was safe for Cerise to continue onward.

The path to the shrine consisted of nothing more than a craggy set of stones to climb, which meant she would have to go the rest of the way alone. She ordered Blue to stay with Daerick and then she peered at the group one last time in hopes that Kian would reappear. After all the effort they had made to reach the shrine, she had wanted to share this moment with him. But as it wasn't meant to be, she patted down her pockets to ensure that her offerings were still there, and she turned to face the rocks.

Before she began her climb, she lowered to one knee and transferred a kiss from her fingertips to the ground in a show of respect for her surroundings. Shiera, the great goddess herself, had once stood on this very summit a thousand years ago when she had taken mortal form. Cerise climbed the first jagged rock and imagined what it might've been like to be there, to regard the goddess in a body of flesh. She pictured Shiera's golden armor gleaming in the sun, her muscled arms folded as she surveyed her creation with dual expressions of mercy and wrath.

It gave Cerise chills.

She continued her climb, ignoring the pain of the sharp stones pressing into her palms. The fantasy of treading in Shiera's footsteps swallowed her so completely that she didn't notice when one of her sandal straps broke in half. The next thing she knew, her left foot slipped out of her shoe, and she was falling backward toward the rocky ground. She barely had time to gasp before she landed hard enough to knock the wind from her lungs.

There was a collective intake of breath from the group. No one spoke or made a sound, except for Blue, who whined and rushed to Cerise's side. Blue helped nudge her into a sitting position, and the rest of the group surrounded her as she probed her body for damage. She found nothing wrong. Miraculously, she wasn't even sore. But as she glanced behind her at the place where she had landed, she discovered a jagged stone protruding from the ground like a serrated blade. The stone should have severed her spine, or at least pierced her from behind. Instead of being impaled on the rock, she seemed to have bounced off of it.

In disbelief, she glanced at the group and found Father Padron bracing his hands on his knees in exhaustion as though he had used his energy to save her life. But he couldn't have. She tasted no magic in the air.

"Did you...?" she asked him.

"No." Father Padron shook his head. "I didn't have time to act."

"Then how are you alive?" Daerick demanded of her. "Not that I'm complaining, mind you, but very few things are beyond my understanding, and your ability to cheat death is quickly becoming one of them."

Cerise felt Nina's pendant warm beneath her shirt. Her sister's necklace had protected her once again, but having been sworn to secrecy, Cerise couldn't say so. "I suppose the goddess—"

"—works in mysterious ways?" Daerick finished with a hint of sarcasm that didn't escape her notice.

"Yes. Her blessings abound," she told him.

Though Daerick was too smart to have been fooled by her excuse, he didn't argue with her. "As blessed as you are," he said, "try to be more careful."

"Perhaps this was a lesson," Cerise said as she removed her other sandal. "I should have taken off my shoes before walking on sacred ground." She glanced at Father Padron and asked, "Don't you agree, Your Grace?"

Father Padron was watching her as though she were an incomplete puzzle. He gave an absent nod, but it was clear that her excuse hadn't fooled him, either.

Before anyone could question her further, she stood and brushed off her hands. She ordered Blue to stay with Daerick, and then she resumed her climb up the rocks, now focused on her handholds and keeping her mind in the present. The craggy stones pierced her tender feet, but the contact gave her a sense of connection that allowed her to scale the ridge without any more missteps. Minutes later, Cerise stood safely at the top of the summit and approached the Blighted Shrine, its onyx surface gleaming in the sunlight despite having burned a thousand years' worth of offerings.

The air around the shrine stood unnaturally still, as though the world held its breath in wonder. Cerise held her breath, too. It struck her that she was nearer to the goddess now than she had ever been. She planted the soles of her bare feet onto the stone and let her flesh absorb the history of this place.

For the first time, she understood the significance of the blighted peak, the reason it was deemed holy. The acts of love and betrayal that had happened on this peak represented the spectrum of light and dark, like Shiera herself. There was a balance to the mountain that Cerise never would have noticed if Nero hadn't shown her the secret oasis in the Below. While the mountain's surface was scorched with blight, deep down, hidden in another dimension, existed a tiny paradise that teemed with beauty.

As above, so below. The goddess embodied all things.

"Mother Shiera, mistress of worlds," Cerise began in a voice thick with emotion, "I come to you with two humble gifts, and in return I ask for your runes to guide me to the Petros Blade." She retrieved the titan hyena tooth and held it toward the sky. "First, I offer you a symbol of darkness, for it is the darkness that defines the light. Without suffering, joy is muted. Without pain, pleasure is meaningless. And without the promise of death, time has no value. Your darkness is a gift."

Cerise placed the incisor atop the onyx shrine, and at once, a black flame consumed the tooth, and it was gone. Her heartbeat ticked with excitement. The goddess had heard her prayer and accepted her first sacrifice.

"Second, I offer you a symbol of light," Cerise said, retrieving the dried lavender blossom that she had plucked from the Below. "For it is through the warmth of the sun and the beauty of your creation that we feel your love. And your love is what makes life worth living. Your light is a gift."

She placed the flower on the shrine, and it, too, was consumed. But even though the offering had been accepted, Cerise felt called to do more, to give more. There was too much gratitude inside her to contain, so she did the first thing that came to mind, and she called out to the goddess in song. It was a simple melody she had learned as a child, but its lyrics perfectly captured the way she felt.

From the golden rays of sunshine to the blackest shade of night,
Your sacred presence fills my heart with sorrow and delight.
Your power is eternal, your hand is cruel and kind,
Your mercy has conceived my soul, and so we are entwined.

Cerise had never been proud of her singing voice, but she closed her eyes, put aside her ego, and infused each note with all of the love and faith in her heart. She finished her song and reopened her eyes.

A pair of ten-sided dice now sat atop the shrine. Each die had been carved from marble, and its stone facets bore symbols in an ancient language Cerise had yet to learn.

The goddess had rewarded her.

Just as she reached for the runes, the goddess surprised her with a second reward. A cool kiss of rain misted down from the heavens, glittering in the sunlight and filling the air with colorful prisms. Cerise spread her arms wide to soak in the mist. She beamed with joy as moisture blurred her vision. She didn't need the Sight to understand that the goddess was singing back to her. She felt it in her very soul, and the warmth that glowed within her chest was more beautiful than she ever could have imagined.

She had been found worthy. Even after her lapse of control with Kian in the tent, the goddess had known what was in her heart.

Pure faith.

When Cerise retrieved the sunset runes and turned toward the group waiting for her below, she discovered that the king had reappeared. Kian stood at the base of the rocks, wearing nothing but a pair of linen pants and a smile filled with so much adoration and pride that Cerise's throat thickened with fresh emotion. Beside him, General Petros placed a hand over his heart, and Nero seemed to be pretending to fish a speck of dust out of his eye. Even Father Padron grinned up at her, though his gaze held an unspoken *I told you so* — a reminder of the lecture he had given her that morning about the risk of forsaking her divine purpose.

Blue was the first one to greet her when she descended to the base of the rocks. Close behind him was Daerick, whose eyes shone with welling tears.

"You did it," Daerick told her. "I didn't think it was possible, but you actually made one good thing happen on this mountain."

Cerise returned his smile as she opened her palm to show him the sunset runes. "Now let's make it two."

18

The sunset runes hadn't come with a set of instructions, but according to what Cerise had learned from Daerick, she was meant to cast the dice at twilight, and then the corresponding runes would indicate how far to travel and in what direction for the following day.

She glanced at the position of the midday sun. With roughly five hours until sunset, there was no way of knowing which direction the caravan should go from the summit. Any time they spent in the saddle might be wasted.

"We have the runes," she said to the group. "Now what?"

Kian thumbed behind him at the steep trail they had scaled earlier that day. "Let's go back to the clearing where we made camp last night. We know it's more or less protected, and the ride is short enough that we can make it there before dark. The altitude has been hard on the horses. They need rest."

"And water," Nero said, nodding in agreement. "There's a spring near the camp. And I reset all of my traps before we left. We should have a kill for supper, even if it's only jackrabbit."

"Then that clinches it," Kian told the group. "We'll retrace our steps back to the clearing and cast the runes at sunset to plan tomorrow's journey."

With that decided, the six of them descended the steep summit path to the thicket where they had tethered their horses and left the wagon. Then they turned around and followed the same packed dirt trail that they had traversed earlier in the day. By late afternoon, they arrived at their previous camp and divided the tasks of pitching tents, building a fire, feeding and watering the horses, and preparing dinner. Nero took Blue with him to check his traps, and they returned with several jackrabbits, which Nero cleaned and roasted on a spit.

Even though jackrabbit was Cerise's least favorite food, she was so famished from the day's ride that her mouth watered the entire time the meat roasted. She slid a jealous glance at Blue, who didn't have to wait for his meal to cook. As Blue gobbled up his raw rabbit, Cerise noticed he had grown again. The sweet puppy she had once cradled in the palm of her hand was now as tall as a mule deer, and he required so much food that she had to let him go hunting alone throughout the day. She wondered when he would reach his full size. The wrinkles on his hide told her he still had yet to grow. If he continued developing at this rate, she might return to the palace on Blue's back instead of Ash's.

As the sun slid closer to the horizon, Cerise and the others gathered around the fire and ate a dinner of roasted potatoes, oatcakes, and seared rabbit. All except for Father Padron, who had elected to fast inside his tent. Nero and General Petros devoured their food wordlessly while Cerise sat in between Kian and Daerick, examining the markings on the sunset runes.

"Can you read these symbols?" Cerise asked Daerick.

Daerick's mouth was full, so he shot her a look of insult.

"Of course you can," she said. "Forgive me."

But there was still one problem. The time to cast the dice was fast approaching, and so was the hour of Kian's nightly disappearance into the shadows. If Cerise wanted to try to follow Kian through the portal again, she would have to fall asleep before sunset. She couldn't be simultaneously awake to cast the runes and asleep to follow Kian into the underworld.

She glanced at the low position of the sun. Perhaps she could cast the runes now. "It's almost twilight," she announced to no one in particular. "The timing is close enough, don't you agree?"

Nero and General Petros shrugged.

"I see no harm in trying," Kian said and looked to Daerick. "Do you?"

"None that I can think of." Daerick swept a permissive hand. "Even if it is too soon to cast the runes, I doubt they'll explode in your face."

"All right. Here we go." Cerise brushed aside the dust from the ground in front of her. "Mother Shiera, mistress of worlds, please guide our path." She tossed the dice gently, careful not to cast them too close to the fire. The dice tumbled forward, but instead of stopping, they reversed direction and rolled back into her hand.

She frowned. Maybe it was too soon.

Nero pointed at her as he paused to swallow a bite of food. "Tell the dice what you seek and then try again."

Cerise lifted the runes to her lips and whispered, "Mother Shiera, mistress of worlds, please take me to the hiding place of the Petros Blade." She cast the dice once again, and this time they tumbled forward and landed firmly in place. "I think it worked!"

Daerick squinted at the symbols facing up on the dice. "It seems we're to travel southwest for twenty clicks."

"Twenty clicks." Nero glanced in a direction that Cerise could only presume was southwest. "That won't be an easy ride. The trail is rough that way."

"Then let's make sure we leave as close to dawn as possible," Kian said. "Everyone, rest well tonight. You'll need your strength."

The king's advice to rest well couldn't have come at a better time, because it gave Cerise an excuse to ask if anyone had a sleeping draft that they could share with her. Even though the day had been exhausting, falling asleep naturally—and into a deep enough sleep to separate her spirit from her body—might require more time than she had to spare.

"I have Hoya leaf." Nero frowned. "But that won't make you sleep. We can look for dream weed…"

"Shiera's bones, no," General Petros said. "We'll all end up in a coma. All she needs is a nip of this." He retrieved a leather flask from his saddlebag and handed it to her. "Arrowroot syrup. My woman at the temple makes it." He lifted a finger. "It works fast, though, so wait until you're ready."

"I'm ready now," Cerise told him. She took the flask from General Petros and thanked him by covering his scarred knuckles with one hand.

"Sleep well, my girl," the general said.

As he had promised, the syrup did its job.

Cerise drank a mouthful of the tonic, and by the time she had finished the other half of her oatcake and a few more bites of jackrabbit, her vision blurred and her dinner plate tilted out of her hand. Fortunately, Blue was there to rescue the meat before it hit the ground. He licked his chops and peered at Cerise for more, and all of a sudden, the sight of his round, black eyes stirred so much emotion inside her that a tear spilled free.

"I love you," she said to Blue. She gathered her enormous pup into her arms and hugged him close, only releasing him when her muscles went slack and allowed him to wriggle free. Then she glanced at Daerick and told him she loved him, too. Daerick snorted a laugh, but she didn't care. One by one, she peered around the group with misty eyes, starting with Kian, the dark and sultry king who captivated her with his bottomless gaze; then General Petros, the warrior with a tender heart; and finally, Nero, brave and strong. They had all carved out a permanent place in her heart.

"I'll feed Blue," Daerick offered, nodding at the tents. "Go ahead and hit the blankets, lover girl."

Cerise tried to stand up too quickly, and the world slanted on its axis. Kian was already there to grip her elbow and guide her to her tent. Once they made it through the canvas flaps, he made a motion to lay her down on the blanket pallet, but she resisted and pointed at a bundle of oversize clothes that she had previously set on the floor.

"First help me put those on," she slurred.

Kian tilted his head in confusion. "You want to change into those clothes?"

"No, put them o-ver," she mumbled.

"Over the clothes you already have on?" Kian asked.

"Mmm-hmm. I'll...'splain...later."

He humored her without argument. Her dizziness made her clumsy, so it took several minutes for him to dress her in the extra layers. When the task was complete, he helped lower her body onto the blanket pallet, and then he cradled the back of her head as she lay on a pillow that she could have sworn hadn't been there before. At once, her body melded with the soft linens, and she couldn't tell herself apart from the bedding.

Kian propped himself up on one elbow beside her, his mouth sliding into a crooked grin. "My lady of the temple, you're painfully adorable when you're drunk."

The canvas roof spun, and Cerise had to shut her eyes to make it stop. Once closed, her eyelids didn't want to reopen. She sank deeper and deeper into a basin of warmth. Soon, her senses went blank and there was nothing.

She didn't know how much time passed before her awareness returned. When she became conscious again, she found herself sitting cross-legged at the foot of her sleeping body, much like she had done the previous evening. She was sober now, and mortified to see how ridiculous she looked passed out with one pant leg covering her sandal, both shirts twisted high around her torso. Kian didn't seem to mind. Still grinning, he moved his gaze over her face with a tenderness she had come to cherish more than her next breath.

Kian skimmed a delicate finger along her lower lip, and then his hand curled into a smoky shadow that quickly claimed the rest of him. The same dark portal appeared behind him, and in a blink, he stood on the other side of it, colorless, naked, fully formed, and peering into the tent as if looking for her. She knew she was invisible to him when his eyes passed twice over her dreaming form. He couldn't see her until she stepped through the portal and joined him. Then, in amazement, he volleyed his gaze back and forth between her two forms until the portal closed.

"I can't believe it," he murmured in awe. "There are two of you."

"I think there's only one of me," she said. "I'm just divided. What you see in the tent is my mortal form. Until I come back to it, my body is like a glove without a hand. But this part of me," she added, palming her chest, "seems to be my spirit."

Kian skimmed a thumb along the outer curve of her neck and raised chills on her skin. "Then how are you solid?"

"Everyone here is solid," she pointed out. "And all of them except for you have been dead for a long time, so they're spirits."

"That's true," Kian said. "Still, I've never seen anyone divide themselves in half, except once at an extremely unfortunate joust that I wish I hadn't attended. You've accomplished something impressive, my lady of the temple."

"Not as impressive as when you turn to shadow," she said. "That's an incredible thing to watch."

"You still win." He nodded at her layers. "You get to keep your clothes."

"Oh, I almost forgot. That's why I wore these." She pulled off the extra shirt and pants and offered them to him. "To make the night a little more comfortable for you."

Kian held the clothes against his chest with the reverence of a child hugging a treasured blanket. "They're still warm!" While putting on the clothes, he gathered the shirt to his nose and then smiled. "It smells like you."

"After a day in the saddle?" she asked with a grin. "Sorry."

"Don't be silly," he told her. "I like everything about you. It's a privilege to know the scent of your body…and the taste of it." His eyes darkened with an emotion she couldn't quite place. "It's a privilege I don't intend to share with anyone else."

The intensity in his lingering gaze made her blush. Her feelings were still tangled up. The goddess had found her worthy, but Father Padron's words about her future rang in her head. And then there was the matter of the Sight. She still wanted it—wanted it badly.

Kian gently ran his hands down her arms, the heat from his palms warming her skin through the thin fabric. He took her hand in both of his and murmured, "I'm yours to command, my lady."

Her pulse pounded in her ears. She caught herself angling her face toward his, parting her lips in anticipation of his touch. Surely, the goddess wouldn't fault her a kiss. She'd proven as much by earning the sunset runes. So she told him, "Kiss me."

And he did.

Their lips met, and her world exploded. The sensations rushed over her, each one headier than the last: the taste of him; the heat of his body pressed tightly against her; the sweeping, seductive motion of his tongue. She opened wider for him, taking him in, exploring his mouth until the need to breathe forced her to break the kiss.

Kian didn't miss a beat. His lips appeared at her ear, the tickle of his warm breath sending a shiver over her as he whispered, "You amaze me. Have I ever told you that?"

She couldn't answer him. She was too dizzy with the pleasure he created as he gently took her earlobe between his teeth and alternated between nibbling her tender flesh and suckling it.

"What you did today at the shrine," he murmured. "It took my breath away. You have a light inside you." He nuzzled the side of her neck. "And in the moments when you let yourself shine…" He paused to lick a sensitive patch of skin, sending her blood rushing to the juncture of her thighs. "You're so radiant I can hardly bear it. You didn't perform a miracle. You *are* the miracle."

She buried her hands in his hair and drew him closer, kissing him with a ferocity she didn't know she had within her. But his words reminded her that they still had much to do, more miracles to perform. So she pulled away from him, even though every part of her body screamed in resistance.

He didn't complain, but his face was at war with the same disappointment and desire that she felt in her bones.

For him, she told herself. *This is for him.*

She cleared her throat and used her fingers to smooth down his tousled hair. Then she looked around at the dark stone walls, trying to find something more innocent to talk about than their previous conversation.

"This place," she finally said. "I think Daerick's theory was right. Coming here must be a gift from the goddess."

Kian huffed a dry laugh. "More a gift to me than to you, I'm afraid. I hate that you were ever exposed to this hell, but if I'm honest, your company is the only thing that makes it bearable." He interlaced their fingers and held up their joined hands for show. "I still don't understand how you can be here, but I'm grateful."

"I don't understand it, either," she admitted. And she was grateful for her time alone with him, too, even though it tested her resolve.

"Come, my lady. Let me show you around." Kian offered a gentlemanly elbow. "The night is long, and there are more comfortable places to spend it than in this tunnel."

Cerise accepted his elbow, and they strolled through the dim corridors, filling the quiet with small talk until they reached the dilapidated courtyard and its four arched doorways. She chose a bench facing the empty fountain and sat down gradually, testing her weight. When the ancient marble didn't crack, she patted the spot beside her. Kian sat down and wrapped an arm around her as she leaned into his warmth to stave off a shiver. She almost preferred the dark stone corridors to this. The crumbling courtyard was like a cold, black mirror to civilization, reminding her with every glance of how far removed she was from anything civil.

"What do you think this place used to be?" she asked. "The

courtyard, I mean. It's the only part of the labyrinth that looks real, like it was something that actually existed."

"I asked myself the same question when I first came here," he told her. "It took me moons to figure it out, but I eventually found a sketch in an old record book that belonged to the distant grandfather of the palace groundskeeper." He indicated the fountain and the marble benches surrounding it. "A thousand years ago, this exact courtyard stood at the heart of the shrubbery maze in the east garden."

"The shrubbery maze." She glanced at the four arched doorways, recalling how many hours she had lost trying to explore their twisted passages. "Does that mean the stone labyrinth is meant to represent the garden maze?"

"I can't say for certain," Kian said. "But it would seem that way."

Cerise tilted her head and studied the fountain, looking for details that might set it apart from any other lawn ornament in the mortal realm. As far as she could tell, there was nothing special about it. The marble benches seemed equally ordinary. The timing, on the other hand, was undeniably significant. "A thousand years ago. That was when the Great Betrayal happened."

"Which I'm sure is no coincidence," Kian said. "I think something sinister happened in this courtyard—something so offensive to your goddess that she recreated the scene here as a reminder to those she condemned to suffer." He released a bitter huff. "A pity she didn't think to give us infinite memory so we would know the reason for our punishment."

Cerise tried to imagine what kind of offense could have taken place in a courtyard at the heart of a garden maze. A forbidden rendezvous, perhaps. Though the courtyard had changed over time, it was still being used for secret meetings. That was where she had stumbled upon Delora and her lover.

"I can only think of one possibility," Cerise said. "No one knows what role the Mortara dynasty played in the betrayal. I always assumed it was house Mortara that brought the other noble houses together. If I'm right, maybe this courtyard was where it happened." She swept a hand toward the scattered benches. "Maybe this is the place where the four noble houses met and agreed to try to murder the goddess. I can't imagine anything more sinister than that."

Kian made a throaty noise of agreement, but his thoughts seemed to have shifted. "I don't want to talk about your goddess anymore," he said quietly.

She matched his smile. "She's your goddess, too."

"As you continue to remind me."

"Because you continue to forget. But I won't hold it against you."

"Then I'll hold you against me," he told her, and he embraced her in his warm, powerful arms. "Not even the blasted Order could object to that."

Cerise nestled against him, resting her cheek against the solid plane of his chest. She couldn't imagine such an objection, either. And she would take refuge in a chaste embrace for now.

Because soon, it would be her Claiming Day.

19

As Nero had warned them, the trail to the southwest grew rougher and more difficult to follow the next day. At times, the path disappeared completely, and the group was forced to leave behind the supply wagon and then dismount the horses and cajole them through sections of dried bramble and brush that were littered with razor-sharp petrified log fragments. But though the hours were slow and tedious, the caravan completed the first day without injury, and then Cerise cast the runes again shortly before twilight.

The runes sent the caravan southwest for another two days. Each night, the group camped under Father Padron's protection, and Cerise continued to drink arrowroot syrup with her dinner so she could fall asleep by sunset. Fortunately, General Petros had plenty of syrup to share, and no one in the group questioned her consumption of it. As strenuous as the journey had become, they all understood the value of a good night's sleep.

But in truth, each night at sunset, Cerise wanted only to follow Kian into the Mortara underworld, where they sought out the most quiet, secluded chambers and passed the hours sharing stories and body heat and kisses that were more or less chaste. Every moment she shared with him was as precious to her as the sunrise that returned them to the tent in the morning. She even came to prefer dusk over dawn. During the day, she and Kian had to share their time with others, but the nights belonged only to them. The nights were her haven, her sanctuary.

It was then that she fell completely in love.

And the emotion really did feel like falling. The exhilaration that lifted her ribs reminded her of the rare, secret opportunities for sledding at the Solon temple. When enough snow had fallen to cover the ground, she had borrowed a flat baking sheet from the kitchen and snuck outside to the hill behind the courtyard. While the others had slept, she'd skidded down the hill at breakneck speeds. In addition to it being a most unladylike thing to do, there had always been a moment when the frosty wind had watered her eyes and whipped her hair and she feared she had gone too fast. But each time she had been tempted to dig in her heels and stop, the thrill of flying had outweighed her fear of the fall, and she held on until the very end.

She held on like that now.

That didn't mean she had deluded herself into thinking her time with Kian could last forever. He was still a king in need of a legitimate heir, and she was still a second-born given in service to the temple. But the way she saw it, she had two choices: she could dig in her heels and protect her heart, or she could dive headlong into love. To her, the choice was clear. There was no thrill in falling slowly. Pain was a natural part of life, so she reminded herself not to fear it. She loved boldly, and by the fourth sunrise, she could honestly say that her heart—the part Blue hadn't claimed—belonged to the king.

She would face the consequences later.

When the dawn of her Claiming Day finally arrived, she awoke in the tent a few moments ahead of Kian. She opened her eyes and held her breath, half afraid of what she would discover. This was the day she had been waiting for…and dreading for most of her life—the day she would learn who and what she was destined to become. But as she sat up in the darkness, she didn't know what outcome she wanted.

A cloud of shadow drifted through the tent flaps and quickly took form into the king's lean, muscled body. At once, he turned to face her, and they sat on the floor, their gazes locked.

"Well?" he whispered. "Do you feel any differently?"

Cerise probed her chest as though receiving the Sight might have physically altered her. She shook her head. She didn't notice any new sensations.

Kian went thoughtful for a moment. "Let's try a test," he whispered. "I'm going to do something. I've already decided what it is, and I'm picturing my actions right now. See if you can predict my path."

Though he couldn't have possibly known it, his suggestion triggered a pang of fear that she recognized all too well. It was the result of having tried—and failed—that same basic test hundreds of times at the temple. But she nodded and began the process. The steps were so ingrained that she performed them without conscious thought: closing her eyes, clearing her mind, and focusing on the warmth and compassion she felt for the king. After she had settled into a state of relaxation, she silently asked the goddess to show her Kian's path.

One moment passed, and then another. She could hear a faint bird call echoing in the distance. She could feel Blue's body heat from where he slept beside her. But the darkness behind her eyelids remained blank.

She inhaled and exhaled slowly. Then she tried again to coax the answer from her mind's eye. *What will the king do? Show me his path.*

Nothing. Not even a flicker of divination passed through her.

She opened her eyes just in time to watch Kian kiss his fingertip and then press that same finger to the bridge of her nose.

"Did you predict that?" he asked.

The familiar sting of failure pricked behind her ribs, but this time, it was multiplied by a thousand. She was giftless. The goddess had deemed her worthy of the sunset runes but not faithful enough to bless her with the Sight.

Maybe the Order had been right after all. Maybe her passion for Kian, even though she hadn't fully acted on it, had distracted her enough to offend the goddess.

Would she be able to break the curses now?

"Do you See anything?" Kian whispered. "Anything at all?"

Cerise peered around the dark tent, looking for a vision or a sign—some hint of a change in her perception that might mean her inner eye had opened. But she saw only the shadowy outlines of her bedding and of Blue resting his head on her blanket pallet.

"No," she told him. Now as much as ever, she was ordinary.

She hadn't received the Sight.

Wait.

She hadn't received the Sight.

There was nothing holding them back anymore.

One good thing could come from her failure.

Tossing a blanket onto his lap, she told him, "Put this on," and then she grasped his hand and towed him out of the tent. She had learned the hard way that noise traveled through canvas walls, and she had no intention of giving anyone a show.

In the dim purple of dawn, she found the other tents tightly closed, but the group would awake soon and begin the morning routine of restarting the fire, preparing breakfast, feeding the horses, and packing up the camp for the day's travel. Wherever she took Kian, they couldn't go far without their absence being noticed.

"Where are we going?" he whispered, doing his best to wrap the blanket around his waist with one hand.

She shushed him and held out a palm to Blue in a command to stay. Blue hesitated briefly, tilting his enormous head at the king as if assessing his intentions, and then he gave a great yawn and padded back into the tent.

Without wasting another second, she towed Kian farther away from camp. She continued to the east, taking him back the way the caravan had come the day before, until they reached an enormous boulder that stood at the head of the trail. She remembered seeing the boulder when she'd passed it on her horse. At least ten feet tall and half as wide, it should block their noise as long as they were careful.

"What are we doing here?" he whispered.

"Gaining distance," she told him.

He opened his mouth to speak but closed it again as she pulled him into her arms. He seemed to get the message then. His blanket fell to the ground. Less than one heartbeat later, she found herself pressed between two walls: one of smooth, solid stone, and the other of hard, naked flesh. With his mouth so close to hers and his warm breath stirring against her lips, all thoughts of failure vanished from her mind. The way he looked at her now—as though she were the only star in a black and endless sky—made her feel anything but ordinary.

"There's not much time," she whispered, running her hands down his back. "Do you want to make the most of it with me?"

A deep rumble sounded from within his chest, and then his hands were in her hair and his mouth at her ear, where he whispered her name with an urgency that brought every soft part of her body to life. He trailed one hand down her arm to her breast and then he palmed it gently, using his thumb to tease her nipple until she groaned and arched against him.

Her reaction seemed to please him. He nuzzled her ear and murmured, "Do you want more, my lady of the temple?"

"Yes," she breathed.

"What shall I do next?"

"Kiss me," she told him.

And so he did. He tipped up her chin and moved his mouth to hers, slow and sweet at first. The brush of his lips was indescribably soft, one tender sweep and then another. He skimmed the tip of his tongue along her upper lip, and when she opened to him, he explored her with shallow licks that tempted her to taste him in return. Their tongues danced and curled. With each warm, wet stroke, she felt her blood heating and rushing through her veins. They went on like this until their mouths moved in desperation and their breaths came in stolen gasps.

Breaking for air, Kian moved his lips to her earlobe and then kissed a trail down the side of her neck. When he reached the middle of her shoulder, he bit down hard, and a loud groan of pleasure arose from her throat. With a growl of his own, he suckled the spot, alternately ravaging it with the scrape of his teeth until she writhed in his arms. He drove her halfway to insanity with his mouth, and when he pulled back, she was dizzy and panting.

"More?" he asked, his eyelids heavy.

She licked her swollen lips and nodded. Whatever he was offering, she wanted it.

Any sliver of space between them was eliminated when he kissed her again. His hands traveled over her curves while he crushed her between his body and the wall of stone. Somehow, the nearness wasn't enough. She tightened her arms around his broad shoulders in a compulsion to feel more of his weight, more of his skin. He seemed to share the same need, because he grasped one of her legs and hooked it around his hip, his fingertips biting into her thigh, his heart thundering against her chest. She could sense his control slipping, and the mystery of what would happen next, of what he would do to her, sent a jolt of anticipation down her spine.

This time, he didn't have to ask what she wanted. She told him, "More," in a voice she barely recognized as her own. She wanted more of the hot rush through her veins, more of his touch and his scent.

She wanted more of *him*.

He released her thigh and grasped the hem of her blouse, which he then lifted over her head with a roughness that thrilled her. After tossing aside her shirt, he hooked his thumbs around the waistband of her linen pants and pushed them to the ground in one swift motion. She kicked them free. Both of them fully naked, he took a step back and admired her. Though his attention made her blush, she fought against her fear and resisted the urge to hide herself. Kian cradled her waist between his hands and gazed at her reverently, taking in the dip of her navel and the outside swell of her thighs. The rising sun cast a glow over his face, highlighting the emotion and the desire etched there as he gazed at her with a silent question.

"More," she commanded again and pulled him back to her with a kiss.

The hair on his body tickled her exposed flesh, and for the first time, she let her hands explore him, *fully* explore him, starting with the contours of his chest and his shoulders, moving lower to trace his rounded backside, and finally trailing a fingertip along the ebony hair that encircled his navel. But she stopped there. She didn't know what to do next, how to touch him. A sudden flush of shyness crept into her cheeks.

Kian seemed to understand. He guided her palm lower and then wrapped her fingers around his flesh. The feel of him was different than she had expected. He was rigid, and yet his skin was softer and more delicate than the rest of him. She loosened her grip, afraid she might hurt him, but he tightened his fingers around hers and then moved her hand slowly up and down. He removed his hand, and she stroked him on her own, letting the sound of his breathing guide her movements. She caressed him until she could hear nothing over the choppy pull of air into his lungs, and then he abruptly stilled her hand and looked to her with the same question in his eyes.

"Yes," she told him. "More."

Now it was his turn to explore her body. She held still, uncertain of what to do as he skimmed one hand down the length of her abdomen and to the juncture of her thighs. Before she could prepare herself for what might happen next, he cupped her in his palm and pulled ever so slightly upward with a firm but gentle motion, and there was no standing still after that. She arched against his palm as he went on massaging a delicious tension into her body. Just when she thought the act could feel no better, he replaced his palm with his fingers, and she tipped back her head, delirious with the sensations of his fingertips stroking and circling and dipping inside her.

She made embarrassing noises—whimpers and whines and guttural moans—but she couldn't bring herself to care about anything except his touch. She didn't know how he did it, how he had mastered her body as though it belonged to him. The longer it went on, the weaker her knees became.

"I can't..." She panted, her legs wobbling.

Kian grasped her by the bottom. "Wrap your legs around me."

She did as he asked and locked her ankles behind his back.

"Are you sure you want this?" He licked his lips and swallowed hard, looking to her with a hunger bordering on desperation. "If not, tell me now."

"I'm more than sure," she whispered. "I want you. All of you."

He settled himself between her thighs, and she felt the smooth tip of him pressing against the slick flesh where his fingers had just been. He lingered there at her entrance, barely nudging inside her, teasing her until she felt swollen and throbbing with need.

"This might hurt," he warned her.

"Oh, stars, I don't care," she breathed. Any discomfort she might feel couldn't possibly be worse than the ache of longing between her thighs. She gripped Kian's shoulders and begged him with her gaze, and then, with a gentle upward motion, he made them one.

She gasped, more at the sudden sensation of fullness than from the brief stab of pain. He stayed still for a long moment, motionless except for his breathing. He let her body adjust to him while he held her gaze, waiting as patiently as ever. When she gave him a nod, he tipped their foreheads together and began to rock gently in and out of her. His rhythm was slow and steady, and even though the motion hurt at times, the pain was mingled with an indescribable pleasure, a sensation that bloomed and strengthened each time he buried himself all the way inside her.

"Are you all right?" he asked.

"Don't stop," she told him.

The wildness in his eyes told her he had no intention of stopping. There was something primal between them now. She felt it in the way she dug her heels into his backside, urging him ever closer. A heavy tension was building inside her, heightening to a near painful intensity. Kian drove her higher with each slow, deliberate stroke. Just when she thought she couldn't bear it another second, he groaned and thrust into her one last time, deeper and harder than before. The pressure between her thighs broke into the sweetest release she had ever known—a set of involuntary tremors, like a convulsion from deep within her core.

She closed her eyes and tilted her face to the heavens, her lips parted in a strangled cry. Her body clenched like a fist. She couldn't move or breathe or think beyond the continuous waves of pleasure washing over her, each one more exquisite than the last. The sensations were so intense that she was almost relieved when the quaking ceased and she drifted back down to herself.

She unlocked her ankles and placed her bare feet on the ground, her legs still weak and trembling. She opened her eyes and peered at Kian to find him watching her with a tired grin, a sheen of sweat glistening on his brow. There was an unmistakable look of satisfaction on his face, and she glowed with pride to know she had put it there. But before she could return his smile, several things happened at once.

A metallic tang of copper coated her tongue. An electric charge lifted the tiny hairs at the nape of her neck. A surge of energy flowed through her from the soles of her feet to the crown of her head, and then a loud *crack* sounded from the tremendous rock behind her.

Kian pulled her out of the way, and she whirled around just in time to watch the stone slab split apart and fall to the ground with a *thud* that shook the earth beneath her feet. She scurried backward and noticed a stream of water bubbling up from the ground where the boulder had just stood.

The water streamed over the cracked, arid dirt, and as Cerise crept closer to the spring, she saw that several green sprouts had already pushed their way up from the soil. She stared in awe as life bloomed in front of her. Two heartbeats later, the sprouts had grown tiny lavender blossoms—exactly like the flower she had offered to the Blighted Shrine.

She felt the sensation of being watched and turned to meet Kian's wide-eyed gaze. The two of them said nothing at first. Then Kian began, "Was that…" He trailed off, shaking his head as though he didn't believe what his eyes had shown him. "Was that *you*?"

"Me?" Cerise touched her chest and remembered she was naked. She darted to her pile of discarded clothes and gathered them up before the water reached them. "How could that have been me?"

While she dressed, Kian retrieved his blanket and wrapped it around his waist. "I don't know, but right before the rock split, I swear I saw you light up."

"Light up?" she asked. "What do you mean?"

"I mean it looked like there was a second sun rising under your skin. At first I thought I imagined it. But then…" He gestured at the split boulder. "But then *that*. It can't be a coincidence."

Cerise absently straightened her blouse while she tried to remember exactly what had happened. She recalled feeling a great surge of pleasure, and then afterward she had tasted copper. "Magic," she realized. "There was magic here. I tasted it in the air. I felt it, too. It was electric. It came up out of the ground and moved through my body."

Kian raised his eyebrows as if prompting her to make a connection.

"Maybe it was Nero," Cerise guessed. "He opens up a spring at every camp."

Kian spread his arms wide. "Do you see our guide here? Because I don't. I think he's still in his tent, like everyone else."

"Maybe he opened the spring from a distance," Cerise said, but even as the words left her lips, she knew that Nero wasn't powerful enough to cast his energy remotely like Father Padron could.

Kian seemed to share her thoughts. "It wasn't Nero, and I don't think it was Father Padron." He thumbed at himself. "And it certainly wasn't me. It's not *my* Claiming Day."

Cerise blinked at him. "Are you implying that instead of the Sight, the goddess gifted me with"—she lowered her voice to a whisper—"magic?"

"You glowed," Kian reminded her, and then an impish grin played on his lips. "And not just because of my superior lovemaking skills."

She didn't return his smile, because unlike Kian, she knew the danger of what he had suggested. Even if he was right and the magic had come from her, for a woman to possess the same gift as priests was unheard of. The Order would consider it sorcery.

Oh, goddess, the Order. Was this why they had tried so hard to keep her a maiden? Not because the act of love was forbidden by scrolls but because of what it might awaken? Had this happened to any other ladies of the temple? She had no way of knowing. There were no oracles around to ask, and even if there were, she didn't know if she could trust any of them with the truth.

One thing was certain: she would never be safe again.

"It's all right," Kian said. He drew her into his embrace, and she nestled her cheek in the hollow where his shoulder met his chest. His touch held an unspoken promise of protection...for as long as his dominion over the priests would last. "There's only one way to know for certain if the magic came from you," he murmured into her hair. "Can you do it again?"

She peered blankly up at him. She didn't know how—or if—she had done it in the first place. "Not here. Not now. Someone will come looking for us."

"Very well," he told her. "Until we know more, we should probably keep this between the two of us."

"And Daerick," she said. "I trust him."

"And Daerick," he agreed. "But if anyone else asks what happened here, we'll tell them you came to the rock to pray for protection, and the goddess gave you a sign."

"A miracle," Cerise muttered.

"No one would question it—not after what they witnessed at the shrine."

She dipped her chin in agreement, but she hoped no one would notice the spring or the lavender blossoms. She didn't want to lie. She wasn't very good at it.

Kian cupped her cheek and lifted her gaze to his. "I won't let any harm come to you. Not as long as I'm alive. I swear it."

"I believe you," she told him.

"Then try not to worry," he said. "At least not in this moment." He brushed a thumb over her skin. "Give this moment to me. One last time before we go back to the others, let the world exist for only the two of us."

He didn't need to say another word. She was already rising onto her toes and circling her arms around his neck. She gave Kian what he wanted—a kiss with her whole heart behind it. She might have little understanding of the ways of the world, but if there was one thing she knew how to do, it was love him.

20

Cerise didn't have to worry about anyone questioning where she and Kian had been. When they returned to camp, each tent was still tightly closed, their occupants too exhausted to wake with the dawn. Not even Blue padded outside to meet her.

"It's still early," Kian whispered, glancing at the sun, which was barely aglow behind the mountain range. "Let them sleep."

They divided the morning tasks between them, and while Kian dressed, stoked a fire, and set a kettle to boil, Cerise fed the horses. She had just dispensed the last of the day's feed when Kian pressed a warm mug of tea into her palm. But it wasn't her usual blend. The liquid was several shades too dark, and it smelled less fragrant and more earthy than she liked.

"What is this?" she asked.

"It's medicinal," he told her.

Cerise sniffed at the tea. She didn't care for the scent, but she took a sip anyway. A horrible flavor crossed her tongue, a taste more bitter than unripe berries.

"Oh, that's awful," she said, making a face.

"Yes, it is utterly vile," Kian agreed. "But trust me, you need this. I'm afraid you have to finish all of it."

She didn't want to drink any more of his terrible tea, but she had tasted far worse. So she tipped back the mug and forced down every last gulp.

She shivered in revulsion. "What *was* that?"

"Crone's weed," he said.

"And why did I have to drink it?"

"Because, my lady of the temple," he began, and then he leaned down, lowering his voice to a whisper, "after what we did this morning, we don't want my seed taking root in your fertile ground, do we?"

"Oh," she said. She hadn't thought of that. But as she glanced into her empty mug, she wondered if she agreed with him. These were unusual times — desperate times. Kian was the last of his dynasty. Only a few moons remained to break the noble curses, and if they failed, he would disappear forever into the shadows and leave no one to control the priests. But if she could give him a firstborn, even an illegitimate one, his child would not only ensure the survival of the Mortara bloodline but also prevent the Order from taking the throne.

She peered up at him and asked, "Or do we?"

Kian blinked once, twice. His eyebrows shot up, and he drew back as though she had physically slapped him. "No," he answered in a cold, hard tone that felt like a slap in return. "We certainly do not."

"Just hear me out."

"I don't need to."

"Please listen," she said, lowering her voice to a whisper so as not to wake the others. "I know it's not ideal…"

"Not ideal?" he hissed. "Have you lost your mind?"

"I understand that a child should be born out of love," she said, "not brought into the world to serve a purpose. But the world needs protection from the Order. Right now, that protection is you. What if we can't break the curse? You've seen what the priests do when your back is turned. Now imagine them without a master. Imagine them *as* the master. You can't let that happen. Our child could be a fail-safe."

"You talk as if we've already lost," Kian said. "Why are you giving up so soon? We have the sunset runes. The goddess obviously favors you. We don't need a fail-safe."

"The runes will only lead us to the blade," she reminded him. "Nero said that to win it, I have to face a test I know nothing about. And the goddess's favor changes every day. Her wrathful eye sees as clearly as her merciful one."

"You asked me to have faith in you," Kian said. "And I did. Now it's your turn to have faith in yourself. There will be no fail-safe. Either we break this curse, or it ends with me. I won't keep passing it on like the plague that it is."

"But that's not fair," she whispered. "The threat of the Order is bigger than a plague. It's bigger than you or me or any of the noble firstborns. You have to think of others. It would be selfish to let your bloodline die out on purpose."

Kian went unnaturally still. His gaze remained locked onto hers, unblinking as his stare quickly transformed from fire and fury into the coldest, blackest of ice. Cerise felt a dropping sensation. She'd pushed him too far.

"How dare you say that to me?" he breathed.

"I didn't mean it like—"

"How *dare* you," he cut in, his eyes narrowing to slits, "tell me to think of others when you've seen where I go at night. You've witnessed that hell. You've watched what your goddess has done to the souls trapped in her purgatory. And after all the nights that I've spent crouched in the corners of that cold labyrinth, you think I haven't considered anyone but myself?"

Anger flashed in his eyes, mingled with a hurt and betrayal that made her long to take back her careless words.

"I assure you that I have thought of others," he said. "I wouldn't send my worst enemy to live in the shadows. So if you truly believe that I would condemn my own child to spend an eternity there, then you don't know me at all. In this case, my lady, *you're* the selfish one."

Cerise dropped her gaze while her cheeks burned with shame. She fidgeted with her mug, twisting it in her grasp and wishing she could disappear inside it. She hated that she had hurt him. And she hated even more the way he looked at her now, as though she were a dust storm on the horizon instead of the only star in his sky. She wanted more than anything to repair what she had damaged so they could go back to loving each other, but she didn't know how.

She started with an apology. "I'm sorry."

"Don't tell me you're sorry," he snapped. "Tell me you understand."

"I understand," she repeated. "I really do. I should have thought it through. I just wanted to consider all the options."

"Then let's not speak of this again."

She snuck a peek at him, hoping he would extend his arms to her in forgiveness. But he didn't. Instead, he turned on his heel and strode to their tent to begin dismantling it. While he pulled the first wooden stake from the ground, she stood alone in front of the fire and wondered how it was possible that only moments earlier, they had been as close as two people could be. Now an invisible barrier divided them, and she didn't know how Kian could stand it. To her, the rift felt like a living thing, a parasite that squirmed beneath her skin and made her want to crawl out of her own body.

She did her best to busy herself while Kian burned off his anger. Gradually, the camp came to life. Blue awoke first, followed by General Petros and Nero, then Daerick and Father Padron. Cerise kept her gaze turned down as she handed each man an oatcake and a mug of tea. There was a hot pressure building behind her eyes, and even with Blue nuzzling her in comfort, she didn't know how long she could hold back her tears.

Then Father Padron called her name, and she reflexively glanced at him. He must have noticed the moisture welling in her eyes, because his gaze widened in concern. Oddly, it was the look of sympathy from him that broke the floodgate holding back her tears, and before she knew it, she was openly sobbing.

"Oh, my child," Father Padron said. He strode to her and gripped her upper arms. "You didn't receive the Sight, did you?"

She had already forgotten it was her Claiming Day, but she let him assume that her tears were of disappointment.

"I'm sorry, Cerise," Father Padron told her, and to his credit, he sounded sincere. He didn't gloat or lecture or make any reference to his warning about her love for the king and what it might cost her. At least not yet. The chiding would doubtlessly come later. For now, he only shook his head. "I was so certain," he said, more to himself than to anyone else. "I sensed something in you... I still do. And I'm so rarely wrong."

General Petros cleared his throat. "I'm sorry, my girl."

"So am I," Daerick added. "But you don't have to be an oracle to change the world. You told me that once."

She nodded and dabbed her face with her shirtsleeve. She had said that.

The only members of the group who didn't offer their condolences were Kian and Nero, who each stood with their arms folded, their heads tilted at a nearly identical angle as they studied her with matching expressions that were impossible to read.

"Yes, well," Kian began, and then he turned to Nero and changed the subject. "We should discuss our provisions before we break down the camp any further. It might be a good idea to take the day to hunt and forage. We lost a lot of supplies when we left behind the wagon. I know the Petros Blade will move again at the next full moon, but we won't find it if we starve to death first."

"I was thinking the same thing," Nero said. "It's best to hunt in the hour before dawn, when the deer are active. But we should be able to track one or two." He nodded at Blue. "If we take the ugly hound with us."

Blue whined. Cerise rubbed behind his ears to assure him that he was the most beautiful pup in her world. She didn't trust herself to speak, so she nodded to give her permission. Blue needed to hunt anyway.

"We can smoke the meat over the fire," Nero went on. "It will take all night, but by tomorrow morning, we could have enough jerky to last us a week."

"Then it's decided," Kian announced. "We'll stay here for one more night. Nero and the general will lead the hunt. Blue will go with them. Father Padron, I want you to ride along as well to protect the kill. We can't have the scent of fresh blood drawing any unwanted attention from predators."

Father Padron pursed his lips in displeasure, but he bowed his head. "As His Majesty commands."

"As for the rest of us," Kian said, "we'll reassemble the tents and then go foraging for sand melon and whatever else we can find." He clapped once. "Let's get to it."

As half of the group prepared for a hunt, no one questioned the king's motives. But Cerise knew what he was really doing—sending them away so she could talk with Daerick in private about what had happened at the boulder. In the wake of her fight with Kian, she had nearly forgotten about that, too.

As she watched Blue lead the hunting party to the west, she almost wished she could go with them. She wasn't in the mood for talking, not even to Daerick, who now sat cross-legged on the other side of the fire and sipped his tea, patiently waiting for someone to inform him of why the group had been divided. As brilliant as Daerick was, he had to know there was a reason Kian had told him to stay behind.

"Well?" Daerick asked Kian.

Instead of answering him, Kian held up an index finger and then slowly made his way around the campfire to where Cerise stood. He stopped in front of her, leaving an arm's length of distance between them.

"Are you really upset about your Claiming Day?" He took a step forward and used his thumb to brush a tear from her cheek. "Or is this because we argued?"

Cerise stared into the distance and folded her arms tightly across her chest. The writhing inside her had died. Now she felt like her ribs might spring open, and it was all she could do to hold her body together.

"Ah, I see." Kian released a sigh. "We had a lovers' quarrel, Cerise. The first of many, I'm sure. Conflict is an inevitable part of life. There's no avoiding it." He tried to tilt her chin to face him. "Will you look at me?"

She jerked free of his grasp.

"Enough of this," he said, his temper flaring. "We don't have time for games. The others won't stay gone forever, and we have bigger problems than a squabble. You have to talk to me so we can move on. Tell me what you're thinking."

Even if she wanted to tell him, she couldn't put her thoughts into words...at least not words that she was willing to say out loud. She didn't want to admit how she truly felt: weak and pathetic, half mad with the fear of losing him. But then an odd sensation came over her, a disconnect between her body and mind, as though she were a puppet with an invisible hand inside her chest. Before she knew what was happening, she whispered, "I'm scared that you'll never see me the same way again. That I let you down so badly this might be the beginning of the end for us."

Oh, goddess, she shouldn't have said any of that!

She didn't know what had come over her, but she clapped a hand over her mouth to stop any more words from slipping out. Silence filled the air, interrupted only by the occasional crackle from the fire. She glanced at Kian to find his face frozen in shock.

"What?" he breathed. "How could you think that?"

She shook her head. She didn't trust herself to speak.

"How?" he repeated, pulling her hand away from her mouth. "Tell me how you could think that."

She swallowed hard. "It was the way you looked at me. And then it was the way you wouldn't look at me. I thought…"

"That I no longer *want* you?" he asked in a tone that implied she had lost all touch with her senses. He dragged a hand over his face. "Gods be damned. I sometimes forget how sheltered you've been." He pinched the bridge of his nose and drew a deep breath. "Have you never had an argument before?"

"Not really," she said. "Not like this." The bickering with other children at the temple didn't count. Those spats hadn't made her feel anything as terrible as she felt now. She had never had a lovers' quarrel, because until this day, she'd never had a lover.

"Tell me this, my lady of the temple," he said. "Do you care for me?"

"Yes."

"And do I sometimes frustrate you?" he asked. "Be honest."

"You frustrate me often," she admitted. "Nearly every day."

In the background, Daerick sniggered.

"All right, then," Kian said dryly. "Every day. And in those frequent moments when I vex you to no end, do you stop caring for me?"

"No," she told him.

"Then why would you expect me to be any different? I'm capable of feeling more than one emotion at a time. Even when I'm upset with you, I never doubt that my spirit is yours. And there's nothing you could do to change that. Nothing at all." He unsheathed his dagger and offered it to her. "You could take this blade and drive it through the heart of every man in existence—my own included—and I would love you no less."

Daerick interjected, "I beg your pardon? *Every* man?"

"Barring Lord Calatris," Kian added. "He's still a boy."

Cerise bit her lip against a smile.

"Do you want proof?" he asked, nodding at the blade.

"Not today," she told him. "Today, the men are safe."

Kian sheathed his dagger and then took her face roughly between his hands. "Listen to me, and listen well," he whispered.

"Our time is over when I take my last breath. Not one moment before. Do you understand?"

"I understand," she told him, relief flowing through her.

Kian kissed her while Daerick made a retching noise.

"Cheers to true love," Daerick called, lifting his mug of tea in a mock toast. "Now that the two of you have settled your differences, perhaps you can tell me the reason you sent everyone else away while I was forced to stay here and watch you kiss and make up."

"My apologies, Lord Calatris," Kian said to him. "I hope the experience hasn't scarred you beyond repair."

"Yes, well, you should be sorry." Daerick pointed back and forth between them. "That was painfully awkward for me, you know."

Cerise hadn't enjoyed it, either. "I hope you didn't overhear too much."

"Only enough to make me wish this were ale," he said into his mug. "Now will you tell me why I'm here?"

Kian led Cerise back to the fire, and the two of them settled cross-legged on the ground beside Daerick, close enough that they could speak in low voices. Even with Father Padron gone, sound carried on the wind.

"Our lady's Claiming Day," Kian began, squeezing Cerise's hand. "It was more eventful than she led you to believe."

"Oh, really?" Daerick asked. "How so?"

"While the rest of you were sleeping, we took a walk to the east," Kian said. "So we could...watch the sunrise."

"So you could watch the sunrise?" Daerick repeated flatly.

Kian glared at him. "The story will take longer if you interrupt me."

Daerick made a buttoning motion across his mouth.

"As I said," Kian went on, "we walked to the east until we reached the boulder at the head of the trail. We stopped there to watch the sunrise, and without warning, magic split the boulder in half and a spring opened up in the ground."

"How do you know it was magic and not an act of nature?"

Daerick asked. "Perhaps the boulder was already damaged and you just happened to be there to see it fall."

"Because I tasted energy," Cerise said. "I felt it, too. It came up from the ground and passed through me. And the spring was enchanted somehow. The water had special properties. Everywhere it touched, flowers grew—the same lavender flower that I sacrificed at the Blighted Shrine."

"So the magic simply appeared out of nowhere, without a reason?" Daerick wrinkled his forehead. "Nothing happened to trigger it?"

"Oh...well." Cerise looked to Kian, her shoulders stiffening. "I wouldn't say *nothing* happened. I was...uh...I was..."

"Overcome with the beauty of the sunrise," Kian finished. "The experience moved her."

"Yes," she agreed. "I was moved."

Daerick made a pained face. "Oh, gods, I think I understand."

"And there was a warning of sorts," Kian said. "Right before it all happened, before the boulder cracked in half, her skin began to glow. I thought I imagined it at first, or that it was a trick of the sun. But it wasn't. She lit up from the inside out, as though—"

"—as though her blood were made of fire?" Daerick guessed. He glanced at Cerise and arched an eyebrow. "It would make sense. I thought the term *umbra sangi* was more symbolic than literal, but perhaps I was wrong."

"Is that what you think?" she asked. "That I'm like Nero?"

"Yes and no," Daerick told her. "He's *umbra sangi* but not like you."

"You're right; he's not like me," she said. "His skin doesn't glow. I've seen him cast magic—you have, too—and nothing about him changes. He doesn't light up."

Daerick shrugged. "He might, if he had more flame in his blood. He told us you have more fire than he does. That's not the difference I'm referring to."

"Then what?" Kian asked.

Daerick pointed at Kian. "*You're* what. Cerise can leave her mortal body and follow you into the underworld. Nero can't. To my knowledge, no one else can. Her spiritual connection to you is what sets her apart from Nero."

"So what are you saying?" she asked. "That I'm *not* descended from the goddess?"

"No, I'm saying you are," Daerick told her. "But I believe you're more than that."

Cerise recalled something Nero had told her the morning after the titan hyena attack—that her blood would burn darker than usual. She decided to see if he was right. "Can I borrow your knife?" she asked Kian. When he handed it to her, she nicked the pad of her index finger and then held her fingertip above the edge of the fire. As soon as the first droplet fell onto the red-hot coals, a tiny flame leaped up, blacker than onyx.

"I think Nero was right," she said. "I'm *umbra sangi*."

"Any theories as to what else she might be?" Kian asked Daerick.

"Actually, yes," Daerick said. "And I'd like to test my theory." He licked his lips, hesitating as if to prepare them for a shock. "I'd like to see if Cerise can refuse a direct order from her king."

Cerise blinked. "You think I might be a priest?"

"A priest*ess*," Daerick corrected. "But yes, the thought crossed my mind."

"That's absurd," she said. There had never been one mention of a female priest in all of recorded history. There hadn't even been rumors of it—at least none that she had heard.

"Is it?" Daerick asked. "Is it any more absurd for you to be a priestess than it is for a goddess of darkness and light to craft a world of mortal beings and then fall in love with one of her own creations? And then to take human form so she could impregnate her mortal lover and sire a race of beings with actual fire in their blood?"

"Don't forget the goddess's mood swings," Kian added. "I find that rather absurd as well."

"I have to agree," Daerick said. "The world is full of absurdities, Cerise."

"All right." She couldn't argue with that. "Go ahead and put your theory to the test."

Daerick picked up a pebble and handed it to Kian, whispering something in his ear. Whatever he said made the king scowl.

"Just do it," Daerick prompted.

"Fine." Kian heaved a sigh and then told Cerise, "You might want to scoot back. This won't work if you're too close."

"Is this part of the test?" she asked.

"Not yet," Daerick said. "More like test preparation."

She scooted back and put more distance between them.

Kian tossed the pebble to her. "Now I command you to pick up this rock and throw it as hard as you can at Lord Calatris."

"Wait," Daerick objected. "She's supposed to throw it at you."

Kian's lips twitched in a grin. "Aim for his face. Really give it your all."

Even as Cerise rolled her eyes at their immature banter, she found herself leaning forward and retrieving the pebble. She didn't know what had prompted her to do it. She hadn't meant to. The act was reflexive, like surrendering to a yawn.

"Try to resist," Daerick said, watching her intently.

She set her mind to a different task: tossing the pebble into the fire. She drew back her arm and took aim at the burning pit, but something stopped her from finishing the motion. It was as though she had forgotten how. Then she unconsciously began rotating toward Daerick. She fought with all her strength to turn away from him, but her body wouldn't obey. The experience was unlike the magic Father Padron had used to force her to drink when she had been sick. She was free to breathe and blink and do anything she wanted...except refuse the king's order. Her muscles tensed, and with all her might, she hurled the pebble at Daerick's face.

Daerick ducked aside, and the pebble bounced into the distance. He let out a low whistle while Cerise and Kian stared at each other in disbelief.

She *was* subject to his command.

But as impossible as it seemed, the bond of obedience began to make sense. She recalled the strange feeling that had come over her earlier—a disconnect between her mind and her body, as though she were a puppet with a hand inside her chest.

"That's why I said all of those things," she realized. "When we argued, you ordered me to tell you what I was thinking. I didn't want to, but I couldn't stop myself."

Kian's lips parted, and he sat still and silent while all of the color drained from his face. Then he pushed up from the ground and strode briskly away from the fire.

Cerise followed him and pulled him to a stop. "What is it?"

"Did you…" he whispered, staring blankly ahead. "Did you really want me?" He turned his gaze to hers. "When we were at the boulder…I wasn't compelling you, was I?"

"What?" She placed a hand on his cheek. "Of course not. I'm the one who took you there. I told you what I wanted. You let me set the pace the whole time."

"Are you sure?" he asked, terror in his eyes. "I want your love, not your obedience."

"And you have it," she told him. "I know what compulsion feels like. It feels wrong and unnatural, and those are the last words I would ever use to describe what we did together. I've had enough shame from the Order. I don't need it from you, too. Please don't take the most beautiful moment of my life and turn it into something ugly."

That seemed to reach him. His gaze softened. "Do you swear that I didn't force you?"

"My king," she said, "you were mine to command, remember?"

He sighed in relief and took her hand once again. "And I forevermore will be. Nothing can happen between us unless you command it."

"All right," she said. "If that's what you want."

"It's what I want," he told her.

And with that, they returned to the fire.

Daerick had finished his tea, but he turned his empty mug over and over in his hands. He glanced at Cerise, his gaze somber. "You have to be careful. More than careful…obsessively vigilant. Whatever gifts you have, you need to learn to control them. Because if you slip up and use magic around the wrong person…"

"He's right," Kian said. "No one can find out."

"Especially not Father Padron," she added. A shiver rolled over her when she remembered his warning. *Betrayers will suffer until the end of days.*

Kian squeezed her palm as if sharing her fear. "I can command the priests to leave you untouched while I'm alive, but…"

"I know," she interrupted. She didn't need to hear the rest. They had already argued about the topic. If she failed to break the curse, the Order would be free to erase her like the anomaly that she was.

"Cerise," Daerick said tentatively. "I heard you say that you resemble your mother but not your father." When she nodded, he bit his lip and apologized with his eyes, reminding her of a healer preparing to lance a boil. "How certain are you that he *is* your father?"

As soon as he spoke the words, a dozen tiles clicked together in her mind to form a picture so distinct she couldn't believe it had taken her so long to see it. Her heart resisted, but she knew Daerick might be right. It would explain why Father had panicked when someone from court had taken an interest in Mama. Mama must have had an affair with a palace lord and become pregnant. Father had obviously known, but instead of shaming Mama and casting her out, he had pretended Cerise was his child.

But why would he do that?

Because second-borns are given to the temple.

She stopped breathing. The answer shook her to her core. Father had claimed her so that he could be rid of her at the temple. She had never belonged there. She should have been raised at home with Nina. But in order for that to happen, Mama and Father would have been forced to admit the truth about her parentage, and that would've spawned the kind of gossip that noble families avoided. So instead of living with the reminder of their shame, they had sent her away—out of sight, out of mind—to a place where they would only have to see her on visiting days.

Her throat constricted while tears burned in her eyes.

Every part of her life had been a lie.

"I'm sorry, Cerise," Daerick said, softer than a rose petal. He gave her an apologetic smile. "Happy Claiming Day. If it's any consolation, mine might be worse."

21

Daerick suggested that the three of them go foraging for sand melon in the opposite direction as that of the hunting party so they could help Cerise experiment with her magic. She agreed, but she asked Daerick and Kian to begin the search without her. She would catch up with them after she had a serious and long-overdue conversation with her family.

As soon as Daerick and Kian left camp, Cerise ducked inside her tent and unpacked her heartrending mirror. She sat on the canvas floor and called out through the looking glass until her mother heard her voice and responded.

"Darling," Mama greeted with a smile that quickly fell when she noticed the redness in Cerise's eyes. "What's wrong?"

"I want to talk to Nina," Cerise said. She knew her sister was still there. Nina's visit wouldn't end for another fortnight.

Mama hesitated. "You look upset."

"Give me to Nina."

Father appeared in the mirror, and Cerise caught herself searching his face for any resemblance to her own. She knew she wouldn't find one—she never had—but her heart sank at the reminder that she wasn't his child. "Where are you?" he asked, peering at the canvas walls behind her. "Is everything all right?"

She could tell that his concern was genuine, but that didn't cool her anger. She couldn't help feeling as though she were a stain on the floor and her parents had used the temple as a rug to cover it up. There was only one person in her family she trusted now.

"I want," she gritted out. "To talk. To Nina."

Father heaved a sigh and then stalked through the house until he found Nina. He passed off the mirror, and a black-veiled face filled the frame.

"What's wrong?" Nina asked.

Cerise waited for Father to leave the room. "Are you alone?"

"Yes," Nina said. "Why?"

"Somewhere no one can hear us?"

"Yes. Now tell me what's wrong."

"*Father* isn't really my father," Cerise said. "That's what's wrong."

Nina didn't balk at the words. She didn't laugh in shock or tell Cerise that she was crazy. Instead, she went still and quiet in a way that hinted she had already known the truth.

"You knew," Cerise breathed. Her heart sank another inch. It seemed she couldn't even trust her own sister. "You knew, and you didn't tell me."

Nina ignored the accusation. "What happened to make you think he's not your father?"

"Does it matter?"

"Yes, it matters," Nina said. "Tell me what happened."

Cerise hesitated. She used to believe that she could share anything with her sister. Now, she wasn't so sure. "If I tell you," she began, "you can't tell anyone else, not even Mama or Father or your husband. You have to keep it a secret."

"All right."

"Promise me. Swear it on the goddess."

Nina held a hand to her heart. "May Shiera strike me dead if I'm lying."

Cerise frowned. She didn't like Nina's choice of words, but she told her sister about her visits to the underworld, her compulsion to obey the king, how her magic had manifested, and the possibility that she was descended from Shiera. By the time she'd finished, Nina seemed to have stopped breathing.

"I couldn't have inherited the fire blood from Mama," Cerise said. "It had to come from my father—my real father. I want to know who he is. If I can find him, maybe I can understand more about what I am and why I have these gifts."

"I already know what you are," Nina said.

Cerise perked up. "You do?"

"Yes. You're my sister, and I love you."

"Oh, stop. This is important. Be serious."

Nina blew out a sigh that billowed her veil. "All right. Here's the truth."

Cerise pulled the mirror closer, listening intently.

"I don't know who your father is," Nina said. "But I do know he's dangerous. When Mama was pregnant, I overheard her and Father arguing about him. It was a long time ago, but I remember thinking they were afraid of him—so afraid that they lied to everyone to keep him from finding out about you."

Cerise cocked her head. That was the last thing she had expected. "So they didn't send me away to the temple to cover up Mama's affair?"

"Affair?" Nina repeated. "Bloody crows, no. It was nothing like that. From the way Mama acted, it sounded like the man took advantage of her."

"You mean he…" Cerise couldn't speak the rest. She didn't want it to be true. "A man forced her? And she had to have *me* afterward?"

"No!" Nina flashed a palm across the mirror. "I don't want you to think that."

"But you said—"

"Forget what I said," Nina snapped. "That isn't what I meant."

"Then what did you mean?"

"That maybe she was taken in by his charm or his power," Nina said. "There are so many ways for people to manipulate each other, Cerise. I have no idea what actually happened because Mama wouldn't talk about it. All I know is that the man was dangerous— Mama and Father didn't want to cross him. So Father claimed you as his, and that meant we had to give you to the temple. But it wasn't to get rid of you. We all love you to the stars and back. I hope you know that."

Cerise felt a flush of guilt rise to her cheeks. During her short time at court, she had gotten so used to lies and manipulation that she'd assumed the worst about her parents, ignoring all evidence to the contrary. Mama and Father had never missed a visiting day at the temple. They had never pressured her to try harder when the other oracles had received their gifts and she hadn't. They had never made her feel unwanted or unloved. In spite of her origins, they had cherished her.

"Oh," was all she could say.

"Listen to me," Nina urged. "Whoever your father is, it's important that he doesn't find out about you. That means you can't go looking for him or ask questions that might get back to him. Do you understand?"

"I can be discreet," Cerise said. She knew better than to generate gossip by asking questions of the wrong people. "The palace has an archive room full of records and diaries and travel logs. I can start by making a list of all the powerful men who visited Solon the year before I was born." But she frowned, realizing her father might have lived in Solon and not at the palace at all, in which case there would be no records of him there. "Did Mama say where he was from?"

"You're not listening to me. Just let it go."

"Did she say where he was from?"

"No. She didn't say anything about him."

"Can you find out something?" Cerise asked. "Maybe look

around in Mama's old letters? Or in her journal? Any detail would help."

Nina huffed another sigh. "I'll try. But only if you promise to let it go."

"Look in Father's journal, too," Cerise added.

"I mean it," Nina said. "Promise me."

Cerise crossed her fingers behind her back. She had no intention of sitting idly by and wondering who had fathered her. His identity was too important to ignore. Breaking the curses might depend on it.

"I promise."

. . .

"So your father is dangerous?" Daerick asked with a glance over his shoulder. He held a shovel like a walking stick, his voice breathy from the exertion of wandering around under the midday sun in search of melon brambles. "In what way?"

"I don't know," Cerise said, a little breathless herself. She wanted to hold Kian's hand, but her palm was too sweaty. "All my sister said was that my parents wanted to hide me from him."

"Interesting," Daerick mused. "From what we know, I think we should consider the possibility that your father is a priest who also has fire blood."

"But I've never heard of priests fathering children." She looked to Kian. "Have you?"

Kian shook his head.

"I haven't, either," Daerick admitted. "They do seem disinterested in the whole business. I noticed it when I visited my brother at his temple. The closer he came to receiving his gift, the less often he turned his head when a pretty girl walked by. Now that he has magic, an entire parade of naked courtesans could dance through the temple and he wouldn't care. It's like that part of him has switched off."

"They're all like that," Kian said. "And I would know. There's not a priest in my service who I haven't met at some point or another."

"Well, to be fair," Daerick said, "they're good at keeping secrets from you. If any of your priests reproduced, I doubt they would volunteer that information to you or even to their own brethren."

"Especially not to their own brethren," Kian said. "But you're right. I can't read their minds. Maybe some of them do have desires of the flesh."

"What about you, Cerise?" Daerick asked. "Not to be indelicate, but have you noticed a change in your…well, in your romantic awareness since your gift manifested?"

Reflexively, her eyes darted to Kian—to the taut muscles of his chest, the rhythmic motion of his stride, and the regal way he carried himself. She recalled the confidence with which he had mastered her body. Her blood rushed with the thought of feeling his touch again.

"No." She fanned her face. "Not at all."

"Then it would seem the rules are different for Shiera's descendants," Daerick said. "That means there could be others like you, Cerise. Any number of priestesses out there in the world, hiding in plain sight. As long as they were careful not to use their magic around the wrong people, no one would know."

She lifted a shoulder. After what she had witnessed, she doubted that anything could surprise her anymore. But she didn't understand why she was the only person they knew of who could travel at will to the Mortara underworld. And then there was the cryptic message left behind by the old emissary: *As above, so below. The flame you seek to dampen will consume you.* Did that mean Cerise was the flame…or the one who would be consumed? And what about the Reverend Mother's warning about false idols? How did that fit in to everything?

She blew out a breath. What was her purpose in all of this?

"If my father was a priest with unusual traits," she said, "that could explain why my parents were afraid of him."

"And why they hid you from him," Kian agreed.

"So who could it be?" she asked. "How do we find him?"

"If your mother spent time at court," Kian said, "your father could be any one of hundreds of priests who served at the palace."

Cerise chewed the inside of her cheek. Her parents had claimed that they'd never visited the palace, but with as many lies as they had told her, she hardly knew what to believe. "Let's assume she was never at court. Do we have records of which priests lived in the Solon temples the year before I was born?"

"I'm sure of it," Kian said. "We can also find out who visited Solon."

Daerick added, "I can think of one priest, even without the records."

Kian and Daerick shared a dark look that immediately told her who they were referring to. The most legendary priest to ever visit Solon was Father Padron. He'd been dispatched there by the old king to put down an insurgence. She couldn't recall what year the rebellion had taken place, but the timing seemed like it could fit.

"How old was he then?" she asked.

Kian shrugged. "I don't know. Roughly our age. It would have been soon after his Claiming Day."

"Not too young to father children," Daerick pointed out.

Twenty years ago. Mama had been a great beauty then. Even now, she turned the heads of many, young and old alike. She could have easily caught Father Padron's eye. But something about the idea felt wrong. As pious as Father Padron was, she couldn't imagine him being tempted by any woman.

"I don't think it's him," she said. "I want to have a look at the records."

Just then, something else occurred to her. She had assumed she hadn't belonged at the temple and that was the reason she had never fit in there. But all gifts of magic, healing, and the Sight were given exclusively to second-borns. So if she was truly a priest—or a priest*ess*—that meant she *had* belonged at the temple, just not with the Seers.

"If I'm a priestess," she said, "then I'm a second-born. That eliminates Father Padron. Because unless he already had a child before he went to Solon, which I doubt, I would be *his* firstborn, if not my mother's."

Daerick frowned in thought. "I've never heard of a priest fathering a child, so it's hard to say. But you make a good point."

Something else niggled at the back of her mind, a realization just beyond her reach. Several moments passed before she pieced together what she had been missing. The man she'd called *Father* wasn't truly her father. She was a Solon in name only. That explained why the soothsayer had detected so little Solon blood within her. She must have inherited a hint of it from her mother but not enough to be of significance.

"I'm not a Solon," she said.

Kian and Daerick peered at her.

"To break the curse," she told them, "each noble dynasty has to offer their blood to the Petros Blade. We have a Calatris here with us, and we have a Mortara and a Petros…"

"But no Solon," Daerick finished. "Flaming hell. I can't believe I didn't think of that. We can't break the curse until we travel all the way back to the castle. We need Cole Solon."

"That slippery bastard," Kian added.

"Our window of time just shrank by a moon," Daerick said.

22

Before they returned to camp, there was one thing left to do. "I want to experiment with my energy," Cerise said. "Now, while Father Padron is gone."

Kian nodded. "You won't get another chance."

"What about over there?" Daerick told her, pointing at a nearby sand melon patch. "You could try raising one from the ground. That seems easy enough."

She didn't know about *easy*, but a melon patch was a good place to start. She knelt on the ground in front of the thorny brush, studying one of the thin, exposed strips of rind peeking out from the dirt. Most of the melon was hidden underground. She couldn't tell how heavy it was or if that even mattered, so she tried to imagine what a priest would do.

She focused hard on the melon, clenched her fists, and strained as if attempting to lift the gourd with her mind. The taste of metal filled her mouth. Power crackled across her flesh. *It was working!* She strained even harder. The rind shook. And then came a great *boom*, and she shielded her face as the melon exploded.

Behind her, Daerick screamed like a monkey, and Kian laughed in shock. She turned to find them being pelted by chunks of melon raining down from the sky.

"Well, it worked," Kian said as he picked a bit of rind out of his hair. "You raised a melon."

"All the way to the sky," Daerick added while brushing debris from his tunic.

"Don't be discouraged, my lady of the temple. All things require practice." Kian winked. "Just don't use me as your next test subject."

"I second that," Daerick said.

Cerise shook the juice from her arms. She hadn't expected instant success, but as she glanced around for another melon, she realized how heavily she was breathing. "That drained me." She pressed a sticky hand to her chest and felt her heart pound. "When I opened the spring this morning, I felt stronger than ever, but now I'm exhausted."

"And rightly so," Daerick said. "You dispatched your first death, didn't you?"

"Oh." She sat back and crossed her legs at the ankles. She hadn't thought of it that way. "I suppose I did."

"If there's ever a fruit uprising," Kian told her, "I'll know who to send."

His joke reminded her of Kian's earlier claim that Father Padron had stopped fifty hearts from beating before breaking a sweat during the Solon rebellion. She hoped the story was exaggerated, because she couldn't fathom such a thing. The simple act of destroying a melon had winded her. And what about the spiritual toll of taking so many lives? He had been so young then. Had the battle changed him? Made him colder than before? Had killing in the name of the throne set him on a path to kill in the name of the Order, too?

She shivered. She didn't want to imagine him using his power against her. "I need to rest before I try again."

"Then rest." Kian jerked his thumb toward another sand melon patch. "Lord Calatris and I can harvest these the old-fashioned way.

We can't go back to camp empty-handed, or it'll look suspicious."

Daerick groaned. "The next time you invent a reason to get rid of Father Padron, choose an excuse that doesn't involve manual labor."

"I'll take that under advisement," Kian said, holding out his hand for the shovel. "Come on. I'll dig. You retrieve."

"I think not." Daerick clutched his shovel and pointed at the thorny brambles. "I'll dig, and you can tear up your arms pulling melons from the ground."

"Need I remind you that I'm the king?"

"Need *I* remind *you*," Daerick said, "that your body restores itself at sunrise? The rest of us don't have that luxury."

"Luxury?" Kian repeated. "Spend one night in the shadows, and then we'll talk about who has the more luxurious..."

Cerise cleared her throat to interrupt their bickering. She needed help with her magic, and she'd just thought of the perfect teacher. "I want to tell Nero the truth."

Kian jerked his gaze to her.

"Before you argue," she said, holding up a palm, "he already knows I have fire blood. He knew it before I did. And he has the same magic, so who better to train me? He showed me a place inside the mountain where time practically stands still. He could teach me everything I need to know before anyone at camp even noticed we were gone."

Daerick slid a glance at Kian. "It's not a bad idea."

"I don't trust him," Kian said.

"Neither do I," Daerick agreed. "We barely know him. But Nero isn't Cerise's biggest threat. You know who the real danger is."

"Padron," Kian spat.

"And if he sees what she can do..."

"Enough." Kian released a long breath and looked to Cerise. "I don't like it, but we don't have much choice. You need to learn how to use your gift, or at least control it so you know how *not* to use it. If Nero can give you that education, then it would be foolish to refuse."

She grinned at him. "Thank you."

"You don't have to thank me," he told her. "I meant what I said before; I don't want your obedience."

"Then thank you for seeing reason," she amended.

Kian laughed dryly. "I'm not unreasonable, and to prove it, I suggest you start your lessons tonight."

"But..." She wanted to spend the night with Kian. She'd come to depend on their time together, and she hated the thought of abandoning him in the darkness.

He gave her a tender smile that told her he understood. "I'll miss your company, my lady of the temple. But I promise I'll be all right. I've lost count of how many nights I spent alone in the dark. I've grown used to it."

His bravery inspired her to make a promise of her own. "It won't be like this forever. Soon you'll spend all of your nights here with the rest of us."

"I hope so," he said.

She shook her head. Hope had nothing to do with it. "We're going to find the Petros Blade. And then we'll take it back to the palace and break the curse. I won't stop until you're restored. I'll free you or die trying. I swear it."

Kian's smile faltered. He said nothing at first, and then he gave a slow, solemn nod and told her, "I believe you."

23

The hunting party returned with a mule deer slung over each of their saddles, along with a new appreciation for Blue's predatory instincts. General Petros said that Blue had scented not only the deer but two rams that had escaped capture. Blue seemed to sense the praise. He held his head high as he proudly loped to Cerise and then dropped a lifeless jackrabbit at her feet. The dried blood around his mouth hinted that he had already consumed several rabbits of his own.

"You saved one for me?" Cerise asked. She rewarded him with a hug and a well-deserved scratch behind the ears. "Thank you, my sweet boy. You're still my hero."

While Blue curled up in the shade to take a nap, the rest of the group worked together to carve the sand melon, butcher the deer, and hang the thin strips of venison over a low fire to smoke. Father Padron cast a protective enchantment over the camp to block the scent of meat from carrying on the wind, and right before sunset, Cerise cast the runes. She had just read the rune's instructions when Kian vanished into the shadows and took half of her heart with him.

At dinner, Cerise pretended to drink her usual sip of arrowroot syrup, but she had no intention of falling asleep. When she retired to her tent, she sat on her blanket pallet and waited as the hours passed, listening to the quiet chatter and the scrape of utensils, then to the rustle of canvas that told her Father Padron had returned to his tent. She waited until she could hear his soft snores before she untied her tent flaps and crept out into the night.

The moon hung in a sliver against a backdrop of stars. The evening air was cool and crisp, scented by the cook fire, which was still smoking. Cerise peered around the darkened camp and found that all but two sets of tent flaps were tied shut—hers and Nero's.

It had to be tonight. There was no time to waste.

She signaled for Blue to stay, and then she strode around the fringes of the encampment to look for Nero. She detected a whiff of burning herbs and followed the scent until she found him sitting against a tree stump, puffing on a wooden pipe and staring beyond the protective enchantment.

With a glance at her, Nero offered his pipe and whispered, "Hoya leaf. Calming to the nerves, if the general's drink wasn't strong enough." He sniffed in amusement. "Though it won't make you drunkenly profess your love for the world."

She sat down beside him and waved away the pipe, but then she changed her mind. Her Claiming Day seemed like it had lasted for a year. And yet time was still running out, even faster now that they had to go back to the palace to break the curse. If her nerves had ever needed calming, it was tonight. She sucked in a mouthful of smoke and let it roll over her tongue. It tasted sweet, but it burned her lungs when she inhaled.

She coughed, her eyes watering as she returned the pipe to Nero. She imagined what the Reverend Mother would say if the woman could see her now: sitting on the cursed ground of the blighted mountain, dressed in pants, sweat-dried dirt on her face, blood beneath her fingernails as she smoked herbs with a heretic.

Most unladylike.

"Why are you awake?" Nero asked. "Is it bad dreams? My aunt taught me how to interpret dreams…or she tried. I'm not very good at it."

Cerise shook her head. "I want to talk to you about something. But first, can we go inside the mountain like we did before?" She darted a glance at Father Padron's tent. "Time passes slower there. We can stay gone for as long as we want, and no one will hear us."

"The Below," Nero said. He chewed his pipe in thought. "Yes, there's a way inside near here. But if someone wakes up and finds us both gone…*together* in the dark?" He slanted her a look. "What would your Half King think about that?"

Cerise resisted the urge to roll her eyes. Nero almost sounded jealous. "Considering we'll only be gone for a few moments, the king would probably think I'm disappointed."

Nero tried to stop from smiling, but a smoky laugh broke free. "Then let's not get caught. No man wants a reputation for that."

He stood up, offering his hand, and then he pulled her to standing as easily as the wind lifting a feather. He set off with his pipe tucked between his teeth and led the way out of the protective barrier. They continued for a few more paces to a cluster of trees that half concealed a stone wall. Unlike other slabs of stone, this one bore a streak of exposed mineral that sparkled in the moonlight. Anyone else might mistake it for ordinary crystal, but Cerise recognized the distinct shimmer of the Below.

Nero held aside a branch for her, jutting his pipe at the stone as if to say, *You know what to do.* She waited for him to explain. It didn't bode well for his teaching skills that he expected her to know something she'd only experienced one time.

"You're *umbra sangi*," he reminded her. "You can do this on your own."

"But how?"

"Your blood is the key."

"How much blood?"

"A few drops," he said. "A few more if you bring someone with you."

She thought back to the first day of the journey, when he had transferred her out of the cave and into the secret cavern. She remembered him cutting his palm and pressing it to the wall as he grabbed her by the wrist. She also remembered the sick sensation of falling afterward. This time, she would be prepared for that.

"One other thing," Nero added. "You have to envision where you want to go. The Below is a vast place with many chambers and passages to explore. Do you remember where I brought you? What the cavern looked like?"

She nodded. "I remember."

"Then take this," he said, giving her a small dagger. "And we'll go together."

Cerise worked up the nerve to nick the tip of her middle finger. She returned the knife to Nero, and they joined hands. Then she imagined the cool, dim cavern where he had taken her before, picturing its glowing walls and its moss-carpeted floor, recalling the babble of water in the background and the electric scent of magic in the air. She held the sensations in her mind and pressed her finger to the stone wall. Gravity gripped her stomach, and one heartbeat later, she and Nero were standing in the cavern.

She smiled as she caught her breath. "I did it!"

Nero took another pull from his pipe. He didn't seem impressed.

The cavern was brighter than she remembered. The walls flowed with turrets of glowing liquid that collected into a stream and followed the downward slope of the mossy floor to somewhere out of sight.

Cerise dipped a finger in the water and smoothed it against her thumb. The droplet was warm, with a slippery consistency that reminded her of the congealed chicken plasma she had once fed to Blue.

"Shiera's blood," Nero said.

"Hmm?"

"This is the mountaintop where she was stabbed. Her wrathful side blighted the Above, and her merciful side created the Below."

"You mean this is her actual..."

"Blood? Yes." Nero teasingly flicked a glowing droplet at her. "It won't bite. It's inside you."

Not so long ago, she would have dismissed the words as superstitious nonsense. Now, she gazed in awe at her hands. "This is what I want to talk to you about. I think the fire in my blood lit up today."

He tilted his head in confusion.

"I received a Claiming Day gift," she admitted. "I have magic."

The transformation on Nero's face put her in mind of a tight bud instantly opening to full bloom. "A woman with *resha*?"

"Does *resha* mean magic?"

"You call it energy."

"Then yes," she told him. "That's what I have."

Nero grinned as he shook his head. "My grandfather—the man who tested you—said magic might come to you, but I didn't believe him. I thought your gift would be different, like my aunt who reads dreams."

"My magic *is* different," she said. "I can't disobey an order from the king. In that way, I'm like the priests. But I can leave my body in dreams. That's my second gift. My spirit can go with the king into the shadows. So I think I have the magic of *umbra sangi* and the magic of priests. That means you and your grandfather were both right."

"I can't wait to tell him." Eyes sparkling with excitement, Nero bent to her height. "He'll assign someone to train you. Maybe my uncle in the city."

"Are there *umbra sangi* in other lands?" she asked. "Like Calatris or Solon?"

"Of course," Nero said. "Shiera's descendants are spread across the world."

"Do they always live in hiding? Or do they mingle in society?"

"I imagine both. Why?"

"I think my father is *umbra sangi*," she said. "My family won't tell me anything about him, except that he's dangerous. But if I can find out where he met my mother — whether it was in Solon or somewhere else — I might be able to narrow down who he is."

Nero frowned. "He could be anyone. Many men are dangerous."

"So I've learned."

"I'll ask my uncle," he said. "He has contacts in other lands. We'll talk to him about it when I take you there for training."

"Actually..." She trailed off and gave him a hopeful look. "I want you to train me."

"Me?" Nero touched his chest. "I'm no teacher."

"I don't have time to be choosy."

"You don't understand," he said. "Sloppy instruction is worse than none at all. You would have to unlearn everything I taught you. My uncle would flay me."

She shook her head. "I need help now, not a fortnight from now. I already lost control once. What if I use magic in front of Father Padron? He'll brand me a sorceress and have me executed. At least show me how to turn my magic off."

"There is no *off.*"

"See how much I have to learn?"

Nero sucked an extra-long pull from his pipe as if drawing fortification for some great test of patience. After two more puffs, he nodded. "Fine. Tell me what happened when you used your energy."

"The first time was an accident," she said. "I was watching the sunrise this morning, and then magic came up through my body and broke the rock I was leaning against."

Nero wrinkled his forehead, but luckily he didn't ask for more details. The last thing she wanted to do was share the events of her sensual awakening with him.

"And the second time?" he asked.

"The second time was on purpose," she said. "I tried to lift a sand melon out of the ground, and it exploded. After that, I had to take—"

"Wait," he interrupted. "Go back to the sand melon. How did you try?"

"What do you mean?"

"Think," he said. "Explain your steps to me."

"I sort of...stared at it really hard." She balled her fists and strained in demonstration. "Then I used my mind to—"

"Ah," he said, nodding. "That was your mistake. You felt tired after, didn't you?"

"Yes. I thought it was because I killed a living thing."

His answering chuckle made her feel like a fool. He lifted an apologetic hand to fend off a glare. "If melons had beating hearts, you would be right. It takes more energy than anything else to stop a heart. You were tired because you used your head to channel your power instead of letting it flow from here." He tapped his chest. "That's like walking on your hands instead of your feet."

She massaged the joining of her ribs. If there was a hidden power within her, she didn't feel it.

"It's easy." He passed her the pipe. "Easier if you relax."

She puffed once, twice, three times. A gradual calm descended over her, unwinding muscles she hadn't known were clenched.

"The power is there, ready and waiting for you to use it. You simply"—he exhaled—"let it out." He took back his pipe and resumed smoking it as he continued the lesson. "Energy isn't a muscle to be flexed."

She had a hard time believing it was really that simple.

"Think about your temple priests," he said. "Have you ever seen them struggle or strain when they cast enchantments?"

"No."

"If it feels like work, you're doing it wrong."

"I've seen them struggle afterward, though," she pointed out. She thought of Father Diaz, who had collapsed after killing a badger at the temple. And the city priest whose knees had given out after he'd calmed the angry crowd. Even Father Padron had fallen off of his horse after he'd dispatched the titan hyena pack. "If the energy is there and using it doesn't take work, why does it make the priests weak?"

Nero nodded as if to say, *Good question.* He removed the waterskin from his hip and poked the tiniest of holes in it before cupping the leak in his palm. "Your magic is like this skin. The energy is there, but you can't use it all at once. You can only draw from what's in your cup." He slurped the water from his hand and flashed a damp palm. "To drain the whole reserve will exhaust you."

She pointed at the leak. "Does it drip that slowly for everyone?"

He gave a casual shrug, but his gaze faltered, and his ears reddened at the tips. "It does for me. That's why I save my energy for important things." He passed a hand over the leather and used his magic to mend it. "For some, it flows quickly. And for others"— he peeked up—"like your high priest, the energy is a torrent of floodwater gushing through the gaps of a broken dam."

Cerise hugged herself. She didn't want to talk about Father Padron. "Show me what to do. Something simple, so we don't drain our cups."

"Motion," he decided, gesturing toward the water that trickled down the wall. "To generate the force to move something light uses almost no magic."

She nodded. "I'm listening."

"We're going to redirect one of these streams." He pointed at a downward rivulet, and the water changed paths right before her eyes.

"See?" he said. "Easy."

"I don't taste any energy."

"That's how little I'm using." He braced himself, planting his feet wide apart. "You'll notice this."

Copper coated her tongue. She tipped back her head to watch the liquid converge into a single glowing waterfall that rippled in luminescent waves and misted her face. The effect lasted for another moment or two before the waterfall vanished and the liquid resumed a scattered dribble.

Nero stepped aside as if giving her the stage. The color in his cheeks showed how much the act had cost him. "Your turn."

She moved closer to the wall and repeated what Nero had done, pointing to a trickle and trying to sway its path. Nothing happened. She imagined her energy as a beam of light escaping her chest and shining at the wall. When that didn't work, she stared hard at the water. Energy filled her mouth. A charge lifted the hair on her forearms. And then the moisture in front of her boiled into steam, forcing her to stumble back from the heat.

"You cheated." Nero pushed her forward. "Do it right this time. Turn off your thoughts and picture what you want."

She did as he asked.

Nothing happened.

"Try exhaling," he suggested. "And when your lungs are almost empty, imagine that the last trace of breath carries your wish."

Shaking out her shoulders, she prepared to try again. She softened her gaze as if searching for a hidden image in the contours of the wet stone. She released a slow breath, and in the last moment, when her lungs could give no more, she envisioned several streams plaiting together like braided hair.

Something warm touched her ribs, as though she had tucked a freshly baked bun beneath her shirt. Focusing her gaze, she found with delight that she had not only succeeded but used so little energy that all she tasted was pride. She smiled, watching the water lace together in a mesmerizing dance. Nero was right. It was easy now that she understood where her energy was and how to let it out.

Giddiness overtook her. She felt like a child with a new toy. She wanted to do more.

She lifted her hands and drew all of the water into a sphere that swirled high above her head. She divided the glowing sphere into two, and then three, and then divided each of those again and again and again until the cavern ceiling resembled a starry night sky. With a sweep of her fingers, she set the stars in motion, orbiting one another. She lowered the clusters to a hundred points throughout the room so they were spinning all around her, the cosmos in motion, and she laughed with the thrill of it. As she raised her hands and face to the heavens she had created, for the first time in her life, she could understand how it felt to be a god.

It was that thought that sobered her.

She waved the water back to the wall and willed the warmth to fade from her chest. She would not—*could* not—forget her purpose. No matter whose blood flowed through her, she was not a goddess but a servant of one.

No false idols.

Now and always, her heart belonged to Shiera.

Brushing the moisture from her cheeks, she turned to Nero, expecting him to reward her with a smile or a nugget of praise. Instead, he fixed her with the same disbelieving stare he had worn the day his grandfather tasted her blood.

His mouth worked mutely before he asked, "Did that tire you?"

"No," she said. "Should it have?"

He didn't answer her, which was answer enough.

The silence between them turned thick in a painfully familiar way. Cerise had stood in the temple and looked at the other girls with the same envy that filled Nero's eyes. She knew it well: the resentment of wanting a power she would never have. If she hadn't tasted that bitterness for so many years, she might not have taken Nero's hand and given it a comforting squeeze. But she did.

"You're not as terrible a teacher as I thought," she said.

Several moments passed, but eventually he smiled. "You're not as slow a learner as I thought."

"I'd like to learn more from you, if you don't mind," she said. "Have you had enough for one night? Do you want to go back to camp?"

"And leave you disappointed?" Something impish gleamed in his eyes. "I already told you. No man wants a reputation for that."

. . .

Cerise returned to her blankets feeling cleaner than before, her hands and face washed by the blood of the goddess, her spirit polished by the joy of accomplishment. Curled on her side with Blue nestled in the bend of her knees, she fell into a blissful sleep and awoke the next morning with the taste of sweet herbs lingering on her tongue.

Eyes closed, she arched her back and reached out to stretch. When her elbow thumped against a warm, solid chest, she grinned because she knew whose it was. She couldn't think of a better way to wake up than sandwiched between her king and her dog. Careful not to disturb Blue, she rolled onto her back and blinked at Kian. He lay facing her, his head propped up on one hand, his black waves tucked behind his ears. He gave her a smile that crinkled the skin around his thundercloud eyes.

"I love to see you happy," he whispered. He stretched out beside her and gathered her in his arms. "Am I to assume your lessons went well?"

"Very well," she said, resting her cheek on his chest and snuggling closer to fill the empty spaces between them. "I only wish I could show you. I learned so much from Nero. And the whole time I was practicing, I never glowed. He said the fire in my blood flashed when it came to life, and now it shouldn't happen anymore."

"That's a relief." Kian kissed the top of her head. There was love in his touch, but there was something more as well—an emotion she couldn't read. His arms tightened harder around her as though he was afraid she might slip through them. "I missed you last night."

"I missed you, too."

"But our time apart gave me a chance to think." His heartbeat thumped below her cheek. "I came to a decision, and I don't know how you're going to feel about it."

She propped her chin on his chest, delivering a questioning look.

"I told you that I don't want your obedience," he went on. "But that's not entirely true. There's one command I have to give you."

She held her breath. She didn't like the sound of that.

"I order you," he said in a firm voice, "to preserve your life by any means necessary. You won't sacrifice yourself to save me."

Reeling, she tried to process the gravity of what he'd said—what it might mean for breaking the curse. His command could restrict her in any number of ways, none of which she could predict. She didn't know the goddess's plan. What if Shiera meant to call her home? What if that was the price required to free Kian and Daerick and Nina's baby? Or the price for keeping the Order off of the throne?

"Kian, you can't," she told him, sitting up. "Too many people are suffering. I have to be able to do whatever it takes to break the curse. I don't know what that is, but if the goddess wants my life—"

"No," he cut off. "She won't have it."

"So you would punish the world to save one person?"

He sat up and took her hand. "Sacrificing lives is part of my duty as king. More people have died in battle throughout the ages than the number who are alive today. But in war, there's always a limit to how much you can lose before you surrender." He squeezed her hand. "You're my limit, Cerise. You have an uncommonly pure soul, and I don't want to live in a world created by any deity who would demand you as a sacrifice. I would rather surrender. I would rather let the world end."

She shook her head. "It's not your place to decide that."

"It is my place," he corrected. "Your goddess made sure of it when she gave me dominion over her priests…and over her priest*ess*. Shiera put this power in my hands. And I command you to live."

"Take it back."

"I won't."

"At least change your wording so I have more freedom."

"I won't," he repeated. He fixed her with a gaze that promised he had given this a great deal of thought and wouldn't be swayed.

Cerise sat there for a while and stared at her lap, her fingers growing limp in his grasp. His decision would haunt them in ways neither of them expected. She sensed it.

"I'm sorry," he murmured.

She drew away her hand. "No, you're not."

"No," he admitted. "I'm not."

24

The sunset runes led the caravan northwest that day, but for only half the distance as the day before. When Cerise cast the dice again at twilight, the runes predicted an even shorter distance for the following morning.

"Only five clicks," she said to the group. She reached out to retrieve the runes, but in the time it took for her to blink, they had vanished. She drew a hopeful breath and looked to Nero. "Does this mean what I think it means?"

Nero nodded, but the flat line of his lips hinted that he didn't share her excitement. "We should reach the Petros Blade tomorrow — probably by midday, if the trail is solid."

"Well, that's good news," Daerick said. He glanced back and forth between them. "Isn't it?"

"It is," Nero told him. "But…"

"I'll be tested," Cerise finished. "And I don't know how. It must be practically impossible, though. If no one has seen the Petros Blade in a thousand years, that must mean no one has ever passed the test."

"Not necessarily," Daerick argued. "I used to think the sunset runes were a myth. I had never seen them, and neither had anyone I'd ever talked to. If I hadn't come on this journey with you, I would be none the wiser. Just because we haven't seen the blade doesn't mean it's been untouched for all this time. Maybe it's been granted and then it disappeared afterward, like the runes just did. Any number of people could have won the blade, and we would never know."

"That's true," Kian said. "Besides, anyone smart enough to earn the Petros Blade would be clever enough to hide it. Only a fool would show off something so valuable and easy to steal."

General Petros grunted while he stoked the fire with a pointed stick. "Laying hands on the most destructive weapon in history isn't supposed to be easy." He glanced at Cerise. "But if anyone deserves to win it, it's you, my girl."

"I agree," Kian said. "I have faith in our lady of the temple."

The tang of energy thickened the air as Father Padron cast his protective enchantment over the camp. Cerise looked to him, expecting to hear his commentary on the subject of faith, but he had no words to offer. He simply turned on his heel and strode to his tent, taking his supper with him. Maybe it was nothing, but she noticed he'd been more quiet than usual since her Claiming Day. And once or twice during the afternoon ride, she'd caught him sneaking a sideways glance at her, almost studying her, as though he had sensed a change in her but couldn't pinpoint the difference.

His silence made her uneasy. It wasn't like Father Padron to hold back his opinions, not even the hurtful ones. *Especially* not the hurtful ones. She would almost prefer to hear his lectures than to wonder what dark thoughts he was hiding from her.

Kian brought her back to present company with a clap of his hands. "Rest well tonight," he told the group. "We'll need all of our strength in the morning."

He gave Cerise a wink as he vanished into the shadows—a silent goodbye and a reminder to study well, since they had decided she would stay behind for one more lesson with Nero.

Cerise repeated her ruse from the night before, pretending to drink arrowroot syrup with her supper and then waiting inside her tent for the rest of the group to fall asleep before she crept out into the darkness to meet Nero on the fringes of camp.

Again, they found a stone slab entrance to the Below, and Nero spent the evening hours teaching her how to cast a defensive shield and how to deliver an offensive blow. Cerise practiced the drills over and over until she learned to protect herself, and when she returned to her tent, it was with a fraction more confidence than before.

The next morning, the group packed up camp and rode northwest for five clicks. Much like their approach to the Blighted Shrine, the path grew steeper and more treacherous as they neared the Petros Blade's hiding place. The horses began to struggle to keep their footing. Cerise was just about to suggest that they stop and tether the horses when Daerick suddenly jerked upright in his saddle and snapped his gaze to hers.

"I see it," Daerick told her, his eyes taking on a dreamy quality.

Dread settled in her stomach. She had seen that faraway look on his face before, and she knew what it meant. His curse was leaking through the veil of time, revealing to him the secrets of the universe and destroying his mind in the process.

"What do you see?" she asked him.

"It's the air here." Daerick turned his eyes to the space in front of him, fanning out his fingers at a phenomenon visible only to himself. "The particles are slippery. Magic won't hold." He laughed in wonder. "I understand how it all works now — how the particles fit together to create the forces of nature. It's so simple. How did I miss it before?"

Cerise glanced around at the rest of the group. Judging by their heavy expressions, everyone understood what was happening.

Even Father Padron put aside his haughtiness long enough to give Daerick a pitying glance.

"Lord Calatris," Kian called, maneuvering near enough to clap Daerick on the shoulder. "Remind me what your sister is called—the tall, busty one with the brown hair. I named my mare after her, but now I've forgotten what to call her when I slap her on the ass."

The teasing seemed to work. Daerick blinked out of his trance and into a scowl. "You say *lower your expectations*," he retorted, "*because I'm not half the man my mother was*."

"That's quite a mouthful," Kian said. "Does she have a nickname?"

Daerick flashed a rude hand gesture. "Is this short enough for you?"

Kian grinned and delivered another pat. "Glad to have you back, my friend."

Daerick turned his face away, clearly embarrassed by his lapse in sanity. "Enchantments won't hold here," he told the group. "So whatever we have to do to get the blade, Father Padron's magic won't work."

That made sense to Cerise, considering the weapon had been hidden to protect it from warmongering kings who might have sent priests to retrieve it. But what she didn't fully understand was how magic could be absent from any place that contained an enchanted object. There had to be *some* magic surrounding the blade—otherwise, it wouldn't be able to move to a new location at each full moon. Perhaps there were multiple kinds of magic in nature, and the energy that protected the blade was different from the energy of priests. She wished she could ask Daerick if he had seen the answer, but she didn't want to make him any more uncomfortable than he already was. Maybe she would ask him later in private.

The group rode in silence for a short while longer, and then they were forced to tether the horses and continue on foot. The higher they climbed, the more Cerise detected a foul scent in the air, an unfamiliar odor that grew stronger and stronger until Blue whined and pawed at his nose. Soon the group crested the next peak and found the cause of the smell.

"Acid," Nero said, waving a hand in front of his face.

Less than ten paces ahead of them stood a bubbling pool of acid so deep that Cerise couldn't see the bottom. Rimmed by a circle of mud, the shallows bore a yellow tint that deepened to a greenish hue at the center. Beads hissed and fizzed where they leaped out of the pool and landed on the cracked soil.

She strode to the pool and inched as close as she dared, peering below the liquid's surface. Something caught her eye—a gleam of sunlight on metal. When she squinted, she could barely make out a double-edged blade with a polished steel hilt. The weapon was smaller than she had imagined, the approximate length of her forearm. It hung suspended within the deep as if gripped in an invisible fist.

"There it is," she said. "The Petros Blade."

Kian pulled her back from the edge. "Careful. You're making me nervous."

"How do I fish it out?" she asked Nero.

"I doubt that you can," Nero said. "That would be too easy. If I had to guess, I would say you have to go in and get it."

"Go in?" Cerise asked. "To a pool of acid?"

Father Padron joined them at the pool's edge and extended a hand as if to will the blade into his grasp. His energy flared, but nothing happened. He tried again. His power surged like an electrical storm. And then from the depths below, the acid bubbled. He smiled in victory, but as he flattened his palm to accept his prize, acid splashed the front of his robes, instantly dissolving the gilded fabric. He staggered back, ripping away the tatters to protect his flesh.

"Magic won't work here," Daerick reminded him.

"Yes, thank you, Lord Calatris," Father Padron snapped. "I can see that now."

"So what do we do?" General Petros asked.

Nero pointed at Cerise. "You're the one who seeks the blade, so you're the one who has to be tested. I think you should start by making an offering."

"What kind of an offering?" she asked.

Nero shrugged. "Blood, maybe?"

"A blood ritual is sorcery," Father Padron warned.

"But I have nothing else to give," she said.

Kian handed her a small knife. "Try a lock of hair."

She pulled a section of hair from her twist and cut it before tossing it into the acid pool. Several moments passed. Nothing happened.

Father Padron cast a glance at Blue and then arched an eyebrow at Cerise, silently reminding her that she did have something else to offer.

"No," she told him. If the goddess wanted Blue, then Shiera would have to come down from the heavens and physically remove him from Cerise's arms.

"Very well," Father Padron said. "Then offer your blood, if that is your wish. But any consequences that arise will be yours to suffer."

Cerise held her breath, silently praying that the fire in her blood would remain invisible as she nicked the pad of her fourth finger with the knife. She extended her hand above the acid. A single red droplet hit the surface.

The group approached from behind to watch.

Like brandy to boiling wine, her blood caused the surrounding acid to froth. She drew back to keep a safe distance until the bubbling ceased, and then she leaned in again to see if anything had changed. Now cutting through the yellow-tinged acid was a path of pure, clean water, and below it, a stone staircase leading down to the blade.

"It looks like your offering was accepted," Nero said.

Kian squinted at the pool. "How can you tell?"

"Because there's a staircase." Cerise traded places with him and pointed. "See?"

"All I see is liquid death."

"Me, too," Daerick added.

General Petros and Father Padron shook their heads. They didn't see the stairs, either. Then a male voice rose from the water. Low and clear, it commanded, "Two must enter."

"Two?" Nero repeated, sharing a glance with Cerise while the rest of the group stared at the pool as though nothing had happened. "Did anyone else hear that?"

"Hear what?" Kian asked.

Cerise told him what he and the others had missed. "I think the voice was talking to Nero and me. We're the only ones who heard it, and no one else can see the staircase. The voice wants us to go inside."

"But why?" Nero asked, shaking his head. "I didn't come here seeking the blade. I didn't make an offering. Why would I be called to enter?"

Kian studied Nero through narrowed eyes. "Maybe the blade knows something about you that the rest of us don't."

Nero tensed as if to take a backward step, but he seemed to think better of it. "I have nothing to hide."

"Then you should have no reason to worry," Kian told him.

Cerise rested a hand on Kian's shoulder to calm him. "Let's remember that Nero risked his life to guide us here."

"He certainly did," Kian said. "At the cost of two satchels of coin from my private treasury." He jutted his chin at Nero. "Now it's time to earn your pay. Go with her, but you enter first. And make sure nothing happens to her while you're down there. If you come out and she doesn't, I'll leave you on this mountain in pieces too small for the insects to notice."

The color drained from Nero's face, but he didn't argue.

Cerise strode ahead of Nero to the watery edge of the pool, where she knelt and poked a testing fingertip through the surface. She felt nothing, not even a hint of moisture. She tried again, this time scooping a hand through the liquid, but it was no more tangible than air. She swung her legs around and tapped the top step with her sandal to make sure the staircase was solid. When her foot met the resistance of stone, she stood up.

"He goes first," Kian reminded her.

Nero brushed past her and descended the steps until his head was submerged beneath the water—or, rather, the illusion of it, because no part of him was wet.

Cerise told Blue to stay, and then she glanced once more at Kian. Their gazes caught and held, an entire conversation passing between them. His eyes urged her to be safe and come back to him. She nodded a silent promise to do her best, and then she followed Nero into the pool.

25

Once Cerise was fully below the surface, she glanced up and saw her own reflection. The group was as invisible to her as the stairway had been to them. Below her, Nero waited on the bottom step, beyond which she could see only blackness.

The Petros Blade had vanished. Everything had vanished.

"Come," Nero called.

As she continued downward, the smell of sulfur gave way to something worse—an odor so rank it triggered her gag reflex. She pulled her collar over her nose. "What is that smell?"

Nero faced away, unfazed. "If I had to guess, probably the ones who came before us."

"The ones who came for the blade? And didn't..." *survive?*

Nero must have heard the fear in her voice, because he thrust out his hand to her. She jogged down the steps and took it. His grasp was loose but steady, a message of support despite having been forced to go into the pool with her.

Together, they stepped into the darkness.

Once their feet met the floor, their surroundings changed. They were no longer inside an acid pool, but instead within the dimly lit walls of an ancient temple. The staircase had changed as well, now constructed from the same dusty clay brick as the floor. There were no structures visible in the open room, at least not in the spaces illuminated by the half dozen flickering wall sconces. What existed in the shadowy corners was anyone's guess. The only other source of light came from the Petros Blade itself, which floated above a great stone dais that was as long and wide as a grown man. There were no visible barriers protecting the blade, but Cerise knew better than to assume she could simply snatch it out of the air.

A voice bellowed, "Prove yourself bold."

Bold? Maybe she should grab the blade after all.

She barely had time to consider the idea before a scraping sound drew her attention to the shadowy rear corner of the room, where a tall, slender man dressed in stained rags limped toward her.

Not a man, she realized as he limped into the torchlight. *A half-decayed corpse.*

She froze, the horror of him locking her in place. She had never seen anything so grotesque. Tufts of black hair pushed up from his scalp in greasy patches. His head, tipped sideways at a curious angle, seemed to have no face. His eyes and lips were gone, his skin decaying like a curtain of putrid lace. Only half of his nose remained, which twitched as he sniffed the air to follow her scent. She planted her feet in a defensive stance and practiced the drill Nero had taught her, summoning her energy and casting it in front of her as a shield. But no sooner had the static wall formed than it dissolved. The magic wouldn't hold, just like Daerick had warned her.

There was nothing to protect them.

She backed away, bumping into Nero. They fled all the way to the dais.

And then a second corpse arose from behind the altar.

This man had both of his eyes, though no light shone from within them. He, too, inclined his head at them; in doing so, he widened the gap where his throat had long ago been slit.

Icy terror gripped Cerise, and she stumbled back a step. The stench was overwhelming. She tried to cover her nose, but something heavy appeared in her palm, dragging it down. She glanced at her hand to find it holding the Petros Blade. In disbelief, she looked above the dais where the blade had just been floating. Nothing was there. It seemed she had the real thing in her possession. She and Nero locked eyes and instantly agreed on their next move.

They ran for the stairs to take the blade back to the group.

As if anticipating what they meant to do, the temple raised a new wall to seal them in. The barrier grew from the floor like a stone hedge, rising so quickly they couldn't stop in time. Shoes skidding, they slammed sideways into the wall with a thump. The impact loosened Cerise's grip on the blade, but instead of falling to the floor, the hilt stayed put. She splayed her fingers and shook her hand. The weapon clung to her palm.

"It's stuck," she shouted, trying to pry it loose.

"Then use it." Nero pointed at the first corpse, sniffing its way toward them. "Pierce his heart. That's how the blade was designed to kill."

"But he's already dead."

"Who cares?" Nero yelled while circling the man to grab him from behind. "Just stab the thing!" He locked the corpse's elbows behind its back. "Do it now!"

Cerise rushed forward and instantly recoiled as the man lunged at her with snapping teeth. The rot from his mouth was suffocating. She cringed, aiming the blade over his heart, but the man moved as he shifted within Nero's grasp.

"Hold him still," she shouted over the man's guttural snarls.

Nero strained, his face reddening. "He's stronger than he…" Trailing off, he glanced behind them, where the second corpse had climbed over the dais and now dragged his feet toward them. "Hurry!"

She closed her eyes and thrust the blade as hard as she could into the man's chest. His ribs splintered, but then the blade wedged there, and her arm jerked as the man thrashed back and forth. She tugged backward, pulling the corpse as well and making Nero stumble.

"Not through the chest!" Nero called while darting glances behind him. "You never stab a man through the chest! His bones will lock your knife."

"Now you tell me!"

"Do it here," he said, keeping one arm around the corpse while using the other to point at its upper stomach. "Go under his rib cage and thrust upward. Pierce the heart from below."

That brief moment was all it took for the corpse to free one hand, which it tangled in Cerise's hair, pulling her face toward his snapping mouth. She held her breath and yanked the blade free. Then, without thinking, she drove it up beneath his ribs so hard that her fist embedded inside his cold, wet, half-rotten body.

The man went limp.

His fingers released her hair. Pulling the blade from his chest was no more enjoyable than putting it there, but with the second corpse advancing, there wasn't time to dwell. She yanked free and tried not to look at the putrid blood that streaked her arm.

Nero circled around behind the other man to restrain him. The second kill was easier now that she knew what to do. Moments later, she was pulling her arm from another chest cavity and resisting the urge to study the men for clues to who they had once been. She didn't want to know.

Suddenly, her arm flung out, and the blade left her palm to float above the dais again, where it shone flawlessly as though she had never used it. She glanced behind her and found the wall still blocking the stairs.

It seemed the temple wasn't finished with them yet.

A voice boomed, "Prove yourself deserving."

Cerise turned to Nero just in time to see his body drift up from the floor. He wheeled his arms and legs as some unknown force carried him to the dais and then slammed him down on his back. Four leather straps appeared and snaked around his wrists and ankles. In the time it took for her to run to him, he was fastened so tightly to the altar that his hands began to redden and swell.

She tugged uselessly on the straps, scanning the dais for some sign of what to do. The answer came when the stone hummed to life beneath Nero's body and illuminated a network of carved channels, roughly a fingertip in width. Like miniature canals, the channels began at his bound wrists and extended down the sides of the dais. The rust-colored stains inside the grooves made it clear what had once flowed there.

She knew what the temple wanted.

Nero's throat shifted. He knew it, too. "Blood. That's why both of us had to enter. So one of us could serve as a..."

Sacrifice.

The unspoken word rang between them.

Cerise glanced over her shoulder at the fallen bodies. The dead men had been sacrificed. Someone had killed them in order to borrow the blade for some important purpose or other. She wondered if the survivors had considered the slaughter worthwhile, if the blade had saved enough lives to justify the murder of innocent men.

The blade emitted a buzzing sound, as if to redirect her attention. Somehow she understood that it wanted to feel her touch again, so she stood on tiptoe and pulled it from the air. This time she was free to move the grip from hand to hand, so she set the blade down next to Nero's shoulder.

Nero glanced at the blade, then to her.

"I'm not going to kill you," she told him, a little insulted that he'd doubted her. "If I wasn't willing to sacrifice my pup for the blade, what makes you think I'm capable of killing you in cold blood?"

"You might not have a choice," he said.

"There's always a choice."

"Yes," he agreed in a dark tone. "Either I die and you live, or we both die together. Technically, it's a choice, but it doesn't seem like saving me is one of your options."

She shushed him and turned in a slow circle, looking for another way out—perhaps a hidden wall or a trapdoor.

"Shiera can't want this," she murmured. "It's wrong to take a life."

"Shiera is half darkness," Nero reminded her. "She takes as many lives as she gives."

Cerise knew that from a logical place, but her heart resisted.

"We won't last long down here," he went on, jerking his gaze to the corner as some hidden creature made a scratching sound. "The best outcome is we'll die of thirst. More likely, other dead ones will tear us apart before that happens."

"I have the blade," she told him. "I can kill anything that comes for us."

"And if they keep coming back to life?"

"Stop talking and let me think."

"Listen to me," Nero urged, and repeated himself when she shushed him again. "I have to tell you this while I can."

"Fine. Hurry up."

"If I don't survive, go back to the city and ask for Ronus," Nero said. "That's my uncle. You can trust him. Tell him what happened to me so he doesn't have to wonder."

Cerise hugged herself against a swelling of fear. She didn't want to hear Nero talk about his death as though it had already happened. No one deserved to die in this terrible place, least of all him. Kian was wrong to think that Nero was motivated by coin. Even now, strapped to a sacrificial altar, Nero cared more about her safety than his own. How could the blade demand the blood of someone so brave? She knew the Petros dynasty had forged the weapon in order to slay the goddess, but she'd never imagined it could be infused with so much evil.

"Whatever happens, don't blame yourself," Nero said. "One way or another, my path is destined to end here. Yours doesn't have to."

"There's only one path," she told him. "And we're both on it. So either we leave here together, or we'll haunt this place together."

"Don't be an idiot. Save your—"

A deep rumbling interrupted him as the temple walls rattled hard enough to fill the air with dust. The Petros Blade vibrated toward the edge of the dais. Cerise caught it before it could hit the floor, but no sooner had she gripped the weapon's hilt than a series of cracks sounded from the great stone walls, where the blocks had split apart and were now spraying water into the chamber. The tremendous pressure caused the cracks to widen even more, allowing torrents of water to gush over the floor, sweeping the dead bodies in its swirling current.

In a blink, Cerise was covered to the ankles.

The temple was forcing her hand.

"Do it," Nero yelled as he peered over the edge of the dais at the rising flood. He tugged uselessly against the leather straps. "Kill me! I would rather bleed to death than drown!"

The Petros Blade warmed in her palm as if urging her to give Nero the quick death he had asked for. Water covered her to the knees. Her hands began to tremble. There was no way out and nothing left to try. If she didn't kill Nero now, they would both drown.

She thought of Kian's command to preserve her life by any means. The absence of magic inside the temple must have disrupted her bond of servitude, because she had free will. But when she pictured Kian and Blue, Mama and Father and Nina—all of the people who would miss her, all of the lives that would be ruined by the curse if she didn't survive long enough to break it—she began to see the logic in Nero's argument. What was the point of both of them dying?

She snuck a glance at him. He was already watching her with a surprising sense of calm. He nodded his consent. "Go ahead," he told her. "You don't know it yet, but you're destined for more than this. I think my role was to bring you here. My fight is over, but yours isn't. So end me. Make it quick. It's what I want."

She tightened her fingers around the hilt. A voice of reason told her that one life was a small price to pay to save the world. With both hands, she raised the weapon as water swirled around her hips. Nero closed his eyes. She focused on his nearest wrist and brought down the blade.

Instead of flesh, she severed a leather restraint. One by one, she slashed the others until Nero was free. His eyes flew wide. He sat up and stared at his hands.

"This is my limit," she told him.

"What?"

"My limit to how much I'm willing to lose," she said, and for the first time, she understood Kian's words to her—his limit before surrender. "The goddess knows what's in my heart. She knows why I want the blade. I don't think she would ask me to do something evil to atone for evil. But if I'm wrong, then so be it."

Nero gripped his forehead and yelled, "Have you lost your mind?"

"Maybe," she said. "But I haven't lost my soul."

To escape the rising water, she climbed onto the stone dais beside Nero. She reached up and returned the Petros Blade to its rightful spot. It glowed and floated peacefully in the air. She supposed she wouldn't need it now.

She threaded an arm through Nero's. She felt like she should say something meaningful, but her fear rose with the water, and all she could do was shiver. Nero didn't say anything, either, until right before the water reached his mouth. He gulped one last breath and used it to call her a fool. Cerise used her last breath to laugh.

26

After that, the flood swallowed them, and there was only blackness and pressure and the all-consuming need to breathe. She soon lost her connection to Nero. The current twisted her body until she didn't know which way was up. Her mouth opened and filled with water. She felt the sensation of falling, and the next thing she knew, sunlight pierced her eyelids, and she hit the ground hard, knocking the last dregs of wind from her lungs.

She sucked in a breath and rolled onto all fours to cough up water. She didn't realize where she was until she smelled sulfur and opened her eyes to the sight of cracked dirt turning to mud beneath her wet hands. Nero lay to her right, hacking up the contents of his own lungs. On her left, Blue licked her face while Kian dropped to his knees and smoothed back her dripping hair. He peppered her with questions that flew to the edges of her senses. Once the shock wore off and the oxygen returned to her brain, she felt something hard against her knee, and she shifted aside to find a length of gleaming steel.

The Petros Blade.

She lifted it by the hilt and shared a glance with Nero, who seemed just as confused as she was. How had they both survived and emerged with the blade if she had failed the final test? She hadn't proved herself deserving at all.

Unless…

Unless the sacrifice had been a different kind of test—the type of challenge that a person had to fail in order to pass. The more she thought about it, the more it made sense. What better way to measure a person's integrity than to require a blood sacrifice in exchange for the blade? Those who sought the weapon for the wrong reasons, for power or for greed, wouldn't hesitate to kill an innocent man to get it. Those with purer motives would resist.

Her lips spread in a smile. "My foolishness won the day!"

Nero flopped onto his back, slinging one arm over his eyes. "I never thought I would thank you for that."

"You still haven't," she pointed out.

"Thank you."

Kian glanced back and forth between them. "Want to share this thrilling story with the rest of us?"

"Yes," Daerick agreed. "I want to hear about your foolishness."

"Me, too," General Petros added.

"I suggest we return to the lower trail first," Father Padron said in an absent voice, his eyes wide with disbelief and fixed on the blade. "I can't protect us here."

"Very well," Kian told him. He cupped Cerise's cheek and asked her, "Are you able to walk?"

She nodded and let him help her to standing. Her knees trembled a bit, but more from the thrill of escaping death than from physical exhaustion. She examined the blade in the sunlight, turning its polished steel to and fro and admiring its gleaming surface. The weapon didn't look so evil in the light of day, but she knew better than to underestimate the damage it could do. She would need to fashion a sheath for the blade and keep it secured to her at all times, just like she had promised Nero at the beginning of their journey.

As if sharing her thoughts, Nero said, "Remember the vow you made."

"I haven't forgotten," she told him.

Nero turned his attention to the king. "My job was to guide you to the blade. Now that you have it, you can't say I haven't earned my pay."

"You've done well," Kian agreed.

"Then this is where we part ways." Nero gestured toward the thicket where the horses were tethered. "The path down the mountain is the same that we took to get here. Our tracks are easy to follow."

"You're not coming with us?" Cerise asked.

"You can find the way," Nero said. "You don't need me to guide you anymore. But if you ever need me in the future, you know where to mention my name."

She nodded.

"Goodbye…for *now*," he told her, as though they were destined to meet again.

"Goodbye for now," she echoed, because she believed him.

"My lady of the temple," Kian called to her after they returned to their horses and began the slow, careful descent back down the mountain. They rode in a single file with General Petros leading the group, followed by Father Padron, Daerick, Cerise and Blue, and Kian riding at the rear of the caravan. "It's time for you to explain how you walked into a pool of acid and then fell out of the sky."

"Yes, do tell," Daerick added over his shoulder. "That was most impressive, and I'm not easily impressed."

Cerise released a breathy laugh when she remembered how clumsily she had faced each of her challenges. She doubted anyone would've been impressed if they'd watched her being tossed back and forth by a rotting corpse with her arm lodged inside its chest. But she told the group what had happened, focusing mainly on the second trial. She wanted them to know that Nero had offered to sacrifice his life for hers. Not that it made much of an impact. When she finished telling her story, Father Padron stared at the trail ahead of him, seemingly as bored as ever. Daerick chewed a thumbnail and gazed off into the distance. A trace of concern lined Kian's forehead, and General Petros turned around and frowned at her so hard that a dimple appeared in his chin.

"I would have killed the boy," the general grumbled. "And I like him."

"You don't know that," Cerise said. "No one knows what they would do in any situation until it happens. If you had been there and seen the look on his face—"

"He would be dead," the general interrupted.

"Actually, you both would be," she told him. "Compassion was the test."

The general pointed at his own face, flushed so hot by the sun that his skin nearly matched the color of the tattooed flames on his head. "Does this look like the face of compassion, my girl?"

Cerise didn't want to lie to him, so she answered with a shrug.

"Clarify something for me," Kian said from behind. "Did you know that you could've preserved your life by taking Nero's?"

She turned to face him. She understood what he was really asking. He wanted to know how she had been able to disobey his direct command to survive by any means necessary. "Enchantments were stripped away, remember?" she quietly reminded him. "The rules of magic were different."

"So you were simply going to die down there?" he asked, his eyebrows knitting together. "You were going to leave the rest of us behind to grieve your loss? Did you give us no consideration when you decided to surrender your life and drown in that wretched place?"

"But I didn't drown," she reminded him. "I'm safe and whole…

and the first person in a thousand years to hold the Petros Blade."

"That we know of," Daerick interjected.

"That we know of," she agreed. "But if I had done anything differently—if I had killed Nero to try to save myself—I would have ruined all of our lives. I'd be dead, Nero would be dead, and we wouldn't have the Petros Blade. I made the right choice—the choice that brought me back to you."

"But you didn't know that at the time," Kian argued. "When the water was rising up to your neck, you had no idea that you'd made the one decision that would save you. Quite the opposite. You had every reason to believe you would drown." There was a dark note of pain in his voice, as though his trust in her had been betrayed. "You seem far too eager to leave this world. That worries me."

Conflicting emotions stirred within her. She hated to see Kian hurting. His pain was her pain. But even though she understood the reason for his hurt, a small part of her resented him for letting his fear of losing her overshadow her triumph. She had accomplished something more remarkable in one day than most people accomplished in a lifetime. And she had done it by trusting her instincts. She had listened to her heart, not to the orders of men. The orders of men would have gotten her killed. She had herself to thank for her survival, and maybe it was petty of her to want credit for that, but she did.

"You asked me to have faith in myself," she reminded him. "So I did, and that's what saved me. I'm not eager to leave this world. I want to live. But it's not fair for you to praise me for having an uncommonly pure soul and then criticize me for refusing to commit murder."

Kian grumbled under his breath.

"Don't you agree?" she prompted. She wanted to hear him say it.

"All right, yes," he told her. "You're right. Your empathy is my favorite thing about you. I shouldn't have faulted you for being exactly who you are. You did well, Cerise."

"Spectacularly well," Daerick added. "We're proud of you."

"Thank you." She sat a bit taller in her saddle and then turned again to face Kian. "Please try not to worry about me," she said, for what little good it would do. It seemed a lover's primary job was to worry. To lighten his mood, she teased, "I have every intention of outliving you."

He laughed without humor. "To outlive a firstborn Mortara is no accomplishment. None of us have lasted beyond our twenty-first birthday. But I do see your point." He lowered his voice so that only she could hear him. "I still command you to preserve your life, but I'm willing to remove murder from the list of necessary means. As long as you don't have to kill an innocent person with your own hands, I order you to do whatever is required to protect yourself."

Cerise heaved a sigh. She hoped he wasn't expecting her to thank him. She had wanted him to remove the compulsion altogether.

"I'm glad that's settled," Daerick said, sliding her a teasing grin. "I do loathe to see Mommy and Daddy fight. Now let's talk about what to do with the Petros Blade."

At the mention of the blade, Cerise felt its weight strapped to her back, held in place by a makeshift sheath that General Petros had constructed out of strips of old rucksack leather. The weapon itself was as light as a dream. What weighed heavily on her shoulders was the urgency to use it before time ran out. With Daerick's Claiming Day and Kian's twenty-first birthday fast approaching, she had to hold herself back from galloping at full speed down the mountain. She wished she didn't need Cole Solon's blood to complete the ritual. The palace had never seemed so far away.

"I think we should have a ceremony," she said. "A proper one. Something lavish to honor the goddess when we ask her forgiveness for the Great Betrayal."

Daerick furrowed his brow. "Do we have to? We're already short on time. I was hoping we could get started as soon as we stable the horses."

"In a *barn*?" she asked.

"Well, maybe not in a barn," he said. "But we shouldn't wait to plan a ceremony. What if it doesn't work? We need to give ourselves plenty of time to keep trying."

Something about his suggestion felt wrong. Almost shameful. "Think about it," she told him. "All of our tests so far have been to prove that we're faithful and brave and worthy. So what message would it send if we rushed the most important part of the process? The goddess would think we're afraid."

"Aren't we?" Daerick asked.

"Of course, but we can't act on it," she said. "The goddess doesn't respect weakness. We have to be strong, and my instincts are telling me we need a ceremony."

Kian told Daerick, "Her instincts have served us well so far."

"Listen to the girl," General Petros added.

Daerick muttered a swear. "All right. We'll have a ceremony, and not in a barn."

"Not in a barn," she agreed. "It should be someplace sacred. Maybe in the palace sanctuary," she called ahead to Father Padron, "if Your Grace will allow it."

Father Padron nodded, wordlessly giving his permission. His silence unsettled her now more than ever. He had all but withdrawn from her life.

"Thank you," she told him, still watching him closely. "We should begin with a prayer, and then it would make sense to give a description of each dynasty's role in the Great Betrayal. That way, the four of you can ask the goddess to forgive the sins of your ancestors."

"'The four of you'?" Father Padron glanced over his shoulder at her. "Are you not participating in the ritual?"

She couldn't tell him the truth. Luckily, she'd prepared an excuse for why Cole should represent house Solon. "I'm not a firstborn like His Majesty, Lord Calatris, and General Petros. I think Cole would make a more fitting representative for our house. As for me, I'd hoped to lead the ceremony, since the goddess entrusted me with the runes and the blade." She forced herself to add, "What do you think, Your Grace?"

Father Padron lifted a shoulder and faced the path ahead of him. "I think that sounds as rational as anything else. Do as you wish, Cerise."

Dread settled in her stomach. His silence was one thing, but for him to carelessly give up control was another. He was the Order's high priest. He enjoyed the attention that came with the role. And more than that, whoever led the ceremony could potentially steer the outcome. If he really did covet the throne or if he wanted the nobles to atone through endless suffering—if it was in his best interests for the ceremony to fail—he should insist on participating in some way, if only to sabotage it.

His complete lack of concern settled like an itch between her shoulder blades. What if he knew something that she didn't?

27

The group traveled for two more days, following their tracks back down the mountain until they reached the supply wagon they had previously abandoned. Half of the oats and all of the rendered fat had been eaten by desert creatures, but the sacks of horse feed and the satchels of herbal tea were more or less untouched, and for that, they were grateful. With a wide, even trail ahead of them, they hitched the wagon to Daerick's mare, and the caravan continued for three more days.

Cerise spent each night in her tent with Blue, missing Kian's company and his touch. As much as she wanted to follow him into the shadows, she had made a vow to protect the blade, and in order to do that, she had to remain inside her physical body. But that didn't stop her from looking for ways to spend time with him. At each camp, she searched for a stone slab entrance to the Below, like Nero had shown her. She eventually found one, and the next morning at sunrise, she handed Kian a pair of linen pants, led him away from the sleeping camp, and then used her blood to transport them to the enchanted caverns Below.

Kian braced himself on his knees, winded from the transfer. After he caught his breath, he peered in wonder at the glowing walls and the moss-carpeted floor. "You described it well," he told her. "I still can't believe this has been here for a thousand years—a whole separate realm that nobody knew about."

She understood the feeling. The *umbra sangi* were good at keeping secrets.

"How slowly does time pass here?" he asked.

"Hours in the Below are like moments Above."

She reminded herself of that as she patiently waited for Kian to take in his surroundings. She had fantasized for so long about bringing him to the cavern, about lying on the cool, mossy ground and feeling him inside her again, and now it was all she could do to stand there and not shuck the pants right off of him. She unstrapped the Petros Blade from her chest and rested it on the floor.

"Then we can stay as long as we like?" he asked.

She nodded.

At that, his thoughts seemed to follow hers. He grinned as something wicked gleamed in his eyes. "How shall we spend our time, my lady of the temple?"

"I thought you'd never ask," she said, sliding her hands up the length of his bare chest and clasping them behind his neck. She stood on tiptoe and angled her mouth toward his.

"Not so fast," he whispered against her lips. "Remember our rule. Nothing happens unless you command it."

She hadn't forgotten. In fact, she had already decided what her first command would be. But for now, she only wanted to kiss him, to reconnect after nights apart, and so she rose higher onto her toes and brushed her lips against his. They melted into each other, tasting and exploring until their breaths turned choppy. When she caught herself straining her hips against him, she broke the kiss and lowered to her heels.

"Here's my first command," she said. "I want you to teach me."

"Teach you...?"

"Everything there is to know about the act of love."

He released a breathy chuckle. "We might need more than one lesson for that. There are so many acts of love that a person could spend a lifetime learning them all. And I'm afraid I don't know the half of it. I'm still a novice."

She arched an eyebrow. *A novice?* She didn't believe him. There was nothing amateurish about what he had done with her on the morning of her Claiming Day.

"Truly," he insisted. "Books have been written on the subject—hundreds of volumes in multiple languages."

"Is it really that complicated?"

"Not complicated," he said. "Diverse. Just like there are different ways to enjoy an apple—my favorite is baked in a pie—there are many ways to please each other."

"Then show me one," she said. "Show me your favorite."

An immediate smile appeared on his face, as if he had been waiting for her to ask. "As my lady commands."

He lowered to the ground and indicated for her to join him. Atop the soft moss, they stretched out on their sides and traded kisses for a while, building back up to the same breathlessness as before. She was more than ready when he slid his fingers beneath the waistband of her pants. She rolled onto her back and parted her thighs for his touch, and luckily, he didn't make her wait. He used his thumb to trace circles over her while his index finger dipped inside. She spread wider, arching her back, silently begging for more. Then he slid his finger deep inside her and found an erotic spot she hadn't known existed. He massaged it while her toes curled, and an animalistic moan rose from her throat.

"I love that sound," he murmured in her ear. "But I love this sound even more," he said, and he added a second finger to amplify the noise of her arousal. "Do you hear how wet you are?"

She nodded, rocking against his hand.

"The body doesn't lie," he said. "When you're dripping into my palm like this, I know that you want me more than your next heartbeat."

He was right. Her body craved nothing except him.

"You asked me to show you my favorite, and this is it." He withdrew his fingers and sucked them clean. "The taste of you, the slippery feel of you. I want to drown in it. I've been dying to do this ever since the first time I kissed you."

She didn't fully understand what he meant to do until he removed her pants and began kissing a trail from her navel to her thigh. Then, with his face between her parted legs, he began using his tongue in the same way he had used his fingers. She tensed at first. But as she relaxed into him, she found that she quite enjoyed the sensation of his tongue. He licked her softly, teasing her delicate bundle of nerves to a stiff peak and then lapping at her with more pressure. He kept repeating the cycle, raising her higher and then bringing her down again, intensifying the ache in her core. When he paused for a moment, she remembered to command him.

"More," she murmured. "And use your fingers inside me, too."

He did as she asked. Nothing could have prepared her for the pleasure of his deep, stroking fingers combined with the lapping of his tongue. She groaned and let her knees fall out to the sides.

"Don't stop," she told him, though the tension was quickly growing unbearable. He kept working her, taking her body higher. Then he drew her into his mouth with a light pull of suction that felt so good she forgot to breathe. It was almost too intense. Just when she was about to tell him to quit, he twisted his fingers around to find that same magical spot, and all of the pressure inside her burst in release. She felt her inner walls tighten around his fingers as waves of pleasure washed over her. The fire in her blood seemed to surge. She couldn't find the words to command him anymore, but somehow he knew exactly what to do, how to lighten his touch until the final quake had passed.

She lay on the ground with her heart pounding. If he was truly a novice, she couldn't imagine what he would be capable of as an expert. He placed kisses on the insides of her thighs and stretched out beside her. She recognized the look of pride on his face, but there was something else behind his smile—a longing for the same touch that he had given to her.

She knew what her next command would be. "Lie back. I want to taste you, too."

He didn't need to be told twice.

She tugged his pants down the length of his legs and tossed them aside. Then she took a moment to admire him: the muscular planes of his chest; his round, strong shoulders; his lean core; and the dark hair that encircled his navel and led to his unmistakable desire for her.

"The body doesn't lie," she repeated as she curled her hand around him.

He was already rigid, but when she stroked him up and down, she felt him grow even harder. A single bead of liquid rose to the surface of him. She used her thumb to spread out the bead and found it slippery, much like her own arousal. She wondered what it tasted like, so she leaned down and licked his velvety tip.

He must have liked that, because he released a groan that echoed through the cavern. The taste of him was salty yet clean. She loved how his body responded to her, the way his muscles tensed with each swirl of her tongue, the guttural moans he released as she stroked him up and down. She had him writhing in pleasure, even though she had never done this before, and that made her feel more powerful than the fire inside her veins.

It also sparked a new ache between her thighs. She wanted him again—all of him this time. A quiet voice warned that it would be greedy of her to take more pleasure so soon, but she silenced the voice. She was in command now. For once in her life, she would take what she wanted and feel no shame about it.

"I'm not done with you," she said as she tugged off her shirt. She repositioned herself astride his hips, and then she slowly glided her wet, aching core along the length of him.

The rumble in his chest told her he didn't mind. "As my lady commands."

She braced her hands on his shoulders and leaned down to align herself with him. Then, one gradual inch at a time, she sank onto his length until she was seated. The fullness inside her was as exquisite as she remembered, but now there was no pain to hold her back. And so she rocked against him, gently at first, testing the way each movement and angle changed the sensations in her body. She discovered that she liked it best when she leaned forward, and even better when she undulated her hips as though she were in the saddle.

Kian gripped her backside. She liked that, too.

"Grab me tighter," she told him.

He did as she asked, all the while clenching his jaw in a struggle for control. His fingers bit into her flesh, but he didn't try to change the pace. He let her experiment with him until she found a natural rhythm, and from there, she let her body take over. She rode his hips faster and increasingly harder. When she craved more pressure, she pushed against his shoulders for leverage, but it wasn't enough.

"Harder," she commanded him.

Their eyes locked and held. She saw her own need reflected in his gaze, the same raw desperation for closeness, as if to collide their bodies into one. He gripped her hips and thrust up from the ground while she sank onto him with all her weight. The impact was exquisite. She crashed into him again, and then again, watching his gaze go wild. With one last thrust, the tension broke, and they cried out together. She tipped back her head as chills cascaded over her skin and pure energy surged in her veins.

Nothing in her world had ever felt so incredible.

Afterward, she lay atop his chest and listened to his heartbeat while he held her in one arm and used his free hand to trace her spine. She waited for his breathing to slow before she propped up her chin and said, "I'm ready for my next lesson."

His chest shook as he chuckled. "My lady of the temple, you can't be serious."

She wagged her eyebrows at him. "Maybe a little bit serious."

"If you have the energy for another lesson right now, then I must not have done my job properly," he said. "You should be spent. I know I am."

Strangely, she wasn't the least bit drained. If anything, she felt stronger than before. The fire in her blood seemed to respond to pleasure, maybe even increase from it. But then again, she had only made love twice. She had no way of knowing if the energy pulsing in her veins was permanent or temporary or related to the act of love at all.

She would need more experience to test her theory.

Biting her lip, she glanced again at him. "I'm ready when you are."

He answered with a weary groan but shifted his weight and rolled her onto her back. He settled above her as a crooked grin formed on his lips. "As my lady commands."

28

In the days that followed, she almost always found an entrance to the Below, and then she and Kian would sneak off at sunrise, enter the cavern, and spend hours talking and embracing and making love.

A lot of love.

True to his word, he had continued his lessons while insisting that she direct his every movement and touch. He showed her a dozen different ways to join their bodies, and with each new, delicious act, she felt her magic grow stronger, not weaker. At times, the power within her cells felt like it would burst her apart if she didn't release it, and so she began to discharge her energy by practicing her defensive drills before she and Kian returned to camp. There was no denying it anymore: the Order had been wrong about the act of love weakening a woman's gift, or at least *her* gift. How could they have been so wrong?

The farther the caravan traveled toward the base of the mountain, the fewer stone slabs she was able to find. She knew that she should be grateful for each click that brought her closer to the palace, but she treasured her time with Kian in the Below. She would miss it.

The final day of their journey arrived. They would reach the palace in the afternoon, leaving them plenty of time to plan and hold a ceremony before sunset. Kian would get another chance if they failed, but Daerick wouldn't. Cerise found her palms sweaty and her hands trembling as she folded her tent into a lumpy square.

Faith, she reminded herself. *Don't lose faith.*

Sometime later, long after she had mounted her horse, she glanced over her shoulder and watched the blighted mountain shrink into the distance. A hint of wistfulness stirred inside her, and at first, she didn't know why. She wouldn't miss the desert heat or the thin air at the mountain summit. She certainly wouldn't miss the shrieks and howls of nocturnal hunters consuming their prey. She wouldn't miss the taste of jackrabbit or the ache in her bones after a day in the saddle. It wasn't until she faced ahead and the palace loomed in the foreground that she realized what had been bothering her.

She didn't want to return to her old life.

She didn't want to change into her black-and-white temple gown. She was more comfortable in breezy linen pants and leather sandals. Her loose travel clothes made breathing easier, as well as climbing and stretching and running—all of the improper things she wasn't supposed to do. Now she would have to learn to glide again, and the thought made her shoulders slump. There would be no more meals around the campfire. Tonight, if everything went well, she would dine at a mile-long table in the company of people she didn't like, or else alone inside her bedchamber, or worse still, in the company of the priests in the sanctuary.

The sanctuary. How ironic that the place where she had once felt safe was now the source of her greatest fear. The priests had never warmed to her, not even when Father Padron had treated her with respect. Now she had lost his favor, and when she returned to the palace and word spread that she was the king's lover, the priests would resent her even more. She would have to be twice as vigilant as usual in hiding her gifts. Her power had grown, but all of the defensive drills in the world wouldn't save her from the collective energy of the Order if they decided to attack her.

Blue must've sensed her agitation, because he nudged her ankle with his snout to get her attention. She glanced down at him, and just like that, her fears gave way to love. The dark eyes peering back at her overflowed with adoration and with another emotion—a fierce determination, as though Blue would protect his mama from whatever threat had made her worry. He didn't seem to know that he was still a pup and it was *her* job to protect *him*. Not that he looked like a pup anymore. He'd grown as tall as a pony and nearly as broad. His bulk had smoothed out the wrinkles from his coat, displaying his namesake blue birthmark. As large as he was, he was bound to raise eyebrows at the palace.

"You're my very best boy," she told him, reaching down to scratch his head. "My sweetest, strongest—"

"*Ha!*" Daerick called out from behind. Just as she glanced over her shoulder at him, he burst into a fit of wild, delirious laughter that turned her blood cold. "I see it now!" he shouted, swaying in the saddle as he pointed at Blue. "The particles of magic from his sire! I've been wondering how a titan hyena could possibly mate with a hound. Now I know!"

All of her worries returned in a rush. This was the first time since leaving the blighted peak that Daerick's curse had touched him. She'd hoped the distance from that dark place had shielded him—and maybe it had, just not completely. Tomorrow was his Claiming Day. If she couldn't break his curse, he would exist like this for the rest of his life, lost inside the fathomless depths of his own mind.

Faith, she reminded herself, though her pulse didn't listen.

"A hyena mating with a hound?" Kian called over his shoulder, using the same loud, taunting voice that had jolted Daerick awake before. "Doesn't that describe your parents' wedding night, Lord Calatris?"

The teasing worked. Daerick blinked and returned to himself, but this time, he didn't have a witty retort to offer. His face was ashen and expressionless. He said nothing until he nudged his horse forward. He rode on the other side of Kian and extended a hand. "Do you have any more of those stomach soothers?"

Kian fished around in his pockets for the tiny tin and then passed it to Daerick, who tossed several tablets into his mouth... and then a few more.

"Hey, now," Kian objected. "Save some for the rest of us."

When Daerick handed over the tin of stomach soothers, Kian hesitated to open it before he ate one. He peered at the sky, rubbing his thumb and forefinger together as he gauged the sun's position, no doubt calculating the hours until dusk.

Cerise reached out and gave his hand a squeeze. She remembered the day Daerick had taken her into the city and what he'd told her about the cruelty of hope. Daerick and Kian had never been closer to breaking the curse, and that had to feel terrifying.

"Not much longer," she told both of them. "We're almost at the palace, and then we'll have the ceremony—today—more than once, if that's what it takes. Try not to worry. We have plenty of time."

But speaking the words didn't make them true. Time was the only thing they lacked, and Daerick surely understood that better than anyone.

They rode in silence until they reached the gatehouse and followed the grassy, tree-lined path to the palace and then to the stables beyond. With her first breath of citrus-scented air, she realized how much the journey had altered her sense of smell. The odor of sweat, dust, and horseflesh had created a new normal for her, and now the air seemed too sweet—and, by contrast, her body even more in need of a washing.

She dismounted her horse and then rubbed her sore backside before she caught herself and remembered to act like a lady. No one seemed to have noticed. The palace servants who had rushed to the stables to meet them were more focused on the king. Kian's steward welcomed him with a moistened towel to wipe the dust from his hands and face, and then the man ordered another servant to prepare a fresh bath for the king in his quarters.

"Mine, too, please," Cerise added.

The servant, a young brunette girl, nodded and curtsied and blushed, reminding Cerise of the reputation she had earned following the palace fire. It seemed like a lifetime had passed since then. She had nearly forgotten about her "sacred lungs"...and also about the repeated attempts on Kian's life. It didn't occur to her until then that breaking his curse would make him more vulnerable than ever. It was his curse that gave him a new body at sunrise. Without it, he could be injured—permanently, like anyone else.

She tried not to dwell on that. She had enough to worry about.

Then she remembered Lady Champlain and how Kian had made Delora his courtesan to spare her from an unwanted marriage. Did that mean he would continue the ruse? She didn't know how she felt about that. They hadn't discussed the matter. But when she looked to Kian and found him peeking through the stable doors at the position of the sun, she knew that Delora was the furthest thing from his mind.

And rightly so.

"We have almost three hours until sunset," Cerise announced to everyone in the stable. She glanced at Kian and then at Father Padron. "We should cleanse ourselves, prepare the sanctuary, and leave at least an hour for the ceremony itself, as well as any further attempts we have to make."

"Don't forget about Cole Solon," Daerick added.

"Right," she said. "He'll need to be notified."

Father Padron brushed the dust from his robes. "I see nothing to prevent it. As long as I'm given the assistance of His Majesty's staff..."

"Take what you need," Kian told him. He gestured at Cerise. "My lady of the temple, I had hoped to escort you to your suite, but I think it would be more prudent of me to remain with my steward and discuss the ceremony preparations. Will you forgive me, my love?"

She smiled at him as she lowered in a curtsy. She understood his gesture. Subtle as it was, he'd publicly acknowledged their relationship. "There is nothing to forgive, Your Highness. I look forward to seeing you at the sanctuary."

A welcome sight awaited her in the sitting room of her suite—a tub of lavender-infused water, along with a tray of soaps, shampoos, towels, and scented oils. She groaned aloud in anticipation, but she needed this to be quick, just cleansing enough to show her respect to the goddess.

She stripped off her clothes and walked toward the footed tub, the Petros Blade still in hand. She slid the blade underneath the tub and then climbed in, submerging herself to the neck. When Blue sat beside her and sniffed curiously at the soap, she told him, "Tonight, you're getting one, too."

He whined and covered his nose with one paw.

"It's nonnegotiable."

Just then, something in the adjoining room caught her eye: a bundle of scarlet fabric resting on the floor next to her bed. Squinting, she realized it was a luggage bag but not one of hers. Suddenly, Blue snapped his head toward the balcony. His ears perked up, and a low growl rumbled from the back of his throat. She recognized that growl from the mornings when Kian had secretly appeared in her suite at sunrise.

Someone was in her bedchamber, but this time, it wasn't the king.

Cerise snatched a towel off the floor, using it to cover herself as she stood up in the tub. "Show yourself," she ordered, resting a hand on the back of Blue's neck. "Or I'll let go of my hound, and I warn you, he's half titan, and his bite is worse than his bark."

A familiar voice teased, "I surrender," and a tall, veiled figure moved into view.

Cerise's jaw fell. She would know her sister anywhere, even with Nina's body softly rounded by pregnancy. Blue must have recognized her, perhaps from the heartrending mirror, because he relaxed and wagged his stumpy tail.

Too shocked to move, Cerise stood there, clutching her towel while she dripped into the tub. "Am I dreaming? Is it really you?"

Nina folded back her veil and removed any doubt that she was real. She smiled, lifting full, rosy cheeks that glowed with more radiance than ever before. Pregnancy had enhanced her beauty, something Cerise hadn't thought was possible. She couldn't breathe, couldn't blink. Her gaze widened uncomfortably as she stared at her sister. Nina's radiance was almost painful to behold, but Cerise would tear out her own eyes before sacrificing a single glimpse of it.

The veil lowered, and for the first time in Cerise's life, she didn't complain. "That was intense," she said, blinking to soothe her eyes. "It actually hurts. How does your husband live with you and not go blind from the staring?"

Nina's silk skirts rustled as she crossed the room and pulled a chair beside the tub. "He doesn't love me as much as you do." She sat down, pointing at the water. "Now, Cerise, darling, I'm glad you're happy to see me, but please get back in. You're filthy."

Cerise grinned. Still in a daze, she dropped her towel and sank into the bath until she was submerged to the chin. She shook water off one of her hands and settled it on Nina's belly. The swell was small but firmer than she had expected, like a sand melon. "You'll have to hide your face from the baby, too. They won't love anyone more than they love—" She cut off as the fog lifted from her brain. "Wait. What are you doing here?"

Nina laughed. "It's good to see you, too, Cerise."

"Did Mama and Father send you?"

Nina didn't answer, which meant *no*.

"Do they even know you're here?"

More silence.

"Does *anyone* know you're here?"

"Well, of course, silly," Nina said. "I've been staying in your room for two nights. I didn't sneak past the guards at the gate. And then there was the maid who let me into your suite and the serving boy who's been bringing me all of my meals."

"Three servants?" Cerise asked. "That's who knows you're here?"

"Four," Nina corrected.

Four was no better. What about Nina's husband? He probably didn't know about her visit, either, or he would've accompanied her to court.

"What's wrong?" Cerise asked. "Did you find something in Mama's journal? Something about my father?"

"No."

"Then what aren't you telling me?"

"Who said there's anything wrong? A girl can't visit her favorite sister?"

"I'm your only sister," Cerise reminded her. "And I'm not a fool. So either tell me the truth, or…" She scrambled for an idle threat and found just the one. "Or I'll compel it out of you."

Nina cringed. "*That's* why I'm here. To stop you from doing something stupid and getting us all killed."

"I was only teasing; I can't compel anyone. I've been careful with my magic."

"Not careful enough," Nina said. "Walls have ears—especially palace walls. You shouldn't say things like that."

Cerise fidgeted with her pendant as she glanced at the suite door. She didn't think she'd spoken loud enough for anyone in the hallway to overhear, but then again, she hadn't known Nina was in the room until a few minutes ago.

"You didn't take off the necklace," Nina said. "Good. At least you listened to me about one thing." She lifted the pendant to inspect it, then shook her veiled head. "I see you've been busy."

"It really works. It saved me from dream weed smoke and a titan hyena attack."

"Bloody crows. This is what you call being careful?"

"Oh, and also from falling off of a cliff face," Cerise added. "How many uses does it have left, do you think?"

"One, maybe two. The link is already worn. Once it breaks, it won't draw from his—" Nina smoothly corrected: "from its power source anymore."

"*His?*" Cerise repeated. "It draws from a person?" She took back the pendant and rubbed her thumb over its gnarled metal, imagining it draining some distant priest each time she'd used it. "I could have killed him."

"No, you couldn't have."

"You don't understand how energy works."

"Trust me. No one was in danger except for you."

There was no point in arguing. Nina wouldn't listen. "If you say so."

"I do." Nina pointed at the water. "Now, tip back that dirty head."

Cerise leaned down so Nina could wash her hair. She was glad to have her sister there, even if Nina had only come to the palace to fuss at her. She'd missed her sister. It didn't seem like that long ago she had promised to break the curse for Nina's baby. Now the time had come to prove it. Maybe Nina could see it happen for herself.

"There's a ceremony in a couple of hours," Cerise said. And then she told her sister everything, starting with Mother Strout's journal and the clues that had led them into the mountains and ending with the test to win the Petros Blade. She left out the battle with the corpses, not wanting to scare Nina. But she didn't leave anything out when she told her sister about Kian. She even included the details that made her blush to say them out loud.

"The king?" Nina asked, washing out the last suds from her hair. "Really, Cerise? After I asked you not to draw too much attention to yourself, you began a torrid affair with the most infamous man in the realm?"

"Yes, really," she said. "And it's not a torrid affair. We're in love."

To Nina's credit, she didn't scoff or laugh. "Well, I can't say that I blame you. He is rather nice to look at."

"He is," Cerise agreed. She imagined Kian getting ready in his royal chambers, washing and dressing and eating stomach soothers like candy. He was counting on her. All of the noble firstborns were. Daerick and General Petros, Nina and her baby—their lives were in her hands.

Tension crept into her shoulders.

"You're nervous," Nina said, starting to towel-dry Cerise's hair. "Just do your best. That's all the king or anyone else can expect of you."

"I'll feel better knowing you're there," Cerise said. "You can stand right up front, where I can see you."

"At the ceremony?" Nina shook her veiled head. "No, Cerise, I can't go with you. No one can know that I'm here."

"But the staff knows."

"No one at *court*," Nina clarified. "This veil doesn't make me invisible. It draws its own kind of attention. The more people see me, the more they'll talk. Word will get around."

"And get back to your husband?"

Nina hesitated as though she'd forgotten about him. "Yes, to my husband."

"Where does he think you are right now?"

"Still visiting Mama and Father. So you can see why I have to be careful. You said it yourself: if the ceremony doesn't work this time, you'll keep trying until the king's last sunset. That could take days, if it even happens at all."

"Wait," Cerise said, ignoring Nina's lack of faith in her. "How long do you plan on hiding out in my suite?"

"Until you break the curse," Nina said. "Or until the king's last day, whichever comes first." She grew still for a long pause. "Father's carriage is parked outside the gatehouse. Do you remember what it looks like?"

"Yes. Why?"

"If anything happens, I'm taking you home."

"What do you mean?" Cerise asked. "And to what home? To the temple?"

"I mean if you can't break the curse," Nina said. "And no, I want to take you to my estate in Calatris. It's more secure. You'll be safer there than anywhere else."

"But the king…" Cerise shook her head. "I won't leave him."

"If he dies, you can't stay here. You have to know that."

"He's not going to die," Cerise insisted. "But even if he did, I can't live with you at your estate. I'm a second-born. I'd have to go back to the temple and to the Reverend—"

"Damn the temple," Nina snapped. "And damn the Reverend Mother! I'm not giving you back to her if there's no one controlling the priests." She seemed to catch herself and lowered her voice to a whisper. "Someone within the Order could very well end up on the throne. Have you thought about that? About what that would mean for a girl like you?"

"Of course I have." She'd thought of little else. The idea of a priest as king—free to use the full force of the Order to persecute anomalies like her to the edge of the realm—robbed her of sleep some nights. "But what I haven't thought about is failure, because it's not an option."

Nina stood from her chair and offered a dry towel. "You're right. There's no reason to panic. Yet."

Yet?

"Let's not get ahead of ourselves," Nina went on. "You rinse off quickly, and I'll lay out your gown for the ceremony. When you go downstairs, I'll stay here and watch Blue so you can focus on what's important." She drew a breath as if to say something more, but she released it and strode into the bedchamber.

Cerise had a good idea of what her sister had left unsaid, because she was thinking it, too. If the ceremony worked, all of their worries would be for nothing. Kian would remain on the throne with the priests bound to him. The threat would end, for her and for everyone else.

She had to break the curse: it was as simple as that.

And as difficult.

29

The Petros Blade had never felt heavier than when Cerise carried it down the stairs and into the foyer, where hundreds of palace workers had gathered outside the corridor that led to the sanctuary. They waited in silence to learn if the king's emissary could perform one last miracle and save them from a deadly curse and the jaws of war. She could swear the slim blade doubled in weight beneath the pressure of all those wide, hopeful gazes.

As the crowd parted and she glided slowly among them, all heads lowered in respect. An occasional hand reached out to touch her skirts. She hurried her pace to discourage the contact. Now more than ever, it was dangerous for anyone to treat her differently. She noticed Lady Delora Champlain standing alone in a quiet corner. Delora wrung her hands but gave Cerise a nod of encouragement.

As she crossed the open-air corridor, the arched sanctuary doorway came into view, and below it, Father Padron stood tall in his gilded robes, both hands folded in front of him. The laws of the realm forbade laymen from entering the sanctuary without permission, so on this side of the threshold stood the king, Daerick, and General Petros. All three of them were the picture of decorum in their uniform jackets and sashes, not a wrinkle or a hem out of place. But none of them could hide their pulsing throats and shifting Adam's apples. And one man was absent—Cole Solon.

In accordance with tradition, Cerise curtsied first to Father Padron and then to the king. Kian gave her a small smile of encouragement as she lowered before him, but the tiny beads of sweat along his upper lip betrayed his anxiety.

She felt it, too.

She stood straight and addressed Father Padron, loud enough for all to hear. "Your Grace, Holiest among Shiera's Order, and Divine Protector of her servants, I ask that you grant these laymen entry into our sanctum, so they may humble themselves before Shiera and atone for the sins of their ancestors."

"I invite them to enter," Father Padron announced, and without further ado, he turned to lead the way as Cerise took her place by his side.

"Do you know where Cole is?" she whispered to him.

Instead of speaking to her, Father Padron did something she hadn't known was possible. He used magic to reply. She flinched as she felt him broach her mind with his voice.

Probably holding back for a grand entrance, he said. *Cole believes mortal eyes only exist to gaze upon his face.*

Cerise looked at Father Padron, but he gazed straight ahead and ignored her startled reaction. Why had he chosen that precise moment to speak to her through magic when he had never done it before? Did he mean to unsettle her? Was it some kind of a test? Or a demonstration of his power, a reminder that he was still in control, despite the fact that she held the Petros Blade? She could only guess. But whatever his motives, he had taught her a valuable lesson. Now that she had experienced the magic, she sensed that all she had to do was think about him and respond. The act was so simple that she could have easily answered him with her mind, though she didn't, of course.

"Should we wait for him?" she asked.

"With less than an hour until sunset?" he whispered aloud. "I think not."

Father Padron confounded her, but on this point, he was right. The strips of light peeking from the curtained windows glowed orange with approaching dusk. It was safer to begin the ceremony and save Cole for last.

Daerick's life depended on it.

"I sent Father Bishop to retrieve him," Father Padron added. "By force, if necessary."

They entered the prayer room, where every priest in residence had assembled for the ritual. The men formed two groups with a wide aisle between them, each priest standing in front of a thin floor cushion. In unison, they knelt upon their cushions and then used their energy to create a hundred tiny flames that floated high above their heads. The light cast a glow upon the animated ceiling murals that depicted the Great Betrayal—the reason that had brought them all there.

From this point on, Cerise would have to trust her instincts.

She strode down the aisle in brisk steps to give the illusion of confidence. When she reached the burning altar, she rested the Petros Blade on the ledge, far from the sacrificial bowl and the flame below it. No one would thank her if the blade was scorching hot when she used it to prick their skin. She indicated for Kian to join her on the left while Daerick and General Petros stood to her right. Father Padron remained in the aisle between his priests, but he gave her a nod as if to say the rest was in her hands.

She began with a prayer, followed by a brief history of creation—the temple-approved version with no mention of Shiera's lover or their mortal descendants. She spoke slowly to give Cole Solon a chance to join them, but by the time she reached the most relevant part of the story—the role each dynasty had played in the Great Betrayal—he was nowhere to be seen.

Unable to delay any longer, she lifted the Petros Blade from the altar and reached for Kian's hand. She would begin with him. "It is believed that house Mortara," she said, her fingers so cold and numb that she could barely feel Kian's touch, "called upon their allies to slay our Holy Creator. They led the noble dynasties into unspeakable sin, and for their treachery, house Mortara was cursed with darkness." She asked the king, "Is your heart filled with repentance?"

Kian glanced at her with a hidden smile. They both knew what his heart contained, and it wasn't love for the goddess. But he answered, "Yes," and laid his palm open for her to slice a scarlet line in his flesh.

The instant his blood appeared, the blade absorbed it and glowed brightly enough to make Cerise shield her eyes. It lasted only a moment before the glow dimmed, but it filled her with the first real hope she had felt all day. She met Kian's gaze as excitement passed between them.

The ceremony was working.

Eagerly, she waved Daerick forward. "House Calatris," she said, taking his hand, "used their superior intelligence to devise a method to slay the goddess. For their treachery, they were cursed with more knowledge than the mortal mind can bear."

"My heart is repentant," Daerick blurted before she could ask.

She sliced his palm and nearly cried with relief when the blade absorbed his blood and glowed once again.

He quickly traded places with General Petros, who offered his meaty palm. Cerise announced, "House Petros, skilled in the military arts, forged the weapon to slay our creator. That weapon is the same blade I hold today. For their treachery, house Petros was cursed with insatiable bloodlust." She tipped back her neck to meet the general's eyes, which shimmered with moisture. It was ironic and somehow fitting that his heart was filled with more repentance than the others. She had to bear down slightly harder to cut his callused skin, but once she did, the blade accepted his blood and dimmed for the final offering.

House Solon.

Cole still wasn't there. She turned to Father Padron and found him at the back of the room, engaged in a conversation with Father Bishop. Father Padron looked at her and shook his head. He hadn't been able to find Cole.

Her stomach sank. She darted a glance at the curtained windows, wondering how much longer she had until sunset. If Cole didn't appear before Kian vanished, would she be able to continue the ceremony, or would she have to start over the next day?

General Petros leaned down to whisper in her ear. "Use your own blood, my girl. Cole's heart is a stone compared to yours."

She didn't doubt that. But General Petros didn't know the truth about her parentage. She wasn't a Solon.

But she knew where to find one.

"Nobody move," she said. "I'll be right back."

Taking the Petros Blade with her, she hitched up her gown and ran down the aisle between the priests, propriety be damned. She streaked past Father Padron and continued through the open-air corridor, into the crowded palace foyer, and up the stairs, ignoring the clamor of confused voices in her wake. She sprinted all the way to her suite and tore open the door so quickly that Nina, who'd been giving Blue a bath, fell onto her backside.

"Are you all right?" Cerise asked.

Nina nodded, rubbing her swollen belly. Her veil was pulled back, both sleeves wet and pushed up to her elbows. "Is it...is it over?"

"No." Cerise helped her sister to her feet. "I need you to come with me."

Nina shook her head wildly as she lowered her veil.

"Listen to me," Cerise said. "The ritual is working, but I need a Solon to finish it. I was going to use my blood, but I'm not a Solon."

"What about Cole?" Nina asked.

"We can't find him."

"There must be another Solon in the palace."

"Maybe, but I don't have time to look." Cerise lifted a hand toward the open balcony, where the daylight had taken a pinkish hue. "The sun will set soon. Please. For Daerick. For me."

Nina's chest rose and fell in rapid breaths.

"No one will know it's you," Cerise promised, reaching for her sister. "Your face will stay hidden, and I won't announce your name. After this, you can go home to your husband, and he'll never know you were here."

Nina was so tense that she'd balled her hands into fists. She took one forward step and stopped before taking another. After a long breath that billowed her veil, she wiped both palms on her skirts and then followed Cerise out the door. With their fingers laced together, they left Blue behind and rushed to the sanctuary.

Nina's fingers trembled as Cerise towed her down the aisle between the priests and to the burning altar, where Kian and the others waited with questioning gazes. Cerise gave them a quick shake of her head—a message that she would explain later.

Right now, there wasn't time.

She turned Nina to face the room and pried loose her fingers. Nina clutched her gown with both hands, shrinking against the altar as if to disappear inside it.

"It's all right," Cerise whispered. "Give me your hand."

Nina obeyed, her palm shaking.

"The Solon dynasty," Cerise called into the prayer room, "put forth the most alluring among them: a mortal whose face was so breathtaking that the goddess was lured from the heavens and seduced into taking vulnerable human form. For their treachery, house Solon was cursed with self-destructive allure." She squeezed Nina's hand. "Do you come before the goddess humbled, seeking her forgiveness?"

Nina nodded her veiled head.

"Say it out loud," Cerise whispered.

"Yes," Nina said in a broken voice.

Cerise brushed a thumb over Nina's delicate skin, and then she nicked her sister's palm just hard enough to break the flesh. Nina didn't so much as flinch as the blade absorbed her blood and glowed brightly enough to render her veil transparent.

In the moment before the light dimmed, Cerise caught a glimpse of her sister's face and saw something that eclipsed fear. Nina's features were frozen in what could only be described as a silent death cry. She reminded Cerise of the rabbit kit at the temple and how it had screamed when the serpent had entered its cage. This couldn't possibly be about Nina's husband.

So if Nina was the rabbit, then who—or *what*—was her serpent?

The question flew to the back of Cerise's mind as the blade dimmed, and everyone glanced around for some sign that the ritual had worked. General Petros studied his hands and arms, flexing them as if testing an injured limb.

"Do you feel any differently?" Daerick asked him.

The general shrugged. "Do you?"

Daerick probed his face and stroked his scraggly beard. "I don't know. Maybe. It's hard to say."

In unison, they all looked to Kian, the only person who could eliminate any doubt as to whether or not the curse was broken. He pushed back his hair and locked eyes with Cerise as the shaded windows darkened with approaching twilight. A glimmer of hope passed between them. She had never wanted anything more than this: for him to remain whole.

Please, she silently begged. *Please let this work.*

The room went silent, every pair of eyes fixed on the king. No one moved, and if anyone breathed, Cerise couldn't hear it. Even time seemed to have gone still. Just when she didn't think she could survive another moment of waiting, the glow faded completely from the windows, and the only light that remained flickered from the enchantments overhead.

Kian exhaled into a shaky smile.

The sun had set, and he was still there.

Cerise drew a breath to thank the goddess, but her lungs were barely half full before Kian's fingertips began to curl into smoke. He raised both hands to his face, watching in horror as they vanished in front of his eyes. He stared at Cerise as if she could explain what had gone wrong. She only shook her head. She couldn't believe what she was seeing, but that didn't stop the shadows from claiming him, faster and faster until there was nothing left of his body. His eyes were the last of him to go—not the storm-cloud gaze of a king but the broken despair of the damned. Those eyes pierced the deepest, most tender part of her soul, and then they were gone.

"No," she cried.

Murmurs erupted in the sanctuary and beyond to the open-air corridor, where a crowd of people had followed and now learned of her failure. Through a haze of grief and shock, she looked across the room to Father Padron, the one person who could help her make sense of what had happened.

But he had no guidance for her. Strangely, he was retreating. He didn't even seem glad that the ceremony had failed. He looked like a captain abandoning a sinking ship as he inched along the hallway leading to his office, his blue eyes radiating fear. Cerise had no idea what could have possibly scared him, but if the high priest of Shiera didn't know what to do, what chance did she have?

"Come with me," Nina urged, brushing the tears from Cerise's cheeks. "Let's take the carriage to the dock. There's a ship bound for Calatris tonight."

"No," Cerise whispered. "There's still time."

Daerick cleared his throat. His face was ashen. "Not for me, there isn't."

"Don't say that," she told him. "We have until midnight."

"To do what?" he asked.

"To keep the fight going." She pointed the blade at the altar. "The ceremony was working. We all saw it. We must have missed something, some final step. Whatever it is, we have to find it."

"Please," Nina said, glancing at the sanctuary entrance, where priests were filing out into the corridor to disperse the crowd. "Let's leave while we can."

Cerise shook her off and focused on Daerick. "Help me figure this out."

"The archives," he said, a flicker of hope in his gaze. "The chamber Father Padron didn't want you to see. There has to be a reason he hid it. Now that you can" — he lowered his voice to a whisper — "use magic, you can open the wall and see what's inside."

"No!" Nina hissed. "It's out of the question!"

Cerise whirled on her sister. "Nina, I'm not going anywhere. Not until every last moment is spent and there's nothing left to try. So either go back to my suite or — "

"I won't leave you."

"Then help me." Cerise nodded at Daerick. "Actually, help *him*."

Daerick raised a questioning eyebrow.

"There's only one way inside the archives, and it's through here." Cerise hooked her thumb toward the sanctuary wall. "With all the priests distracted, no one will notice my energy, but they'll hear it if I split the wall." And that was assuming she had the skill to do it. "I need you to think of a reason to clear the sanctuary."

Daerick nodded slowly. "I might have an idea."

"*And*," she added, "keep the priests out until I'm finished. Especially Father Padron. He's been watching me since my Claiming Day. I can tell he knows there's something different about me."

Nina clutched the fabric over her heart so hard that her knuckles turned white. Even so, she nodded. "We'll find a way to make it work."

"Are you sure you don't want to wait in my suite?" Cerise asked. Whatever had terrified Nina during the ceremony, it hadn't let go. "Blue will protect you. Or if you want, you can take Father's carriage someplace safe."

"Oh, Cerise," Nina said in an exasperated voice that skated the line between laughter and tears. "There's nowhere I would feel safe if you weren't with me." She cradled her swollen belly and went quiet for a moment. "I won't leave you, so don't ask me to."

There was a dark undercurrent in Nina's tone that Cerise didn't like. Something was happening inside her sister's mind that she wasn't privy to—something unsettling. She desperately wished she could read Nina's face without falling into a trance.

"Is there something you want to tell me?" Cerise asked her sister.

"Yes." Nina folded her arms, as stubborn as ever. "Be ready to do your job, because I'm ready to do mine."

30

They enlisted the help of General Petros, who issued an evacuation order under the guise of inspecting the sanctuary for potentially harmful cracks he claimed to have seen in the ceiling during the ceremony. Cerise had worried that Father Padron would object, but oddly, he was still so shaken that he didn't argue. He shuffled with the other priests to the dining hall for supper while Cerise took advantage of the empty prayer room.

With the Petros Blade strapped to her back, she stood in front of the massive stone wall and tried to recall where the seams had been when Father Padron moved it. She needed to visualize the act before releasing her energy, like Nero had taught her, but enough time had passed that she couldn't remember the details. She checked over her shoulder. She was still alone, but Daerick and Nina wouldn't be able to keep the priests away forever.

She would have to try.

Exhaling long and slow, she widened her stance and stared at the wall with a soft focus, thinking of the corridor on the other side. She let her energy flow and commanded the stone to part.

The tang of copper coated her tongue. A charge raised chills of pleasure on her skin. And to her great surprise, the wall slid in half with a grinding rumble that she felt through the soles of her shoes. She grinned while waving away the dust. She had done it, and she didn't feel the least bit tired. Nero would be proud of her…if not a bit jealous.

She strode into the corridor and illuminated the wall sconces with nothing more than a flick of her hand. It was strange to remember how awe-stricken she had felt during her last visit, when Father Padron had led her on his arm and told her not to worry about being "late to bloom." At the time, she had considered herself more of a weed than a flower. She had never imagined that one day her strength would resemble a mighty oak tree with branches stretching toward the sun. She could still hardly believe it.

She hurried to the end of the corridor, where she crossed beneath the marble archway leading to the mausoleum. She remembered the corner walls that Father Padron had opened to access the archives. She parted the walls and squeezed through the slim gap, but she stopped short in surprise. The room was already lit. Someone had been in the archives. Her pulse thumped. Whoever had lit the torches had yet to extinguish them, which meant the person might still be down there.

She scanned the dusty floor for the partial boot print she had seen before. Instead of one partial heel, an entire trail of prints led to a far wall between two flickering sconces. She crouched down to study the boot prints. All of them looked identical. It would seem that one person had been coming and going from the hidden chamber—more than likely, it was Father Padron. If she was right, then she didn't have to worry about him waiting for her on the other side of the wall.

If she was wrong…then she would run.

She parted the wall, and the marble slid apart to reveal a lighted hallway. Peeking down the corridor, she detected no movement or sound. As she crept slowly inside the hidden chamber, the scents of dust and damp blended with something else—there was energy in the air, clouds of it, along with the stench of a washroom privy. She covered her nose and continued to the end of the hallway, where she hugged the wall and glanced around the corner.

What she saw turned her stomach.

On the other side of a small, stony chamber, a man and a woman were half naked and bloodied, both of them spread flat against the wall and bound there by some invisible force of magic. The woman's dull, matted head hung slack between her shoulders, hiding her face. Loose skin sagged from her bones, as if she had starved. Cerise couldn't tell if the woman was dead or alive. Each outline of her ribs was visible, but her chest didn't seem to be moving.

The man's head hung low, too, but as Cerise crept closer, she noticed he was breathing. He must not have been hanging on the wall for very long, because his body was corded with the lean muscle of someone well-fed. But that was where his good fortune ended. His shirt was torn down the front, exposing a chest mutilated by hundreds of weeping boils that looked too unnatural to have been caused by anything but magic of the cruelest kind.

Is that what you think happens under my watch? Abuse? Murder?

Father Padron had asked her that once. Now she knew exactly what happened under his watchful eye. She didn't know what crimes the man and woman had committed, but they didn't deserve to suffer torture, especially not at the hands of the Order. Holy magic was a gift, and for a priest to abuse his power was the foulest form of blasphemy she could imagine. She would tell the king as soon as the sun rose. The priests were still beholden to his command—for now, at least. If Father Padron wanted a reformation, he would have one.

Starting with himself.

She approached the victims while scanning the rest of the room. Aside from filth and waste, all that caught her eye was a discarded bundle of clothes and rubbish in the corner. That wouldn't ordinarily strike her as important, but someone had cast an energy shield around the pile, so she made a note to take a closer look at it.

The nearer she moved to the wall, the stronger the smell of decay grew, leaving no doubt that the woman's soul had returned to Shiera. The woman's hair was gray, her skin withered with age. Cerise began to suspect who the woman was, and she was right. She recognized the face of the elderly maid who had touched her skirts the first night she'd arrived at the palace—the maid Father Padron claimed to have discharged from her post and then relocated into the city.

Revulsion and horror clawed up inside her. Cerise hadn't fully believed him. She had expected Father Padron to punish the woman, but not like this.

He was crueler, far crueler, than she'd ever imagined.

She whispered a prayer of peace for the departed maid. Her words stirred the man, who groaned and lifted his face toward her...a face so handsome that not even bruises could disfigure it.

"Cole," she breathed.

He licked his cracked lips and begged in a hoarse whisper, "Mercy, please. I repented." His eyes were swollen and bleary. He didn't seem to know who she was. "Mercy, please," he repeated, his voice breaking in a sob. "I repented. You said I would be forgiven."

"Lord Solon, it's me," she said. "Cerise."

Cole blinked. His eyes focused on her and lit with recognition. "My lady?"

"Yes. Tell me who brought you here. Was it Father Padron?"

Cole nodded. "I repented."

"I'm sure you did," she said, wincing as she studied the wounds on his chest. Cole couldn't have been hanging on the wall for longer than a few hours. Father Padron had accomplished a disturbing amount of torture in the short time since his return to the palace. And he had hidden Cole from her. Perhaps he had tried to sabotage the ceremony after all.

"My lady," Cole said. "Please—will you let me go if I confess my crimes to you?"

She would release him no matter what, but his words made her curious to know what he might have done. "Yes, I promise."

"I committed treason, my lady," he said in a rush, darting a glance at the entrance to the hallway as if afraid that Father Padron would return. "Treason and murder."

She found that hard to believe. Torture would make a man confess to anything. But she asked him to go on while she calculated the best way to lower him to the ground without hurting him.

"I was the queen's lover," he told her.

"That's no secret."

"But I fed her herbs—crone's weed so she wouldn't conceive another child with the king. It went on for years until she caught me putting the herbs in her wine. She was furious. She ordered me to leave the palace at first light. But I was afraid she would tell the king what I had done, so I poisoned them both."

Cerise froze. "His Majesty's parents… That was you?"

"Yes," Cole admitted. "I tried to kill His Majesty, too. More than once."

As Cole went on to describe the predawn attacks involving the desert panther and the dream weed fire, Cerise no longer doubted his confession. What she didn't understand was the reason for any of it. Cole didn't seem motivated by self-preservation or money or revenge. He seemed to have wanted to end the royal line.

"But why?" she asked.

"Because the priests can't do it themselves."

"Do you mean someone compelled you to murder the king?"

Cole's gaze wandered back to the corridor. "No, the priests can't compel anyone to harm the king. I had an arrangement with Father Padron."

"What kind of arrangement?"

"We agreed that if I helped the Order take the throne by ending the Mortara line, the Order would give me more lands."

"More lands?" she repeated, shaking her head in disbelief. "Are you telling me that you risked execution, you betrayed your king and your realm, and you committed murder for *more lands*?"

"No, you don't understand," he said. "The Mortaras have been dwindling for years. That's not my fault. The Order is bound to take the throne. It's only a matter of time, and when that time comes, I would rather be in their good favor than be their target. You know what they'll do." He peeked at the dead woman. "You know what they've already done. I had a choice to be Padron's ally or his enemy."

"And look what that choice got you," she reminded him. "Your ally doesn't want you to repent. He doesn't care about your soul. He only wanted to use you and then send your secrets to the grave."

"I was wrong, and I'm sorry," Cole cried. "I'll pay for my crimes, I swear, but not like this. Please not like this."

"What about the old emissary?" she asked. "Did you kill her, too?"

"No, I swear," Cole said. "She poisoned herself."

Cerise doubted that, now more than ever. Mother Strout had gathered so much information, and it was only by her own guile that she'd been able to hide any of it. Maybe during the course of her investigations, someone had caught her asking the wrong questions. Any number of Father Padron's men could have poisoned her. Or Father Padron himself. He could have compelled her to drink poison, just like he'd compelled Cerise to drink water when she was sick.

"My lady, please have mercy," Cole said.

"I will," she assured him. "Just help me understand something. Why would Father Padron risk committing treason when no one knows for certain what will happen if the last Mortara dies? The priests might be bound to a different king."

Cole shook his head. "They won't. I don't know how or why, but he told me the Order can only be bound to a firstborn Mortara. He said it was part of the curse, and if the priests can't break it, then they have to stay bound until—"

"Wait," she interrupted. "The priests have been trying to break the curse?"

"Yes, for decades," Cole said. "It's the only other way to free themselves."

Cerise felt her heart drop into her stomach. If that was true, then she'd had it all wrong. Breaking the curse wouldn't stop the Order from taking the throne. It would give the priests their freedom even sooner. No matter what she did, the priests would be free. If she failed to break the curse, then Kian's death would unbind them. If she succeeded, then Kian would lose his power to control the same men who had been plotting to kill him for years. Even if she saved Kian's life, the priests could take it—easily—and then rule in his stead.

Either way, the Order would win.

But no, she thought. One thing didn't make sense. If Father Padron had all but won, then why had he looked so shaken after the ceremony? He should be gloating and planning a coup with his men, not hiding in fear.

Cerise shook her head. She was still missing something.

"My lady, please," Cole said. He must have mistaken her silence for hesitation to release him. "Please have mercy. Will you let me down?"

"Of course I will," she told him.

She studied the open wounds on his chest. Moving him might send him into shock from the pain. She needed to heal him first, a skill she hadn't learned. She remembered what Nero taught her, how to imagine what she wanted, and then she held both palms forward and willed Cole's flesh to mend. The magic in his wounds resisted her; it took two tries to clear the boils. But she soothed his skin and then gradually eased him down from the wall until his bare feet touched the floor. He was so overcome by relief that he didn't question how she had cast the magic. He wasted no time in wobbling on weak legs toward the corridor. She began to follow him, but then she remembered the pile of objects in the corner.

"You go ahead," she told him. "I'll be right behind you."

Cole didn't need telling twice. He was already gone.

She rushed to the corner and crouched down to peer through the static shield at the bundle on the other side. The tip of an aged scroll peeked through the folds of fabric, but beyond that, she couldn't discern what the objects were or why Father Padron might want to guard them. She tried using her energy to disperse the shield, but the protection he had cast was too strong. Glancing over her shoulder, she thought of the gap she had left in the sanctuary wall. The priests would finish their dinner soon, and then Daerick and Nina wouldn't be able to keep them away for much longer.

She faced the corner for one last attempt. Instead of scattering the energy, she focused on creating an opening large enough to fit her hand inside. It worked. She reached in and grabbed the bundle, pulling it free before the static re-formed. She snuck a glance at the scroll and found it filled with jumbled text in a language she couldn't read. She would need Daerick to interpret it.

She tucked the scroll deep into her dress pocket and held on to the fabric, just in case it might provide a clue. As she turned to leave, a rumbling noise pulsed through the room, originating from the shield she had just breached.

She had triggered an alarm.

She bolted across the chamber and down the hallway without sparing a second glance at the rest of the bundle in her hand. She didn't even stop to close the walls behind her as she left the torture chamber and the archive room. Her shoes skidded over the dusty mausoleum floor. She righted herself and barreled down the long, upward-sloping corridor leading to the sanctuary. Ahead of her, Cole noticed her clomping footfalls, and then he glanced over his shoulder at her and hurried his own steps in response.

She nearly burst with relief when she crossed into the prayer room and found it empty. She immediately spun around and used her energy to pull both halves of the wall together. It was then that Cole noticed the anomaly of a young woman wielding magic.

"How…" He trailed off in shock. "I've never seen an oracle do that."

"Forget what you saw." She glanced around for a place to hide the cloth. If the priests found her with it, there would be no denying that she was the one who had triggered the alarm. "Get as far away from here as you can."

"I'm grateful to you, my lady."

She nodded absently. Her gaze landed on the burning altar, and she tossed the cloth onto it. In the moment before the fabric ignited, she recognized a pattern of gilded threads peeking between patches of dried blood. She knew the garment. It was the robe Father Padron had worn the night he'd dispatched the titan hyena pack. She had cut the robe off of him before treating his lacerated back. She'd meant to burn all of the bloody clothes that night, but clearly she had missed one.

The robe ignited, and the blood-encrusted fabric erupted into a roaring black flame that rose to the ceiling and held there, snaking back and forth while the fabric shrank to ash.

Cold overcame her. Right down to her bones.

Now she knew why Father Padron had hidden the robe. Why he hadn't wanted her to burn it with the rest of the clothes.

His blood burned black.

Just like hers did.

Because he was *umbra sangi*, too.

If there had been any doubt regarding the identity of her father, it vanished into the smoke that thickened the air. There was no use denying it anymore. Her father was a monster.

A low voice from behind asked her, "Where did you get that?"

She whirled around with a gasp.

The monster had found her.

31

"Never mind. Obviously, *he* gave it to you." Father Padron stood ten paces away, holding Cole still in a magical grasp. No one else was with him. He must have responded to the alarm alone to hide his secrets from the other priests.

Secrets he would kill to protect.

Even so, Cerise didn't run. Some irrational need for connection forced her to search his face for similarities to hers. She found them in the shape of his eyes—the left one ever so slightly higher than the right—and in the way his lips pulled a little more to one side than the other. She looked more like Mama, but her father had filled in the details.

"Now you know my shame," he said with a bitter glare at the last ebony flames lingering above the ashes. "My blood burns black because I committed a sin so vile that twenty years of atonement can't erase it. I broke my vow of abstinence, Cerise. The goddess won't forgive me."

She shook her head. He had it all wrong.

"She rejects all of my offerings," he went on. "I gave her my blood and my pain. I prayed my throat raw. I converted the faithless and slaughtered heretics for her, and still it's not enough."

As Cerise pictured his lacerated back, she began to understand what had twisted him into the cold, cruel man he had become. He didn't know that he was *umbra sangi*, that he had the blood of the goddess in addition to the priesthood. No one had ever told him that the goddess had meant for him to love so he could continue her bloodline. He had always believed that the act of love was forbidden to him, and so he thought he had sinned with Mama.

And he'd been punishing himself for it ever since.

Cerise couldn't stop a flicker of sympathy from rising inside her. Despite everything he had done, she understood him better than anyone; the Order had used lies and fear to control her, to weaken her power, to make her think that something as natural as the tides was a sin. And how ironic that the same fear Father Padron had used against her—claiming that the act of love would dull her gift—had harmed him, too. He had believed the Order's lie, and so his own guilt and shame had compounded for twenty years. He'd woven a cloak of scars over his back and carried its burden for half of his life. That made him no less of a monster, but one born from pain instead of evil. Perhaps something tender had survived beneath the scars—a part of him that she could touch.

Perhaps she could pull him back from the darkness.

"You're wrong about the black flame," she said. "It's not a sign that the goddess rejected your offerings. It's a sign that you're different from other priests."

He drew back, hitching his upper lip. "Do not presume to explain the signs to *me*, you Sightless infant. You know nothing."

"I know it's not a sin for you to love," she said. "Or for me to love, or for anyone who desires it. The goddess is passionate. She made us in her image, to be like her."

"Be careful, Cerise. You're sliding dangerously close to apostasy."

"Please listen to me," she begged. "The flame burns black because you're not an ordinary priest. You're descended from Shiera. That's why you're so powerful and why you can do things that other priests can't. You have the blood of the goddess in your veins."

As soon as she mentioned the goddess by name, she knew she had pushed too far beyond the limits of his faith. She should have known he wouldn't believe her. She hadn't believed the truth, either, when Nero had first told it to her.

Father Padron's gaze turned so hard and cold that she cringed under its weight. "Heretic," he hissed, hurtling a jolt of energy at her. Before she could block the attack, her lips sealed shut. "I'll hear no more from you."

Cerise closed her eyes and imagined his enchantment melting away. She freed her voice and shouted, "You *will* listen! What you did all those years ago was no crime. You have to forgive yourself and stop projecting your"—two more enchantments whizzed at her, but she deflected them—"guilt onto everyone else."

His jaw dropped. "How did you do that?"

"The goddess wants you to hear me."

He seemed to have forgotten his enchantment over Cole, who had freed one leg and was trying to drag himself out of the prayer room. As Father Padron shook his head in bewilderment, he noticed the motion. With no more attention than a man would pay to a fly, he waved a hand, and in response, Cole's neck snapped in half and his body crumpled to the floor.

Cerise covered her mouth.

"It was a cleaner death than he deserved," Father Padron mused, nudging Cole with his shoe. "If you repent, I can spare you from this, Cerise."

The lie slid so smoothly from his lips that she almost believed him. "Did you do this to Mother Strout, too?" she asked, and as she pictured the late emissary's black-and-white journal, she finally realized why Mother Strout had hidden the ritual for breaking the curse. She had known the priests were a threat, and she had wanted to delay their freedom from bondage to the king for as long as she could. "Did she find out the truth about you and Cole?"

Father Padron didn't say *yes*, but he didn't deny it.

That was answer enough. He had murdered a Seer—a devoted lady of the temple, revered by all who had known her, and the former emissary to two kings. Father Padron's crimes went beyond the unlawful torture and killing of laymen. Not even sisters of Shiera's Order were safe from this man.

Cerise retreated a pace toward the altar. She still wore the Petros Blade on her back. She didn't want to use it, but unless she could find a way to make him listen, she might have to.

She knew she wouldn't reach him by contradicting his beliefs; he would only accuse her of heresy. She had to find a different approach. But before she had a chance to try, Nina came sprinting so quickly into the prayer room that her veil molded to her face.

Nina threw herself in front of Cerise and shouted, "Stay away from her!"

Tensing, Cerise prepared to defend her sister, but Nina didn't need her help. Father Padron rocked back on his heels as if Nina had physically struck him. Then Nina threw back her veil, and he cried out in anguish, shielding his eyes like a creature of the night shrinking away from the sun.

What was happening?

All Cerise could do was volley her gaze back and forth between her sister and Father Padron for some sign as to what had brought him to his knees. She couldn't figure it out. Nina's heaving chest and trembling hands said she was just as terrified of him as he was of her.

Why were they so afraid of each other?

As Nina stood over him, Father Padron peeked at her from between his fingers. His glances were tentative at first, brief glimpses that turned longer and bolder until he lowered both hands and straightened to full height. A smile unfurled across his mouth, a grin so full of venom that it raised chills on the back of Cerise's neck.

"It doesn't work anymore," he told Nina, who cradled her rounded belly while inching backward. "Your power over me is dead." He spoke as if they knew each other, which didn't make sense. Until he raised a triumphant chin and added, "You won't seduce me again."

The full force of realization struck Cerise with a blow that knocked her breathless. She collapsed in front of the altar, barely noticing when her knees gave out. The truth was too big to make room for her senses. She had been wrong, so very wrong. It wasn't Mama who had caught Father Padron's eye in Solon all those years ago.

It was Nina.

The floor seemed to tilt. Cerise gripped the tiles, but it was in vain. Her whole axis had shifted, and now she didn't know which way was up. Mama was her grandmother. And Father was her grandfather, which meant she was a Solon after all.

And her sister…

She raised her gaze to Nina's belly. That was where she would find her sibling. She peered at Nina's face just long enough to see a hundred apologies written in the lines around her mouth. *My mother.* Cerise couldn't reconcile it with the truth. Her brain refused to allow it. Nina shook her head in a reminder that Father Padron hadn't made the connection. He still didn't know that he had a child.

"You might as well hear the rest," he said, his narrowed eyes fixed on Nina. "This is the reason for my sin. She used sorcery to seduce me."

"No," Nina whispered. "That's not what happened."

"Don't deny it," he snapped. "No one else has ever tempted me. Even when I met you, I was unimpressed by your face. But you kept coming back, bringing me sweet cakes and smiling and watching me with those eyes, making it harder to turn away until the sight of you consumed me. You invaded my every thought. How do you explain that if not by sorcery?"

"Love," Cerise said, scrambling up from the floor. "It makes the Solon allure stronger. That's why her face entranced you—because you loved her. But you don't feel that way anymore, so the allure doesn't work." Cerise took another step forward, approaching him as though he were a wounded animal. She hadn't expected him to listen to her, but when he furrowed his brow in consideration, she saw her chance and kept going. "It didn't happen overnight, did it? The first time you met her, you thought she was beautiful but nothing more. Then, as you got to know her, she became more and more striking until you couldn't bear it."

His silence told her she was right.

"I know the feeling because I love her, too," she went on. "Nina doesn't want to hurt anyone. If she did, she would use her face as a weapon instead of hiding it behind a veil." Cerise pulled her necklace from beneath her dress and showed him the battered pendant that had been protecting her since her arrival at the palace. Now she understood where it had come from and why Father Padron had looked so drained each time it had saved her life. He had tied it to his own energy. "You gave this to her, didn't you? You made a ring, and then you linked your power to it to protect her. You wanted to keep her safe because you loved her. The goddess wouldn't fault you for that."

For two long heartbeats, she held her breath and watched him digest her words, weighing them against the certainty he had clung to for his entire life. She knew firsthand the fear of letting go, like falling backward with no safe place to land. His eyes gave her hope. There was an open window inside them, barely wide enough to admit a breeze of doubt.

But in the end, the window slammed shut, and just like that, she lost him.

"You didn't fool me about the black flame, and you won't fool me about *her*, either." He turned a glare on Nina that could melt iron. "She will confess to seducing me, and then I will deliver her punishment."

Cerise glanced at Cole's body, bruised and bloodied from the torture chamber wall. She had witnessed Father Padron's idea of justice, and she wouldn't allow him to punish an insect, let alone her sister. Or her mother. Whatever Nina was to her didn't matter, because nothing had changed. She loved Nina more than life, more than any purpose or doctrine or prophecy, and infinitely more than the man who had fathered her.

Without hesitating, Cerise unsheathed the Petros Blade and lunged at him. But with a flick of his wrist, Father Padron sent the blade flying across the room. She attacked him again, this time with a burst of energy that knocked him backward twenty paces. He struck the floor and skidded until he hit the rear wall. When he righted himself, he was too stunned to retaliate. He inhaled through his mouth, no doubt tasting her residual energy and questioning how it was possible for a woman to wield magic.

She saw no reason not to tell him.

"I'm not a heretic or a sorceress," she said and lifted her chin. "But I *am* my father's daughter."

He blinked once, twice, three times before he pieced together the truth. It gave her a perverse sense of satisfaction to watch the color drain from his face. He had kept so many secrets from her, but just this once, when it really mattered, he was the last to know.

"Impossible," he murmured, even as he scanned her face exactly the way she had searched his only moments earlier.

"I'm not pleased about it, either," she told him.

"Impossible," he repeated. "It's a lie. It has to be. I never lay with another woman. If you were my child, you would be a firstborn. You would bear your mother's curse."

Nina spoke in a trembling voice. "She was a twin. The first baby was born sleeping." She looked to Cerise. "You were the second."

"Impossible," Father Padron murmured again.

Cerise repeated something Daerick had told her once, when she had used her faith like a blindfold to block out what frightened her. "It's not faith to ignore common sense. It's foolishness."

In the span of half a breath, his face hardened with rage. Nina shouted a warning that came too late. His energy struck Cerise in the chest before she could brace herself, but instead of knocking her backward, the charge lingered on her ribcage, buzzing like a swarm of bees. An odd pressure moved across her skin, as if the magic was trying to penetrate her. Because it was. With a gasp, she looked to Father Padron. He was trying to stop her heart. That shouldn't have surprised her, but it did. He knew that she was his daughter, and still, he despised her.

Heat bloomed from the pendant resting against her dress. In one final act of protection, it dispersed the static and cracked in half. As the metal pieces clinked to the floor, they drained a surge of magic from their power source, and Father Padron slouched against the wall, weakened by the force of his own attack.

Cerise didn't give him a chance to recover. He was beyond saving. The only way to protect herself and the people she loved was to kill him—now, while he was weak. She stretched out her arms and imagined her energy closing around his chest, crushing his heart, like he had tried to do to her. Energy flowed from her in torrents, gushing out faster than she could control it. She wasn't prepared for how quickly her energy drained. Soon her hands trembled and sweat beaded on her upper lip. She tried to give more, but he blocked her magic and used the wall to push himself to his feet.

As he stood, she collapsed.

The room spun around her. She had enough strength to conjure a shield before his next attack, but she struggled to hold it through a haze of dizziness and nausea. She heard running footsteps and glanced up to find Nina on the other side of the sanctuary, picking up the Petros Blade.

Nina charged Father Padron with a battle cry that echoed through the high ceilings. She only made it a few steps before he cast her aside, and she fell to the floor with a grunt of pain, gripping her distended belly.

Cerise launched to her feet, and in doing so, she dropped her shield. Father Padron took advantage of the slip and cast a ring of fire around her. The flames closed in so quickly that they singed her skirts before she could shield herself again. He held the inferno in place. Through the shield, she caught glimpses of his face as the flames flickered and danced. He wore an arrogant smile that tightened her stomach. It was the look of someone who knew he had won.

"Let's end this, Cerise," he said. "I have an offer for you." He parted the flames wide enough to give her a view of Nina, who now clutched her throat as if choked by an invisible fist. "Give yourself up. Confess your sins of heresy and sorcery. Accept your punishment, and I'll let her live. Fight me, and she'll die where she stands."

Cerise pressed both palms to the shield wall and locked eyes with Nina. The answer came at once. *Yes.* A thousand times yes. She knew the cost, and she would pay it. To trade her life for Nina's and the baby's was a bargain. But when she opened her mouth to speak, no sound came out. She tried again to shout, *Yes!* but her lips wouldn't so much as form the word.

The king's command to preserve her life—it wouldn't let her surrender. She knew full well that Father Padron would kill her if she gave herself up to him, and so she was physically unable to do it.

She shoved a trembling hand through her hair, pins tearing at her scalp. She had to find a way around the compulsion. Closing her eyes, she willed the shield to lower, but she couldn't control her own magic. It flowed from her in a steady stream to feed the protective barrier. A sob rose from her throat. When she opened her eyes, Nina's face had turned red.

"I can't let down my shield!" Cerise shouted. "The king's compulsion won't let me."

Padron scoffed. "I don't believe you."

"It's true!" she said. "He ordered me to preserve my life by any means. I'm a priestess. I'm bound to obey him as much as—"

"You dare call yourself a priestess?" Padron hissed. "I don't know what manner of abomination you are, but you won't live to darken another day. Either surrender now and save your mother, or resist and join her in hell. Make your choice."

Nina shook her head and mouthed *no.* She didn't want Cerise to give up her life. But that choice didn't belong to Nina or to the king. It belonged to Cerise, and she didn't want to live in a world without Nina in it.

"I swear I'm telling the truth," Cerise promised. "Just let her breathe! She's with child. If you kill her, the baby will die, too."

Father Padron lifted a shoulder. "One fewer heretic to root out later."

With panic screaming along her nerves, Cerise searched for the Petros Blade. As soon as she found it, she used her energy to send it flying through the air toward Padron's chest. But her power was divided, weakened by holding the shield, and he easily knocked the blade aside with a teasing *tsk, tsk, tsk.*

"You're wasting time, Cerise," he said, nodding at Nina. "And she doesn't have much left."

Nina sank to the floor, her eyes bulging and watering. Fear shone in her gaze, but she pressed a hand over her heart and mouthed, *I love you.*

"No!" Cerise pounded her fists against the shield that had become her cage. Her mind raced for another solution. She thought of Nero and called out to him mentally, but she knew he couldn't possibly reach her in time. She had just begun to focus on Daerick when he ran into the sanctuary, followed by General Petros. As their eyes widened to take in the scene, she pointed at Father Padron and shouted, "Kill him!"

The general moved with lightning grace, drawing a dagger to take aim. He had no way of sensing the energy that Father Padron fired at him, and Cerise wasn't strong enough to block it. The dagger exploded in the general's hand, and the force of the blow knocked him to the floor so violently it rendered him unconscious.

Daerick covered his head. "They're coming!"

The priests.

"Don't let them in!" Cerise yelled. She pulled the scroll from her pocket, stared at it to form a mental image of its markings, and then sent the image to Daerick with her mind. *Translate this*, she told him. She prayed that the information in the scroll would help her break the curse. It was the only way to free herself from the king's compulsion and trade her life for Nina's.

As Daerick nodded and ran out of sight, Cerise knelt on the floor to peer between the flames at Nina, who lay on her side, peering back with tears in her bloodshot eyes. There was a new calm in her gaze—the peace that came from a dimming light. Cerise slapped the tile and screamed at Nina to hold on. Then she summoned the image of her last ally in the castle and prayed that she would answer.

Delora, she called. *Let Blue out of my suite and come to the sanctuary. Kill Father Padron if you can. Do it now!*

"This is your last chance, Cerise." Father Padron knelt down to taunt her, a smile curving the face she had once thought so handsome. "Your mother's soul won't stay with us for much—"

Cerise had enough energy to cast a blow through the shield and break his nose, which she did with pleasure.

While he stumbled back and cupped blood in his hand, she heard Daerick shout, "The priests!"

"I know!" Cerise said. "Don't let them in!"

"No, that's the missing element!" he yelled. "It wasn't just the Mortaras who planned the Great Betrayal. It was the priests. The priests didn't want to serve the people. They wanted to rule the people. They wanted power, and so their curse was bondage."

Cerise scanned the floor for the Petros Blade. Using every last drop of her energy, she summoned the blade to her outstretched hand. It slid across the tile and through the ring of fire. The hilt burned her palm when she picked it up, but she ignored the pain. She stood tall, meeting Father Padron's gaze as she slid the blade across her forearm.

"Shiera's priests colluded with house Mortara," she said as her blood flowed into the blade, "to usurp her holy authority and rule in her place. For their treachery, they were cursed to serve the whims of others. The priests are still undeserving, but this priestess is repentant."

The blade glowed with the light of ten suns, forcing her to shut her eyes.

The compulsion blinked out.

She had done it. She'd broken the curses.

Now she was free from her bond of service to the king, and she didn't need her eyes to drop her shield and slash at her father. She felt the connection with his robes and slashed out again, forcing him back. She was stronger now, in control of her magic. She extinguished the flames and slashed at him once more. When he cried out and stumbled to the floor, she took a moment to squint through the smoke and find Nina.

Cerise felt her arms go limp. She was too late.

Nina lay in exactly the same position as before: one slim hand resting near her heart and the other tucked lovingly beneath her womb. Her eyes were half open and sightless, her red lips parted as if she had fallen asleep. But she wasn't asleep, and all of the magic in the world couldn't change that.

Or could it?

Cerise sheathed the blade, ran to Nina, and skidded to her knees. Placing a hand on Nina's chest, she channeled her energy inside it, willing Nina's heart to beat. Nothing happened. She tried again, and again, and then again, even leaning down to blow air into Nina's lungs.

Nina didn't stir.

Cerise sank back, staring at her useless hands.

All this power, and for what?

For what?

All this power, and she couldn't save Nina.

In the moment before the pain came, it struck her how graceful Nina looked in death. Even with the curse broken, she could still stare at Nina for hours and never get her fill.

Then the grief hit.

It started as a pinprick of pain at the base of her throat and spread in both directions—up into her face, where it pressed her eyes and squeezed her temples, and down into her chest, where it stretched her ribs until she feared they might crack. Something inside her shifted and broke. Instinctively, she knew she would never be whole again. Part of her life had ended. The sweetest part. The time of love and light and laughter was over. Now she existed in the dark, with nothing but emptiness all around.

She hadn't simply lost a mother or a sister. She had lost the sun and every star in the sky.

32

Cerise stumbled away from Nina's body.

"Mother Shiera, mistress of worlds," she heard herself say. Her voice broke. She couldn't finish the prayer for the departed. She wasn't ready to recite the words. Praying for Nina would mean admitting she was dead, and she simply couldn't do that. Not yet.

Maybe not ever.

Noises and flashes of light surrounded her, muted as though she were underwater. From the opposite end of the prayer room, the motion of fabric and the sound of shoes told her the priests had breached the sanctuary. Kian materialized by her side, naked and flinching with the shock of the chaos he'd appeared into—smoke in the air, bodies on the floor, General Petros unconscious, Father Padron wounded, and the priests scurrying to his aid.

"What in damnation?" Kian asked her. "Whose blood is this? What's happening? Did you break the curse—is that why I'm here?"

Yes, she had broken the curse. Along with her own heart.

She faced away from him. She couldn't look him in the eyes. The logical part of her knew that his command had saved her life.

Father Padron would have killed her if she'd surrendered, and he probably would have killed Nina, too. But she also knew that her survival had come at a price.

It had cost her the sun.

Kian pulled her back to him, wrapping both arms around her waist and tackling her to the floor. The blow jarred her senses into place.

She glanced up and watched magic rend the air where she had just stood. Father Padron had made it to his feet, swaying visibly as he clutched a scarlet gash low on his abdomen. Blood flowed between his fingers. Sweat covered his face, his gaze shifting focus, but like the feral beast that he was, his wounds were bound to make him even more dangerous.

Cerise pushed to her knees and prepared to defend her king. From behind her, she heard Kian order Father Padron to stand down—impotent words that went ignored. Father Padron released a bitter laugh, and the next thing Cerise knew, she tasted energy, and her body stiffened where she knelt on the floor. She hadn't defended herself in time. Her grief had made her slow, but not Father Padron. He had already paralyzed her, starting with her limbs and ending with her lungs. Unable to move or breathe, she saw Kian in her peripheral vision. He was trapped under the same enchantment, frozen beneath Father Padron's glare.

"You don't command me, *Your Highness*," Father Padron spat. "And you never will again. By this night's end, I'll make you wish you had surrendered into the shadows for all of eternity."

Grief gave way to fear. Cerise ached to breathe, but she couldn't reach her own energy. Padron had somehow paralyzed that, too. He closed the distance between them and then leaned aside as much as his wound would allow, bending to look her in the eyes, to savor her suffering. A smile had barely curved his lips when something struck his shoulder hard enough to spin him around. Cerise heard the tearing of flesh, and his enchantment broke. All of a sudden, she and Kian were free.

She drew a breath and glanced behind Father Padron to find Delora holding a bow, already nocking a second arrow. Two priests used their magic to disarm Delora, and in a flash, she was face down on the floor with her wrists behind her back—but Blue charged ahead, snarling at Father Padron.

Padron cast a shield around himself, and Blue skidded to a halt and clawed at it. When Blue couldn't penetrate the magic, he loped to Cerise and whined in agitation. The violence in the air had triggered his predatory instincts, and he didn't seem to know what to do with himself. From somewhere in the distance, a bell tolled to summon the royal guard, and Blue tipped back his head and released a savage howl.

"Let her go," Kian ordered the priests while pointing at Delora. "Your high priest has committed treason. You will assist me in taking—"

"You will do no such thing!" Father Padron called to his priests. "You will kill the emissary, her beast, and anyone who stands in your way!" He yanked the arrow from his shoulder and then thrust it toward her. "Cerise Solon is a heretic and a sorceress!"

At once, Cerise cast a shield in front of herself, Blue, and the king. Hiding her magic was no longer an option.

Kian had torn a strip of fabric from the curtains and tied it around his waist. "You will stand down," he repeated to the priests. "And assist the royal guard in—"

"Kian Mortara no longer commands you," Father Padron shouted. "Your chains are broken. Test your magic and see! You are beholden to no layman—and to no false king! This is the day I have promised you! The day we reclaim our divine right to rule after a thousand years of oppression!"

Daerick shouted from the sanctuary entrance, "The royal guard is coming, and so is every man and woman in the palace capable of holding a blade. I don't think any of you want to fight a bloody battle in this room tonight—I know I don't—but unless you bend the knee to your king, that will happen. People will die here. I guarantee some of them will be you."

Daerick had just finished his warning when the first squadron of the royal guard arrived. Dozens of uniformed soldiers armed with swords and bows gathered outside the sanctuary, seemingly unsure if they should enter. Through the crowd, Cerise could see servants, stable hands, and cooks, each of them bearing a makeshift weapon of their own—a shovel, a kitchen knife, a pitchfork. The workers looked to one another in confusion. Kian extended a palm to hold them off.

"Choose your next actions carefully," Kian told the priests, who outnumbered his royal guard. Even if more guards arrived, their swords and arrows couldn't match the combined magic of the Order.

Daerick had been right. People would die if the priests turned against the king. Cerise's body went numb as her gaze was drawn once more to Nina. *All of them* might die if the priests turned against the king.

"The penalty for treason is death," Kian continued. "Obey me, go and stand with my guard, and all will be forgiven."

"Your faith is your king," Father Padron told his men. "The goddess delivered your freedom so that you may carry out her will. Now let her will be done. The emissary is an abomination. You can see the forbidden magic she uses to shield herself. It is our duty to dispatch her and anyone who stands in the way of divine justice."

"Divine *justice*?" Cerise called out. The numb places inside her body began to fill with heat. She pointed at Cole and then at Nina. "Your high priest is a murderer and a hypocrite. He killed an innocent woman with a child in her womb!"

"Cole Solon killed the woman," Father Padron smoothly lied. "Because she carried his bastard. I couldn't stop him, but I dispatched him for his crimes."

Rage boiled Cerise's blood. Every part of her felt ready to combust. "The only bastard she ever carried was *yours*!"

There was a collective intake of breath.

"That woman was my mother," Cerise yelled, pointing at Nina. "And this"—thrusting an index finger at the high priest—"is the man who stole her heart and fathered me."

"Lies!" Father Padron shouted.

"I wish it was a lie!" she shouted back at him. "I hate that your blood runs in my veins! But it does." To prove it, she conjured a flame in her hand. "Where do you think my magic came from?"

"From sorcery," Father Padron spat. "You convict yourself even as you speak."

She ignored him and addressed the priests. For once, they would know what kind of man they served. The fire of her fury had engulfed her, consumed her. "He killed my mother to hide his secret. He murdered Cole Solon after using him to poison the late king and queen. And when Mother Strout discovered his treason, he poisoned her, too. His evil has no limits. I can't stop him alone, but together we can bind him. You have to help me."

"Help you?" Father Padron asked, scoffing. "A heretic who would say anything to save herself?"

"I don't need saving." Cerise unsheathed the Petros Blade. "The goddess entrusted me with the most destructive weapon in all of creation—*me*, not Father Padron—because I alone was worthy to wield it." As she spoke, the blade began to vanish, exactly like the sunset runes had done, and she held it high for all to see the last glimpse of it. "Shiera gifted me with her favor so I could break the noble curses. She guided my path and blessed me along every step of the journey. *That* is what the will of the goddess looks like." Cerise paused. "Listen to your hearts. Who do you think she would want you to follow? A priestess created in her own image? Or a man who perverts her holy magic by using it to torture and murder innocents?"

Kian stood beside her and clasped her hand. To anyone watching, the gesture probably looked like an act of solidarity. But there was love in his touch, a silent *I'm sorry, and I'm here for you* in the squeeze of his palm and the brush of his thumb against her inner wrist. She squeezed him in return while settling her other hand atop Blue's head. If not for the two of them, she didn't know how she would have the strength to stand.

As she scanned the crowd of priests, she was met with dozens of cold, hard gazes from the men whose loyalty belonged to Father Padron. Even now, knowing the evil he had done, they were willing to overlook his crimes in exchange for whatever he had promised them. There were more of his kind than she had hoped. The Reverend Mother's words echoed in her ears. *Nameless, faceless men who served false idols.* It wasn't the Triad. It was the Order.

A few pockets of men traded wary glances with one another, hesitating to act, clearly torn between the treason Father Padron had asked them to commit and the risk to their own safety if they refused. Cerise remembered what Cole had told her—that he had chosen to be Father Padron's ally instead of his enemy. She could only hope the priests would be braver than Cole had been.

While the men wrestled with their morals, one priest backed away and strode briskly to join the royal guard at the sanctuary entrance. Cerise recognized him as Father Bishop. She held her breath and silently prayed that other men would follow his lead, that his bravery would embolden them to do the right thing. But in the end, every other priest remained in the room. One by one, each man made his decision until all of them stood tall and clasped their hands in front of Father Padron, collectively declaring their allegiance to the Order.

The priests had listened to their hearts, and they had chosen cowardice.

They shamed the mighty goddess they claimed to serve.

"I fight for the king and his priestess!" shouted a young woman from the crowd that had gathered behind the royal guard. Other voices clamored with hers in support.

Kian looked to Cerise. "Are you ready, my love?"

She nodded at him and said, "If we survived the blighted mountain, we can survive this." And then she dropped her shield.

The priests formed a tight huddle and worked together to raise a shield of their own, but Cerise was prepared for them, and she used her energy to strike it down. Then Kian gave the signal for his royal guard to attack, and the sanctuary erupted into chaos.

The battalion surrounded the priests and slashed out at the men on the fringes, who scrambled to defend themselves with their limited magic. A lone priest could be defeated, but collectively, they were unstoppable, and so Cerise focused her efforts on blocking them from pooling their energy. Blue barked and snarled, tensing on his haunches and all but begging her to release him into the crowd. She told him, "Go," and at once, he launched into the fray and tore into his first victim.

Daerick ran to Kian's side and handed him a sword, and the two of them joined the fight. In the brief moment that Cerise looked at them and away from the battle, one of the priests killed a guard and used magic to duplicate his weapon—two blades, then four, eight, sixteen, until more priests were armed than not—and then the sound of clanking metal filled the sanctuary, punctuated by feral shouts and groans of pain. The tang of magic and the smell of sweat thickened the air, and then it struck Cerise: she had lost sight of Father Padron.

She peered through the chaos for his gilded robes. When she couldn't find him, she lowered to one knee and searched the floor for his body. All that remained of Father Padron was a set of bloodred shoe prints leading to a side door.

Cerise drew a hopeful breath. He never would have abandoned the fight unless he was vulnerable. Judging by the trail of blood he had left behind, he hadn't been able to heal himself from his wounds. Perhaps the magic infused into the Petros Blade had prevented it. If so, that meant this was her chance to end him, to cut the head off the beast and restore balance to Shiera's holy Order.

Cerise glanced at Kian as he thrust his sword into his opponent's chest. He didn't need her help, at least not now, and so she seized the moment and went after Father Padron. She crouched low and followed the trail of blood to the side door, then pushed the door open and left it partly ajar—just wide enough for her to see the battle on the other side.

As her eyes adjusted to the moonlight, she stepped into what appeared to be a private garden. Shorn grass stretched out for roughly half the length of the prayer room, bordered by tall, leafy hedges that blocked the space from view. It was a simple garden with no flowering vines or fountains on display. The highlight of the space was a small carriage resting in the corner, already tethered to a pair of horses.

A shadowy figure limped toward the carriage. His steps were clumsy and uneven. He clutched his side with one hand, the other hanging limp from the shoulder where an arrow had landed. He had nearly reached his escape.

Cerise clenched her jaw. He was going to be disappointed.

She strode across the lawn while raising her hands toward the hedges, willing them to stretch forth their branches and cover the carriage wheels. They sprouted, one branch atop another, thicker and thicker until not a glimpse of wood or metal remained.

"You're not going anywhere," she said. "Except to the goddess. Then she can deliver the justice that you deserve."

Father Padron turned around and leaned against the hedges for support. Though he was weak and bleeding, he laughed at her, a reaction that struck her as odd. It was then that she realized her mistake. He'd predicted that she would follow him.

He had lured her there and set a trap, and she'd just walked into it.

The space around her formed an invisible cylinder, and then dirt began to fill it from the ground up. It seemed Father Padron lacked the strength to stop her heart, so he meant to suffocate her.

Thinking fast, she conjured a bubble of air around her head. Dirt rose up to her face, blocking her view. She imagined the cylinder bursting apart. When that didn't work, she envisioned a hole opening up at the bottom of it, wide enough for her to crawl through. It

took two tries to pierce Father Padron's magic and another two
tries before she managed to squeeze out onto the grass. She stood
up, shaking the soil from her body, and found half of the carriage
wheels uncovered.

"I told you," she gritted out. "You're not going anywhere."

She braided the hedges back together, this time trapping him
between the branches. Her mouth watered with the metallic tang
of magic. She could choke him, make him suffer the same death
as Nina. *Yes*, she decided. But as she willed the branches to wrap
around his throat, a sharp howl rang out from inside the sanctuary,
and she whirled toward the sound.

Blue.

She squinted through the open doorway, but the air had turned
hazy, and she struggled to make out Blue in the distance. He seemed
to be writhing on the floor, surrounded by the sandaled feet of
priests.

Cerise tensed to run to him, but she hesitated. Father Padron
would never be this weak again. This was her chance to end him,
to make him pay for what he'd done to Nina. If she left to go and
fight the priests, she might not have the strength to kill him when
she returned.

She was still wavering when Blue cried out in agony, and the
decision made itself. She wove another thicket of branches around
Father Padron to hold him in place, and then she spun around and
bolted back inside the sanctuary.

The room was in ruin.

Someone had knocked the sacrificial bowl into the curtains,
which had caught flame and filled the air with smoke. Figures ran
to and fro, but she couldn't discern who anyone was. She dropped
to her knees to peer below the haze and crawled closer to Blue. She
counted ten pairs of feet around him—too many priests for her to
fight alone. Then she noticed the faces of the fallen, some of whom
she recognized.

There in front of her was Father Bishop with his neck broken, and beside him lay sweet Lark, the young, freckled maid who had once braided Cerise's hair, now slain, her eyes open and sightless, exactly like Nina's. Another girl of no more than fifteen lay sprawled beneath the weight of a stone slab that a priest had cast onto her chest. Sandaled feet trampled over the girls as more priests gathered to surround Blue and combine their magic against him. When one of the priests stepped on Lark's face, Cerise felt her heart rend in two, and she realized something that had eluded her before.

Lark meant nothing to the priest. He didn't value her life. He didn't respect her in death. And he never would. None of them would.

So it was within the Order. These were the same men who had rejected Cerise in favor of a monster of their own kind. They would never accept her as a priestess, because to them, women were objects to be tamed and controlled or else threats to be cut down. Even the goddess had been no exception. The priests of long ago had resented Shiera's power so deeply that they'd tried to dampen her flame. A thousand years later, the Order still hadn't learned, hadn't changed. They would rather extinguish a woman's flame than stand in her warmth.

As above, so below. The flame you seek to dampen will consume you.

Cerise finally understood her purpose. It wasn't to restore balance to the Order; it was to raze it to the ground and build something new.

She turned her gaze to the enchanted murals on the ceiling. Through the smoky haze, she found the vengeful side of Shiera's face—one eye blazing, her upper lip hitched above a lethal incisor. Cerise didn't shrink away from the sight. For the first time in her life, she understood the value of wrath over mercy.

"Mother Shiera, mistress of worlds," she called out in a voice that matched the goddess's fury. "You are darkness and light, balance in all things. You foresaw that to give more power to your own sex would create instability, and so you favored the priests with magic. But now, balance is lost. Power has rotted them. They use their holy gift to dominate and murder your daughters. Hear me; make me your vessel. Punish my enemies and yours. Fill me with your flame, and let them be consumed!"

Ebony fire erupted from the burning altar. Cerise yanked free the golden chain Nina had given her. She sent the chain slithering across the floor and commanded it to lengthen and loop around the ankle of every priest left standing. Then she reached a hand toward the burning altar and imagined a link between herself and the flames. She opened herself like a conduit, channeling the flames through her body and into the metal necklace.

Scorching heat flowed through her. The black flame seemed to boil the blood inside her veins. She screamed out in agony, her limbs trembling while she held the connection. Throughout the room, bodies stiffened and fell. The smell of burned hair and flesh rose above the smoke. Even still, Cerise willed the goddess to give her more fire, more vengeance, until the final priest dropped and she broke the link.

She collapsed onto the tile floor. In the wake of the sudden deaths, shouts of confusion broke out, followed by retreating boots. She dragged herself to Blue's body and gently skimmed her palm over his hide. His tongue was lolled to the side, his eyes rolled back in his head. He didn't even try to sit up, and that scared her the most. The priests had wounded him in places she couldn't see.

She darted a glance at the garden door while stroking Blue's head.

"I'm here, sweet boy," she murmured. "They can't hurt you anymore." Closing her eyes, she poured what remained of her energy into his body, imagining his broken bones mending and his severed tissue knitting back together. She gave him everything she had, and with her last drop of magic, she enchanted him to sleep so he wouldn't suffer.

When she had healed Blue to the best of her ability, she stood up and swayed for a moment, gripping her thighs for support. The curtains had burned out, and with nothing else in the prayer room to catch flame, the air was beginning to clear. She followed her own trail of dirt back to the garden. Along the way, she passed a discarded sword and picked it up, but she had little hope of using it. She had been gone for too long, and Father Padron was too clever to have stayed where she'd put him.

She stepped outside, and her shoulders rounded. The carriage was gone, the hedges shredded into piles of leaves. She didn't bother walking to the hedge wall to scan the horizon for him. Even if she knew which direction he had gone, she was too weak to ride after him. She plunged the blade into the grass and raised her face to the moon.

Tonight, she had broken more than a curse.

She had broken everything that mattered.

33

The sun rose the next morning, and life went on.

Those who had died in battle had already been conveyed to the temple in preparation for burial. Those who had survived now worked to repair the damage. Palace maids aired out smoky rugs and scrubbed blood from the floor tiles while royal guards fortified the windows and gates against the possibility of an attack.

The palace was vulnerable for the first time in a thousand years. Its main source of protection was gone, including Father Padron, whose abandoned carriage had been found on the outskirts of the city. No one knew where he'd traveled from there. Kian and General Petros had rallied allies, gathered troops, and dispatched search parties with orders to kill Father Padron on sight. As for the surviving priests throughout the temples of the realm—men like Daerick's brother—they had been summoned to the palace for an interview with Shiera's high priestess to determine their place within the new Order.

Shiera's high priestess. That was Cerise's title.

Now she had to earn it, which meant gathering the strength to pick herself up from the sanctuary floor. She hadn't moved from the spot where she had curled up in between Blue, who was still sleeping, and Nina, who would never wake. At some point during the night, she must have dozed off, because her head was currently resting on Delora's lap, and she couldn't recall how that had happened.

Delora hummed absently while stroking Cerise's hair. She had been doing that for a while, and Cerise liked it, both for the comfort and for the observance that came from sitting still. Delora was the only other person who had stopped, who hadn't gone about her morning as though Nina had never existed. Kian had come to visit once or twice, but he hadn't stayed for long. Cerise couldn't fault him, not when the entire palace looked to him for reassurance and leadership. Daerick was off researching something or other, and everyone else bustled on with their tasks.

It was sacrilege. Didn't anyone notice there was less beauty in the world today? Less sweetness? Hadn't they woken up a little colder beneath their blankets?

"Do you think…" Delora softly cleared her throat. "Well, that maybe…"

"No." Cerise reached out and grabbed Nina's hand. It was cold, and she released it just as quickly. "Not yet. Please."

"All right," Delora murmured.

"I need a little longer."

"It's all right," Delora repeated.

But it wasn't all right. Someone from the palace had traveled through the night as a courtesy to notify Mama and Father of Nina's death, but Nina's remains belonged to her husband. Soon he would come from Calatris to take Nina away. Then he would seal her up in a tomb with his first wife, and Cerise wouldn't even have a grave to visit.

Just thinking about it made her chest ache with a tension that kept building with no release. It reminded her of what Kian had once said: *You have too much love in you. If you don't find an outlet for it, you might explode.* That was exactly the problem. All of the love she felt for Nina was trapped inside her with no way out.

"You were right," Delora said, leaning slightly aside to peer at Nina. "She does cast a shadow over beauty."

Cerise nodded.

"I can tell that she loved you." Delora resumed her gentle stroking. "I'm sorry that you lost her. I know what it is to lose a mother."

A mother.

The term still sounded foreign to Cerise's ears. She'd barely had time to think of Nina as a mother before Father Padron had snatched her away. He'd taken so much from her, but even more from Nina. He had stolen Nina's love. He had stripped away her happiness and her security. He'd cut her life short, and in doing so, he'd killed the baby that she had wanted for so long. In a way, he had even taken Cerise from her. It was because of him that Nina had pretended to be a sister to her own child.

It wasn't fair.

Cerise rested a palm on Nina's rounded belly and wondered if what Nina had said about her twin was true. Had her older sibling really died at birth, or had Nina hidden the baby with a different family? Had he stolen that child from her, too? Cerise would ask Mama and Father if they knew the truth, but as private as Nina had been, her secrets had likely died with her.

"I feel like I barely knew her," Cerise said. "And now I never will. She's gone. The person who loved me most in the world is gone." Nina had been so brave in coming to the palace. She had put herself within reach of her greatest fear because her love had outweighed her terror. And Cerise had forced Nina out of her suite, forced her right into the serpent's jaws.

"She spent half her life protecting me," she whispered, "and I couldn't keep her safe for a single day."

"Don't talk like that," Delora said. "I never met Nina, but I know she wouldn't want you to blame yourself, and she definitely wouldn't want you to feel alone. You're loved by so many people: your family, and your friends, and Kian. He's—" She cut off at the sound of approaching footsteps and smoothly finished, "Here to check on you again."

Two shiny, black boots stopped in front of Cerise, followed by breech-clad legs as Kian knelt down and blocked her view of Nina. "I'm afraid it's time, my love," he said. "Her carriage is here. The crew needs to prepare her for the voyage home."

"Home," Cerise repeated. That was why Nina had come to the palace. "She wanted to take me home with her, but I wouldn't leave you."

Kian extended a hand toward her face but must have thought better of it. "I wish I could give her back to you. I would trade places with her if I could."

Trade places with her?

Cerise snapped her gaze to his. It was the first time she'd glimpsed his face since the night before, and he looked terrible. His eyes were bloodshot and weary, rimmed by dark circles of exhaustion. But despite that, her anger flared. Kian knew that his command to survive had forced her to watch Nina die. So how could he wish to make the same sacrifice that he had robbed her of making?

"You don't get to say that," she told him. "I was the one who had to watch her die, not you. I'm the one who loved her, not you. Don't talk to me about trading places with her when you took that choice away from me."

"Cerise," Delora interjected from behind her.

"No, it's fine," Kian said, but that wasn't true. His color had dulled, his throat shifting as he tried to swallow. "Padron lied to you, Cerise. You have to know that. You and Nina were the living proof of his darkest secret. He could only erase that secret by erasing both of you. If you had surrendered, he would have killed Nina anyway. Two would have died instead of one, and you wouldn't have broken the curse or driven him into hiding or defeated the Order. You wouldn't have survived to save us all."

A small voice told Cerise that he was right. Father Padron hadn't kept his promise to Cole, and he wouldn't have kept his promise to her. But the wound was too fresh and the grief too intense. She had to let some of it out. She hardened her gaze and told him, "At least you don't command me anymore."

Pain flashed in Kian's eyes, but it didn't take away from hers. If anything, the pressure in her chest only compounded from knowing she had hurt him. He seemed to shrink in the moment before he turned away from her. He reached into his pocket and bent low over Nina's head. She didn't understand what he was doing until she heard a *snip*, and then she watched him tuck a chestnut curl of hair inside an oval locket that dangled from a fine golden chain.

Still facing away, he handed her the necklace. "This belonged to my mother. I thought you might like to have it. Now a part of Nina will always be with you."

Cerise stared at the locket while shame leaked from her eyes. She had hurt Kian—on purpose—and in return, he had given her a keepsake from his own mother. How quickly she had forgotten that he'd lost a mother, too—and at the hands of Father Padron.

"Thank you." Cerise let her touch linger when she accepted his gift, prompting him to look at her. There was no need for words when their eyes met. They exchanged apologies in a single glance, each of them understanding the other. He was sorry for her loss but didn't regret compelling her to survive. She was sorry for blaming him but wasn't ready to admit that nothing could have saved Nina. So for now, they made peace.

"You're welcome," he told her.

He moved aside so she could say goodbye.

Cerise closed her eyes. She decided not to remember Nina like this, with her cheeks colorless and her exquisite face frozen in death. After everything that Father Padron had stolen from her, she refused to let him taint her memory of Nina, too. She summoned the image that she treasured most: the smiling, bright-eyed Nina who loved fiercely. That was *her* Nina, the secret side of the veiled beauty that few had seen and no one could take away.

"Goodbye, Nina," she said. "Thank you for loving me."

She felt blindly for Nina's veil and lowered it for the very last time. And then she finally confronted the task she had been avoiding. She rose onto her knees, lifted her face to the ceiling, and recited the prayer for the departed.

"Mother Shiera, mistress of worlds," Cerise called out as loudly and as clearly as her tear-roughened voice would allow. "Please welcome your servant Nina into your arms and grant her mercy for any offenses she committed against you." A fresh sob squeezed her windpipe. The prayer was complete, but deep in her chest, she felt the swelling of words left unsaid, a pressure that would not be contained. And so she broke with tradition and pleaded with the goddess from her heart.

"I know that darkness is as sacred as the light. I know that pain is as necessary as pleasure. I know that many of your faithful servants have died in ways that were cruel and unfair. But not like this. Nina was the best of your daughters. She was strong and loyal and kind—a woman made in the image of a mighty goddess—and her life was taken by a man. And not simply a man, but an unholy, undeserving priest who resented her flame as much as the priests of a thousand years ago resented yours. That man didn't deserve to stand in Nina's warmth, let alone to steal it. Don't let him win. Let there be justice for Nina. That is what I ask of you."

"I ask it as well," Kian murmured and clasped her hand.

"As do I," Delora said.

Cerise wiped her eyes on her sleeve. She didn't know which side of Shiera might be listening that day. In mercy or in wrath, she only hoped her prayer had been heard.

34

Because there was no one left to scold her, Cerise dressed for the day in a gauzy linen tunic and leggings and then gathered her hair at the nape of her neck in a plain braid that was more befitting of a lady's maid than a lady of the temple. She didn't care. She was the high priestess of Shiera now, and she could do as she pleased. She wasn't going back to the temple—not now, not ever—and to prove it, she pulled her black-and-white gowns from the closet and tossed them off the balcony. When the last dress had flittered over the railing, she donned a pair of sandals and returned to the sanctuary to see if Blue was awake.

She tried to stop her gaze from wandering to the empty spot inside the prayer room where Nina's body had lain, but naturally that was the first place she looked. A deep throb was her punishment. The floor tiles were scrubbed to a high shine, all traces of fire and death removed. The sanctuary looked the same as ever, aside from the missing curtains…and the presence of a massive dog snoring in the middle of the room.

She knelt down next to Blue. Settling a hand on his head, she willed him to wake slowly, for his mind to stir and his body to rest. As her magic passed over him, his snores quieted and his eyelids fluttered. Blue opened and closed his eyes several times before he blinked alert and sharpened his gaze. He peered first at the floor and the walls as if to orient himself. When he eventually focused on her face, his stumpy tail wagged in a *thump thump thump* against the tile.

She smiled. "Feeling better?"

The thumping quickened.

"Good. Let's get you on your feet." She awoke the rest of him and warned, "Slowly, now. Don't jump—"

Instantly, he leaped to his enormous paws and shook out his pelt. He arched his back in a stretch and then bounced in excitement as if waiting for her to throw a stick. She laughed and pressed a silencing hand over her mouth. It seemed too soon for laughter, almost like a betrayal. But her ribs continued to quake, and each chuckle released so much pressure from her chest that she refused to hold it back. She ruffled Blue's head and laughed until her stomach hurt. Then Blue's own stomach rumbled loud enough to quake the ground.

"Healing is hard work. No wonder you're hungry. Come on," she said, standing. "If we hurry, there might be leftover sausages from breakfast."

She crossed the threshold into the open-air corridor and found a palace guard waiting for her there, scratching his jaw and peering into the sanctuary as if he didn't know whether or not he was allowed inside now that the priests were gone.

"My lady," he greeted. "Or should I say *Your Grace*?"

Cerise shook her head. She refused to be called *Your Grace*. It reminded her too much of Father Padron or the Reverend Mother. "*My lady* will suffice."

"Very well, my lady," the guard told her. "We apprehended a young man at the gates. He says he's here to see you."

"A young man?" she asked.

"Yes, a local boy, by the look of him. Tall, built like a bull, not very talkative. He claims you summoned him here."

She drew a sharp breath. *Nero.* "That's right. I did. Where is he now?"

"At the front gate, my lady."

"I'll meet him there," she said as Blue's stomach growled even louder than before. "Will you please take Blue to the kitchens and ask them to spare as many sausages as they can? If there aren't enough sausages, raw chickens will do."

The guard cast a wary glance at Blue, who likely outweighed the man by ten stones.

"He'll be on his best behavior," Cerise promised. "Won't you, sweet boy?"

Blue yipped in response and then heeled next to the guard, eager for his breakfast. The two of them departed for the kitchens, and Cerise made her way toward the gatehouse.

She soon identified Nero in the distance, walking alongside Kian and General Petros. She watched the group ambling along the tree-lined path leading to the castle. None of them had noticed her yet, and the sight of them reminded her of an afternoon they had spent hunting jackrabbits on the mountain. She had watched them return from the hunt, and she had smiled at how boyish they had looked then, swinging their arms, pelts draped over their shoulders, their heads tipped back in laughter.

They weren't laughing now.

Nero's shoulders were stiff and raised. Clearly, he had heard about the battle with the priests and—more importantly—the news that Father Padron had escaped into the city and was now free to use his magic in any way that he chose. The threat of a rogue priest would worry any rational person, but it had to worry Nero in particular. He and other wielders of "unusual" gifts still weren't safe from persecution. If anything, Nero and the other fire bloods were more vulnerable now that Kian no longer had control over Father Padron—or any of the surviving priests that Padron might be able to recruit.

Cerise hated the idea of having to fight again, but she had to prepare herself for it. Transitions of power were rarely smooth, and Father Padron wasn't the kind of man who would quietly surrender. One battle had ended, but another would soon begin.

General Petros likely knew it. He still hadn't recovered fully from his injuries, but he was on his feet, limping along while favoring his left hand. He kept the pace a few steps behind Kian, who moved with a slow, deliberate gait that hinted at more than just exhaustion. He must have injured himself in the battle, too.

Cerise waved at them and met them on the palace lawn.

General Petros was the first to speak. He cupped her shoulder and said, "I'm sorry, my girl. I heard about what happened to your mother, and I said a prayer for you when I visited my healer at the temple."

"Thank you," she told him. "I appreciate that."

The general peered down at her with a sad smile. It was the first time since breaking the curse that she paid attention to him, and she noticed that his eyes were soft and warm, his hands no longer trembling with pent-up rage. She had never seen him so free.

At least she had done one thing right.

"I'm sorry, too," Nero added in a voice that sounded as numb and as blank as the expression on his face. "The high priest of Shiera is your father. It explains much, but I still can't believe it."

Neither could Cerise. She didn't want to think of Padron as her father. He wasn't worthy of the role. "The *former* high priest," she corrected. "He's a common fugitive now."

"Common?" Nero asked, raising an eyebrow.

"Not common," she admitted. "But one that bleeds."

Kian stood beside her and settled a hand on her lower back. He brushed his thumb over her thin blouse, and the comfort of his touch made her relax the shoulder muscles she hadn't known were clenched. "We've been gathering allies," he told Nero. "But what we really need is magic. If you would be willing to recruit more of your kind to fight with us, we stand a better chance of ending Padron with minimal casualties."

Nero frowned and went thoughtful for a moment. "The *umbra sangi* are private and scattered. But I can try. The high priest is a threat to us all."

"The *former* high priest," Cerise reminded him. "Titles carry power and legitimacy. Padron doesn't deserve our respect. Call him a sadist or a traitor or anything you like, but not a high priest."

Nero nodded in agreement, and then the discussion turned to his recruitment of fire bloods, how long the journey might last, and the supplies he would need along the way. While they spoke, Daerick came outside to join them. He listened for a while before offering a suggestion of his own.

"I want to board the next ship to Calatris and visit my brother before he leaves his temple," Daerick said. "To give him a firsthand account of what happened here. We don't know what rumors are spreading, but we can be sure that Padron will twist the truth to his advantage."

Cerise realized how right Daerick was. "He won't even have to twist the truth. All he has to do is tell it simply. I killed every priest in the palace, I stabbed him with the Petros Blade, and then I took his place as the head of the Order. If that's all the priests hear, they'll think *I'm* the monster."

"We need to get ahead of the rumors," Daerick said. "My brother will believe me. He trusts me, and the others trust him."

"Then go to him," Kian told Daerick. "Hire a private ship if you have to. Take as much from the treasury as you need."

"Let's send word to my old temple, too," Cerise said. "The Reverend Mother foresaw something like this. She probably knows what's coming, but we should warn her anyway."

"I'll handle it," Daerick said.

Kian clapped him on the shoulder. "Safe journey."

"Just one thing first," Daerick said, turning his attention to Cerise. He smiled at her warmly and wrapped one arm around her in a hug. "Thank you," he whispered in her ear. "You saved me from a lifetime of torment, and I know what it cost you. I can never repay my debt to you, but I can make sure every noble family in the realm knows that you're the one who broke their curse."

She returned his hug while tears of gratitude welled in her eyes. She'd been so focused on what she had lost that she hadn't seen all she'd gained. Daerick was restored, and Kian, and General Petros, and all of the other noble firstborns who had suffered for the crimes of their ancestors. They were all free because of her, and so was the realm—free from the old ways of the Order. She had done more than one thing right.

"I can't take all the praise," she told Daerick. "I had a good teacher."

Sometime later, Cerise and Kian snuck into the hedge maze and hid themselves away in the secret courtyard at the center. They sat side by side on a stone bench facing the fountain, and as Cerise rested her head on Kian's shoulder, she thought of all the nights they had spent in the shadows, sitting on a dark replica of that same stone bench. She would miss their quiet hours together but not that place. She shivered just to imagine it.

"There's something I haven't told you," Kian said. "I was waiting for the right time, and now that we've had a chance to slow down and catch our breath, I think you'll be happy to hear it."

"What's that?" she asked.

"It's something I saw in the underworld, right before you broke the curse," he said. "I was walking in the labyrinth, pacing away the hours, much like any other night. I passed the souls of the damned, and they didn't see me. They never did. And then, out of nowhere, all of them vanished. Every last soul that I could see was gone, just like that." He snapped his fingers. "And then I blinked, and I was standing next to you in the sanctuary. I didn't understand what was happening at the time, but now I think I do."

Cerise peered up at him, hope stirring in her chest. "Their souls are free?"

"So it seems," he said. "Free from a thousand years of torment. You wondered why you were able to follow me into the shadows, and now we know what purpose your gift served. I believe your presence there had something to do with their release."

"I *am* happy to hear that," she told him. More than happy. The souls of the Mortara firstborns never should have been trapped at all. Only the priests and the nobles with whom they had colluded deserved to be punished, and not even forever. "I suppose we were right about the replica of the courtyard in the underworld." She glanced around them. "This must have been where it happened all those centuries ago—where the priests and the Mortaras met."

"Undoubtedly," Kian said. He shifted on the bench and then winced in pain, massaging his knee. "Damnation. I almost forgot how long it takes for an injury to heal. I might need your help with this, if you don't mind. It hurts more than anything else."

"Of course I don't mind." She was glad he had finally asked. She held a palm above his leg and willed her energy to mend his flesh.

He tested his knee, moving it to and fro.

"Better?" she asked.

"Much. Thank you, my love."

She laced their fingers together and warned, "Be careful; you don't get a new body at sunrise anymore. This one has to last, and I'm rather attached to it."

"Are you?" he asked. He made a show of pondering her advice before he delivered a mockingly serious look. "Well, in that case, I'm afraid I have to rescind my offer to let you stab me in the heart."

That made her smile. "A pity I missed my chance."

"Indeed," he said, then added a *tsk*. "Those who hesitate are lost."

She leaned aside to scan his body for visible signs of damage. "Are you hurt anywhere else? I'm getting better at healing, I think."

"I don't want to drain you."

"You won't," she told him, and then she explained what Nero

had taught her about accessing her supply of magic. "My magic is like a flagon of water. The energy is there, but I can't use it all at once. I can only draw from what's in my cup. Last night, I drained every last drop. That's why I was exhausted. But today, my cup is almost full again."

Kian made a noise of contemplation. "So in what way does love make your gift stronger? Does it increase the volume of the flagon or the cup?"

"Both, I think. But it's hard to know."

"Then yes," he said. "You may heal me."

She raised an eyebrow. "Oh, may I?"

He winked at her. "I will permit it."

"All right. Where does it hurt?"

"Everywhere."

"Everywhere?"

"Everywhere," he repeated. "I might actually be dying."

She bit her lip against a grin. He truly had no tolerance for pain. She placed her palms on Kian's chest and closed her eyes, imagining her energy traveling through his body and mending him, much like she had done for Blue. When she finished, she sat back and watched his reaction.

Kian groaned in relief as he stretched his muscles and tested his limbs. He thanked her again and placed a kiss on the back of her hand, and then he gave her a smile so warm and genuine that the rest of the world fell away, and for one suspended heartbeat, there was only the two of them. "If the act of love strengthens your gift," he said with a teasing gleam in his eyes, "then I'm ready to do my part in helping you become the most powerful wielder of magic who ever lived."

She chuckled. "That's quite generous of you."

"As always, I'm yours to command, my lady."

"Then you had better rest up," she said, examining the dark circles beneath his eyes. "You look tired."

"I am tired," he admitted. "I've forgotten what it's like to need sleep." He grinned as if he had just realized something. "And to dream. I haven't had a proper one of those in ages."

Cerise hadn't considered that. Now that his body had been restored, other things would change, too. He would spend his nights in a real bed instead of in the underworld, and at sunrise, he would awake in that same bed instead of materializing by her side. The two of them would no longer spend their dreaming hours together—at least she didn't think so. She assumed her gift of dream walking had ended with the curse.

She sighed. "I've gotten used to you appearing next to me each morning. I'm going to miss our sunrises together."

"Miss them?" Kian asked. "Nonsense. All of my sunrises belong to you. Will you stay with me tonight?"

She pretended to think it over. "Is Blue invited?"

"Will he bite me again?"

"Quite possibly."

"For you, I'll risk it."

"Then yes," she told him. "I'll stay with you tonight."

"And all the nights after that?"

There was a serious undertone beneath his teasing, a question she wasn't prepared to answer because she'd never allowed herself to consider it. She had always known their time together would end. Much had changed in their lives, but he was still a king in need of legitimate heirs, and high priestess or not, she was a second-born given in service to the temple.

Her life belonged to the goddess.

Kian's throat shifted as he swallowed. Her silence seemed to unnerve him. "Do you still love me?"

She drew a sharp breath and took his face between her hands. "Always," she told him, mortified that he had felt the need to ask. She moved her gaze over the planes of his face, drinking in the storm-cloud eyes that had never failed to see the heart of her. Now more than ever, she loved him. She would die loving him, and in the afterlife, her spirit would love him still. "Always," she told him again.

He looked to her with urgency. "Then be my queen."

"But ladies of the temple aren't—"

"The old ways are gone," he interrupted. "Don't you think the old rules should go with them?"

Her lips parted. She hadn't thought of it like that.

"I'm the king," he said. "You're the high priestess of Shiera. If anyone deserves to write their own rules, it's us. Let's decide for ourselves which path to take."

A warmth appeared inside her chest—a gentle glow, like an embrace from within. She recognized the sensation because she'd felt it a hundred times before, in quiet temple corners or on jagged mountain summits, where she had knelt in prayer.

Shiera had given her blessing.

"Be my queen," Kian repeated. "You have my soul. I won't share the throne with anyone but you. Look at what we've already accomplished. The two of us could do anything."

Cerise didn't need to think any more about it. "Yes," she told him as she gazed in wonder at her love, her future husband, her "half king" made whole. She'd never imagined her heart could feel so full.

He was right. Together, they would be unstoppable.

Epilogue

The slain beauty had not heard the girl's prayer.

In body and in mind, she was no more sentient than the carriage that bore her. All around, motion vibrated the carriage walls and trembled the plush velvet cushion upon which she rested. Her veil had been pulled back, baring her legendary face to anyone fortunate enough to catch a glimpse of her through the carriage windows. As the horses trotted onward, wheels rumbled, hooves clopped, and axles squeaked.

The slain beauty did not hear those sounds, either.

Nor did she see the point of light when it appeared above her or feel its heat as the tiny point multiplied into a miniature star that bathed her in its glow. She was oblivious to her blood thinning and warming inside her veins and equally ignorant of her organs mending and her damaged flesh weaving together.

She did not sense the babe stirring to life within her womb. Her first sensation came as her heart squeezed into a rhythmic beat. But true awareness didn't dawn until a moment later, when she drew a great, heaving breath that rent the silence, and she opened her eyes.

The slain beauty had not heard the girl's prayer.

But the goddess had.

And in a rare twist of fate, her merciful and vengeful sides were both listening that day, the perfect balance of darkness and light to grant a prayer so double-edged as justice, for there could be no change without battle, no battle without pain.

Though the girl didn't know it, she had prayed for catastrophe.

Tomorrow, she would have it.

Acknowledgments

Writing a book is a solitary job, but *publishing* a book is a team effort. Several talented people have collaborated to bring *The Half King* to life, and I'm grateful to every single one of them.

First, to my editors Molly Majumder and Mary Lindsey: Thank you for loving this book and for giving me thoughtful suggestions that elevated my craft. I couldn't have done it without you. Added thanks to Hannah Lindsey and Rae Swain, whose keen eyes caught everything I missed, and to Britt Marczak, Jessica Meigs, Claire Andress, and Aimee Lim for stellar formatting and proofreading.

Much appreciation to Bree Archer for my stunning cover, to Elizabeth Turner Stokes for a gorgeous case design, to Zarin Baksh for those dreamy end papers, and to Amy Acosta for the beautiful map art. People really do judge a book by its packaging, and you all knocked it out of the park!

A special round of thanks to Heather Riccio and Curtis Svehlak for keeping the production process rolling smoothly. And a huge shout-out to Ashley Doliber, Lizzy Mason, Meredith Johnson, and Brittany Zimmerman for being real-life social media and marketing wizards. I can't overstate how glad I am to have your support. Thank you for spreading the word about this book!

I'm so very grateful to my literary agent, Nicole Resciniti, who's been my champion for more than a decade, and to my savvy, hardworking publisher, Liz Pelletier, who made this book possible. Both of you are an inspiration to me!

Big hugs to my friend, critique partner, and talented author Lorie Langdon for taking the time to read and evaluate my work, and more importantly, for reminding me that writing is a gift. I sometimes forget how far I've come and how lucky I am to make up stories for a living. Thank you for keeping me grounded.

As always, much love to my family and friends for their unfailing support, and especially to my husband, Kevin, who never misses an opportunity to brag about me and my books to any person willing (or unwilling) to listen. You're my biggest fan, and it's one of the many reasons I love you!

CONNECT WITH US ONLINE

@REDTOWERBOOKS

@REDTOWERBOOKS

@REDTOWERBOOKS

RED TOWER
BOOKS™